George M. Fenn

The Tiger Lily

a story of two passions

George M. Fenn

The Tiger Lily
a story of two passions

ISBN/EAN: 9783337851286

Printed in Europe, USA, Canada, Australia, Japan

Cover: Foto ©Andreas Hilbeck / pixelio.de

More available books at **www.hansebooks.com**

A STORY OF TWO PASSIONS

BY

G. MANVILLE FENN

AUTHOR OF "THE NEW MISTRESS," "WITNESS TO THE DEED," ETC.

A NEW EDITION

LONDON
CHATTO & WINDUS, PICCADILLY
1896

CONTENTS

CONTENTS.

THE TIGER LILY.

CHAPTER I.

MODERN SKILL.

" Hallo, Sawbones ! "

The speaker raised his head from the white pillow of the massive, old-fashioned four-post bed, and set the ornamental bobs and tags of the heavy bullion fringe upon the great cornice quivering. He was a sharp-faced, cleanly shaven man, freshly scraped, and the barber who had been operating was in the act of replacing his razor and strop as these words were spoken to the calm, thoughtful-looking person who entered the substantially furnished room.

" Good morning, Mr. Masters. Had a quiet night ? "

" Bah ! You know I haven't. How is a man to have a good night when ten thousand imps are boring into him with red-hot iron, and jigging his nerves till he is half mad ! Here, you : be off ! "

" Without brushing your hair, sir ? "

A

"Brush a birch broom! My head never wants brushing. You know that."

He gave himself a jerk, and the short, crisp, wavy grey locks glistened in the bright morning sun, which streamed in through the window.

"Look here; you can cut it to-morrow when you come—if I'm not dead. If I am, you may have a bit to keep in remembrance."

"Oh, not so bad as that, sir, I hope. Dr. Thorpe is too——"

"That'll do," said the man in the bed sharply. "I kept to you because you didn't chatter like the ordinary barber brood. I may get better, so don't spoil your character. Be off!"

The barber smiled, bowed, and left the room to doctor and patient.

"Well?" said the latter, meeting his attendant's searching eye. "I'm not gone."

"No; and I do not mean to let you go if I can help it."

"Ho!—But perhaps you can't."

"God knows, sir; but I shall do my best. I would rather, though, that you would let me bring in some one in consultation."

"And I wouldn't. If you can't set me right, Thorpe, no one in Boston can. Look here; brought your tools?"

The young doctor smiled.

"Ah, it's nothing to grin about."

“No; it is serious enough, my dear sir.”

“Then answer my question.   Brought your tools ? ”

“I have come quite prepared.”

“Then I shan’t have it done.”

Michael Thorpe looked at his patient as if he did not believe him, and the latter continued—

“I say : it’s confoundedly hard that I should suffer like this.   Spent all my life slaving, and now at sixty, when I want a little peace and enjoyment, this cursed trouble comes on.   Look here, Thorpe ; don’t fool about with me.   Charge me what you like, but tell me ; couldn’t you give me some stuff that would cure it without this operation ? ”

“Do you want me to be perfectly plain with you, sir, once more ? ”

“Of course.   Do I look the sort of man to be humbugged ? ”

“Then I must tell you, sir, the simple truth. You may go on for months, perhaps a year, as you are.   That is the outside.”

“I wouldn’t go on for a week as I have been, my lad.—But if I have it done ? ”

“There is no reason why you should not live to be eighty, or a hundred, if you can.”

“Right ; I’ll go in for the hundred, Thorpe.   I’m tough enough.   There, get it over.”

“You will have it done ? ”

“Of course I will.   Don’t kill me, or I’ll come back and haunt you.”

"I should be too glad to see a dear old friend again, so that wouldn't alarm me," said Thorpe, examining his patient, who smiled grimly. "I shall not kill you. All I'm afraid of is that I may perform the operation so unskilfully that my labour and your suffering will have been in vain."

"And then I'll call you a miserable pretender, and shan't pay you a cent. Bah! You can do it. I know you, Michael Thorpe, and haven't watched you for nothing."

The young surgeon held out his hands to his patient.

"Give me your full confidence, Mr. Masters," he said, " work with me, and I can cure you."

"Right, my lad. But you had it before," he cried, grasping the hands extended to him. "I trust you, boy, as I always did your father—God bless him! Now, no more talking. Get to work. I won't holloa. Where are you going?"

"Only down to the drawing-room to fetch the nurse."

" Ring for her—she's downstairs."

"I mean the other—the professional nurse whom I brought with me."

" What for?"

"To help me now, and to attend you for a few days afterwards exactly as I wish."

"Two nurses? One has nearly killed me. Two will be downright murder."

"No, sir," said Michael Thorpe, smiling. "The good in one will neutralise all the ill that there may be in the other."

"Fetch her up, then; and look here, Thorpe; I'm a man, not a weak hysterical girl. None of your confounded chloroform, or anything of that kind."

"You leave yourself in my hands, please," said the surgeon, smiling, and going across to the door, which he left open, and then uttering a sharp cough, returned.

A minute later there was a faint rustling sound beyond the heavy curtains, and the patient, frowning heavily, turned his head in the direction of the door. Then the scowl upon his sharp face gave place to a look of wonder and delight as a rather slight, dark-haired girl, in a closely fitting black dress and white-bibbed apron, advanced towards him, with her large dark eyes beaming sympathy, and a smile, half pity-ing, half affectionate, played about her well-formed, expressive lips.

"Cornel!" he cried. "Why, my dear little girl, this is good of you to come and see me. I thought it was the nurse."

He stretched out his hands, drew the girl to him, and kissed her tenderly on both cheeks, and then on the lips, before sinking back with the tears in his eyes—two utter strangers, which, possibly find-ing their position novel, hurriedly quitted their temporary resting-place, fell over the sides, and trickled down his cheeks.

"I am the nurse," came now, in a sweet, silvery voice, as the new-comer began to arrange the pillow in that peculiarly refreshing way only given by loving hands.

"You? Impossible!"

"Oh no, Mr. Masters. Michael told me every-thing, and I was going to offer, when he asked me if I would come and help him."

"Oh, but nonsense! You, my child! It would be too horrible and disgusting for a young girl like you."

"Why?" she replied gently. "Michael trusts me, and thinks I carry out his wishes better than a paid servant would."

"That's it, my dear sir. I want, both for the sake of an old friend and for my reputation, to make my operation perfectly successful. Cornel here will carry out my instructions to the letter. She will help me too in the operation."

"But an operation is not fit——not the place for a young girl."

"Why not?" said Cornel, smiling.

"It is unsexing you, my child."

"Unsexing me, when I come to help to calm your pain, to nurse you back to health and strength! A woman never unsexes herself in proving a help to those who suffer. Besides, I have often helped my brother before."

Meanwhile the surgeon had busied himself at a table upon which he had placed a mahogany case. He had had his back to them, but now turned and advanced to the bed, with a little silver implement in his hand.

"Now, my dear sir, a little manly fortitude and patience, and you may believe me when I tell you that there is nothing to fear."

"Who is afraid?" said the old man sharply. "But what's that?"

"A little apparatus for injecting an anæsthetic."

"I said I wouldn't have anything of the kind," cried the patient angrily. "I can and will bear it."

"But I cannot and will not," said the surgeon, smiling. "You could not help wincing and showing your suffering. That would trouble, perhaps unnerve me, and I could not work so well."

"What are you going to do?—give me chloroform?"

"No; I am going to inject a fluid that will dull the sensitive nerves of the part, and place you in such a condition that you will lose all sense of suffering."

"And if I don't come to?"

"You will not for some time. Now, old friend, show me your confidence. Are you ready?"

There was a long, deep-drawn breath, a look at the young girl's patient, trust-giving face and then

Ezekiel Masters, one of the wealthiest men in Boston, said calmly—

"Yes."

A few minutes later he was lying perfectly insensible, and breathing as gently as an infant.

"Can you repeat that from time to time, as I tell you?" said the surgeon.

"Yes, dear."

"Without flinching?"

"Yes.   It is to save him.   I shall not shrink."

"Then I depend upon you."

Busy minutes followed, with the patient lying perfectly unconscious.

"How long could he be kept like this, Michael?" whispered Cornel, whose face looked very white.

"As long as you wished—comparatively.   Don't talk ; you hinder me."

"As long as I liked," thought Cornel, with her eyes dilating as she gazed at the patient, with the little syringe in her hand, and the stoppered bottle, from which the fluid was taken, close by—"as long as I liked, and he as if quite dead.   What an awful power to hold within one's grasp!"

CHAPTER II.

"Hah!"

A long-drawn sigh of content, which made Cornelia Thorpe emerge from her chair behind the bed-curtains, and bend over to lay her soft white hand upon the patient's forehead, but only for it to be taken and held to his lips.

"Well, angel?" he said quietly.

"Your head is quite cool; there is no fever. Have you had a good night's rest?"

"Good, my child? It has been heavenly. I seemed to sink at once into a delicious dreamless sleep, such as I have not known for a year, and I feel as if I had not stirred all night."

"You have not."

"Then you have watched by me?"

"Oh, yes."

"Hah!" There was a pause. Then: "You must have given me a strong dose?"

"No," said Cornel, smiling. "Your sleep was quite natural. Why should it not be? Michael says the cause of all your suffering is completely removed, and that he has been successful beyond his hopes."

The old man lay holding his nurse's hand, and gazing at her fair, innocent face intently for some minutes before breaking the silence again.

"When was it?" he said at last.

"A week to-day, and in another month you may be up again."

"Hah! And they say there are no miracles now, and no angels upon earth," said the patient, half to himself. Then more loudly, "Cornel, my child, I think I must turn over a new leaf."

"Don't," she said, smiling. "I like the old page. You have always been my father's dear friend—always good and kind."

"I? Bah! A regular money-scraping, harsh tyrant. A regular miser."

"Nonsense, Mr. Masters."

"Then I'll prove it. I won't pay Michael his fees, nor you your wages for nursing me—not till I'm dead. Well, have I said something funny? Why do you laugh?"

"I smiled because I felt pleased."

"Because I'm better?"

"Yes; and because you are not going to insult Michael, nor your nurse, by offering us——"

"Dollars? Humph! There, let's talk about something else. Does Michael still hold to that insane notion of going to Europe?"

"Oh yes; we should have been there now, if it had not been for your illness."

"Then he gave it up for a time, because I wanted him to attend me?"

Cornel bowed her head.

"Humph! Sort of madness to want to go at all. Isn't America big enough for him?"

"Of course," said Cornel, laughing gently; and now the air of the nurse appeared to have dropped away, to give place to the bright happy look of a girl of twenty. "Surely it is not madness to want to increase his knowledge by a little study at the English and French hospitals. Besides, it was our father's wish."

"Yes; Jack was very mad about the English doctors, when there was not one who could touch him. I say, though: Michael is going to be as clever."

"I hope so," said Cornel, with animation. "He studies very hard."

"Yes, he's a clever one, girl; and Jack Thorpe would have been very proud of him if he had lived. But, I say——"

Cornel looked inquiringly in the keen eyes which searched her face.

"You really want to go with your brother?"

"Yes," she said with animation—"I should very much like to go."

"To study with him in the English and French hospitals?"

"I should like him to take me round with him," she said, with her cheeks growing slightly tinged. "I am always interested in his cases, and surely a woman is none the worse for a little surgical and medical knowledge."

"A precious deal better, my dear. But, I say——"

"Yes, dear guardian," she said, with a sweet, thrilling modulation now in her tones, as her eyes grew dim, and she laid both her little hands in the patient's.

"I promised your father I'd always have an eye on you two, and I don't think I ought to let you think of going, Cornel dear."

She was silent.

"Isn't it a sort of madness for you—to—eh? You know."

"To love and keep my faith to Armstrong Dale?" she said gently; and the love-light shone brightly in the eyes which met the old man's now without shrinking.

"Yes; that's what I meant, little one. I don't know how you could get yourself engaged to him."

Cornel laughed gently—a pleasant, silvery little laugh, which seemed to do the patient good, for he smiled and listened to the last note of the musical sounds. But he grew serious, and there was a cynicism in his tones as he went on.

"I don't believe in him, my girl. He's good-looking and a bit clever; but when you have said that, you have said all."

A little white finger was laid upon the speaker's lips, but he went on.

"I know: he gammoned you with his love nonsense, but if he had been the fellow I took him for, he'd have stayed here in Boston and painted and glazed. Painted you. Painted me—glazed me too, if he had liked. What did he want to go and study at Rome and Paris and London for? We've cleverer people in the States than out there."

"To get breadth, and learn his own failings," said Cornel gently.

"Hadn't any—I mean he was full of 'em, of course. Couldn't have loved you, or he'd have stopped at home."

"It was to show his love for me, and to try and make himself a master of his art, that he went away," said Cornel, with a look of faith and pride in her eyes.

"Bah! He has forgotten you by this time. Give him up, puss. He'll never come back. He'll marry some fine madam in the old country."

Cornel winced, and her eyes dilated as these words stung her; but the pang was momentary, and she laughed in the full tide of her happy trust in the man she loved.

"You mark my words, Cornel," said the old man; "that fellow will throw you over, and then that will set your monkey up, and you'll come and ask me to marry you, and I will. The folks 'll all laugh, but let 'em. We shall be all right, little one. I shall have a sweet little nurse and housekeeper to take care of me to the end, and you'll have an ugly, cantankerous old husband, who won't live very long, and will die and leave you a million dollars, so that you can laugh at the whole world, and be the prettiest little widow in Boston—bah! in the whole States—and with too much good sense to throw yourself away.—Who's that?"

"Doctor," said Michael Thorpe, entering. "How is he, Cornel?"

"Getting better fast; so well this morning that he is saying all kinds of harsh and cruel things."

"Capital sign," said the young surgeon.—"Yes, capital. Why, you are splendid, Mr. Masters, and at the end of only a week."

"Oh, I'm better. Only said you were mad to want to go to Europe; and that she's worse to pin her faith to a gad-about artist who'll only break her heart."

Michael Thorpe's stern, thoughtful face expanded into a pleasant smile.

"Yes, Cornel dear," he said; "there's no doubt about it; he's mending fast. I'll book my cabin in one of the Allan boats for about the beginning of next month. You will not be able to go."

CHAPTER III.

A FAIR CLIENT.

A noble-looking specimen of humanity, with a grand grizzly head, and strongly marked aquiline features, lit up by deeply set, piercing eyes, got out of a four-wheeler at No. 409 Portland Place, knocking off a very shabby hat in the process.

"Mind the nap, guv'nor," said the battered-looking driver with a laugh, as his fare stooped to pick up the fallen edifice; and as he spoke, the man's look took in the ill-fitting coat and patched boots of him whom he had driven only from Fitzroy Square.

"Not the first time that's been down, cabby. Hand 'em off."

A minute later, Daniel Jaggs, familiarly known in art circles as "The Emperor," and by visitors to the Royal Academy from his noble face, which had appeared over the bodies of noble Romans and heroes of great variety, stood on the pavement with an easel under one arm, a large blank canvas under the other, and a flat japanned box of oil colours and case of brushes held half-hidden by beard, beneath his chin.

He walked up to the door of the great mansion, whose window-sills and portico were gay with fresh flowers, and gave a vigorous tug at the bell.

The double doors flew open almost directly, and "The Emperor" was faced by a portly butler, who was flanked by a couple of men in livery.

"Oh! the painter's traps," said the former. "Look here, my good fellow; you should have rung the other bell. Step inside."

"The Emperor" obeyed, and, leaving the visitor waiting in the handsome hall, in company with the footman and under-butler, who looked rather superciliously at the well-worn garments of the artist's model, the out-of-livery servant walked slowly up the broad staircase to the drawing-room, and as slowly returned, to stand beckoning.

"You are to bring them up yourself," he said haughtily.

Daniel Jaggs placed his hat upon one of the crest-blazoned hall chairs, loaded himself well with the artistic impedimenta, and then went forward to the foot of the stairs up which the butler was leading the way, when, hearing a sound, he turned sharply.

"Here! Hi!" he cried loudly; "what are you going to do with that 'at?"

For one of the footmen was putting it out of sight, disgusted with the appearance of the dirty lining.

" Hush ! Recollect where you are," whispered the butler. " Her ladyship will hear."

" But that's my best 'at," grumbled the model, and then he subsided into silence as he was ushered into a magnificently furnished room; the door was closed behind him, and he stood staring round, thinking of backgrounds, when there was the rustling of silk, and " The Emperor" was dazzled, staring, as he told himself, at the most beautiful woman he had ever seen in his life.

Valentina, Contessa Dellatoria, was worthy of the man's admiration as she stood there with her dark eyes half veiled by their long lashes, in all the proud matured beauty of a woman of thirty, who could command every resource of jewel and robe to heighten the charms with which nature had liberally endowed her. She was beautiful; she knew it; and at those moments, eager with anticipations which had heightened the colour in her creamy cheeks, and the lustre in her eyes, she stood ready to be amused as she thoroughly grasped the meaning of the man's astonished gaze.

" You have brought those from Mr. Dale, have you not ? " she said at last, in a rich, soft voice.

" Yes, my lady. I 've, my lady. The heasel and canvas, my lady."

" Perhaps you had better bring them into this room."

" Yes, my lady—of course, my lady," said the

model eagerly, as he blundered after the Contessa, "The Emperor's" rather shambling movements, being due to a general looseness of joint, in no wise according with the majesty of his head and face.

" Yes; about there. That will do; they are sure to be moved."

" Oh yes, my lady, on account of the light. Mr. Dale's very partickler."

" Indeed ? Will he be here soon ?"

" Direc'ly, I should say, my lady. He hordered me to bring on his traps."

" From his studio ?" said the lady, sinking into a chair, and taking a purse from a little basket on a table.

" The Emperor's" eyesight was very good, and the movement suggested pleasant things. The lady, too, seemed disposed to question him, and he winked to himself mentally, as he glanced at the beautiful face before him, thought of his employer's youth and good looks, and then had sundry other thoughts, such as might occur to a man of a very ordinary world.

But his hands were not idle; they were as busy as his thoughts, and he spread the legs of the easel, and altered the position of the pegs ready for the canvas.

" Will you take this—for your trouble ?" came in that soft, rich, thrilling voice.

" Oh no—thank you, my lady—that ain't necessary," said the man hastily, as his fingers closed over the coin extended with a smile by fingers glittering with jewels.—"A suv, by jingo," he added to himself.

"Are you Mr. Dale's servant?"

"No, ma'am—my lady. Oh, dear, no. An old friend—that is, you know, I sit for him—and stand. I'm in a many of his pictures."

"Oh, I see. He takes your portrait?"

"Well, no, my lady; portraits is quite another line. I meant for his gennery pictures."

"*Genre?*"

"Yes, my lady. I was standing for Crackticus that day when you and his lordship come to the studio."

"Indeed? I did not see you."

"No, my lady. I had to go into the next room. You see I was a hancient Briton, and not sootable for or'nary society 'cept in a picture.—I think that'll do, my lady. He'll alter it to his taste."

"Yes, but—er—does Mr. Dale paint many portraits of ladies?" said the Contessa, detaining the model as he made as if to depart.

"Oh no, my lady. I never knew him do such a thing afore. He never works away from his studio, and he went on a deal about having to come here —er—that is—of course, he did not know," added the man hastily.

The Contessa smiled.

"But he has painted the human countenance a great deal? I mean the faces of ladies. There were several of nymphs in his Academy picture this year —beautiful women."

"The Emperor" smiled and shook his head.

"On'y or'nary models, my lady. He made 'em look beautiful. That's art, my lady."

"Then he had sitters for that picture?" she asked, rather eagerly.

"Oh yes, my lady; but Lor' bless you! it isn't much you'd think of them. He's a doing a picture now—a tayblow about Juno making a discovery over something. Her good man wasn't quite what he ought to have been, my lady, and she's in a reg'lar rage."

"Indeed?"

"Yes, my lady; and he tried all the reg'lar lady models—spent no end on 'em, but they none of 'em wouldn't do."

"Not beautiful enough?"

"He didn't think so, my lady, though, as I told him, it was too much to expeck to get one as was perfeck. You see in art, to make our best studies, we has to do a deal of patching."

"Painting the picture over and over again?"

"Your ladyship does not understand. It's like this: many of our best tayblows of goddesses and nymphs is made up. One model does for the face, another for the arms and hands, another for busties and—I beg your ladyship's pardon ; I was only talking art."

"I understand. I take a grcat deal of interest in the subject."

"Thankye, my lady. I told Mr. Dale as it was expecting too much to get a perfeck woman for a model, for there wasn't such a thing in nature. But, all hignorance, my lady, all hignorance. I hadn't scon your ladyship then. I beg your ladyship's pardon for being so bold."

"The Emperor" had seen the dreamy dark eyes open wide and flash angrily, but the look changed back to the listless, half-contemptuous again, and the lady said with a smile—

"Granted.—That will do. I suppose you will fetch Mr. Dale's easel when it is removed ?"

"I hope so, my lady, and thank you kindly. So generous! Never forget it, and——oh! I beg your pardon, sir."

"The Emperor" had been backing toward the door, and nearly came in contact with a short, slight, carefully dressed, middle-aged man—that is to say, he was about forty-five, looked sixty-five the last thing at night, and as near thirty-five as his valet could make him in the day.

He gazed keenly at the noble features of the man who towered over him, and "The Emperor" returned the gaze, noting, from a professional point of view, the rather classic Italian mould of the features, disfigured by a rather weak sensual mouth, and dark eyes too closely set.

"Two sizes larger, and what a Yago he would have made to my Brabantio," muttered "The Emperor," as he was let out by one of the footmen; and at the same moment Armstrong Dale, artist, strode up—a manly, handsome, carelessly dressed, typical Saxon Englishman in appearance, generations of his family, settled in America since the Puritan days, having undergone no change.

"Traps all there, Jaggs?"

"Yes, sir, everything," said the man confidentially, "and oh! sir——"

"That will do. Say what you have to say when I return: I'm late. Take my card up to the Contessa," he continued, turning sharply to the servant; and there was so much stern decision in his manner that the door was held wide, and the artist entered.

Meanwhile a few words passed in the drawing-room.

"Who's that fellow, Tina?" said the man too small, in "The Emperor's" estimation, for Iago.

The Contessa had sunk back in her lounge, and a listless, weary air had come over her face like a cloud, as she said, with a slight shrug of her shoulders—

"Mr. Dale's man."

"Who the dickens is Mr. Dale?"

Twenty years of life in London society had so

thoroughly Anglicised Conte Cesare Dellatoria, that his conversation had become perfectly insular, and the Italian accent was only noticeable at times.

"You know—the artist whom we visited."

"Oh, him! I'd forgotten. That his litter?"

"Yes."

"Humph! I haven't much faith in English artists. Better have waited till we went to Rome in the winter. Why, Tina, you look lovely this morning. That dress suits you exactly, beloved one."

He bent down and kissed the softly rounded cheek, with the effect that the lady's dark brows rose slightly, but enough to make a couple of creases across her forehead. Then, as a dull, cracking noise, as of the giving of some form of stay or stiffening was heard, the gentleman rose upright quickly, and glanced at himself in one of the many mirrors.

"Well, make him do you justice. But no—he cannot."

"You are amiable this morning," said the lady contemptuously.

"Always most amiable in your presence, my queen," he replied.

"Oh, I see! You are going out?"

"Yes, dearest. By the way, don't wait lunch, and I shall not be back to dinner."

"Do you dine with Lady Grayson?"

The Conte laughed.

"Delightful!" he cried. "Jealousy. And of her dearest, most confidential friend."

"No," said the lady quietly. "I have only one confidential friend."

"Meaning me. Thank you, dearest."

"Meaning myself," said the lady to herself. Then haughtily: "Yes?"

This to one of the servants who brought in a card on a waiter.

"Caller?" exclaimed the Conte. "Here, stop a moment; I've an engagement;" and he hurried out through the back drawing-room, while the lady's eyes closed a little more as she took the card from the silver waiter, and sat up, listening intently, as she said in a low voice—

"Where is Mr. Dale?"

"In the library, my lady."

There was a pause, during which the Contessa turned her head toward the back room, and let her eyes pass over the preparations that had been made for her sitting.

"Move that easel a little forward," she said.

The man crossed to the back room and altered the position of the tripod and canvas.

"A little more toward the middle of the room."

At that moment there was the faintly heard sound of a whistle, followed by the rattle of wheels, which stopped in front of the house. A few moments later the rattle of the wheels began again, and there was the faint, dull, heavy sound of the closing front door.

"I think that will do," said the Contessa carelessly. "Show Mr. Dale up."

The man left the room, and the change was instantaneous. His mistress sprang up eager and animated, stepped to one of the mirrors, gave a quick glance at her flushed cheeks and sparkling eyes, laid her hand for a moment upon her heaving bosom, and then hurriedly resumed her seat, with her head averted from the door. She took up a book, with which she half screened her face, the hand which held open the leaves trembling slightly from the agitation imparted by her quickened pulses.

The door opened silently, and the servant announced loudly—"Mr. Dale," and withdrew.

The artist took a step or two forward, and then waited for a sign of recognition, which did not come for a few moments, during which there was a quick nervous palpitation going on in the lady's temples.

Then she rose quickly, letting fall the book, and advanced towards the visitor.

"You are late," she said, in a low, deep, emotional voice.

"I beg your ladyship's pardon," said Dale, looking wonderingly, and with all an artist's admiration for the beautiful in nature, at the glowing beauty of the woman whose eyes were turned with a soft appealing look in his, while the parted lips curved into a smile which revealed her purely white teeth.

"I forgive you," she said softly, as she held out her hand—"now that you have come."

Armstrong Dale's action was the most natural in the world. He was in London, and it was two years since he left Boston to increase his knowledge of the world of art. He took the hand held out to him, and for the moment was fascinated by the spell of the eyes which looked so strangely deep down into his own. Then he was conscious of the soft white hand clinging tightly to his with a pressure to which it had been a stranger since he left the States.

CHAPTER IV

AN UNEXPECTED SCENE.

ARMSTRONG DALE walked up and down his grim-looking, soot-smudged studio, as if he had determined to wear a track on one side similar to that made by a wild beast in his cage.

"I won't go again," he said; "it's a kind of madness. Heavens! how beautiful she is! And that man—that wretched, effete, miserable little piece of conceit, with his insolent criticisms of my work. I felt as if I could strangle him. If it had not been for her appealing looks, I should have had a row with him before now. I will not put up with it. But how she seems to hate him; how she——

"Bah! Brute! Idiot! Ass! Conceited fool! Because nature has given you a decent face, can't a handsome woman look at you without your thinking she admires you—can't she speak gently, and in her graceful refined way, without your thinking that she is in love with you?

"It's all right, Cornel, my darling! I've been a fool—a conceited fool; but I've got your sweet, innocent little face always before me, the remembrance

of your dear arms about my neck, and your kisses
—armour, all of them, to guard me against folly.
Pish! Fancy and conceit! I will go, finish my
painting, get it exhibited if I can, and pile up Phili-
stine gold as spoil to bear home to her who is to
be my very own."

It was the third time of making this declaration,
and, full of his self-confidence, Dale made his way
for the fourth time to Portland Place, to find his
pulses, which had been accelerating their rate, calm
down at once, for his reception by the Contessa was
perfect, but there was a mingling of annoyance with
his satisfaction on finding that his hostess was not
alone.

Lady Grayson, one of Valentina's greatest inti-
mates, was there, a handsome, arch-looking woman,
widow of a wealthy old general, who, after a long
life of warfare in the East, had commenced another
in the West, but this was not even of seven years'
duration before he fell.

Lady Grayson smiled sweetly upon the artist as
he entered; and he felt that there was as much
meaning in her words as in her looks.

"I forgot this was your sitting day, Tina. Do
you know, I thought ladies always had to go to an
artist's studio to be painted. There, I suppose you
two want to be alone?"

"Pray, don't go," said Valentina calmly. "I do
not suppose Mr. Dale will mind you being present."

"I? Not at all," said Armstrong. "It will not make any difference to me."

"Indeed!" said the lady archly, "I thought you might both want to talk."

Armstrong Dale turned to his palette and brushes; and, as the Contessa took up her position, he crossed to the window, half closed the shutters, and drew a curtain, so as to get the exact light upon his sitter, whose eyes had met those of her dearest friend, and a silent skirmish, none the less sharp for no words being spoken, went on.

Dale returned to the front of his easel, and after a few words of request to his sitter respecting her position, to which she responded by a pained look, which made him shiver, he began to paint.

"Oh, how clever!" cried Lady Grayson, who had resumed her seat.

"Then she is waiting to see Cesare," thought the Contessa, smiling at her friend.

"Did you mean that dab I just made with my brush, Lady Grayson?" said Armstrong coldly.

"Fie! to speak so slightingly of your work. Dab, indeed! why, I have had lessons in painting and ought to know. Every touch you give that canvas shows real talent."

"And with all due respect, Lady Grayson, I, as a man who has studied hard in New York, Paris, Rome, and here in London, confidently say that you are no judge"

"I declare I am, sir," cried Lady Grayson merrily. "The fact is, you are too modest.—Don't you think he is far too modest, dear?"

"I am debarred from entering into the discussion," said the Contessa, with a fixed smile.

"Then I must do all the talking.—Capital! The portrait grows more like at every touch. By the way, Mr. Dale, how is your big picture getting on— the one I saw at your studio?"

In spite of her self-command, Valentina turned pale, and a flash darted from her eyes.

She at his studio!

Then she drew a long breath, the light in her eyes grew fixed, and there was a peculiar hardening in her smile, as Armstrong went on painting, and said calmly—

"The large mythological study I showed you and the Conte?"

"Yes, that one," said Lady Grayson, who, in spite of her assurance, did not dare to look at her friend, whose smile grew a little harder now, though there was a feeling of triumph glowing at her heart, as she detected her friend's slip.

"Badly," said Armstrong quietly. "I beg your pardon, Lady Dellatoria; that smile is too hard. Are you fatigued?"

"Oh no," she replied; and the smile he was trying to transfer to the canvas came back with a look which he avoided, and he continued hastily—

"I cannot satisfy myself with my sitters. I want a good—a beautiful, intense-looking—face, full of majesty, passion, and refinement; but the models are all so hard and commonplace. I can find beautiful women to sit, but there is a vulgarity in their faces where I want something ethereal or spiritual."

"Why not get the Contessa to sit?"

"Or Lady Grayson?" said Valentina scornfully.

"Oh, I should sit for Mr. Dale with pleasure."

"My dear Henriette, how can you be so absurd?"

"Oh, but I do not mean until you have quite done with him, dear."

"You would not do," said Dale bluntly.—"Quite still now, please, Lady Dellatoria."

"Alack and alas! not to be beautiful. But would your present sitter do?"

"I should not presume to ask Lady Dellatoria to sit for a study in a picture to be publicly exhibited," said the young man coldly.

"But you—so famous.—Ah, here is the Conte!"

"Yes; what is it?" said Dellatoria, entering. "Want me?"

"I knew it," thought the Contessa. "It was an appointment."

"Yes, to judge. That picture of Mr. Dale's. You know—the one we saw that day at his studio."

The Conte's eyes contracted a little, and he glanced at his wife, whose face was calm and smiling.

"Oh yes, I remember," he said—then, in an

aside, "You little fool.—What about it?" he added aloud.

"Mr. Dale can't find a model who would do for Juno. I was suggesting that dearest Valentina should sit."

"Very good of you, Lady Grayson," said the Conte shortly ; "but her ladyship does not sit for artists."

"And Mr. Dale does not wish her ladyship to do so, sir," said the artist, as haughtily as the Conte.

"There, I've said something wrong," cried Lady Grayson. "Poor me! It's time I went. I had no business to stay and hinder the painting. Good morning, Mr. Dale. Good-bye, Valentina, dear. Ask the Conte to forgive me."

She bent down and kissed the beautiful face, which did not wince, but there was war between two pairs of eyes. Then, turning round, she held out her hand.

"Good-bye, dreadful man. I'm too awfully sorry I cannot give you a lift on my way back to the park."

"No, thanks. By-the-by, yes ; I want to go to Albert Gate. Would it be taking you out of your way?"

"Oh no. Delighted. My horses don't have half enough to do."

"Then come along."

Armstrong could not help glancing at the couple as they crossed towards the door; and then as he turned back to the canvas his heart began to beat painfully, for he heard a peculiar hissing sound as of a long deep breath being drawn through teeth closely set, and a dangerous feeling of pity entered his breast. He could not paint, but stood fixed with the brush raised, completely mastered by the flood of thought which rushed through his brain. He saw plainly how great cause there was for the coldness and contempt with which the Contessa viewed her husband, and he realised fully the truth of the rumours he had heard of how she—a beautiful English girl—had been hurried into a fashionable marriage with this contemptible, wealthy, titled man. What else could come of it but such a life as he saw too plainly that they led!

He fought against these thoughts, but vainly; and they only opened the way to others still more dangerous. The first time he had met Lady Dellatoria, when she visited his studio in company with her husband, she had seemed attracted to him, and he had felt flattered by the eagerness with which she listened to his words. Then came an invitation to dinner at Portland Place, for the discussion of his undertaking the portrait. That night, the Conte was called away to an engagement, and he was left in that luxurious drawing-room, talking to the clever, refined, and beautiful woman who seemed to hang upon his words.

Soon after he went back to his studio half

intoxicated by her smiles; but the next morning he had grown more himself, and had a long talk with Joe Pacey, his greatest intimate, and been advised to paint the portrait by all means, but to hit hard for price.

"Do you no end of good, boy; but take care of yourself; she's the most beautiful woman in society."

Dale had laughed contemptuously, accepted the commission, and matters had gone on till it had come to this. He had been forced to be a witness of the breach between husband and wife, the cruelty of the treatment she received, and he had heard that painful drawing in of the breath, as she sat there almost within touch. She, the suffering woman, who had from the first accorded to him what had seemed to be the warmest friendship; and now the blood rose to his brain, and his resolutions, his fierce accusations, appeared to have been all in vain.

He dared not look round in the terrible silence which had ensued. He could only think that he was alone with the woman against whom his friend had warned him, and for the moment, in the giddy sensation that attacked him, he felt that he must rush from the room.

Then he started, and the brush fell from his hand, for there was a quick movement in the chair on his left, and he turned sharply, to find Valentina's eyes filled with tears, but not dimmed so that he could not read the yearning, passionate look with which she gazed at him, as she said in a low, thrilling whisper—

"You heard—you saw—all. Have you no pity for me—no word to say?"

For a few moments not a word.

The Contessa rose and took a step toward him, with her hands raised appealingly.

"You do not—you cannot—understand," she half whispered, "or you would speak to me. Can you not see how alone I am in the world, insulted, out-raged, by that man whose wife I was almost forced to become? Wife!" she cried, "no, his slave, loaded with fetters of gold, which cut into my flesh till my life becomes insufferable. Mr. Dale—Arm-strong, I thought you sympathised with me in my unhappy state. Have I not shown you, since fate threw us so strangely together, that my life has been renewed—that everything has seemed changed?"

He looked at her wildly, and the palette he held fell upon the rich thick carpet in the struggle going on within his breast.

"Are you dumb?" she whispered softly; "have you been blind to my sufferings?"

"No, no!" he cried. "Indeed, I have not. But you must not speak like this. It is madness. I have seen and pitied. I have felt that your hus-band——"

"Husband!" she said contemptuously.

“Oh, hush!” he cried. “Lady Dellatoria, you are angry—excited. Yes, I see and know everything, but for your own sake, don’t—for Heaven’s sake, don’t speak to me like this.”

“Why,” she said bitterly, “are you not honest and true?”

“No,” he cried wildly. “It is mere folly. It has all been a terrible mistake my coming here. I cannot —I will not continue this work. It is impossible. The Conte insults me. He is dissatisfied. Lady Dellatoria, I cannot submit to all his——”

He shrank from her, for her hand was laid upon his arm.

“Yes,” she said, as she raised her face towards his; “he insults you, as he insults me; he—poor, weak, pitiful creature—insults you who are so true and manly. I am not blind. I have seen all that you try to hide. You pity me; you have shown yourself my sympathetic friend. Yes, and I have seen more—all that you have tried so hard to hide in your veneration—your love for a despairing woman. Mr. Dale—Armstrong,” she whispered— and her voice was low, tender, and caressing; her eyes seeking his with a passionate, yearning look, which thrilled him—“don’t leave me now; I could not bear it.”

“Lady Dellatoria!” he panted wildly, as honour made one more stand in his behalf.

“Valentina,” she whispered, “who casts off all a

woman's reserve for you, the first who ever taught her that, after all, there is such a thing as love in this weary world, and with it hope and joy."

The hands which had rested upon his arm rose to his shoulders, and tightened about his neck, as she laid her burning face upon his breast.

CHAPTER V

WITH one quick motion, Armstrong threw Valentina back into her seat, and snatched up palette and brushes, mad with rage and shame, as he made an effort to go on painting. For the drawing-room door had been opened with a good deal of rattling of the handle, and he expected that the next minute he would have to turn and face the husband.

But it was a woman's voice, full of irony and sarcasm, and he turned sharply, to see that the Contessa sat back in her chair with a strangely angry light in her dark eyes, gazing at Lady Grayson.

"Pray forgive me, dear," said the latter mockingly. "So sorry to disturb you. I was obliged to come back, for I have lost my purse. Did I leave it here?"

"How could you have left it here?" said the Contessa coldly, as she quivered beneath her friend's gaze.

"I thought, love, that perhaps I had drawn it out with my handkerchief. It is so tiresome to lose one's purse; is it not, Mr. Dale?"

"Worse, madam, not to have one to lose," said Armstrong, who was placing his brushes in their case.

"How droll you are," said Lady Grayson; "as if anybody except a beggar could be without a purse. But surely you have not done painting the portrait?"

"Yes, Lady Grayson, I have done painting the portrait," replied Dale gravely.

"And all through my interruption. Oh, my dearest Valentina, how could I be so indiscreet as to come and interrupt your charming sitting."

"Would it be a sin to strangle this mocking wretch, who is triumphing over her shame and my disgrace?" thought Dale.

The Contessa was silent, and the situation growing maddening, when Lady Grayson suddenly exclaimed—

"Why, there! I told the dear Conte that I felt sure I had dropped it here; and when I am influenced about anything happening, as I was in this case, I am pretty sure to be right."

She said this meaningly, with a smile at the other actors in the scene, and then took a few steps toward the couch she had occupied, and, picking from it the missing purse, held it up in triumph, and with her eyes sparkling with malicious glee.

"I am so glad," she cried; "I was so sure. Good-bye once more, dearest Valentina. Good morning, Mr. Dale. Oh, you fortunate man," she continued, gazing at the canvas. "To paint like that. Ah, well, perhaps it may be my turn next," she added, with a mocking glance at the Contessa. "What, you going too, Mr. Dale?   Then I did spoil the sitting."

"No, madam," said Armstrong coldly; "your arrival was most opportune.   Lady Dellatoria, my man shall come for the canvas."

Valentina darted a wildly reproachful look at him, which he met for a moment, flushed, and turned from with a shiver.

"May I see you to your carriage, Lady Grayson?" he said.

"Oh, thank you, Mr. Dale: if you would.   Good-bye, dearest," she cried, with a triumphant mocking look at the fierce, beautiful face.   "You must let me drop you at your studio, Mr. Dale," she continued; and as the door closed behind them, Valentina started from her chair to press her hands to her temples, uttering a low, piteous moan.

"Cast off! and for her!" she cried wildly.   "She has always been trying to lure him from me—him —my husband; and she could not rest in her suspicions without coming back."

She ran to the window to stand unseen, gazing down, and to her agony she saw Dale step into the carriage, take his seat beside Lady Grayson, and be carried off.

Valentina turned from the window with her face convulsed, but it grew smooth and beautiful, and there was a dreamy look in her eyes, and a smile upon her parted, humid lips.

"I am mad," she said to herself, with a mocking laugh. "He care for her! Absurd! He loves me! In his brave fight he struggled hard, but—he loves me. His arms did hold me to his breast; his lips did press mine. And she?—poor weak fool, with her transparent trick, to return and play the spy. Let her know, and have a hold upon me, and defy me about Cesare. She will threaten me some day if I revile her. Poor fool! I am the stronger —stronger than ever now. I could defy the world, for, in spite of his cold looks, his anger against himself—he loves me."

She raised her eyes and stood looking straight before her for some moments, and then started, but recovered herself and smiled as she gazed at the figure before her in one of the mirror-filled panels of the room.

For she saw reflected there a face and figure that she felt no man could resist, and the smile upon her face grew brighter, the dreamy look intensified, as she murmured—

"At last! After these long, barren, weary years, love, the desire of a woman's life;" and closing her eyes, she slowly extended her arms as, in a whisper soft as the breath of eve, she murmured, "At last! Come back to me, my love—my life—my god."

CHAPTER VI.

THREE weeks soon pass in busy London, but to
Armstrong Dale the twenty-one days which ensued
after the scene at Portland Place were like months
of misery.

Stern in his resolve to avoid all further entanglement, and to keep faith to her whom in his heart
of hearts he loved, he shut himself up in his studio,
and made a desperate attack upon his great mythological picture, a broad high canvas, at which
Keren-Happuch stared open-mouthed, when she
went into the studio every morning "to do Mr.
Dale up"—a feat which consisted in brushing the
fluff about from one corner to another, and resulted
in a good deal of sniffing, and the lodging of more
dust upon casts, ledges, furniture, and above all, upon
Keren-Happuch's by no means classical features,
where it adhered, consequent upon a certain labour-
and-exercise-produced moisture which exuded from
the maiden's skin.

"I can't help looking smudgy," she used to say;
and directly after, "Comin', mum," for her name

was shouted in an acid voice by Mrs. Dunster, the elderly lady who let the studio and rooms in Fitzroy Square to any artist who would take them for a time.

But the poor little slavey was Keren-Happuch to that lady alone. To Armstrong she was always Miranda, on account of her friend, the dirty-white cat of the kitchen; to his artist friends such names as seemed good to them, and suited to their bizarre thoughts.

To Armstrong one morning came Keren-Happuch, as he was painting out his previous day's work upon his great picture, and she stood staring with her mouth open.

"Oh, Mr. Dale, sir, what a shame! What would Miss Montmorency say?"

"What about, Miranda?"

"You a-smudging out her beautiful figure as you took such pains to paint. Why, she was a-talking to me 'bout it, sir, when she was a-goin' yesterday, and said she was goin' to be Queen June-ho at the 'cademy."

"But she will not be, Miranda," said Armstrong sadly; "it was execrable. Ah, my little lass, what a pity it is that you could not stand for the figure."

"Me, sir! Oh, my!" cried the girl, giggling. "Why, I'm a perfect sight. And, oh!—I couldn't, you know. I mustn't stop, sir. I on'y come to tell you I was opening the front top winder, and see your funny friend, Mr. Pacey, go into Smithson's. He always do before he comes here."

" Keren-Hap-puch!" came faintly from below.

" Comin', mum," cried the girl, and she dashed out of the studio.

" Poor, patient little drudge!" said Armstrong. half aloud. "Well washed, neatly clothed, spoken to kindly, and not worked to death, what a good faithful little lassie she would be for a house. I wish Cornel could see her, and see her with my eyes."

He turned sharply, for there was a step—a heavy step—on the stair, and the artist's sad face brightened.

"Good little prophetess too. Here's old Joe at last. Where's the incense-box?"

He took a tobacco jar from a cupboard and placed it upon the nearest table, just as the door opened and a big, heavy, rough, grey-haired man entered, nodded, and, placing his soft felt hat upon his heavy stick, dropped into an easy-chair.

"Welcome, little stranger!" cried Armstrong merrily. "Why tarried the wheels of your chariot so long?"

There was no answer, but the visitor fixed his deeply set piercing eyes upon his brother artist.

"Was there a smoke somewhere last night, old lad, and the whisky of an evil brew?"

"No!" said the visitor shortly.

"Why, Joe, old lad, what's the matter? Coin run out?"

"No!"

"But there is something, old fellow," said Armstrong. "Can I help you?" And, passing his brush into the hand which held his palette, he grasped the other by the shoulder.

"Don't touch me," cried the visitor angrily, and he struck Armstrong's hand aside.

There was a pause, and then the latter said gravely—

"Joe, old fellow, I don't want to pry into your affairs, but if I can counsel or help you, don't shrink from asking. Can I do anything?"

"Yes—much."

"Hah! that's better," cried Armstrong, as if relieved. "What's the good of an Orestes, if P does not come to him when he is in a hole! But you are upset. There's no hurry. Fill your pipe, and give me a few words about my confounded picture while you calm down. Joe, old man, it's mythological, and it's going to turn out a myth. Isn't there a woman in London who could sit for my Juno?"

"Damn all women!" cried the visitor, in a deep hoarse tone.

"Well, that's rather too large an order, old fellow. Come, fill your pipe. Now, let's have it. What's wrong—landlady?"

The eyes of the man to whom he had been attracted from his first arrival in London, the big, large-hearted, unsuccessful artist, who yet possessed more ability than any one he knew, and whose advice was eagerly sought by a large circle of rising painters, were fixed upon him so intently that the colour rose in Armstrong Dale's cheeks, and, in spite of his self-control, the younger man looked conscious.

"Then it's all true," said Pacey bitterly.

"What's all true?" cried Dale.

"Armstrong, lad, I passed a bitter night, and I thought I would come on."

The young artist was silent, but his brow knit, and there was a twitching about the corner of his eyes.

"I sat smoking hard—ounces of strong tobacco; and in the clouds I saw a frank, good-looking young fellow, engaged to as sweet and pure a woman as ever breathed, coming up to this hell or heaven, London, whichever one makes of it, and going wrong. Ulysses among the Sirens, lad; and they sang too sweetly for him—that is, one did. The temptation was terribly strong, and he went under."

Armstrong's brow was dark as night now, and he drew his breath hard.

"Do you know what that meant, Armstrong? You are silent. I'll tell you. It meant breaking the heart of a true woman, and the wrecking of a man. He had ability—as a painter—and he could have made a name, but as soon as he woke from his mad dream, all was over. The zest had gone out of life. You know the song, lad—' A kiss too long—and life is never the same again.'"

"I made you my friend, Joe Pacey," said Armstrong huskily, "but by what right do you dare to come preaching your parables here?"

"Parable, man? It is the truth. Right? I have a right to tell you what wrecked my life—the story of twenty years ago."

"Joe!"

There was a gripping of hands.

"Ah! That's better. I tell you because history will repeat itself. Armstrong, lad, you have often talked to me of the one who is waiting and watching across the seas. Look at me—the wreck I am. For God's sake—for hers—your own, don't follow in my steps."

Neither spoke for a few minutes, and then with his voice changed—

"I can't humbug, Joe," said Armstrong. "Of course I understand you. You mean about—my commission."

"Yes, and I did warn you, lad. It is the talk of every set I've been into lately. There is nothing against her, but her position with that miserable hound, Dellatoria, is well known. He insults her with his mistresses time after time. Her beauty renders her open to scandal, and they say what I feared is true."

"What? Speak out."

"That she is madly taken with our handsome young artist."

"They say that?"

"Yes, and I gave them the lie. Last night I had it, though more definitely. I was at the Van Hagues —all artistic London goes there, and a spiteful, vindictive woman contrived, by hints and innuendoes, as she knew I was your friend, to let me know the state of affairs."

"Lady Grayson?"

"The same."

"The Jezebel!"

"And worse, lad. But, Armstrong, my lad—I have come then too late?"

Pride and resentment kept Dale silent for a few moments, and then he said huskily—

"It is false."

"But it is the talk of London, my lad, and it means when it comes to Dellatoria's ears—Bah! a miserable organ-grinder by rights—endless trouble. Perhaps a challenge. Brutes who have no right to name the word honour yell most about their own, as they call it."

"It is not true—or—there, I tell you it is not true."

"Not true?"

For answer Armstrong walked to the side of the studio, took a large canvas from where it stood face to the wall, and turned it to show the Contessa's face half painted.

"Good," said Pacey involuntarily, "but——"

"Don't ask me any more, Joe," said Dale. "Be satisfied that history is not going to repeat itself. I have declined to go on with the commission."

"Armstrong, lad," cried Pacey, springing from his seat, and clapping his hands on the young man's shoulders to look him intently in the eyes. "Bah!" he literally roared, "and I spoiled my night's rest, and——Here: got any whisky, old man? 'Bacco? Oh, here we are;" and he dragged a large black briar-root, well burned, from his breast and began to fill it. Then, taking a common box of matches from his pocket—a box he had bought an hour before from a beggar in the street, he threw himself back in the big chair, lifted one leg, and gave the match a sharp rub on his trousers, lit up, sending forth volumes of cloud, and in an entirely different tone of voice, said quite blusteringly—

"Now then, about that goddess canvas; let's have a smell at it. Hah! yes, you want a Juno—a living, breathing divinity, all beauty, scorn, passion, hatred. No, my lad, there are plenty of flesh subjects who would do as well as one of Titian's, and you could beat an Etty into fits; but there isn't a model in London who could sit for the divine face you want.

Your only chance is to evolve it from your mind as you paint another head."

"Yes; perhaps you are right," said Dale dreamily.

"Sure I am.　There, go in and win, my lad. You'll do it.—Hah! that's good whisky.—My dear old fellow, I might have known.　I ought to have trusted you."

"Don't say any more about it."

"But I must, to ease my mind.　I ought to have known that my young Samson would not yield to any Delilah, and be shorn of his manly locks. —Yes, that's capital whisky.　I haven't had a drop since yesterday afternoon.　A toast: 'Confound the wrong woman.'　Hang them," he continued after a long draught, "they're always coming to you with rosy apples in their hands or cheeks, and saying, 'Have a bite.'　You don't want to paint portraits.　You can paint angels from clay to bring you cash and fame.　Aha, my goddess of beauty and brightness, I salute thee, Bella Donna, in Hippocrene!"

"Oh, do adone, Mr. Pacey," said the lady addressed, to wit, Keren-Happuch.　"I never do know what you mean, I declare "—(sniff)—" I wouldn't come into the studio when you're here if I wasn't obliged. Please, Mr. Dale, sir, here's that French Mossoo gentleman.　He says, his compliments, and are you too busy to see him ? "

"No, Hebe the fair, he is not," cried Pacey.　"Tell

him there is a symposium on the way, and he is to
ascend."

"A which, sir ? Sym—sym——"

"Sym—whisky, Bella Donna."

The girl glanced at Dale, who nodded his head,
and she hurried out. The door opened the next
minute to admit a slight little man, most carefully
dressed, and whose keen, refined features, essentially
French, were full of animation.

"Ah, you smoke, and are at rest," he said. "Then
I am welcome. Dear boys, both of you. And the
picture ?"

He stood, cigarette in teeth, gazing at the large
canvas for a few moments.

"Excellent ! So good !" he cried. "Ah, Dale, my
friend, you would be great, but you do so paint
backwards."

"Eh ?" cried Pacey.

"I mean, my faith, he was much more in advance
a month ago. There was a goddess here. Where
is she now ?"

"Behind the clouds," said Pacey, forming one of
a goodly size; and the others helped in a more
modest way, as an animated conversation ensued
upon art, Pacey giving his opinions loudly, and
with the decision of a judge, while the young
Frenchman listened to his criticism, much of
it being directed at a flower-painting he had in
progress.

The debate was at its height, when the little maid again appeared with a note in her hand.

"Aha!" cried Pacey, who was in the highest spirits—"maid of honour to the duchess—the flower of her sex again. Hah! how sweet the perfume of her presence wafted to my sense of smell."

"Oh, do adone, please, Mr. Pacey, sir. You're always making game of me. I'll tell missus you call her the duchess—see if I don't. It ain't me as smells: it's this here letter, quite strong. Please, Mr. Dale, sir, it was left by that lady in her carriage."

"Keren-Happuch!" came from below stairs as the girl handed Dale the note, and his countenance changed as he involuntarily turned his eyes to his friend.

"Keren-Happuch!" came again.

"Comin', mum," shouted the girl, thrusting her head for a moment through the ajar door, and turning back again.

"Said there wasn't no answer, sir."

"Keren-Happuch!"

"A call from the Duchess of Fitzroy Square," said Pacey merrily.

"No, sir, it was that Hightalian lady, her as is painted there," said the girl innocently, and pointing to the canvas leaning against the wall, as she ran out.

"Confound her!" roared Pacey, springing to his feet, and turning upon his friend, with his eyes flashing beneath his shaggy brows; "is there no such thing as truth in this cursed world?"

"What do you mean?" cried Dale hotly, as he crushed the scented note in his hand.

"Samson and Delilah," said Pacey, with savage mockery in his tones. "Here, Leronde, lad," he continued, taking up his glass, "a toast for you—Vive la gallantry. Bah!"

He lifted the glass high above his head, but did not drink. He gave Armstrong a fierce, contemptuous look, and dashed the glass into the grate, where it was shivered to atoms.

CHAPTER VII.

LERONDE stood for a moment watching his friends excitedly; and then, as Pacey moved towards the door, he sprang before it.

"No, no!" he cried; "you two shall not quarrel. I will not see it. You, my two artist friends who took pity on me when I fly—I, a communard—for my life from Paris. You, Pacie, who say I am brother of the crayon, and help me to sell to the dcalaire; you, Dale, dear friend, who say, 'Come, ole boy, and here is papaire and tobacco for cigarette,' and at times the dinner and the bock of bière, and sometimes wine—you shake hands, both of you. I, Alexis Leronde, say you muss."

"Silence!" roared Pacey. "Whoever heard of good coming of French mediation?"

"Be quiet, Leronde," cried Armstrong firmly. "Joe, old fellow, let me—a word—explain."

"Explain?" growled Pacey, as the young Parisian shrugged his shoulders and stood aside to begin rolling up a cigarette with his thin deft fingers.

"Stop, Joe!" cried Armstrong, "you shall not go.

The letter is some request about the picture—for another artist to finish it. Here, read it, and satisfy yourself."

He tore open the scented missive, glanced at it, and was about to hand it over to his friend; but a few words caught his eye, and he crushed the paper in his hand, to stand flushed and frowning before his friend.

"All right: I see," said the latter, with a bitter, contemptuous laugh. "We're a paltry, weak lot, we men. Poor little daughter of the stars and stripes across the herring-pond! I'm sorry, for I did think I could believe your word."

"Dear boys—ole men!" cried Leronde, advancing once more to play mediator.

"Shut up!" roared Pacey, so fiercely that the young Frenchman frowned, folded his arms across his chest, and puffed out a cloud of smoke in defiance.

"Joe, I swear——"

"Thank you," said Pacey ironically. "I can do enough of that as I go home;" and, swinging open the door, he strode out and went down-stairs, whistling loudly the last popular music-hall air.

"Aha! he flies," cried Leronde, biting through his cigarette, the lighted end falling to the floor, while he ground up the other between his teeth. "I go down. He insult me—he insult you, my

dear friend. I pull his nose on ze door mat, and say damn."

"Be quiet, lad!" cried Armstrong fiercely. "It is nothing to do with you. It is my affair."

"Yes, I understand, dear ole man," said Leronde, placing his fingers to his lips, and nodding his head a great deal, while Armstrong stood dreamy and thoughtful, frowning, as if undecided what to do. "I know I am French—man of the whole world, my friend. I love the big Pacie. So good, so noble, but he is not young and handsome. The lady, she prefaire my other good friend. What marvel? And the good Pacie is jealous."

"No, no; you do not understand."

"But, yes. Cherchez la femme! It is so always. They make all the mischief in the great world, but we love them always the same."

"I tell you that you do not understand," cried Armstrong angrily.

"Well, no; but enough, my friend. Ah, there is so much in a lettaire that is perfumed. I do not like it; you two are such good friends—my best friends; you, the American, he, the big honest Jean Bull. I do not like you to fight, but there, what is it?—a meeting for the honour in Hyde Park, a few minutes wiz the small sword, a scratch, and then you embrace, and we go to the déjeûner better friends than before. You are silent. I will make another cigarette."

"I was thinking," said Dale slowly.

"What—you fear to ask me to be your second? Be of good courage, my friend. I will bear your cartel of defiance, and ask him who is his friend."

"Bah!" ejaculated Dale, so roughly that Leronde frowned. "There, don't take any notice of me, old fellow," he cried. "Sit down and smoke. You will excuse me."

Leronde bowed, and Armstrong hurried into his inner room, where he smoothed out the note, and read half aloud and in a disconnected way :—

> "*How can you stay away—these long weary weeks —my unhappy state—force me to write humbly— appealingly—my wretched thoughts—Lady Grayson —her double looks of triumph over me—will not believe it of you—could not be so base for such a heartless woman as that—heartbroken—my first and only love—won from me my shameless avowal—not shameless—a love as true as ever given—for you so good and noble. In despair—no rest but in the grave—forgive your coldness. Come back to me or I shall die—die now when hope, love, and joy are before me. You must—you shall—I pray by all that is true and manly in your nature—or in my mad recklessness and despair I shall cast consequences to the winds and come to you.*"

Dale crushed up the letter once again, and as he stood frowning and thoughtful, he struck a match, lit the paper, and held it in his hand till it had completely burned out, scorching his hand the while.

Then, going to the window, he blew the tinder out and saw it fall.

"The ashes of a dead love," he muttered; and then quickly, "No, it was not love. The mad fancy of the moment. There, it is all over. Poor woman! if all she says is honest truth, she must fight it down, and forgive me if I have been to blame. Yes; some day I can tell her. She will not forgive me, for there is nothing to forgive. Poor little woman! Ah, if the one who loves us could see and know all—the life, the thoughts of the wisest and best man who ever breathed! Nature, you are a hard mistress. Well, that is over; but poor old Joe! He will find out the truth, though, and ask my pardon. Everything comes to the man who waits."

He crossed to a desk lying on a table by his bed, opened it, took out a photograph, and gazed at it for a few moments before replacing it with a sigh.

"You can be at rest, little one. Surely I am strong enough to keep my word."

Then he started and bit his lip, for a hot flush came to his temples as the last words in the letter he had burned rose before him: "*cast consequences to the winds and come to you.*"

He shivered at the idea, as for the moment he saw the beautiful, passionate woman standing before him with her pleading eyes and outstretched hands.

"No!" he cried aloud, "she would not go to the man who treats her with silence and——"

"Did you call me, mon ami?" said a voice at the door.

"No, old fellow; I'm coming," cried Dale; and then to himself, as one who has mastered self, "That is all past and gone—in ashes to the winds. Now for work."

CHAPTER VIII.

"Nothing like hard work.   I've conquered," said
Dale to himself one morning, as he sat toiling away
at his big picture, whose minor portions were standing out definitely round the principal figure, which
had been painted in again and again, but always to
be cleaned off in disgust, and was now merely
sketched in charcoal.

He was waiting patiently for the model who was
to attend to stand for that figure—the figure only
—for Pacey's idea had taken hold, and, though
he could not dwell upon it without a nervous
feeling of dread, and asking himself whether it
was not dangerous ground to take, he had determined, as he thought, to prove his strength, to
endeavour to idealise the Contessa's features for
his Juno.   It was the very countenance he wished
to produce, and if he could have caught her expression and fixed it upon canvas that day when
the Conte entered, so evidently by preconcerted
arrangement with Lady Grayson, the picture would
have been perfect.

"It need not be like her," he argued; "it is the expression I want."

He knew that in very few hours he could produce that face with its scornful eyes, but he always put it off.

After a time, when the trouble there was not so fresh, it would be more easy—"and the power to paint it as I saw it then have grown faint," he added in despair, with the consequence that between the desire to paint a masterpiece, and the temptation to which he had been exposed, the face of Lady Dellatoria was always before him, sleeping and waking; though had he made a strong effort to cast out the recollection of those passionate, yearning eyes, the letters he received from time to time would have kept the memory fresh.

"At last!" he cried that morning, as steps were heard upon the stairs. "But she has not a light foot. I remember, though: they told me that she was a fine, majestic-looking woman."

There was a tap at the door.

"Come in."

Jupiter himself, in the person of Daniel Jaggs, thrust in his noble head.

"All right, Emperor, come in," said Dale, going on painting, giving touches to the background of his Olympian scene, with its group of glowing beauties, who were to be surpassed by the majesty of the principal figure still to come. "What is it? Don't want you to-day."

"No, sir. I knowed it was a lady day, but I've come with a message from one."

"Not from Lady——"

He ceased speaking, and his heart beat heavily. Jaggs had been to and from Portland Place with the canvas. Had she made him her messenger?

"Yes, sir; from Lady Somers Town."

"What?" cried Dale, with a sigh of relief, though, to his agony, he felt that he longed to hear from the Contessa again.

"Lady Somers Town, sir; that's what Mr. Pacey used to call her. Miss Vere Montesquieu of the Kaiserinn."

"Miss Vere Montesquieu!" said Dale contemptuously.

"Well, that's what she calls herself, sir. Did you say what was her real name, sir?"

"No, I didn't, but I thought it. Oh, by the way, Jaggs, I must have another sitting or two from you. We haven't quite caught the expression of Jupiter's lips."

"No, sir, we haven't, sir," said the model, looking at the canvas wistfully. "I know azactly what you want, but it's so hard to put it on."

"It is, Jaggs."

"You want him to be looking as he would if he

was afraid of his missus, and she'd just found him out at one of his games."

" That's it."

" Well, sir, I'll try again. Perhaps I can manage it next time. I was a bit on the other night, and I did get it pretty warm when I went home. I'll try and feel like I did then, next time I'm a settin'."

" Yes, do," said Dale, who kept on with his work. "Ah, that's better. Well, you were going to say something. Is anything wrong ? "

" Well, sir, I'm only a poor model, and it ain't for me to presoom."

" Lookers-on see most of the game, Jaggs. What is it ? "

" Well, sir, I was looking at Jupiter's corpus."

" Eh ? See something out of drawing ? "

" No, sir; your nattomy's all right, of course. Never see it wrong. You're splendid on 'ticulation, muskle, and flesh. But that's Sam Spraggs as sat for the body, wasn't it ? "

" Yes; I've fitted it to your head."

" Well, sir, not to presoom, do you feel sure as it wouldn't be more god-like, more Jupitery as you may say, if you let me set, painted that out, and give the head the proper body. Be more nat'ral like, wouldn't it ? "

" No. What's the matter with that ?—the composition of a more muscular man with your head is, I think, excellent."

"But it ain't nat'ral like, sir. You see, Sam's too fat."

"Oh no, Jaggs. He only looks as if Hebe and Ganymede had poured him out good potions of a prime vintage, and as if the honey of Hybla often melted in his mouth."

"Well, sir, you knows best. Maria Budd says—"

"Who?"

"Miss Montesquieu, sir. She's old Budd's—the Somers Town greengrocer's—gal."

"Humph! Idiot! Well, what message has she sent? Not coming again?"

"No, sir. She's very sorry, sir; but she's got an engagement to early dinner at Brighton to-day, and won't only be back in time to take her place in the chorus to-night."

"Confound the woman! I shall never get the figure done. Do you know of any one else, Jaggs?"

"No, sir; and I'm afraid that you won't after all be satisfied with her."

"Ah, well, you needn't wait. Seen Mr. Pacey lately?"

"Yes, sir. Looks very ill, he do. Good morning, sir."

"Good morning."

"Beg pardon, sir; but my missus——"

"There, there, I don't want to hear a long string of your inventions, Jaggs. How much do you want?"

"Oh, thankye, sir. If you could manage to let me have five shillings on account.—Thankye, sir. You are a gentleman."

"The Emperor" departed, winking to himself as if he had something on his mind; and Dale threw down brushes and palette, sat back with his hands clasped behind his head, gazing at the blank place in his great canvas, till by slow degrees it was filled, and in all her majestic angry beauty Juno stood there, with her attendants shrinking and looking on, while she seemed to be flashing at her lord lightnings more terrible than those he held in his hand.

The face, the wondrous figure, in all its glow of mature womanhood, were there; and then the eyes seemed to turn upon Dale a look of love and appeal to him to think upon her piteous state, vowed to love and honour such a man as that.

Armstrong shuddered and wrenched his eyes away, wondering at the power of his vivid imagination, which had conjured up before him the Contessa in all the pride of her womanly beauty; and strive how he might to think of her only in connection with his picture, as he felt that he could produce her exactly there, and make the group a triumph of his work, he knew that his thoughts were of another cast, and that, in spite of all, this woman had inspired him with a passion that enthralled his very soul.

He started up, for the maid entered with a letter, and he fancied that she seemed to read his thoughts, as he took it and threw it carelessly on the table.

He did not look at the address. There was the Conte's florid crest, face upward, and it lay there ready to be burned as soon as he left his seat, for the matches were over the fireless grate.

Keren-Happuch had reached the door.

"'Tain't scented up like some on 'em," she said to herself; and then she turned to look wistfully at the artist, whose eyes were fixed upon vacancy, for he was reading the letter in imagination. He knew every word of sorrowful reproach it would contain, for the letters were little varied. She would tell him of her solitary state, beg him to reconsider his decision, and ask him whether, in spite of the world and its laws, it was not a man's duty to take compassion upon the woman who loved him with all her heart. Yes: he could read it all.

"Must get away," he said to himself. "Why not go back home, and seek for safety behind the armour of her innocency? My poor darling, I want to be true to you, but I am sorely tempted now. It cannot be love; only a vile, degrading passion from which I must flee, for I am—Heaven knows, how weak."

"Ain't yer well, sir?" said Keren-Happuch, in commiserating tones.

He started, not knowing that the girl was there.

"Well? Oh yes, Miranda, quite well."

"No, you ain't, sir, I know; and it ain't because you smokes too much, nor comes home all tipsy like some artisses does, for I never let you in when you wasn't just what you are now, the nicest gent we ever had here."

"Why, you wicked little flatterer, what does this mean?" cried Dale merrily.

"No, sir, and that won't do," said the girl. "I'm little, but I'm precious old, and I've seen and knows a deal. You ain't well, sir!"

"Nonsense, girl! I'm quite well. There, run away."

"No, sir, there ain't no need; she's out. There's no one at home but me and puss. I can talk to you to-day without her knowing and shouting after me. She 'ates me talking to the lodgers.—I knows you ain't well."

"What rubbish, my girl! I'm well enough."

"Oh no; you ain't, sir. I don't mean poorly, and wants physic, but ill with wherritin', same as I feels sometimes when I gets it extry from missus. I know what's the matter; you've got what Mr. Branton had when he spent six months over his 'cademy picture as was lovely, and they sent it back. He said it was the blues. That's what you've got, because you can't get on with yours, which is too lovely to be sent back. I know what a bother you've had to get a model for the middle there, and it worries you."

"Well, yes, Miranda, my girl, I'll confess it does."

"I knowed it," she cried, clapping her hands; "and just because you're bothered, none of the gents don't seem to come and see you now. Mr. Leerondec ain't been, and Mr. Pacey don't seem to come anigh you. Sometimes I feel glad, because he teases me so, and allus says things I don't understand. But I don't mind: I wish he'd come now and cheer you up."

"Oh, I shall be all right, Mirandy, my little lassie, as soon——"

"Yes, that you will, sir, because you must get it done, you know. It is lovely."

"Think so?" said Dale, who felt amused by the poor, thin, smutty little object's interest in his welfare.

"Think so! Oh, there ain't no thinking about it. I heard Mr. Pacey tell Mr. Leerondec that it was the best thing he ever sec o' yours. I do want you to get it done, sir. It seems such a pity for that big bit in the middle not to be painted."

"Yes, girl; but it must wait."

"Mr. Dale, sir, you won't think anything, will you?"

"Eh? What about?"

"'Cause of what I'm going to say, sir," she said

bashfully. "I do want you to get that picture well hung, sir, and make your fortune, and get to be a R. A."

"Thank you. What were you going to say?"

"Only, sir, as I wouldn't for any one else; no, not if it was for the Prince o' Wales, or the Dook o' Edinburgh hisself, but I would for you."

"I don't understand you," said Dale, wondering at the girl's manner.

"I meant, sir, as sooner — sooner — than you shouldn't get that picture done and painted proper, I'd come and stand for that there figure myself."

Dale wanted to burst out laughing at the idea of the poor, ill-nurtured, grubby little creature becoming his model for the mature, graceful Juno; but there was so much genuine desire to help him, so much naïve innocency in the poor little drudge's words, that he contained himself, and before he could think of how to refuse without hurting her feelings, there was a resonant double knock and ring at the front door.

"Why, if it ain't the postman again," cried the girl. "He was here just now. I know: it's one o' them mail letters, as they calls 'em, from foreign abroad."

Keren-Happuch was right, for she came panting up directly with a thin paper envelope in her hand, branded "Boston, U.S.A."

"For you, sir," she said; and she looked at him

wistfully, as in an emotional way he snatched the letter from her hand and pressed it to his lips.

"Salvation!" he muttered, as he turned away to go to the inner room. "God bless you, darling! You are with me once again. I never wanted you worse."

"It's from his sweetheart over acrost the seas," said Keren-Happuch, as she spread her dirty apron on the balustrade, so as not to soil the mahogany with her hand as she leaned upon it to go down, sadly "And he's in love, too; that's what's the matter with him.   Puss, puss, puss!"

There was a soft mew, and a dirty white cat trotted up to meet her, and leaped up to climb to her thin shoulders, and then rub its head affectionately against her head, to the disarrangement of her dirty cap.

"Ah! don't stick your claws through my thin clothes.—Yes," she mused, "he's in love. Wonder what people feel like who are in love, and whether anybody'll ever love me. Don't suppose any one ever will: I'm such a poor-looking sort o' thing. But it don't matter. You like me, don't you, puss ? And them as is in love don't seem to be very happy after all."

CHAPTER IX.

THE MODEL.

ARMSTRONG Dale did not hear the door close.
Picture—the Contessa—everything was forgotten,
and for the time he was back in Boston. For he
had thrown himself into a chair, and torn open the
envelope. But he could not rest like that. He
wanted room, and he came back to begin striding
about his studio, reading as he walked.

But it did not seem to him like reading, for the
words he scanned took life and light and tone as he
grasped the pure, sweet, trusting words of the writer,
breathing her intense love for the man to whom she
had plighted her troth. And as in imagination he
listened to the sweet breathings of her affection, and
revelled in her homely prattle about those he knew,
and her hopeful talk of the future, when he would
have grown famous and returned home to the
honours which would be showered upon him by his
people—to the welcome for him in that one true
throbbing heart, his own throbbed, too, heavily, and
his eyes grew moist and dim.

"God bless you, darling!" he cried passionately; "you have saved me when I was tottering on the brink and ready to fall. The touch of your dear hand has drawn me back when all was over, as I thought. I will keep faith with you, Cornel. Forgive me, love! Heaven help me; how could I be so mad!"

There was a brightness directly after in his eyes, as he carefully bestowed the letter in his pocketbook and placed it in his breast.

"And they say the day of miracles is past, and that there is no magic in the world," he cried proudly. "Poor fools! they don't know. Lie there, little talisman. You are only a scrap of paper stained with ink, but you are a charm of the strongest magic. Bah! It was all a passing madness, and I have won. What a silly, weak, morbid state I was in," he continued, as he stood in front of his picture, and snatched up palette and brushes. "Why, Cornel darling, you have burned up all the clouds with the bright sun of your dear love. And I can finish you now, my good old daub. Jupiter can easily have that hang-dog, cowardly, found-out look imported into his phiz. I feel as if I can see, and do it now. The nymphs are as good as anything I have done. I don't always satisfy myself, but that background is jolly. I've got so much light and sunshine into it, such a dreamy, golden atmosphere effect, that it brightens the whole thing, and what a nuisance it is that old Turner ever lived! If he had never been born, my background would have been grand. As it is—well, it's only an imitation. No, no; come, old fellow: say, a good bit of work by an honest student of old Turner's style. Yes," he continued, drawing back, "I think it will do. Even dear old Joe praised that; he said it wasn't so bad. Poor old chap! I wish we were friends again. And as for my Juno, I think I can manage her. Montesquieu shall come —esquieu—askew—no, not askew; I'll get her into a noble, dignified position somehow. I hope she has a good figure. While her face—why, Cornel, my darling, it shall be yours."

He paused to stand thoughtfully before the great canvas, drawn out upon its easel into the best light cast down from the sky panes above, and let his mahlstick rest upon the picture just above the blank, paint-stained portion left for the principal figure.

"Queer way of working," he said with a laugh, "finishing the surroundings before putting in the mainspring of my theme. That's hardly fair, though, for I painted my Juno first—ah! how many times, and rubbed her out. Never mind; she must come strong now to stand out well in front of these figures. She must—she shall."

He stood there motionless for a few minutes; and then, quite eagerly—

"Why not?" he said. "Too soft, sweet, and gentle-looking? Cornel, darling, it shall be an expiation of a fault, and some day in the future you shall stand before it and gaze in your own true face as I have painted you—made grand, crushing, majestic, full of scorn and contempt, as it would have been, had you stood face to face with me, awaking to the fact that I was utterly lost, unworthy of your love. I can—I will—paint that face, and that day, darling, when you turn to me with those questioning eyes, and tell me you could not have looked like this, you shall know the truth."

The inspiration was there, and with wonderful skill and rapidity he began to sketch in the face glowing before him in his imagination. No model could have given him the power to paint in so swiftly those lineaments, which began to live upon the canvas as the hours went on. For he was lost to everything but the task before him, and he grew flushed and excited as the noble frowning brow threatened, and then by a few deft touches those wonderful liquid eyes began to blaze with passionate scorn. The ruddy, beautifully curved lips were parted, revealing the glistening teeth; and at last, how long after he could not tell, he shrank away from the great canvas, to gaze at the features he had limned, trembling, awe-stricken, knowing that his work was masterly, but asking himself whether the painting was his, or some occult spiritual deed of which he had been the mere animal mechanism, worked by the powers of evil to blast him for ever.

His lips were parched, his tongue and throat felt dry with the fever which burned within him, as he stood trying to gather the courage to seize a cloth and wipe out the face that gazed at him and made him shrink in his despair.

He dragged his eyes from the canvas, and looked wildly round the great studio, where all was silent as the grave. The bright light had passed away; and he knew that it must be about sunset, for all was cold and grey, save the shadows in the corners of the room, and they were black. Everything was growing dim and misty, save the face upon his canvas, and that stood out with its scornful, fierce anger, though, through it all, so wonderful had been the inspiration beneath whose influence he had worked, there was an intense look of passionate love and forgiveness; the eyes, while scornfully condemning and upbraiding, seemed to say, " I love you still, for you are and always will be mine."

"Cornel!" he groaned. "Heaven help me! and I have fought so hard. Ah!" he cried, with a sigh of relief, for there were hurried footsteps on the stairs, and the fancied dimness of the studio seemed to pass away as little, meagre Keren-Happuch gave one sharp tap on the door, and then ran in, to stop short, looking wonderingly at the artist's ghastly, troubled face.

"Oh, Mr. Dale, sir, you do work too hard," she cried reproachfully. Then, in an eager whisper, "It's all right, sir. The model's come. I told her she was too late for to-day, but she said she'd see you all the same."

"Where is she?" said Armstrong, in a voice which startled him.

"In the 'all, sir. I made her wait while I come to know if you'd see her. She's got on a thick wail, but sech a figger, sir. She'll do."

"Send her up," said Dale, " but tell her I cannot be trifled with like this."

"Yes, sir. I'll tell her you're in a horful rage 'cause she didn't come this morning."

Dale hardly heard the words, but turned away as the girl left the room, to stand gazing at the face which had so magically sprung from the end of his brush; and he still stood gazing dreamily at the canvas when the door was once more opened, there was the rustling of a dress, and Keren-Happuch's voice was heard, saying snappishly—

"There's Mr. Dale."

Then the door was shut, and muttering, "Stuck-up, orty minx," the girl went down to her own region.

Dale did not stir, but still stood gazing at the canvas, fascinated by his work. But his lips moved, and he spoke half-angrily, but in a weary voice.

"I had given you up, Miss Montesquieu. I want you for this figure, but if you cannot keep faith with me——yes," he said, as his visitor stepped toward him, drawing off her veil—"for this."

He turned sharply then, as if influenced in some unaccountable way, and started back in horror and despair.

"Valentina !"

"Armstrong !" came in a low, passionate moan, as she flung herself upon his breast—"at last, at last !"

The palette and brushes dropped from his hands —he was but man—and she uttered a low sigh of content as his arms closed round her soft yielding form, and his lips joined hers in a long, passionate, clinging kiss.

Then reason mastered once more, and he thrust her from him.

"No, no," he gasped; "for God's sake, go! Why have you come ?"

"A cold welcome," she said, smiling. "I come to beg that you will grant his prayer."

"I do not understand you."

"My husband wrote begging you to reconsider your determination, and come to finish my portrait."

"Impossible ! He did not write."

She pointed to the unopened letter lying upon a table, with the florid crest plainly showing.

"I had not opened it," he said. "I thought——"

"That it was from me. How cruel men can be! He asks you to come back."

"At your persuasion?" cried Dale fiercely.

"Yes, at my persuasion, and you will come. You must—you shall." She clung closer to him. "Armstrong," she whispered, "I cannot live without you. You have drawn me to you; I could bear it no longer;" and she held to him once more in spite of his repellent hands.

"It is madness—your husband—your—your title —your fair fame as a woman."

"Empty words to me now," she said in a low, thrilling whisper. "I could not stay. You are my world—everything to me now."

"Woman, I tell you again, this is madness—your husband?"

"With Lady Grayson, I believe. What does it matter? I am here—with you. Armstrong, am I to go on my knees to you? I will—you have humbled me so. Why are you so cruel, when you love me too?"

"I—love you—no!"

She laughed softly as, in spite of his shrinking, her arms enfolded him once more, and her words came in a low sweet murmur to his ear.

"Yes; you love me—as wildly and passionately

as I love you. I knew it—I could feel it, though you would not answer my appeals. Look," she whispered, "it is as I felt; you are always thinking of me.. I am ever in your thoughts. But am I as beautiful as that? Yes: to you. But look from the picture to my eyes. They could not gaze so fiercely and scornfully as that. Now, tell me that you do not love me, and I was not in your thoughts."

She pointed to the features, glowing—almost speaking, from the canvas—her faithful portrait, full of the angry majesty he had sought to convey.

Alas! poor Cornel. Not a lineament was hers.

Armstrong groaned.

"Heaven help me!" he muttered. "Is it fate?"

His hands repulsed her no longer, and he stood holding her at arm's length, gazing into the eyes which fascinated, lost to everything but her influence over him, till with a hasty gesture, full of anger, she shrank away and sought her veil from the floor.

"Some one!" she whispered fiercely, for there was a step upon the stair.

"The Conte," cried Dale, startled at the interruption.

"Hide me, quick! That room," cried the Contessa; and she took a step toward it as she veiled her face. "No," she cried, turning proudly, and resisting an inclination to step behind the great canvas close to which she stood, " Let him see me. His faithlessness has divorced us, and given me to the man I love. You will protect me. Kill him if you wish. I am not afraid."

This in a hasty whisper as the steps came nearer, and Valentina's eyes glistened through her veil as she saw the artist draw himself up, and take a step forward to meet the intruder.

" Better that it should be so at once," she whispered. " Let him come."

The door was thrown quickly open as she spoke.

CHAPTER X.

ARMSTRONG'S teeth and hands were clenched for
the encounter with the angry husband who had
tracked his wife to the studio, and he was ready to
accept his fate, for he told himself that he could
fight no more against his destiny. The woman had
told him that he would defend her, and he must—
he would.

There was no feeling of dread, then, in his breast
as he advanced to the encounter, but only to stop
speechless with amazement as Pacey entered in
his abrupt, noisy manner, to grasp his hand and
clap him on the shoulder.

"Armstrong, old man," he cried loudly, "I could
not stand it any longer. You and I must be friends.
I believe you told me the truth, lad, I do from my
soul. La Bella Donna told me Miss Montesquieu
was here, but I thought that wouldn't matter, as she
wouldn't be sitting at this time."

Dale could not speak : he was paralysed.

"Don't hold off, old lad," said Pacey, in a low tone.

“We must make it up. Any apology when she's gone.”

He turned sharply to where the Contessa stood, closely veiled, and nodded to her familiarly.

“Glad you and Mr. Dale have come to terms. Many engagements on the way?”

There was no reply, but the tall proud figure seemed to stiffen, and there was a flash of the eyes through the veil at Armstrong, who now recovered his voice, while his heart sank low within him.

“Go now,” he said, “at once.”

“Oh, Montesquieu won't mind my being here. But do you really——”

Pacey stopped speaking, as he realised for the first time that it was not the model he had heard was sitting to his friend. He stared at her hard, as if puzzled, then at the canvas, where the beautiful sketch gazed at him fiercely, and he grasped in his own mind the situation.

The paint was wet and glistening: this was the model who had been sitting for the face, and it could be none other than the Contessa.

A change came over him on the instant. His brows knit, the free, noisy manner was gone, and he took off his hat, to say with quiet dignity, as he bent his head, but in a voice husky with the pain he felt—

“I beg Lady Dellatoria's pardon for my rudeness. I was mistaken,” and he turned to go.

"Stay, sir," she cried, in her low, deep, and musical tones; "my visit to your friend is over. Mr. Dale, will you see me to my carriage? It is waiting."

Valentina held out her hand, and, pale now with emotion, Armstrong advanced to the door, which he opened, and then offered his arm. This she took, and he led her down to the hall in silence.

"Your imprudence has ruined you," he said then, bitterly, "and disgraced me in the eyes of my friend."

"No," she said softly. "You can trust that man. He would die sooner than injure a woman because she loves. Now I am at rest. You will come to me, for I have won. You see," she continued, as Armstrong mechanically opened the door, and she stepped out proudly on to the steps, "I have no fear. Let the world talk as it will."

A handsomely appointed carriage drew up, and the footman sprang down to open the door, while Dale, who moved as if he were in a dream, handed her in, she touching his arm lightly, and sinking back upon the cushions.

"I shall expect you to-morrow then, Mr. Dale," she said aloud, "at the usual time." Then to the servant, "Home."

Armstrong stood at the edge of the pavement, bareheaded, till the carriage turned the corner out of the square; and then, still as if in a dream, he walked in, closed the door, and ascended to the studio to face his friend.

Pacey was standing with his hands behind him, gazing at the face upon the canvas. He did not stir when Dale took a couple of steps forward into the great, gloomy, darkening room, waiting for an angry outburst of reproaches.

A full minute must have elapsed before a single word was uttered, and then Pacey said slowly, and in the voice of one deeply moved—

"Is she as beautiful as this?"

Dale started, and looked wonderingly at his friend.

"I say, is she as beautiful as this?" repeated Pacey, still without turning his head.

"Yes: I have hardly done her justice."

"A woman to win empires—to bring the world to her feet," said Pacey slowly. "'Beautiful as an angel' is a blunder, lad. Such as she cannot be of Heaven's mould, but sent to drag men down to perdition. Armstrong, lad, I pity you. I suppose there are men who would come scathless through such a trial as this, but they must be few."

There was another long pause, and Pacey still gazed at the luminous face upon the canvas.

"Is that all you have to say?" said Dale at last.

"Yes, that is all, man. How can I attack you now? I knew that you had been tempted, and, in spite of appearances, I believed your word. I thought you had not fallen, and that I had been too hasty in all I said. Now I can only say once more, I pity you, and feel that I must forgive."

Dale drew a deep breath, which came sighing through his teeth as if he were in pain.

"Let's talk Art now, boy," said Pacey, taking out his pipe, and, going to the tall mantelpiece, he took down the tobacco-jar, filled the bowl, lit up, and began to smoke with feverish haste, as he threw one leg over a chair, resting his hands upon the back, and gazing frowningly at the face, while Dale stood near him with folded arms.

"From the earliest days men gained their inspiration in painting and sculpture from that which moved them to the core," said Pacey, slowly and didactically. "Yes, I believe in inspiration, lad. We can go on working, and studying, and painting, as you Yankees say, 'our level best,' but something more is needed to produce a face like that."

He was silent again, and sat as if fascinated by the work before him.

"What am I to say to you, lad?" he continued at last. "It is like sacrificing everything—honour, manhood, all a man should hold dear, to his art; but as a brother artist, what am I to say? I am dumb as a man, for I have seen her here and felt her presence. There was no need for me to look upon her face. It is beautiful indeed. I say that as the man. As the artist who has done so little for myself——"

"So much for others," said Dale quickly.

"Well, you fellows all believe in me and the hints I give, and some of you have made your mark pretty deep. Yes, as the man who has studied art these five and twenty years, I say this is wonderful. It did not take you long?"

"No."

"Of course not. There is life and passion in every touch. You must finish that, my lad, and we will keep it quiet. No one must see that but us till you send it in. Armstrong, boy, you are one of the great ones of earth. I knew that you had a deal in you, but this is all a master's touch."

"You think it is so good, then?" said Dale sadly.

"Think it good? You know how good it is. Better, perhaps, than you will ever paint again; but would to God, my lad, that you had not sunk so low to rise so high."

Dale sank into a chair, and let his face fall forward upon his hands, while Pacey went on slowly, still gazing at the canvas.

"Yes," he said, "it wanted that. All the rest is excellent. That bit of imitation of Turner comes out well. The man wants more feeling in the face —a little more of the unmasked—but this dwarfs all the rest, as it should. Armstrong, lad, it is the picture of the year. There," he continued, "my pipe's out, and I think I'll go. But be careful, lad. Don't touch that face more than you can help, and only when she is here."

Dale laughed bitterly.

"Why do you laugh? Is it such bad advice?"

"Yes."

And he partly told his friend how the work was done—leaving out all allusion to Cornel—Pacey hearing him quietly to the end.

"I am not surprised," he said at last. "What you say only endorses my ideas. Good-bye, lad; I'll go."

He rose from the chair, tapped the ashes out of his pipe, looking at them thoughtfully, and picked up his hat from where he had cast it upon the dusty floor. He then turned to face Dale, holding out his hand, but the artist did not see it, and sat buried in thought.

"Good-bye, old lad," said Pacey again.

Dale sprang to his feet, saw the outstretched hand, and drew back, shaking his head.

"Shake hands," said Pacey again, more loudly.

"No," said Dale bitterly; "you cannot think of me as of old."

"No; but more warmly perhaps, for there is pity mingled with the old friendship that I felt. I came here this afternoon, as schoolboys say, to make it up. I was in ignorance then; now I have eaten of the bitter fruit and know. Armstrong, lad, knowing all this, and as one who, with all his reck-less Bohemianism and worldliness, has kept up one little habit taught by her long dead, how can I say 'forgive me my trespasses' to-night if, with such a temptation as yours, I can't forgive ?"

Dale gazed at him wildly, and Pacey went on.

"The bond between us two is stronger now, lad, so strong that I think it would take death to snap the cord. Good-bye. If you do not see me soon, it is not that we are no longer friends."

Then their hands joined in a firm grip, and Pacey slowly left the room, muttering to himself as he passed out into the square—

"Fallen so low, to rise so high. Yes, I must save him, and there is only one way in which it can be done."

CHAPTER XI.

JAGGS MAKES A DISCOVERY.

LETTER after letter, which had remained un-answered.

"Their scent sickens me," Dale cried passionately, as he committed them to the flames unread, for he frankly owned to himself that he dare not read one, lest he should falter in the resolution he had made.

For he had struggled hard to fight against his fate, and though tied and tangled by the threads which still clung to him, he had mockingly told himself that he was not mad enough to venture into the spider's web again.

Then, twice over, he had hastily drawn a curtain in front of his great picture upon Keren-Happuch coming up to the studio to bring in a card—the Conte's—and bit his lip with rage and mortification as that gentleman was shown up, in company with Lady Grayson.

The visit on the first occasion was to complain about Dale's curt refusal to go on with the picture;

while the young artist haltingly gave as his reason that it was impossible for him to complete Lady Dellatoria's portrait on account of a large work that he was compelled to finish. And all the while Lady Grayson, with the reckless effrontery of her nature, looked at him mockingly, her eyes laughingly telling him that he was a poor weak coward, and that she could read him through and through.

Then came the second visit with the wretched Italian, blindly, or knowingly, to use him as a screen for his own amours, almost imploring him to come.

"Lady Dellatoria is so disappointed," he said volubly. "She takes the matter quite to heart. No doubt, Mr. Dale, there is a little vanity in the matter—the desire to be seen in the exhibition, painted by the famous young American artist."

"There are plenty of men, sir, who would gladly undertake the commission," said Dale angrily. "I beg that you will not ask me again."

"Mr. Dale, you are cruel," cried Lady Grayson. "Our poor Contessa will be desolate. Let me plead for you to come and finish the work."

"Aha! yes," cried the Conte, wrinkling up his face, though it was full enough before of premature lines. "A lady pleads. You cannot refuse her."

Dale gave the woman a look so full of contempt

and disgust that she coloured and then turned away, shrugging her shoulders.

"He is immovable," she said to the Conte.

"No, no! Body of Bacchus! I understand;" and he placed his finger to his lips, and half closing his eyes, signed to Dale to step aside with him. "Mr. Dale," he whispered, "Lady Dellatoria has set her mind upon this, and I see now: a much more highly paid commission that you wish to do for some one. That shall not stand in the way. Come, I double the amount for which we—what do you name it? Ah, yes—bargained."

Dale turned upon him fiercely.

"No, sir!" he cried; "it is not a question of money. No sum would induce me to finish that portrait."

"Ah, well: we shall see," said the Conte. "Do not be angry, my young friend. Lady Dellatoria will be eaten by chagrin. But we will discuss the matter no more to-day. Good morning."

He held out his hand to Lady Grayson, but she did not take it. She moved toward Dale, and held out her gloved fingers.

"Good morning, Mr. Dale," she said merrily. "You great men in oil are less approachable than a Prime Minister." Then in a low tone: "It is not true, all this show of opposition. I am not blind."

She turned and gave her hand to the Conte, and

they left the studio, Armstrong making no effort
to show them out, but standing motionless till he
heard the door close, when, with a gesture of contempt and disgust, he threw open the windows and
lit his pipe.

A minute later he had thrown the pipe aside
and taken out Cornel's letter to read; but the words
swam before his eyes, and he could only see the
face hidden behind that curtain.

"Poor little talisman!" he said, sadly apostro-
phising the letter, "you have lost your power. Evil
is stronger than good, after all."

"Good-bye, little one," he continued, "for ever.
You would forgive me if you knew all, for I am
drifting—drifting, and my strength has gone."

Two days passed—a week, and hour by hour he
had waited, fully expecting that Valentina would
come. He shrank from the meeting, but felt
that it must be, for her influence seemed to be over
him sleeping or waking, her eyes always gazing
into his.

But she did not come. Only another note, and
this he read in its brevity, for it contained but
these words—

"You will drive me to my death."

"Or me to mine," he muttered, as he burned the
letter; and then, in a raging desire to crush down
the thoughts which troubled him, he turned to his
work.

"Never!" he cried fiercely. "I will not go. If she comes here—well, if she does. That mockery of a man will track her some day, and then, in spite of English law, there will be a meeting, and he will kill me. I hope so. Then there would be rest."

The picture which he had now stubbornly set himself to finish, as if he were urged by some unseen power, progressed but slowly. "The Emperor" came to sit, and tried to mould his features into the desired aspect with more or less success; but, in spite of inquiries, and interview after interview with different models recommended by brother artists as suitable to stand for the figure, Dale's taste was too fastidious to be satisfied, and Juno's face alone looked scornfully from the canvas.

Pacey had been again and again, but only in a friendly way, to chat as of old, sometimes bringing with him Leronde to gossip and fence with, at other times alone. No reference was made to the picture or the past.

"I shall never finish it," said Dale, as he sat alone one day gazing at his canvas. "What shall I do— go abroad? Joe would come with me, and all this horrible dream might slowly die away."

"No," he muttered, after a pause; "it would not die. Better seek the true forgetfulness. Do all men at some time in their lives suffer from such a madness as mine?"

His musings were interrupted by a step upon the

stairs, and he hastily drew the curtain before his canvas.

A single rap, which sounded as if it had been given with the knob of a walking-stick, came upon the door panel, and directly afterwards, in answer to a loud "Come in," Jaggs entered with the knocker in his hand, to wit, a silk umbrella—one of those ingenious affairs formed by sewing all the folds where they have been slit up by wear and tear, and declared by the kerb vendor as being better than new—a fact as regards the price.

"Ah, Jaggs, good morning," said Dale. "But I don't want you. I shall let your face go as it is."

"Quite right, sir," said the man, glancing at the curtain. "Couldn't be better; but I didn't come about that."

"Oh, I see," said Dale sarcastically. "Your banker gone on the Continent?"

"The Emperor" drew himself up, and looked majestic in the face and pose of the head, shambling as to his legs, and extremely deferential in the curve of his body and the position of his hands and arms.

"Mr. Dale," he said, "I don't deny, sir, as there 'ave been times when a half-crown has been a little heaven, and a double florin a delight, but I was not agoing to ask assistance now, though I am still a strugglin' man, and been accustomed to better things. It was not to ask help, sir, as I'd come, but to bestow it, if so be as you'd condescend to accept it of your humble servant, as always feels a pride in your success, not to hide the fack that it does me good, sir, to be seen upon the line."

" Well, what do you mean ? " said Dale gruffly.

" I want to see that picture done, sir. It'll make our fortune, sir. I'm sure on it, and I say it with pride, there isn't anything as'll touch it for a mile round."

" Thank you, Jaggs ; you are very complimentary," said Dale ironically, but the tone was not observed.

" It's on'y justice, sir, and I ain't set going on for twenty years for artists without knowing a good picture when I see one. But that ain't business, sir. You want a model, sir, and that Miss Montesquieu, as she calls herself, won't be here for a month or two, and you needn't expect her. Did you try her as Mr. Pacey calls the Honourable Miss Brill ? "

" Pish ! I don't want to paint a fishwife, man."

" No, sir, you don't ; and of couise Miss Varsey Vavasour wouldn't do ? "

" No, no, no ! there is not one of them I'd care to have, Jaggs. If I go on with the figure, I shall work from some cast at first, and finish afterward from a model."

" No, sir, don't, pr'y don't," cried Jaggs. " You'll only myke it stiff and hard. It wouldn't be worthy on you, Mr. Dale, sir ; and besides, there ain't no need. You're a lion, sir, a reg'lar lion 'mong artises, sir, and you was caught in a net, sir, and couldn't get free, and all the time, sir, there was a little mouse a nibblin' and a nibblin' to get you out, sir, though you didn't know it, sir, and that mouse's nyme was Jaggs."

"What! You don't mean to say you know of a suitable model?"

"But I just do, sir. That's what I do say, sir."

"No, no," cried Armstrong peevishly. "I don't want to be worried into seeing one of your friends, Jaggs. Your taste and mine are too different for a lady of your choice to suit my work."

"Don't s'y that, sir," cried Jaggs, in an aggrieved tone of voice. "I'm on'y a common sort o' man, I own, sir, but I do know a good model when I see one—I mean one as shows breed. I don't mean one o' your pretty East End girls, with the bad stock showing through, but one as has got good furren breed in her."

"Is this a foreign woman, then?"

"That's it, sir. Comes from that place last where they ketch the little fishes as they sends over here for breakfast—not bloaters, sir, them furren ones."

"Anchovies?"

"No, sir, t'other ones in tins."

"Sardines?"

"That's it, sir: comes from Sardineyer last, but her father was a Ruman. Sort o' patriot kind o' chap as got into trouble for trying to free his country. Them furren chaps is always up to their

games, sir, like that theer Mr. Lerondy, and then
their country's so grateful that they has to come
over here to save themselves from being shot."

" But the woman ?"

" Oh, she come along with her father, sir, and he's
been trying to give Hightalian lessons, and don't get
on 'cause they say he don't talk pure, and he's too
proud to go out as a waiter and earn a honest living,
so the gal's begun going out to sit. But she don't
get on nayther, 'cause her figure's too high."

" What ! a great giraffe of a woman ?"

" Lor' bless you, no, sir ! 'bout five feet two half,
I should say. I meant charges stiff; won't go out
for less nor arf crown a hour, and them as tried her
don't like her 'cause she's so stuck up."

" Look here, Jaggs ; is she a finely formed, handsome woman ?"

" Well, Mr. Dale, sir, I won't deceive you, for from
what I hear her face ain't up to much ; but she don't
make a pynte o' faces, and I'm told as she's real good
for anything, from a Greek statoo to a hangel."

" Well, I'll see her. Where does she live ?"

" Leather Lane way, sir."

" Address ?"

" Ah, that I don't know, sir. I b'leeve it's
her father as does the business and takes the
money."

" He is her father ?"

" Oh yes, sir, it's all square. I'm told they're very
G

'spectable people.   Old man's quite the seedy furren gent, and the gal orful stand-off-ish."

"Tell him to come and bring his daughter.   If I don't like her, I'll pay for one sitting and she can go."

"Right, sir; and speaking 'onest, sir, I do hope as she will turn out all right."

"Thank you.   There's a crown for your trouble."

"Raly, sir, that ain't nessary," said "The Emperor," holding out his hand.—"Oh, well, sir, if you will be so gen'rous, why, 'tain't for me to stop you.—Good mornin', sir, good mornin'."

CHAPTER XII.

Two days passed, and Dale was standing, brush in hand, before his canvas, thinking. He had made up his mind to trust to his imagination to a great extent for the finishing of Juno's figure: this, with the many classic sketches he had made in Greece and Rome, would, he believed, enable him to be pretty well independent. He was in better spirits, for he had heard nothing from Portland Place, and flattered himself that the impression which had troubled him was growing fainter.

"Come in," he cried, as there was a tap at the door, and Keren-Happuch appeared, evidently fresh from a study in black-lead, and holding a card between a finger and thumb, guarded by her apron.

"Here's a model, sir, and she give me this."

Dale took a very dirty card, which looked as if it had been for some time in an old waistcoat pocket. Printed thereon were the words—"D. Jaggs. Head and face. Roman fathers, &c.," and written on the back in pencil, in Jaggs' cramped hand—

"Signora Azatchy Figgers."

"Where is she, Miranda?"

"On the front door mat, sir. And please, Mr. Dale, sir, mayn't I bring you some beef-tea?"

"No, thank you, Miranda. Bring up the visitor instead."

"Oh, dear! he do worry me," muttered Keren-Happuch. "I do hope he ain't going into a decline."

Dale smiled at the dirty card, and waited for the entrance of the new model, who was shown in directly by the grimy maid, and immediately, in a quick, jerky, excited way, looked sharply round the room before turning her face to the artist as the girl closed the door.

On his side he gazed with cold indifference at his visitor, who, after taking a couple of steps forward, stopped short, and he saw that she was rather tall, wore a closely fitting bonnet, over which a thick dark Shetland wool veil was drawn, and was draped from head to foot in a long black cloak, which had evidently seen a good deal of service.

"Signora Azacci?" said Dale, glancing at the card again, and making a good shot at her name.

It was evidently correct, for the woman said, in a husky voice, as if suffering from intense nervousness—

"Si, si."

"You are willing to stand for me—for this picture ?" said Dale, scanning her closely, but learning nothing respecting her figure on account of the cloak; and he spoke very coldly, for the woman's actions on entering struck him as being angular and awkward; now they were jerky, as she raised her hands to her temples.

"No Inglese, signore," she said then, excitedly; and again, after an embarrassed pause, "Parlate Italiano ?—No ?"

"No," said Dale, shaking his head.

Her hands again came from beneath her cloak in a despairing gesture. Then, placing one to her forehead, she looked round at the lumber of paintings and properties, as if seeking for a way to express herself, till her eyes lit upon the great uncovered canvas. Bending forward in a quick, alert way, she uttered a low, peculiar cry, and almost ran to it, leaned forward again, as if examining, and then, with extreme rapidity, pointed to the blank place in the picture where Lady Dellatoria's face stood out weirdly. She then took a few quick steps aside from where Dale stood, frowning and annoyed at what seemed to be a hopeless waste of time. Then, with a rapid movement, she unclasped the cloak, swept it from her shoulders, and holding it only with her left hand, let it fall in many folds to the floor, while as she stood before him now in a plainly made, tightly fitting black cloth princess dress, she

instinctively fell into almost the very attitude Dale
had in his mind's eye, and he saw at once that her
figure must be all that he wished.

"Bravo!" he cried involuntarily, and with an
artist's pleasure in an intelligence that grasps his
ideas.

At the word "Bravo!" the woman turned her
head quickly.

"Excellent," he continued; "that promises well."

Her face was hidden, but as she shrugged up
her shoulders nearly to her ears, and raised her
hands with the fingers contracted and toward him,
he felt that she must be wrinkling up her forehead and making a grimace expressive of her
vexation.

"Yes, it is tiresome," he said; "but we don't
want to talk. I dare say I can make you understand. But I've forgotten every word I picked up
in Rome."

"Ah!" cried the woman, with quick pantomimic
action, as she changed her attitude again, and leant
toward him—"Roma—Roma?"

"Si, si."

"My lord has been in Rome?" she cried in
Italian.

"I think I understand that," muttered Dale, "and
if your form proves to be equal to your quick
intelligence, my picture will be painted. Now
then, signora, this is a language I dare say you can

understand. Here are two half-crowns. For two hours—'due ore.'"

"Si, si," she cried eagerly, and she almost snatched the coins and held them to her veiled lips.

"Silver keys to your understanding, madam," he muttered, taking a mahlstick from where it stood against a chair. "Humph! I begin to be hopeful. Yes, more than hopeful," he continued, as the model was rapidly drawing off her shabby, carefully mended gloves, before taking a little common portemonnaie from her pocket and dropping the coins in one by one. Then aloud, as he pointed with the mahlstick, "La bella mano."

"Aha!" she cried quickly. But she gave her shoulders another shrug, and shook the purse, saying sadly—"Pel povero padre."

"'Padre.' For her father," muttered Dale. "Not so sordid as I thought, poor thing. Will you remove your veil?"

She leaned toward him.

"I said, Will you remove your veil?—Hang it, what is veil in Italian? 'Velum' in Latin."

She was evidently trying hard to grasp his meaning, and at the Latin "velum" she clapped her beautifully formed hands to her veil.

"No, no!" she cried haughtily; and then volubly, in Italian—"I am compelled to do this for bread. I do not know you, neither need you know me. My face is not beautiful, and we are strangers.

You wish to paint my figure. I will retain my veil."

"I do not understand you, signora, and yet I have a glimmering of what you wish to express," said Dale, as gravely as if his visitor could grasp every word. "There, you seem to be a lady, and—hang it all, this is very absurd, my preaching to you, and you to me. I wish Pacey were here. He speaks Italian like a native. No, poor lass, I suppose they must be starving nearly, or she would not stoop to this. I don't wish Joe Pacey were here."

Then quietly bowing as if acceding to her wishes, he made a sign to his visitor to take her attention, and as she watched him from behind her thick veil, he walked to the entrance and turned the key.

Crossing the studio to the farther door, he threw it open, and then drew forward from the end of the great room a large folding-screen, which he placed at the back of the dais and opened wide.

"There, signora," he said, "I am at your service;" and he pointed to the inner room, turned from her, and walked to the canvas.

The model stood motionless for a moment or two, and then caught up the great cloak from where it lay upon the floor.

"Grazie, Signore," she said then, with quiet dignity,

and she was hurrying across to the inner room, but he arrested her.

"One moment," he said, with grave respect, and the chivalrous manner of a true gentleman toward one whose tones seemed to suggest that she trusted him. "Let us arrange the pose first. Look at the picture: study it well. You see the subject."

Dale continued speaking, but kept on pointing to the scene he had depicted, and, to his intense gratification, she threw the cloak across a chair back, gazed intently at the picture for a few moments, letting her eyes rest longest upon the beautiful, scornful face, and then went quickly to the dais, stepped up, turned, and with rare intelligence fell once more into the very position he desired, bettering in fact that which she had sketched at first.

"Eccellentissimo!" he cried; and then she stepped down quickly, and glided into the inner room, while Dale gazed at his painting with a feeling of triumph sweeping away the morbid thoughts which had troubled him so long.

"Art is my mistress after all," he said to himself, as he glanced upward to see that the skylight was properly blinded, and then, going to a box, rapidly prepared his palette, armed himself with a sheaf of brushes, and altered the position of his easel a little.

He was hardly ready when he heard the slight

rattle of the handle, a faint rustling sound, and the swinging of the door again.

But he did not turn as a light step passed behind him, and a faint creaking sound announced that the model had mounted upon the dais.

He raised his eyes, and she was standing there apparently as he had seen her first, closely veiled, and still draped in the long, heavy, black cloak.

Then, with a quick movement, the long garment was thrown aside, and the model stood before him in the very attitude, and the perfection of her womanly beauty—a beauty made hideous in the ghastly effect produced by the black face and head swathed in the thick veil.

But this passed unnoticed by the artist, who, with a triumphant ejaculation, began to sketch rapidly, as he muttered to himself without vanity—

"Pacey is right : my canvas must be a success."

CHAPTER XIII.

A STRANGE SITTING.

"Yes," said Dale to himself again, "Art is my mistress. I have betrayed one, fought clear of the web of another, and now I am free to keep true to the only one I love."

And all through that visit of the Italian, he worked on with a strange eagerness, till, at what seemed to be the end of an hour at most, his model made a sudden movement.

"I beg your pardon," he said, "I ought to have told you to rest more often. Stanca?" For he recalled a word meaning fatigued or wearied.

"Si—si," she said quickly, and pointed to the clock on the mantelpiece, when, to Dale's astonishment, he saw that the two hours had elapsed, and that his model had quickly resumed her cloak. Then, without a word, she crossed to the door of the inner room, and about a quarter of an hour later emerged, to find him standing back studying his morning's work.

"Grazie," he cried, and then pointed to the

roughly sketched in figure. "Bravo!" he added, smiling.

She bent her head in a quiet, dignified manner, and raking up another Italian word or two, Armstrong said—

"A rivederla—au revoir."

"Ah, monsieur speaks French!" she cried in that tongue, but with a very peculiar accent.

"Yes, badly," he replied, also in French. "That is good; now we can get on better. Can you come to-morrow at the same time?"

"I am at monsieur's service."

"Then I shall expect you. Thank you for your patient attention. Another time, pray rest when you are fatigued."

She bowed in a stately manner, and pointed to the door which he had locked, and as soon as it was unfastened, passed out without turning her head.

Dale stood working at his sketch for another hour, and then turned it to the wall, to light his pipe and begin thinking about his model now that he had ceased work.

It was quite mysterious her insisting upon keeping her face covered. Why was it? Had she some terrible disfigurement, or was it from modesty? Possibly Her manner was perfect. She was evidently miserably poor, and seemed eager to gain money to support her father—he had quite grasped that—and the poor creature being compelled to stoop to this way of earning a livelihood, she naturally desired to remain incognito. Well, it was creditable, he thought; but the first idea came back. She was evidently a woman gifted by nature with an exquisite form, and at the same time, by accident or disease, her countenance was so marked that she was afraid of her clients being repelled, and declining to engage her.

"Ah, well, signora, the mysterious Italienne, I will respect your desire to remain incog. It is nothing to me," said Dale, half aloud, as he sent a cloud of blue vapour upward. "I may congratulate myself, though, on my good fortune in finding such a model."

He sat back in his chair, dwelling upon the figure, and then went twice over to his canvas, to compare his work with the figure in his imagination, and returned to his seat more than satisfied.

Then he put work aside, and began thinking of home, and the sweet sad face he could always picture, with its eyes gazing reproachfully at him.

"Yes," he said, with a sigh; "poor darling! It was fate. I was not worthy of her. When the misery and disappointment have died away—Heaven bless her!—she will love and be the wife of a better man, unless—unless some day she forgives me—some day when I have told her all."

The next morning he was all in readiness and

expectant. The light was good for painting, and his mind was more **at** rest, for there was no letter from the Contessa. But for a few moments he was angry with himself on finding that he felt a kind of pique at the readiness with which she had given up writing her reproaches. But that passed off, and as the time was near for the coming of the model, he drew the easel forward to see whether, after the night's rest, he felt as satisfied with his work as he did the previous day. But he hardly glanced at the figure, for the eyes were gazing at him in a terribly life-like way, full of scorn and reproach ; and as he met them, literally fascinated by the work to which his imagination lent so much reality, he shuddered and asked himself whether he had after all been able to free himself from the glamour—dragged himself loose from the spell of the Circe who had so suddenly altered the even course of his life.

He was still contemplating the face, and wondering whether others would look upon it with the fascination it exercised upon him, when Keren-Happuch came up to announce the arrival of his model, who entered directly after, to look at him sharply through her thick veil.

He uttered a low sigh full of satisfaction, for her coming was most welcome. It would force his attention to his work.

"Good morning," he said gravely and distinctly, in French. "You are very punctual."

She bowed distantly, and then her attention seemed to be caught by the face upon the canvas, and she drew near to stand gazing at it attentively.

She turned to him sharply. "The lady who sat for that: why did she not stay for you to finish the portrait?"

Dale started, half wondering, half annoyed by his model's imperious manner.

"It is great!" she said. Then in a quick, eager tone: "The lady you love?"

He was so startled by the suddenness of the question, that he replied as quickly—

"No, no. It is not from a model. It is imagination."

"Ah!" she said, and she looked at the picture more closely. "You thought of her and painted. You are very able, monsieur, but I like it not. It makes me to shiver, I know not why. It makes me afraid to look."

"Then don't look," said Dale, in an annoyed tone.

"You will cover it, please, monsieur. The face is so angry; it gives me dread."

"Pish!" ejaculated Dale. "Very well, though. Get ready, please. I want to do a long morning's work."

"Monsieur will pay me," she said, holding out her hand in its well-mended glove.

He took out a couple of half-crowns, which she almost snatched, and then, without a word, pointed to the door almost imperiously.

He nodded shortly, and went to fasten it, while she glided into the inner room, and in a wonderfully short space of time returned ready, took her place upon the dais, dropped the cloak, and he began to paint.

"Monsieur has not covered the dreadful head," she said hoarsely.

Without a word he took a square of brown paper, gummed it, and covered the face; then in perfect silence he went on painting, deeply interested in his work as his sketch took softer form and grew rapidly beneath his brush.

But the work did not progress so fast as on the previous day: he was painting well, but the black head, so incongruous and weird of aspect, posed upon the beautiful female form he was transferring to canvas, irritated him, and as he looked at his model from time to time, he could see that a pair of piercing eyes were watching him.

Half-an-hour had passed, when there was a low, weary sigh.

"We will rest a little," he said quietly, and pointing to a chair and the screen, he devoted himself to an unimportant part of the work for some ten minutes, but to be brought back to his model by her words—

"I am waiting, monsieur."

He started and resumed his work, remembering to pause for his patient model to rest twice over, and then to continue, and grow so excited over his efforts—painting so rapidly—that when he heard another weary sigh he glanced at the clock, and found that he had kept his model quite a quarter of an hour over her time.

"I beg your pardon, mademoiselle," he said. "You must be very weary."

"Yes, very weary," she said sadly, as she moved towards the door, glancing over her right shoulder at the picture. "It is better now. I can look at your work; the dreadful face makes me too much alarmed."

"A strange sitting," he said. "Two veiled faces."

There was a quick look through the thick veil, but she walked on into the room, and in due time passed him on her way, bowed distantly, and went out, leaving Dale motionless by his canvas, gazing after her at the door, and conjuring up in his mind the figure he had so lately had before him.

He recovered himself with a start, and raised one hand to his forehead.

CHAPTER XIV

It was with a novel feeling of anxiety that Dale waited for the coming of his model. A peculiar feverish desire to know more of her position had come over him, and he made up his mind to question her about her father and the cause of his exile. Jaggs had said that he had had to flee for life and liberty, and if he questioned her about these she would, foreigner-like, become communicative.

It was nothing to him, of course. This woman—lady perhaps, for her words bespoke refinement—would answer his purpose till the picture was finished. She was paid for her services, and when she was no longer required, there was an end of the visits to his studio.

He told himself all this as he sat before his great canvas, working patiently, filling up portions, and preparing for his model's coming. And as he worked on, with the figure as strongly marked as the model, the softly rounded contour of the graceful form began to glow in imagination with life, and at last Dale sprang from his seat, threw down palette and brushes, and shook his head as if to clear it from some strange confusion of intellect.

"How absurd!" he said aloud, and trying to turn the current of his thoughts, they drifted back at once to his model, and he gazed at his work, wondering which of his ideas was correct about her persistently keeping her face covered.

"She cannot be disfigured," he muttered. "It must be for reasons of her own.—She is, as I thought, forced to undertake a task that must be hateful to her. — I wonder whether her face is beautiful too?"

"Bah! what is it to me?" he muttered angrily. "I do not want to paint her face, and yet she must be very beautiful."

He sat down again before his canvas, thoughtful and dreamy, picturing to himself what her face might be, and the next minute he had seized a drawing-board upon which grey paper was already stretched, picked up a crayon, and with great rapidity sketched in memories of dark aquiline faces that he had studied in Rome and Paris, with one of later time—one of the women of the Italian colony which lives by the patronage of artists.

These soon covered the paper, and he sat gazing at them, wondering which would be suited to the figure he was painting.

Then, throwing the board aside, he began to pace the studio impatiently.

"What nonsense!" he muttered. "What craze is this! Her face is nothing to me. I'm overwrought. Worry and work are having their effect. I have had no exercise either lately. Yes: that's it: I'm overdone."

He stood hesitating for a few moments, and then thrust his hand into his pocket, and drew out five shillings.

"I'll rout out Pacey and Leronde, and we'll go up the river for a row."

He rang the bell and waited, giving one more glance at his picture, and then turning it face to the wall, with the curtain drawn.

He had hardly finished when Keren-Happuch's step was heard at the door, and she knocked and entered.

"You ring, please, sir?"

"Yes. Take this money. No—no—stop a moment. She would be hurt," he muttered, and, hastily wrapping it in a sheet of note-paper at the side table, he thrust the packet into an envelope, fastened it down, and directed it to La Signora Azacci.

"There, Keren-Happuch," he said.

"Don't call me that now, please, Mr. Dale, sir. I likes the other best, 'cause you don't do it to tease me, like Mr. Pacey."

"Well then, Miranda, my little child of toil," he said merrily, "I have wrapped up this money because the young lady might not like it given to her loose. It isn't that I don't trust you."

The girl laughed.

"Zif I didn't know that, sir. Why, you give me a fi'pun' note to get changed once."

"So I did, Miranda, and will again."

"And sovrins lots o' times. I don't mind."

"Give this to the Italian lady."

"Is she a lady, sir? I think she is sometimes, and sometimes I don't, 'cause she's so shabby. Why, some o' them models as comes could buy her up out and out."

"Yes, Miranda; but don't be so loquacious."

"No, sir, I won't," said Keren-Happuch, wondering the while what the word meant.

"Tell her that I'm not well this morning, and have gone into the country for a day, but I hope to see her at the same time to-morrow morning."

"There, I knowed you wasn't well, sir," cried the girl eagerly.

"Pooh! only a little seedy."

"But was she to come at the reg'lar time this morning, sir?"

"Yes, of course."

"Then she ain't comin', sir, for it's nearly an hour behind by the kitchen clock."

Dale glanced at his watch in astonishment, then at the clock on the mantelpiece.

Keren-Happuch was quite correct in every respect, for the model did not come, and Dale felt so startled by this that he did not leave the studio all day, but spent it with a growing feeling of trouble.

That night, to get rid of the anxiety which kept his brain working, he sought out his two friends and dined with them at one of the cafés, eating little, drinking a good deal, and sitting at last smoking, morose and silent, listening to Leronde's excited disquisitions on art, and Pacey's bantering of the Frenchman, till it was time to return to his studio, which he entered with a shudder, to cross to his room.

Keren-Happuch had been up and lit the gas, leaving one jet burning with a ghastly blue flame, and when this was turned up, the place seemed to be full of shadows, out of which the various casts and busts looked at him weirdly.

"Phew! how hot and stuffy the place is," he muttered. "Am I going to be ill—sickening for a fever? Bah! Rubbish! I drank too much of that Chianti."

The Italian name of the wine of which he had freely partaken suggested the Conte, but only for a moment, and then he was brooding again over the failure of the model to keep her appointment.

"Surely she is not ill," he said excitedly; then,

with an angry gesticulation, "well, if she is, what is it to me? Poor woman! she will get better, and I must wait."

He hurried into his room, and turned up the gas there, but he could not rest without going back into the studio and turning the gas on full before dragging round the great easel, and throwing back the curtains to unveil the picture, with its graceful white figure standing right out from the group like sunlit ivory. But a shadow was cast upon the upper part by a portion of the curtain whose rings had caught upon the rod, and a strange shudder ran through him, for the paper he had used to hide the face looked dark, and, to his excited vision, took the form of the close black veil, through which a pair of brilliant eyes appeared to flash.

Snatching back the curtain, he wheeled the easel into its place, with its face to the wall, turned down the gas after fastening the door, and threw himself upon his bed to lie tossing hour after hour, never once going right off to sleep, but thinking incessantly of the beautiful model, and the masked face whose eyes burned into his brain.

AFTER THE LAPSE.

DALE'S hands trembled, and there were feverish marks in his cheeks as he dressed next morning, and then walked into his sitting-room and rang.

The breakfast things were laid, and in a few minutes Keren-Happuch came through the studio with his coffee and toast, while an hour later, without daring to speak to him, she bore the almost untouched breakfast away.

As soon as he was alone, he made an effort to master himself, and walked firmly into the studio, drew forward his easel, and after removing the curtain, stood there to study his work and criticise and mark its failings.

He found none to mark, but stood there waiting for its living, breathing model, knowing well enough that he must check the madness attacking him—at once, in its incipient stage.

"I'm as weak a fool as other men," he muttered. "Bah! I can easily disillusionise myself. I'll insist upon her removing her veil to-day. It is that and the foolish wish to see her face that has upset me, I being in a weak, nervous state. Once I've finished and had the work framed, I really will give up painting for a few weeks and rest."

That maddening day passed, but no model came, and as soon as it was dark he went out, but not until the last post had come in that was likely to bring him a letter of excuse from his sitter.

He went straight to the street where Jaggs lodged, to learn that he was away from home. The people of the house thought that he had gone down somewhere in the country to sit for an artist who was doing a sea-picture, but they were not sure whether it was Surrey or Cornwall.

Somewhere Leather Lane way, Jaggs had told him that the father lived. Perhaps he was ill, and his child was nursing him. But how could he go about asking at random in that neighbourhood about the missing model?

But he did, seeking out first one and then another handsome picturesque vagabond belonging to the artistic Italian colony, and questioning them, but without avail. They had never heard the name.

He tried a lodging-house or two, upon whose steps Italian women were seated, dark-eyed, black-haired, and with showy glass bead necklaces about their throats. But no; those who could understand him neither knew the name, nor had they heard of a Sardinian patriot whose daughter went out to sit.

Dale returned to his rooms to pass another sleepless night, hoping that the next morning would put an end to his anxiety, fever, or excitement, whichever it was—for he savagely refrained from confessing to himself that he grasped what his trouble might be.

But the morning came, and seven more mornings, to find him seated before his unfinished picture, practising a kind of self-deceit, and telling himself that he was feverish, haggard, and mentally careworn on account of his dread of not being able to finish his picture as satisfactorily as he could wish.

He had tried hard during the interval, but, in spite of all his efforts, he had been able to get tidings of neither Jaggs nor the model the man had introduced; while to make his state the more wretched, Pacey had not been near him, and for some unaccountable reason Leronde, too, had stayed away.

He was seated, wild-eyed and despairing, one morning, when Keren-Happuch came running in, breathless with her exertions to reach the studio, and bear the news which she felt would be like life to the young artist.

"Here she is, sir!" panted the girl, "she's come

at last;" and then ran down to open the front door.

Dale staggered and turned giddy, but listened with eyes fixed upon the door, hardly daring to believe till he saw it open, and the dark, closely veiled figure enter quickly.

Then there was a reaction, and he asked himself why he had suffered like this. What was the poorly dressed woman who had just entered to him?

His lips parted, but he did not speak, only waited.

"Am I too late?" she said, in her strongly accented French. "Some other? The picture finished?"

"No," he said coldly; and he wondered at her collected manner as he caught the glint of a pair of searching eyes. "I have waited for you. Why have you been so long?"

"I have been ill," she said simply, and her tones suggested suffering.

"Ill?" he cried excitedly; and he took a step towards her with outstretched hand. "I am very sorry."

"Thank you," she said quietly, and ignoring the extended hand. ' I am once more well, and I must be quick. Shall I stay one more hour every day and you pay me more? Oh, no. For the same!"

"Yes, pray do," he said huskily, and he thrust his hand into his pocket to pay her in advance according to his custom, but she ignored the money as she had previously passed his hand without notice, and after pointing to the door, she hurried through into his room, to return in a wonderfully short space of time and take her place upon the dais.

Dale began to paint eagerly, feverishly, so as to lose himself in his work, but in a few minutes he raised his eyes to see the glint of those which seemed to be watching him suspiciously through the thick veil, as if ready to take alarm at the slightest word or gesture on his part, and at once the power to continue his work was gone. He felt that he must speak, and in a deep husky voice he began—

"You have been very ill, then?"

"Yes, monsieur," curtly and distantly.

"I wondered very much at not seeing you. I was alarmed."

"I do not see why monsieur should feel alarm."

"Of course, on account of my picture," he said awkwardly. Then laying down his palette and brushes, he saw that the model gave a sudden start, but once more stood motionless as he took out his pocket-book, and withdrew the pencil.

"Will you give me your address?"

"Why should monsieur wish for my address?"

"To communicate with you. If I had known, I should have been spared much anxiety. Tell me, and I will write it down."

"With that of the women who wait monsieur's orders? No!"

This was spoken so imperiously that Dale replaced the pencil and book, and took up palette and brushes.

"As you will," he said, and he began to paint once more.

But the power to convey all he wished to the canvas had gone, and he turned to her again.

"Tell me more about yourself," he said. "You are a foreigner, and friendless here in England: I know that, but tell me more. I may be of service to you."

"Monsieur is being of service to me. He pays me for occupying this degrading position to which I am driven."

There was so much angry bitterness in her tones that Dale was again silenced; but his pulse beat high, and as he applied his brush to his canvas from time to time, there were only results that he would have to wipe away.

"I am sorry you consider the task degrading," he said at last. "I have endeavoured to make it as little irksome as I could."

"Monsieur has been most kind till now," she said quickly; and then, in a bitterly contemptuous tone, "monsieur forgets that I am waiting. His pencil is idle."

He started angrily, and went on painting, but the eyes were still watching him, and, strive all he would, there was the intense desire growing once more to see that face which was hidden from him so closely. He knew that he ought to respect his visitor's scruples, but he could not, and again and again he shivered with a sensation nearly approaching to dread. But the wish was still supreme. That black woollen veil piqued him, and after a few minutes of worthless work, he asked her if she was weary.

"Yes," she replied.

"Then we will rest a few minutes."

"No, monsieur; go on. I am your slave for the time."

He started at her words, and as much at her tone, which was as full of hauteur as if she were some princess. But now, instead of this driving him in very shame to continue his work, it only impressed him the more. There was a mystery about her and her ways. The almost insolent contempt with which she treated him made him angry, and his anger increased to rage as he fully realised how weak and mortal he was as man. He tried not to own it to himself, but he knew that a strange passion had developed itself within him, and with mingled pleasure and pain he felt that this beautiful woman could read him through and through, and that hour by hour her feelings toward him became more and more those of contempt.

He did not stop to reason, for he was rapidly becoming blind to everything but his unconquerable desire to see her face. There were moments when he felt ready to rage against himself for his weakness and, as he called it, folly; but all this was swept away, and at last, as the sitting went on and the model haughtily refused to leave the dais for a time to rest, he found himself asking whether there was not after all truth in the old legends, and whether, enraged by his shrinking from Lady Dellatoria's passionate avowals, the author of all evil had not sent some beautiful demon to tempt him and show him how weak he was after all. It was maddening, and at last he threw down palette and brushes to begin striding up and down the room, carefully averting his eyes from his model, who stood there as motionless as if she were some lovely statue.

At last he returned to his canvas.

"You must be tired now," he said hurriedly. "Rest for a while."

"I'm not tired now," she replied coldly, "if monsieur will continue."

"I cannot paint to-day," he said hoarsely. "You trouble me. What I have done is valueless."

"I trouble monsieur?" she said coldly. "Am I not patient?—can I be more still?"

He made a mighty effort over self, and for the moment conquered. Seizing his brushes and palette, he began to paint once more, but in a reckless way, as if merely to keep himself occupied, but as he turned his eyes from his canvas from time to time to study the beautiful model, standing there in that imperious attitude, strange, mysterious, and weird, with the black enmasking above the graceful voluptuous figure, he lost more and more the self-command he had maintained.

For a few minutes he told himself that he was mistaken, that her eyes must be closed; but it was, he knew too well, a mere mental subterfuge: they were gleaming through that black network, and piercing him to the very soul

He could bear it no longer, and again throwing down brushes and palette, he paced the room for a minute or two before turning to the marble figure standing so motionless before him.

"I tell you I cannot paint," he cried angrily. "It is as if you were casting some spell over me. I must see your face. Why do you persist in this fancy? Your masked countenance takes off my attention. I beg—I insist—remove that veil."

"I do not quite understand monsieur," she said coldly. "He speaks in a language that is not mine, neither is it his. He confuses me. I am trying to be a patient model, but everything is wrong to-day. Will he tell me what I should do to give him satisfaction?"

"Take off that veil!" cried Dale.

The model caught up the cloak and flung it around her shoulders.

"Now, quick!" cried Dale excitedly, "that veil!"

"Monsieur is ill. Shall I call for help?"

"No, no, I am not ill. Once more I beg, I pray of you—take off that veil."

"But monsieur is so strange—so unlike himself," she cried, as, taking another step forward, Dale caught the hand which held the cloak in his.

"Now!" he cried wildly, with his eyes flashing, and trying to pierce the woollen mask—"that veil!"

For a moment the warm soft hand clung to his convulsively, and the other rose with the arm in a graceful movement towards the shrouded face; but, as if angry with herself for being about to yield to his mad importunity, she snatched away the hand he held, and with the other thrust him back violently

"It is infamous!" she cried, with her eyes flashing through the veil. "It is an insult. Monsieur, it is to the woman you love that you should speak those words;" and, with an imperious gesture, she stepped down from the dais as if it had been her throne, and with her face turned toward Dale, she walked with calm dignity, her head thrown back, and the folds of the cloak gathered round her, to the inner door, passed through, and for the first time, when it was closed, he heard the lock give a sharp snap as it was shot into the socket.

Dale stood motionless in the middle of the studio, his eyes bloodshot and his pulses throbbing heavily, unable for some little time either to think or move.

"Yes," he muttered, as he grew calmer; "it was an insult, and she revenges herself upon me. An hour ago I was to her a chivalrous man in whose honour she could have faith. Now I am degraded in her eyes to the level of the brute, and—she trusts me no longer. Do I love this woman whose face I have never seen, or am I going mad?"

But he was alone now, and he grew more calm as the minutes glided by; and once more making a tremendous effort to command himself, he waited as patiently as he could for the opening of the door.

In a few minutes there was the sharp snap again of the lock being turned, the door was thrown open, and the tall dark figure swept out into the great studio with head erect and indignant mien.

She had to pass close by him to reach the farther door, but she looked straight before her, completely ignoring his presence till in excited tones he said—

"One moment—pray stop."

She had passed him, but she arrested her steps and half turned her head as a queen might, to listen to some suppliant who was about to offer his petition.

"Forgive me," he panted. "I was not myself. You will forget all this. Do not let my madness drive you away."

He was standing with his hands extended as if to seize her again, but she gathered her cloak tightly round her, so that he could see once more the curves and contour of the form he had transferred to canvas, as she passed on to the door, where she stopped and waited for him, according to his custom, to turn the key.

Her mute action and gesture dragged him to the door as if he were completely under her influence; and, throwing it open, he once more said pleadingly, and in a low deep voice which trembled from the emotion by which he was overcome—

"Forgive me: I was half mad."

But she made no sign. Walking swiftly now, she passed out on to the landing, descended the staircase, and as he stood listening, he heard the light step and the rustling of her garments, till she reached the heavy front door, which was opened and closed with a heavy, dull, echoing sound.

But still Dale did not move. He stood as if bound there by the spell of which he had spoken, till all at once he uttered a faint cry, snatched his hat, and followed her out into the street.

Too late. There was no sign of the black cloaked

figure, and, after hurrying in different directions for several minutes, he returned to his studio utterly crushed.

"Gone!" he muttered, as he threw himself into a chair. "I shall never see her more. Great heavens! Do I love this woman? Am I so vile?"

"Please, sir, may I come in?"

Dale started up and tried to look composed, as little Keren-Happuch entered with a note in her hand.

"One o' them scented ones, sir," said the girl. "It was in the letter-box. I found it two hours ago, but I did not like to bring it in."

As soon as Dale was alone, his eyes fell upon the Contessa's well-known hand, and, without opening the letter, he gazed at it, and recalled the past.

At last his lips parted, and he said thoughtfully—

"Loved me with an unholy love. It is retribution! She must have felt as I do now."

JOE PACEY AT HOME.

PACEY sat back in a shabby old chair, in a shabby room. The surroundings were poor and yet rich— the former applying to the furniture, the latter to the many clever little gems presented to him by his artist friends, many of whom were still poor as he, others high up on the steps leading to the temple of fame.

Joseph Pacey's hair needed cutting, and his beard looked tangled and wild; and as he sat back in his slippers, he looked the very opposite of his *vis-à-vis*, the exquisitely neat, waxed-moustached, closely clipped young Frenchman who assisted briskly in the formation of the cloud of smoke which floated overhead by making and consuming cigarettes, what time the tenant of the shabby rooms nursed a huge meerschaum pipe, which he kept in a glow and replenished, as he would an ordinary fire, by putting a pinch of fresh fuel on the top from time to time.

" Humph ! " he ejaculated, frowning. " And

so you think he has got the feminine fever badly ? "

"But you do say it funny, my friend," said Leronde. "Why, of course. Toujours—always the same. As we say—'cherchez la femme.' Vive la femme! But helas! How she do prove our ruin, and turn us as you say round your tum."

There was silence for a few moments, during which, as he sat shaggy and frowning in the smoke, Pacey looked as if some magician were gradually turning his head into that of a lion.

"Seen him the last day or two ? "

"Yes," said Leronde, putting out his tongue and running the edge of a newly rolled cigarette paper along the moist tip. "I go to see him yesterday."

"Well. What did he say ? "

"And I ask him to come for an hour to the Vivarium to see the new ballet."

"I asked you what he said."

"He say—'Go to the devil.'"

"Well, did you go ? "

"Yes. I come on here at once."

Pacey glowered at him, but his French friend was innocent of any double entendre; and at that moment there was a sharp knock at the outer door—the well-worn oak on the staircase of No. 9 Bolt Inn.

"Aha! Vive la compagnie!" cried Leronde.

"Humph! Some one for money," muttered Pacey. "Who can it be? Well, it doesn't matter: I've got none.—Here, dandy," he said aloud, "open the door. Shut the other first, and tell whoever it is that I cannot see him. Engaged—ill—anything you like."

"Yes, I see. I am a fly," said the young Frenchman, and, passing through the inner door, he closed it after him and opened the outer, to return in a minute with two cards.

"Who was it?" growled Pacey.

"A lady and gentleman. I told them you could not see any one, and they are gone."

Pacey snatched the cards, glanced at them, uttered an ejaculation, and springing up, he threw down his pipe, and nearly did the same by his companion as he rushed to the door, passed out on to the landing, and began to run down the stairs.

"My faith, but he is a droll of a man," muttered Leronde, pointing his moustache; "but I love him. Aha! always the woman. How he run as soon as he read the name. We are all alike, we men. What was it? Mees Torpe and—faith of a man—she was pretty. Mees! I thought it was her husband at first. H'm! The lover perhaps."

The door flew open again and Pacey returned, showing in Cornel Thorpe and her brother.

"Here, Leronde," cried Pacey excitedly. "Excuse me—very particular business, old fellow."

"You wish me to go?" said Leronde stiffly, as he waited for an introduction.

"If you wouldn't mind, and—look here," continued Pacey, drawing him outside. "Don't be hurt, old fellow—this is very particular. You saw the names on the cards?"

"Oh yes."

"Not a word then to Armstrong."

"I do not tiddle-taddle," said Leronde stiffly.

"That's right. I trust you, old fellow. Come back at six, and we'll go and dine in Soho."

"But—the lady?"

"Bah! Nonsense, man! This is business. Au revoir—till six."

Pacey hurried back and closed both doors, to find his visitors standing in the middle of the room, Cornel pale and anxious, and her brother stern, distant, and angry of eye.

"I did not expect you, Miss Thorpe," cried Pacey warmly. "Pray sit down."

"I think my sister and I can finish our interview without sitting down, sir. You are Mr. Joseph Pacey?"

"I am," said the artist, as coldly now as the speaker.

"And you wrote to my sister——"

"Michael, dear, I will speak to Mr. Pacey,

please," said Cornel, and she turned to the artist and held out her hand. "Thank you for writing to me, Mr. Pacey," she continued. "I thought it better, as my brother was coming to England, to accompany him and see you myself."

She sank into the chair Pacey had placed for her, and after a contemptuous look round at the shabby surroundings, the doctor followed her example.

"My brother is angry, Mr. Pacey; he is indignant on my behalf. He thinks me foolish and obstinate in coming here to see you, and that I am lowering myself, and not displaying proper pride."

"I do," said the doctor firmly.

"Out of his tender love for me, Mr Pacey," Cornel continued, with her sweet pathetic voice seeming to ring and find an echo in the old artist's heart; "but I felt it to be my duty to come to know the truth."

"You have done wisely, madam," said Pacey. "When I wrote you it was in the hope that you would come and save a man whom I have liked—there, call it sentimentality if you please—loved as a brother—I ought to say, I suppose, as a son."

"Your letter, sir, suggested that my old schoolfellow—the man who was betrothed to my sister—has in some way gone wrong."

Pacey bowed his head.

"Cornel, dear, you hear this. It is sufficient. We do not wish to pry into Armstrong Dale's affairs. We know enough. Now, are you satisfied?"

"No.—Mr. Pacey, your words have formed a bond between us greater than existed before. I have heard of you so often from Armstrong, and come to you as our friend, in obedience to your letter. I ask you then to keep nothing back, but to speak to me plainly. Please remember that I am an American girl. I think we are different from your ladies here. Not bolder, but firm, plain-spoken, honest and true. We feel a true shame as keenly as the proudest of your patrician maidens; but we crush down false, and that is why I come to you instead of writing to and making appeals to the man whom I have known from childhood—the man who was betrothed to me, and who loved me dearly, as I loved him, only so short a time ago. There, you see how simply and plainly I speak, the more so that I know you have Armstrong Dale's welfare at heart."

"God knows I have," said Pacey fervently.

"Then tell me plainly, Mr. Pacey."

"Cornel!"

"I will speak, Michael," she said gently. "His happiness and mine depend upon my knowing the truth.—Mr. Pacey, I am waiting."

Pacey gazed at her with his face full of reverence for the woman before whom he stood, but no words left his lips.

"You are silent," she said calmly. "You fear to tell me the worst. He is not ill: you said so. He cannot be in want of money. Then it is as I gathered from your letter: he has been led into some terrible temptation."

Pacey bowed his head gravely.

"Now, are you satisfied?" said Thorpe earnestly. "I knew that it was so."

"And I clung so fondly to the hope that it was not," said Cornel, gazing straight before her, and as if she were thinking aloud. Then, turning to Pacey—"He was becoming famous, was he not?"

"Yes."

"Succeeding wonderfully with his art?"

"Grandly."

"And now this has all come like a cloud," sighed Cornel dreamily. Then again to Pacey, in spite of her brother's frown, "Is she very beautiful?"

Pacey paused for a moment, and then said sadly—

"Very beautiful."

"And does she love him as——he does her?"

"I fear so," said Pacey at last.

Cornel drew a long and piteous sigh, and they saw the tears brimming in her eyes, run over, and trickle down her cheeks.

"Let us go, dear," she said softly. "I was too happy for it to last. Forgive me: I felt that I must know—all. Good-bye, Mr. Pacey," she continued, holding out her hand, while her face was of a deadly white. "I am glad you wrote. You thought it would be best, but he must love her better than ever he loved me, and perhaps it is for his advancement."

"It is for his ruin, I tell you," cried Pacey fiercely.

"But you said she loved him. Is she not true and good?"

"Girl!" cried Pacey, with his brows knotted by the swelling veins, "can the devil who tempts a man in woman's form be true and good?"

"Ah!"

Ejaculation as much as sigh, and accompanied by a wild look of horror. Then, with her manner completely changed, Cornel laid her hand upon Pacey's arm.

"Who is this woman?" she said firmly.

Pacey compressed his lips, but the beautiful eyes fixed upon him forced the words to come, and in a low voice he muttered the Contessa's name.

Then he stood looking at his visitor wonderingly, as, with her lips now white as if all the blood within them had fled to her heart, she said firmly—

"And the Conte?"

"Is a man of fashion—a dog—a scoundrel whom I could crush beneath my heel."

"Cornel," cried her brother firmly, "you have heard enough: you shall not degrade yourself by listening to these wretched details."

"Yes, I have heard enough," she said firmly; but she did not stir, only stood with her brows knit, gazing straight before her.

"Then now you will come back to the hotel," cried the doctor eagerly.

"No: not yet," she said, drawing herself up.

"Not yet?" cried Thorpe, in wonder at the firmness and determination she displayed.

"Not yet: I am going to see Armstrong Dale."

"No," cried Pacey excitedly. "You must not do that. I will see him and tell him you are here. It may bring him to his senses, and he will come to you."

Cornel turned to him, smiling sadly.

"You tell me that he is slipping away into the gulf, and when I would go to hold out my hands to save him, you say, ' Wait, and he will come to you!'"

"At any rate you cannot go," cried Thorpe.

"Armstrong Dale is my affianced husband, and at heart, in his weakness and despair, he calls to me for help. I am going to him now."

"And God speed your work!" cried Pacey excitedly.

"for if ever angel came to help man in his sorest need, it is now."

The next minute, without a word, Cornel Thorpe was walking alone down the old staircase to the street, while Pacey and her brother followed, as if they were in a dream.

CHAPTER XVII.

Four days had passed, and Armstrong had not left his place, but waited, hoping against hope, and at last sinking into a wild state of despair.

"I must have been mad," he said again and again. "One false step leads to another, and I am going downward rapidly enough now."

He smiled bitterly as he sat with his head resting upon his hand, feeling that he had driven his beautiful model away for ever, and vainly asking himself how it could be that so mad a passion had sprung up within him for a woman whose face he had never seen.

Then all at once he sprang to his feet, with his eyes flashing as he listened eagerly, and then a strange look of triumph began to glow in his countenance. "I must be more guarded," he said to himself, "or she will take flight again:" and catching up palette and brush, he made a pretence of painting as he waited with his back to the door for the entrance of her whose step was heard ascending the stairs in company with Keren-Happuch. Then he heard the girl's voice, and his heart sank like lead in doubt, for he felt that the model would have come up without being shown.

But the next moment he was full of hope as the door was opened, closed, and he heard the familiar rustle of the drapery, and the step across the floor.

He did not turn, but stood there with his heart beating violently, and a wild desire bidding him turn round quickly and snatch the veil from his model's face. He was a coward, he told himself, not to have done so before. What did her anger matter? Had she not come back—penitent —friendly——

His heart gave a great leap.

—Loving, for she laid her hand upon his shoulder, and he turned round with a smile of triumph, to drop palette and brushes and turn white as ashes.

"Cornel!"

"Yes, Armstrong. The world grows very small now. You wanted me, and I am here."

"I—I wanted you?" he faltered, as she took a step or two back, and then stood gazing at him wistfully, with her hands clasped before her, and a look of love, pity, and despair in her eyes that stung him through and through.

"Yes, Armstrong, I heard that you were in great

peril. We were children together. Armstrong—you wanted help—and—I have come."

He sank into the nearest chair with a groan, and she advanced slowly and stood close to him.

"I have felt for weeks that there was something: your letters were so different. Then they became fewer; then they ceased. But I said you were busy, and I waited so patiently, Armstrong, till that message came."

"What message?" he cried hoarsely.

"That which told me I ought to join Michael, and help you in this time of need."

"Who—who wrote to you?" he cried.

"There is no need to hide his name. Your dearest friend, Mr. Pacey."

"The wretched meddler!"

"The true, honest gentleman you have always said he was, Armstrong. I have come from him now."

"The cowardly hound!" muttered Dale.

"No; your truest and best friend. He wrote to me for your sake and mine, Armstrong, and I have come."

"What for?—to treat me with scorn and contempt?" he cried angrily, snatching at a chance to speak; "to tell me that all is over between us? Why have you not brought your brother with you, to horsewhip me and add his insults to your upbraidings?"

"Michael is here"—Dale started, and looked with a coward's glance at the door—"he is in London, but it was not his duty to come to the man who is my betrothed. I came alone to ask you—if it is all true?"

He drew a hoarse breath, and then forced himself to speak brutally, to hide the shame and agony he felt.

"Yes," he said roughly; "it is all true."

She winced as if he had struck her, and there was silence for a few moments before she spoke again, and then in a curiously changed voice, from her agony of heart.

"No, no," she whispered at last; "it cannot be true. It is a strange dream. I cannot—I will not believe it."

He strove again and again to speak, but no words would come. He tried to speak gently and ask her to forgive him, but in vain; and at last, even more brutally than before, he cried—

"I tell you it is true! If you knew all this, how could you come?"

There was a pause before Cornel spoke again, and then she drew herself up with an imperious gesture, and her words came firmly and full of defiance of the world.

"I came because I heard the man I loved was beaten down and wounded in the fight of life, and I said—'What is it to me?—he loved me very dearly, and if he has been met by a strange tempta-tion, and has fallen, my place is there. I will go to him, and remind him of the past, and point out again the forward way.' Armstrong, that is why I have come."

He groaned, and his voice was softened now, and half-choked by the agony and despair at his heart.

"Go back," he said, "and forget me, Cornel; I am not the man you thought. I left you strong in my belief in self, ready for the fight, but your knight of truth and honour has turned out to be only a sorry pawn. I don't ask you to forgive me: I only say, for your own sake, go, and forget that such a villain ever lived."

"Then it is all true?" she said sternly.

"I don't know what Joe Pacey has said," he cried bitterly, as he gazed in the sweet womanly face before him, "but I make the only reparation that I can. I speak frankly, Cornel dear, and tell you that the worst he could say of me would not exceed the truth. Utterly unworthy—utterly base —I am not fit to touch your hand."

As he spoke now in his excitement, he took a step toward her, and she drew back.

"Yes!" he cried bitterly; "you are right. Shrink from me and go."

"No," she said, after another pause, "I will not shrink from you; I will not upbraid; I will only say to you, Tear these scales from your eyes, and see, as Armstrong Dale, my old playfellow—brother—lover—used to see. Break from the entanglement, like the man you always were, and be yourself again."

"No!" he groaned, "I am no longer master of myself. For God's sake, go!"

"And leave you to this—caught in these toils, to struggle wildly for a time, and for what?—a life of misery and repentance? It is not true; you are too strong for this. Armstrong, for your own sake—for all at home—one brave effort. Pluck her from your heart."

He looked at her sadly for a few moments, and then shook his head.

"Impossible!" he groaned. "It is too late."

"No!" she cried excitedly; "even on the very edge there is time to drag you away. Armstrong—I cannot bear it—come with me, dearest. You loved me once; you made me care for you and think of you as all the world to me. This woman—she cannot love you as I do, dear. For I do love you with all my poor heart. Don't quite break it, dear, for I forgive you everything, only come back with me now. Do you not hear me? I forgive you everything, and you will come."

She staggered toward him with her arms open to clasp him to her breast, but he shrank away with a groan of despair.

"No," he said; "it is too late—too late!"

She heaved a piteous sigh, and her hands fell to her sides. Then, with her head bent, she walked slowly to the door, passed out, and he heard her steps descending. A few moments later there were voices in the hall, followed by the heavy closing of the door, which seemed to shut him for ever from all that was good and true, alone with his despair as he turned to his canvas, where he gazed upon the form he had created, apparently the only memory of a mad passion which had crushed him to the earth.

CHAPTER XVIII.

"You, Mr. Pacey? Where is my brother?"

"Gone back to the hotel. Left me to wait till you came out.—Seen him? Bah! I needn't have asked that."

Cornel was silent for a few moments as she walked on side by side with her strange-looking companion.

"Why did my brother go back to the hotel?"

"To cool himself."

Cornel looked round wonderingly.

"Temper," said Pacey shortly. "Said he couldn't contain himself; that he was mad to let you come to see Armstrong; and at last I persuaded him to go back, and said I'd see you safely to the hotel."

"And do you think I was doing wrong to go, Mr. Pacey?" she said, turning upon him her candid eyes.

"No: I stood out here feeling more religious than I have these twenty years. Ah! you don't understand. Never mind. Tell me you've brought him to his senses."

Cornel's brow contracted, and she shook her head.

"Oh, but you should have done, my dear," cried Pacey angrily. "You've been too hard upon him. Try and forgive him just a little bit. It's life and death, ruin and destruction to as fine a lad as ever stepped."

"Yes," said Cornel piteously.

"Then you shouldn't have been so stern with him, you know. He has been a blackguard; he deserves something. I am more bitter with him than ever, but, my dear—don't flinch because I speak so familiarly: I'm old enough to be your father—I say, if there is to be no forgiveness, there'll be very few of us men in heaven, I'm afraid, for we're a bad lot, my child, a very bad lot, though I don't think it's all our fault."

Cornel looked up at him again, with her nether lip quivering.

"That's right," said Pacey; "I don't know much about women, but that means being sorry for him just a little. Now, look here: don't you think you and I might go back together, and I leave you with him five minutes while you bring him to his knees, and then promise to forgive him some day?"

Pacey stopped short to say this, and took a half

turn to go back. To his surprise, Cornel placed her hand upon his arm.

"Take me out of this busy street," she whispered, "or I shall break down. You do not know how I pleaded to him and offered him forgiveness."

"You did?"

"Yes," in a faint whisper, "I offered to forgive everything if he would come away."

"And he wouldn't? You tell me he wouldn't?"

"No!" in the faintest of whispers.

"Oh!" ejaculated Pacey, as he hurried her along. "That settles it then. You offered to forgive him, and he refused? Then you've had an escape, my dear. He is not worthy of another thought. There, let me take you back to your brother. I thought better of him, and that the sight of the sweetest, truest little woman who ever breathed would bring him to his senses—make a man of him again. There, I'm very sorry—no, I'm not, for I've done my duty by him, and you've done yours."

"No, we have not," said Cornel, growing firmer once more. "There is much to do yet. This lady —this Contessa?"

"Well, what about her?" said Pacey, frowning.

"You told me that she is very beautiful."

"Yes, and so is some poison—clear as crystal."

"You know, then, where she lives?"

"Oh yes, I know where she lives," growled Pacey savagely.

"Take me to her."

Pacey shook himself free, and literally glared at the plainly dressed girl at his side.

"I wish you would take me to her, Mr. Pacey. I must see her at once."

"You? You see her? That tiger lily of a woman! No, that won't do at all."

"Mr. Pacey, I must see her. I have failed with Armstrong, but something tells me that I may succeed with her."

"But do you know what sort of a woman she is?"

"A lady of title, beautiful and rich."

"Oh yes; but, my dear child, you who are as fresh as a little lily-of-the-valley, what could you say to her? Why, she is a heartless woman of fashion, proud as a female Lucifer, and you would only be exposing yourself to insult."

"She would injure herself more than me," replied Cornel. Then, after they had walked a few yards in silence, she turned to her companion.

"Mr. Pacey, you are Armstrong's most trusted friend?"

"I was once, but that's over now."

"No; true friends do not leave those they love when they are in their sorest need. I must—I will save Armstrong from this woman's toils. He has ceased to love me, but I cannot, when a word might save him, keep back that word. Take me to this lady's home."

"But, my dear Miss Thorpe——"

"I have known you for over a year, Mr. Pacey, though we only met to-day for the first time."

"Yes; and I've known you, my dear," said Pacey, "though he never half did you justice."

"Then I am Cornel Thorpe to you. Now listen: we must save him."

"But——"

"What is this lady's name?"

"The Contessa Dellatoria."

"Take me to her at once."

"And she could not master him?" muttered Pacey. "She masters me."

He was already walking her on fast towards Portland Place, where fortune favoured the mission, for a carriage and pair passed them, driven rapidly, as they were close to the house, and Pacey told his companion that the fashionably dressed lady leaning back was the Contessa, with the effect of making Cornel hasten her pace after quitting Pacey's arm; while, resigning himself to the inevitable, he advanced more slowly, watching the scene before him as the carriage stopped. The footman ran up and gave a thundering knock and heavy peal, with the result that the door was thrown open at once, two more servants waiting to receive their lady.

By the time the steps were rattled down, and Valentina had alighted, Cornel was at her side, pale and trembling, in her simple, plainly cut black dress, cloak, and bonnet with its thin silk veil.

"Can I speak to you, madam?" she said faintly.

The Contessa turned upon her in wonder, and Cornel shrank for the moment from the beautiful, magnificently dressed woman.

"Speak to me?" she said haughtily, as her eyes swept over the American girl. Then, as she walked towards the door, "Who are you? what are you—a hospital nurse?"

"Sometimes," said Cornel, fighting hard to be firm.

"Oh, I see: then you want a subscription for your charity. This is neither the time nor the place."

The Contessa swept on, but Cornel was at her side again before she could reach the door.

"No, no, madam, you are mistaken," she cried in a low voice. "I wish to—I must see you."

Valentina's eyes dilated a little, and she looked wonderingly at the speaker.

"I—I have a message for you. I must speak to you. Take me to your room, for Heaven's sake."

A policeman was approaching, and the butler stepped out, saying significantly—

"Shall I speak to the young person, my lady?"

No answer was vouchsafed, for just then Cornel caught the Contessa by the arm and whispered—

"You must see me, madam. It is life or death to one you know—one whom, I believe, you would not injure."

"Hush! Who are you?"

"A stranger from a distant land, madam."

Valentina started, and the rich blood flushed to her cheeks.

"I landed from America yesterday. Pray hear me. Your future depends upon it, and—perhaps—my life."

The Contessa made a sign to Cornel to follow, and entered the door; and a minute after, as Pacey passed slowly by, he ground his teeth when he heard the coachman say to the footman, who was crossing the pavement with a shawl over one arm, and a basket containing a carriage clock, scent bottle, card case, and Court Guide—

"I say, Dicky, what game do you call that?"

"Last noo dodge for raising the wind," said the footman, and he went in and closed the door.

"A hurricane, I should say," muttered Pacey. "Poor little girl, can she face the storm?—I don't know though—there's a strength in her that masters me."

Meanwhile Lady Dellatoria led the way to the boudoir, held aside the portière, and signed to Cornel to enter. Then following, the great velvet curtain was dropped, and they stood face to face, scanning each other's features, and measuring the one whom a natural instinct taught each to consider the great enemy of her life. Cornel's heart sank as she stood thus in the presence of her beautiful rival. For the moment, she was ready to sink into one of the luxurious lounges, and sob for very despair as she felt how unlikely it was that Armstrong could still care for the simple homely girl who had come across the wide ocean to save him—him, a willing victim to one who gazed at her with such contempt, and who at last broke the silence.

"Well," she said, "I have granted your request. Why do you not speak?"

"I was thinking, madam, how beautiful you are."

Valentina smiled faintly, and raised her eyebrows. It was such an old compliment paid to her.

"You wished to speak to me about some one I know. Have you brought a message? Who are you?"

"I am the poor American girl to whom Armstrong Dale plighted his troth before he left us to make his name and fame."

The Contessa's eyes were slightly veiled. It was no message then from him, and she avoided the searching eyes, so full of innocence and truth, that gazed at her, as she said huskily—

"Well, what is that to me?"

Cornel looked at her wonderingly, asking herself

whether there was a mistake; but growing confident, she went on—

"This, madam: my lover—I speak to you in the homely fashion of our people—my lover came here to England, and his success was beyond my wildest dreams. We wrote to each other, and we were happy in the expectation of our future, till he saw you, and then—all was changed."

"Is this the beginning of some romance? But, of course—your love-story."

"Yes, madam, and no romance. But I do not come to speak angrily to you — I do not heap reproaches upon your head. I come to you simply as one woman in suffering should appeal to another."

The Contessa made a contemptuous gesture.

" In my simple, faithful love for the man pledged to be my husband—the man who has sinned against me in what is but a base love for you—I am ready to forgive him, and look upon the past as dead. And now I come as a suppliant to you, asking you to set him free, that he may sin no more."

"What! How dare you?" cried the Contessa. "Such words to me!"

"From his promised wife, madam! Yes: I dare tell you, because, with all your wealth and beauty, even your power over his weakness, I am stronger in my right. You have blinded him—turned him from the path of duty—you are the destroyer of his future."

"Absurd, girl! This Mr. Dale, the artist employed by my husband—surely in his vanity he has not dared——"

She ceased speaking, and shrank from Cornel's clear, candid gaze.

"No, madam, he has not dared—he has not spoken. He does not know that I have taken this step."

"Most unwisely."

"No, madam, I know that I am acting wisely—in his interest and yours."

"My good girl, this is insufferable. If you were not a stranger to our customs in England, I would not listen to you."

"There is no custom, madam, in a woman's love, here or in America. Heart speaks to heart. He is my promised husband: give him back to me. I plead to you for your own sake as well as mine."

"This is mere romance."

"Again I say no, madam, but the truth. Think of your peril, too."

"Silence!"

"I will not be silent," said Cornel firmly. "You love him: I see it in your quivering lips, and the blood that comes and goes in your cheek. You hate me, madam, as a rival. Well, let me prove your love for him."

"Will you be silent, girl?" cried the Contessa hastily.

"No; I must speak now. You would not have listened to me so long had I not spoken truth. You love him—you dare not deny it. Well, I love him too, and I tell you that your love came like a blight upon his life."

"Woman, will you——"

"No; I will not be silent," said Cornel firmly · "but even if I ceased to speak, my words would ring in your ears. It is not love that holds him to you, or you to him, but a blind mad passion, the destroyer of you both. Call it love if you will, but prove that love by giving him up to return to his old, peaceful life."

"And your arms?" whispered the Contessa maliciously.

"Ah! The proof!" cried Cornel. "No one but a spiteful rival could have spoken that. But your love is not as mine. I will not ask you to give him back to me, but to set him free before some horror descends upon you both. Your husband——"

"Hush!"

Valentina gave a quick look round, and Cornel flushed in her eagerness as she exclaimed—

"The shadow over both your lives! You know it. Now, madam, prove your love by freeing him from such a risk. How can you call it love that threatens him with danger and disgrace!"

"And if I tell you that you, a foolish, jealous girl, are conjuring up all this in your excited brain —that I have listened to you patiently—and that I will hear no more ?"

"I will tell you that your love for Armstrong is a mockery and snare, that you throw down the gage, and that I will save him from you yet."

" And how ? Bring some false charge against him to my husband ? Set about some lying slander on my name ?"

" Bring you to public shame—bring disgrace upon the head of the man I love ? No, madam. You refuse my offer ?—No : you will hear me. Give him up, as I will for his sake—woman—sister—am I to plead in vain ?"

The Contessa pointed to the door.

"Yes," said Cornel quietly. "I will go, but I will save him yet."

"Then it is war," muttered the Contessa, whose eyes contracted as she stood listening as if expecting a return; "and you will save him ? Yes : to take to your heart ? Not yet."

She hurried to the window as the faint sound of the closing door was heard, and held aside the curtain, so as to gaze down the wide place, and see Cornel take Pacey's arm, and, as if weak and suffering, walk slowly away.

"Bah ! What is she to me, with her pitiful school-girl love ?—'Save him yet !'"

She crossed the room and rang. Then, throwing herself into a lounge, she waited till the servant entered.

"Is your master in?"

"No, my lady. Lady Grayson called. Gone to the Academy, I think."

"That will do."

Left alone, Valentina sprang to her feet, and pressed her temples.

The next minute, with a smile upon her lip, and an intense look as of a set purpose in her eye, she went slowly from the room.

CHAPTER XIX.

CHECK.

WHAT to do?

Armstrong's constant question to himself.

His determination, arrived at again and again, was to flee at once from the horrible passion which was sapping the life out of him—his insane love for a woman who evidently despised him, and whose face he had never seen.

He argued that, by going right away to Rome, Florence, or even merely to Paris, he would avoid Lady Dellatoria, who would soon forget him as he would forget this Italian woman, who —he could not explain to himself why—had, as it were, woven some spell round him and made him half mad.

He reasoned with himself, called upon the teaching of his early life, mocked at his folly, and told himself that he had got the better of the insane passion—that he had disgusted this woman by his insults, and that he was free, for she would come no more. But in another hour he was watching for her coming, and trying to contrive some means of tracing her, and begging her to come again.

Why?—that he might stand spell-bound again before that masked face, tortured, enslaved, and in greater despair than ever?

"It is of no use!" he muttered passionately. "I have not the mental strength of a child. I must go right away from the horrible temptation—and at once."

He made a step or two toward his room. He had money enough; a few things could be packed, and in an hour he might be on his way to Dover. After that the world was before him, so that he could seek for peace.

No. Michael Thorpe and his sister were in London. It would be the act of a coward to flee now, and be dragging himself down lower still in their eyes. He could not go: Michael Thorpe would be sure to come before long, he felt, and he wished he would. It would be a relief to have some savage quarrel. Hah! there was an opportunity: Pacey, who had betrayed him and brought Cornel over for that shameful scene, after which he had felt that his life had better end.

"No," he said half aloud, "I can't quarrel with poor old Joe. He meant well, and he was right. But I cannot leave London now."

He burst into a mocking laugh the next minute, for he would not indulge in self-deceit. He knew that it was not merely the dread of being thought cowardly which kept him there, but his mad passion for this woman, who treated him as if he were a dog.

Then he grew calmer, and tried to reason with himself. She had not treated him as a dog. Her conduct had been irreproachable. No lady could have been more modest or refined in her conduct throughout. She had come there merely as a model, and he had conceived this strange passion for her in spite of distant coldness, and complete disdain. He remembered in a score of things how she had borne herself as if conferring a favour by coming and taking his money; and he knew, too, how it was forced upon her by her filial affection.

"No!" he groaned, "she is not to blame. I shall never see her more, thank Heaven! and in time the recollection will die out."

His eyes reverted to the picture, as this thought held him for the moment, and he again laughed bitterly and cried aloud, while gazing at the beautiful figure which inspiration and the work of his brush had placed upon the canvas.

"Die out, while she is there to renew my passion hour by hour, minute by minute! Curse the picture!" he raged. "Why did I ever conceive the vile thought?"

He stepped to it and tore off the paper which covered the face.

The next moment he had stepped back, startled and wondering at the perfection of his art, as Lady Dellatoria's eyes seemed to be gazing passionately into his.

He shivered and turned away, holding one hand to his brow.

"I am ill," he said, in a low, muttering tone "unstrung, half wild. Well, this shall be the first step toward a cure;" and, taking a large Spanish knife from among the knick-knacks upon the table, he felt the point and edge, stepped forward, and was in the act of thrusting the blade through the canvas close to the frame, when the door-handle rattled, and the grimy face of Keren-Happuch was thrust in.

"She's come again," said the girl gleefully.

"The lady who was here yesterday?" cried Dale, throwing the knife from him.

"No, sir; her!" cried the girl. "She's coming up now."

She pointed to the canvas as she spoke, and Dale involuntarily turned to see the counterfeit presentment of Lady Dellatoria looking at him from the group with indignant scorn, and as if enraged at his mad passion for the model whose steps were now heard as the girl slipped out.

"It is fate!" muttered Dale, as the door was flung

open, and the closely veiled and cloaked figure stood before him.

For some moments neither spoke. The model stood just within the closed door, proud and imperious in her pose, and with the glint of her eyes flashing through the thick veil, while, a prey to his emotion, Armstrong strove to find words as the struggle within him continued.

He would master himself, he thought. It was madness, and he called upon his manhood to protect this woman, who trusted to him, from a repetition of his last insult.

"You have returned, then," he said to her coldly, but with his voice trembling.

"Yes, monsieur," she replied, in her peculiarly accented French. "It was necessary. Monsieur wishes me to continue?"

He made a sign toward the door at the other end of the studio, and she seemed to hesitate, but the next moment she walked firmly across to the room and disappeared, while Dale fastened the outer door.

Then mechanically drawing the easel into its proper position in the light, he took up palette and brushes, and stood gazing straight before him, his nerves astrain, and pulses beating with a heavy dull throb.

His back was to the entrance of his room, and with a mist before his eyes he waited, ignorant of how the time passed till he heard the door behind him open, and the rustling sound of the heavy cloak as it swept over the rug-covered floor.

Then, with every sense at its acutest pitch, he felt her approach till she was close behind his chair on her way to the dais.

The model stopped suddenly, and he turned to see that she was gazing fixedly at the uncovered face upon the canvas, as if struck by the intense gaze of the goddess's eyes.

It was almost momentary, that pause. Then she continued her way to the dais, and mounted it to resume her familiar attitude, and, once more, Dale began to paint; a quarter of an hour before about to destroy, now eagerly bent upon finishing the task, while the piercing eyes gleamed through the veil, and seemed to pierce him.

"It is fate!" he muttered, as those eyes fixed his, meeting them through the veil; but was it lovingly tempting him, or watching him in dread —a dread born of the doubt he inspired at the last visit?

He could not tell, but everything of the past died away in that present, and in a voice which he hardly knew as his own, he said softly—

"Why were you so angry with me last time?"

There was no reply, but the eyes gleamed distrustfully through the veil.

"You are angry still," he continued. "Was

it so great an offence to ask you to discard your
veil?"

"Monsieur is wasting time," was the reply, and
he went on using his brush angrily for a few
minutes.

"Tell me," he said at last, "why you are so
obstinate? Do you not wish me to see your
face?"

She shook her head quickly, and he watched her,
telling himself that there was something coquettish
in the act.

"But you will not refuse me now?" he said. "I
beg—I pray of you—let me see your face."

"It is not possible. I do not wish you to know
me again if we ever meet."

"Why not?" he said eagerly. "For Heaven's
sake, do not be so distant with me."

"I come here at your wish, monsieur, and you
pay me to be your model.—Monsieur insults me
once more."

"No!" he cried passionately, as he threw down
palette and brush; "a man cannot insult a woman
he loves with all his soul."

He took a step or two towards her, but with one
quick movement, she stooped and swung the great
cloak about her shoulders, and, unseen by him,
caught up the knife he had so recently held. The
next moment she made for the inner room, but he
intercepted her.

"No, no!" he cried wildly. "You must not leave me again like this. Listen: you will hear me. Once for all, you shall remove that veil."

"I—will—not," she cried firmly. "Why does monsieur wish to see my face?"

"You, as a woman, know," he cried, in a low, excited voice. "It is of no use. I must speak now. I tell you again, I love you."

"It is not true!" she whispered. "You dare to tell me that, when I know that it is not true. That is the woman whom you love, monsieur!" and she pointed scornfully at the face upon the canvas.

"No!" he cried, half startled by her manner, "I swear that you are wrong."

"It is her portrait, monsieur."

"It is no one's portrait. Imagination, every stroke," he cried. "Now let me see the face of the woman I really love."

He raised one hand to snatch off the veil, but with a quick movement she sprang from him, and, with her eyes gleaming through the film, flung one white arm from the cloak, gave her wrist a turn, and he saw that she was holding the great Spanish knife dagger-wise, with the point towards his breast.

"Don't come near me, or it will be your death," she panted.

"Ah!" he said, with a half-laugh, as, stirred now to the deepest depths, he bent forward trying to penetrate her disguise, but without avail; "can you punish me so cruelly as that for loving you? Well, you have made me yours, and it is my fate. Better death than the misery I have suffered, the despair of losing you and not seeing you again."

"It is a mockery!" she cried, and her voice now was strangely altered. "A man cannot love a woman whose face he has not seen."

"You know that is not true," he whispered, as he still advanced, and she now began to retreat—"you know I love you with all my soul. I have told you so, and you know it in your heart."

"Keep back!" she cried huskily, as she retreated, keeping the knife-point toward his breast.

"No! Remove your veil."

"Bah!" she cried contemptuously, and with her voice resuming its former tone. "Go, monsieur; dwell upon and love your picture when I am gone."

"No; I love you, the living, breathing embodiment. Now, if I die for it, I will see your face."

He stretched out one hand, and touched her veil, but it was tightly knotted behind her head, and with her left hand she caught his fingers and held them firmly, their warm contact sending a thrill through every nerve.

At the same moment, he felt the point of the

knife touch his breast, but he did not shrink, only struggled to free his hand.

Then, as if moved by the same impulse, they remained motionless, gazing into each other's eyes, and he felt her warm breath upon his lips.

"Then you do love me?" she whispered in a voice that, in its soft passionate tones, made every fibre vibrate in strange music to the melody of her utterance.

"More than life," he whispered back. "You see."

A low mocking laugh came from her lips as she loosened her grasp, flung up her hands, and the knife fell far away upon the floor. Then, with a sudden movement, as he seized her waist and drew her to him, she threw herself back, snatched off the veil, flung it upon the dais, and clasped her arms about his neck.

"Valentina!—You!"

CHAPTER XX.

A MINGLING of rage, passion, disappointment, and delight swept over Dale at the revelation. One moment he wondered at his blindness in not divining long before that it was she; then at her daring recklessness, and the skill with which she had played her part, deceiving him completely to the very end.

And as she gazed in his eyes, clasped then in his arms, yielding as he did to what he told himself again was fate, a mystery which he could not unravel, he asked himself the question, did he love her or did he not? His passion had been for another woman, and paradoxically it was she from whom he had literally fled, and from whom, had she come openly, he would have turned in disgust.

And yet how beautiful she was. What love and passion beamed from the half-closed eyes that sought his, as her lips murmured words that told him she was his at last, as he was hers, her very own; while, mastered by her tenderness, he found no words then of angry reproach or blame.

"Venus victrix." She had brought him to her feet, but there was no sound of triumph in her tones. Every word was a caress, and he found himself wondering that he could ever have treated her with the coldness he had shown.

"I knew you loved me," she murmured in his ear, "and that in your mad belief in what you told yourself was your duty, you were punishing yourself and me. It was a mere schoolboy friendship pledged years ago, against which nature rebelled. For the first time in my unhappy life I knew what it was to love, and knowing, as a woman soon divines, that you loved me, I felt a new joy in my heart that I was so beautiful, and that it pleased you, the only man I ever felt that I cared for—that I did love, for I knew that you were mine as I was yours. And so I had no hesitation about running all the risks I have, deceiving even Lady Grayson, who watches me like a cat. I said in my heart that I would dare all, even to degrading myself—no: it was no degradation, for it was for the sake of him I loved. But tell me now; you did know me from the beginning?"

"I swear I had not the least idea," he said angrily.

"You had not," she sighed; and then mockingly, "and, cruel to the last, you began to love another as you thought. I saw it growing from the first, and for a minute it made me angry, and ready to turn and revile you, instead of carrying on the deceit; but a feeling of intense joy ran through me, for was not all your loving passion for me —was I not winning you to confess the love you always did feel, though blindly thinking that you had conquered self? You did love me—did you not?"

"Yes, I always loved you," he whispered, "and I fought so hard for both our sakes."

"And lost," she said with a laugh. "I have won. No, no," she whispered caressingly, "don't repulse me now. You are so much to me. But yes, if you will. I do not mind. Strike your poor slave if you wish; she will never murmur or complain. Your blows would be like tender caresses to me now, for your words have dragged me forth from an age of misery and despair into a new life of hope and brightness and joy. You told me you loved me with all your soul."

"No, no," he cried angrily, in his last struggle for truth and honour; "it is not true. It was all an imaginary passion for an imaginary being."

"Am I an imaginary being?" she whispered, as she wreathed her arms about him and drew him to her breast. "No, no; it was all a solemn truth, the outspeaking of your heart to the only woman you love. You could not lie to me, my hero—my idol. What is the world to us, Armstrong? You cannot retract your words. I have won you—my own—my own. You can never leave me now."

As those words left her lips, Dale started from her arms, for a carriage had stopped, and a heavy double knock resounded through the house.

Valentina stood listening as Dale crossed rapidly to the door, unlocked it, and returned, after relocking it, silently.

"Well?" she said calmly, "a visitor? Send him away."

"Your husband," he whispered.

"Bah!" she cried contemptuously. "The man the world calls my husband—the wretch who bought me as he would some trinket that gratified his eye."

"But the risk—the scandal," he whispered. "For your sake—there, dearest, for your sake," he whispered, as he clasped her to his breast.

"Yes, you do love me," she said softly

"There, quick! in there! He must not know."

"And why?" she said calmly, as she clung to him. "I do not fear him; and as for you," she cried, with a look of pride, "you are brave and strong. Let him come: kill him as you would some wretched snake."

He gazed at her half in wonder, half in horror, as she laughed mockingly, but there was a look of intense hatred and disgust in her eyes which told him how truly earnest were her words—how great her loathing for this man.

At that moment there was a tapping at the door, and Dale crossed to it quickly.

"Yes?" he said.

"This gent would like to see you, sir," came in Keren-Happuch's voice, and a card was shot under the door.

He caught it up, and hesitated a moment.

"Not at home," he said.

"Please, sir, I said as you was."

"Then show him up," said Dale desperately, and darting across to where Valentina stood, he pointed to the inner door.

"Quick!" he cried.

"For your sake, yes," she said, smiling calmly enough; but as he threw open the door, she flung one arm about his neck, and pressed her lips to his before he closed it upon her.

Then crossing quickly, he unfastened the other, caught up palette and brush, and dragged his great canvas round with its face to the wall.

He had not a moment to spare, for as he faced round, firm and defiant now, ready for anything that might come, Keren-Happuch entered, looked round wide-eyed and wondering for the model, and held the door wide for the Conte to enter.

Her position and the glance she gave round were

not lost upon Armstrong, who frowned at her so severely that she hurried out.

"The crisis!" thought Dale, growing firm now that he was face to face with danger; and his eyes involuntarily measured his visitor's physique.

The Conte's first words set him wondering whether they were genuine or part of a plan laid by the wily Italian. For his face was smooth and smiling, and he came forward offering his hand in the frankest manner.

"Ah! my dear Mr. Dale," he cried, "it is a pleasure to see you again."

Armstrong could not help taking the hand, but his grasp was cold and limp as that of his visitor.

Then, unasked, the Conte placed his glass in his eye, took out a cigarette, and gave it a wave.

"May I?" he said.

Armstrong bowed coldly, and the little, wrinkled, elderly-looking man struck a scented fusee, lit his cigarette, glanced round and seated himself.

"And how do the fine arts march?" he said cheerily. "By the way," he continued, without waiting to be answered, "my dear Mr. Dale, I was close by, and I thought I would call to ask if you have reconsidered that decision of yours?"

"My decision?" said Dale, following his example.

"Yes; about her ladyship's portrait. We were discussing it this morning. I believe I introduced the subject, but her ladyship took to it eagerly. You will go on with it?"

"Surely, my lord, there are plenty of better artists in London who will be glad to undertake the commission," said Dale quietly.

"Perhaps so, but you began the sketch, and we were so well satisfied that we wish you to continue it."

"Then he suspects nothing," Armstrong said to himself; and for the moment he felt ready to agree to the proposal. But directly after, a suspicious idea came to him. Suppose this were a deeply laid plan to entice him to the Conte's place, so that an opportunity might be afforded for a discovery?

He had gone through so much excitement of late that his brain felt confused, and he was unable to calculate coolly. At the first he had decided in his own mind that the Conte must be aware of his wife's visits to the studio, and had now tracked her there. All this talk then was for some ulterior reason, and in all probability he was waiting for an excuse to search the place, or else to trap her when she tried to leave. For aught the young artist knew, there might be half-a-dozen spies about the place, waiting to see her go, and his brow grew rugged with the intensity of his thoughts.

The Conte rose from his seat, and Dale started up.

"No, no; don't move," said the Conte.   "I was only about to look round while you thought the matter over.   Ah! you object?   Good.   I will reserve myself for your show day.   Pardon, a thousand times."

He resumed his seat, smiling, while in agony Dale thought of the great picture not twenty feet from where his visitor had stood.

"My proposal troubles you, I see; but why let it, my friend?   Let us consider it as men of the world—as we did at first.   It will do you good as an artist—it will do me good amongst my friends, for I shall be proud to see the face of my beautiful wife—a lady of society—upon the Academy walls. We made our little arrangement—I will not insult you by talking of money—and all was well.   Then came this little pique.   I affronted you by some thoughtless remark, and you retired."

Dale was about to speak, but the Conte interrupted him.

"One word, my friend, and I have done.   It is my wife's wish that the picture should be finished; it is mine.   I apologise as one gentleman to another.   Now, say that I am pardoned, and that you will do it."

The temptation was terribly strong.   This man begged him to come; it meant endless freedom, the run of the house, and constant meetings with Valentina; but Dale's manly instincts rose in revolt against so degrading an intimacy. He and the Conte could only be deadly enemies, and he rose slowly from his seat.

"It is impossible, sir," he said. "I thank you for your consideration and your apology, but I must hold to my decision. I cannot—I will not commence the portrait again."

"You are too hasty, Mr. Dale. Take time. With your permission I will smoke another cigarette. Let us talk of other things."

"No, sir," replied Armstrong; "let us talk of this, and let me tell you plainly that I cannot and will not undertake this commission."

"But, my dear friend, you did undertake it."

"And repented almost at once," said Armstrong bitterly.

"You English—I mean you Americans—are too hard and decisive," said the Conte, with a smile and shrug. "Ah, as you know, everything depends upon the diplomat. I am a poor ambassador. I should have brought Madame the Contessa here to plead to you."

Armstrong could not suppress a start, and he looked keenly at the Conte, whose eyes seemed to be fixed searchingly upon his, as if to read the secret thoughts of his heart. And now he felt sure that all this was subterfuge—a means of gaining time for some reason. He had tracked his wife there, and was waiting for the moment when the eruption ought to break forth; and a quarrel with a foreigner and for such a cause could only mean one thing.

"Ah," said the Conte gaily, "the mention of madame has, I see, its effect. Say, if she comes and pleads you will yield?"

"This man is too subtle for me," thought Armstrong. "He is playing with and torturing me before he strikes. Heavens! what have I done to bring me into such a position?"

"Come, you are giving way," cried the Conte gaily, "and I may go back soon—after our friendly chat, as you people call it, and tell her ladyship that I have made our peace."

"No, sir," began Armstrong, keeping well upon his guard, in the full conviction that there was another motive for the visit, and determined to strike his visitor down if he approached the inner room. But he was interrupted again.

"By the way—in passing—apropos of portraits —Lady Grayson s—is it commenced?"

"Lady Grayson's?"

"Yes; you know her; you met her at our house. My wife's bosom friend."

"I remember Lady Grayson, of course, perfectly."

"And you are painting her portrait?"

"I regret to say that you have been misinformed, sir."

"But—how strange! Lady Grayson told us

that she was going to ask you to undertake the commission. Of course—yes—and she said, laughingly—I remember now, perfectly—that she should visit you at your studio, be a most perfect sitter, and that there would be no giant—no, no, it was ogre of a husband—to pass criticisms and offend the artist."

He laughed merrily as he spoke, and twisted his cane about in a peculiar way, suggesting to Armstrong that he meant to strike with it at first; and then, as he saw a gold garter-like band around it about six inches from the knob, his heart gave one throb, for he felt certain that there was a keen rapier-like blade concealed within.

But he spoke quite calmly.

"Lady Grayson has been premature in her announcement, Conte. I am under no promise to paint any such portrait, neither shall I undertake the commission."

"Body of Bacchus!" cried the Conte, laughing, "how droll! Truth is more strange than romance, as you people say. Come, now, confess you have been too scrupulous—too secretive.—My dear Lady Grayson, this is wonderful. Your name was on our lips."

For as he was speaking, Keren-Happuch ushered in the fashionably dressed woman, gave Dale an imploring look, which plainly said, " Forgive me," glanced at the fastened door, next at the dais, and then disappeared.

"Ah, Conte, you here! Mr. Dale, pray forgive me for coming unannounced. I want to make a petition—to lay an appeal before you."

She held out her hand with a most winning smile, and then turned and shook hands with the Conte.

"What he has been waiting for," thought Dale —"her coming—she, his mistress, to be a witness of his own wife's shame."

There was an angry, determined look in his eyes. A minute before, a feeling of misery and despair troubled him. There was a sensation akin to pity in his breast for the man who was being basely deceived; but now rage took its place, compunction was gone, and he felt hard as steel, as he prepared himself for the fight, determined at all hazards to save Valentina from such a humiliation as this.

The thoughts flew like lightning through his brain as, in her most silky tones, Lady Grayson addressed him.

"May I lay my petition before you now, Mr. Dale?"

"Oh, I will not be *de trop*," cried the Conte. "I am going. My dear Mr. Dale, you will think over that, and write to me, I am sure?"

"I assure you, sir," began Dale; and then he

bit his lip savagely, for in a playful, girlish way, Lady Grayson had stepped aside, ostensibly that the gentlemen might speak together; really to obtain a glimpse of the picture on the easel.

She succeeded, and turned back directly.

"I beg pardon," she cried. "Oh, do forgive me, Mr. Dale; it was very rude."

Their eyes met, and he saw a look of malicious triumph in hers, which told him that this woman had recognised the face upon the canvas, and that her suspicion of the Contessa coming to sit for him was confirmed.

"I do so love pictures!" she cried. "But you need not go, Conte. I will stand aside till you have finished with Mr. Dale."

"Conte Dellatoria has finished his proposal to me, madam," said Armstrong firmly. "I regret, sir, that I must hold to my decision."

"Oh!" cried Lady Grayson, "don't say that you have refused to continue my dearest friend's portrait!"

"Yes, madam, I have declined decisively."

"Oh, but that is too cruel," cried Lady Grayson, looking quickly round the studio; and once more there was a look of triumph in her eyes which met his sparkling with malice, as they both cast them on the same object, which he too saw for the first time.

The thick veil Valentina had snatched off, lay

upon the edge of the dais, where she had thrown it, and a chill of horror ran through Armstrong as he felt that they were in this woman's power, even if he were wrong, and she had not been brought, as he had imagined.

Then a fresh idea struck him. He was perhaps mistaken, and his feeling of rage increased. It was an assignation; they had arranged to meet there for some reason—why they had chosen his studio, he could not divine.

"I am so sorry," said Lady Grayson, after an awkward pause. "It augurs so badly for my success."

"Shall I leave you to discuss the matter, my dear Lady Grayson? Mr. Dale is a tyrant—an emperor among artists. As for me, I am crushed."

"No, no; you will stay and help me to plead. My dear Mr. Dale, do not be so cruel. I do so want to be on the line this year, and if you would consent to paint a poor, forlorn, helpless widow, I cannot tell you how grateful I should be."

"It is impossible, madam," said Armstrong coldly, but with a burning feeling of rage against his visitors seething in his breast. It was an assignation then, but Lady Grayson had divined Valentina's presence, and he had seen her glance again and again at the further door. He was in a dilemma too: for if he refused this woman's prayer, she would perhaps spitefully declare all she knew to the husband. But he cast that aside. If she did not speak now, she would at some other time, and in his then frame of mind he could only fight. He could not fence.

"Impossible!—you hear this cruel man, Conte? he is a tyrant indeed. Mr. Dale, is it really in vain to plead?"

"I tell you again, madam, it is impossible."

"But if I wait a week—a month—any time you like?"

"My answer would only be the same, madam, as I have given Conte Dellatoria. I can paint no more portraits for any one. I have, I think I may say, painted my last."

"I am disappointed," she said, giving him a peculiar look. "But, no—you will not refuse me. Come, Mr. Dale—for the Exhibition. Only this one portrait at your own terms, and I will promise to preserve secrecy."

The malicious look in her eyes intensified as she said these words, telling him plainly that she knew all, but that the Conte was, after all, still in ignorance.

His answer would have been a promise, for the sake of the unhappy woman within that room; but at that moment there was a sharp rap at the door, Keren-Happuch opened it, and blurted out—

"Oh, if you please, sir, here's that there lady as you began to paint."

Dale turned upon her dumbfounded.

"Who?"

"That there countess, sir, from Portland Place."

The Conte turned excitedly to Lady Grayson.

"She must not find me here," he whispered.

"Show the lady up," said Armstrong recklessly, for, whoever it might be, it would rid him of his visitors.

"Yes, sir;" and the door closed.

"My dear Mr. Dale," said the Conte quickly, "I must speak plainly. I have reasons for not wishing to meet my wife here this morning. You will not ask me to explain, but let me step in here for a few minutes till she is gone. Remain here and meet her," he said in a low voice to Lady Grayson, and as steps were heard upon the stairs, he stepped quickly to the inner door.

CHAPTER XXI.

THE RUSE.

THERE was a puzzled look in Lady Grayson's face as
Dale sprang at the Conte, and swung him round,
sending him staggering from the door, before which
he placed himself, his face dark with wrath.

For the moment, the Italian looked utterly as-
tounded. Then, with a fierce ejaculation, he made
at Dale with his cane raised, and his countenance
convulsed.

"Dog!" he muttered in Italian; and the artist
clenched his fist, ready to proceed to any extremities
now in Lady Dellatoria's defence.

But Lady Grayson flew between them, whispering to the Conte eagerly, and Dale caught a word
or two here and there—

"Scandal—mistake—my sake—meet her now."

The Conte drew himself up and pressed Lady
Grayson's hand, as he gave her a significant look.
Then, veiling his anger with a peculiar smile, he
turned to Dale.

"Lady Grayson is right," he said, with grave

courtesy; "it was a mistake. I was quite in the wrong, Mr. Dale. I ought not to have attempted to break in upon your privacy. We all have our little secrets, eh? There, it is quite past. An accident, that Lady Dellatoria should be calling now when we are here?"

"Yes—a very strange accident," said Lady Grayson, with a malicious look at the artist.

"It does not matter," continued the Count. "All this contretemps because ladies are vain enough to wish the world to see how beautiful they are. But she is long coming, this wife of mine."

No one spoke for a few moments, all standing listening for the steps upon the stairs, and the rustling sound of the Contessa's dress, but everything was perfectly still, and at last, with a shrug of the shoulders, the Conte turned to Armstrong.

"Is the lady in some ante-room waiting for our departure?"

"No," said Dale sharply.

"Because we would relieve you of our company, but we would rather meet the lady now."

"Of course," cried Lady Grayson. "We do not wish our visit to be misconstrued."

"I do not understand it," said Dale; and going to the bell, he rang sharply. Then once more there was silence, till shuffling steps were heard, then a tap at the door, and Keren-Happuch entered in answer to a loud "Come in," wiping her hands upon her apron, and with her face scarlet.

"Where is the lady you announced just now?" said Dale sharply.

"Plee, sir, she's gone, sir."

"Gone?"

"Yes, sir."

Lady Grayson uttered a low sigh of satisfaction.

"What did she say?"

"Nothin', sir."

"Did you tell her that this lady and gentleman were here?"

"Oh no, sir. I never said nothin' to her, sir."

"But she said she would call again?"

"That she didn't, sir. She couldn't. She just comed and goed," faltered the girl.

"But did she not hear our voices in the studio?"

"No, sir; she couldn't. Why, she never come no further than the street door mat, and you can't hear no talking in here, even if you stand just outside."

"Oh, you have tried?" said the Conte laughingly.

"That I hain't, sir, but I've seed missus more'n once."

"That will do."

"Yes, sir," said Keren-Happuch, but Dale checked her.

"Don't go," he said.

"Ah, well then, Mr. Dale, as the lady is not coming up to see us, we will go and see her:

Mahomet to the mountain, eh! my dear Lady Grayson? May I see you to your carriage?"

"I have no carriage here," she said quickly. "Yes, we had better go."

"After our double failure to-day; but Mr. Dale will alter his decision on our behalf. Good day, my dear modern representative of Fra Lippo Lippi. It is grand to be a handsome young artist," the Conte continued, as he took a step toward the dais, and raised something on the end of his cane, "supplicated by beautiful ladies to transfer their features to canvas; but you should warn them not to leave their veils behind when they take refuge in another room. Look, my dear Lady Grayson;" and he held the veil toward her on the end of his cane, "thick—secretive—admirable for a disguise.— Come."

He tossed the veil back on to the dais, and opened the door for his companion to pass out, while Dale stood fuming with rage, and Lady Grayson gave him a mocking look as he advanced.

"Good morning, Mr. Dale," she said laughingly, and then in a whisper—"secret for secret, my handsome friend. You and I cannot play at telling tales out of school."

"Lor, if it ain't like being at the theayter,' thought Keren-Happuch, as the door was shut, and Dale crossed quickly to reopen it, and stand listening till the front door closed. Then he came back to where the little maid stood waiting, while, faintly heard, came a call from below.

"Keren—Hap—puch!"

"Comin', mum. Please, Mr. Dale, sir, missus is a callin' of me; may I go?"

"Who was the lady who came just now?"

Keren-Happuch writhed slightly, as she looked in a frightened way in the artist's face.

"Do you hear me? I said, Who was the lady who came just now?   It was not the Contessa?"

"No, sir."

"Was it that—that American lady?"

"What! her with the pretty face, who went away crying, sir?   Oh no; it wasn't her."

The girl's words sent a sting through him.

"Then who was it?"

"Please, Mr. Dale, sir, I don't like to tell you."

"Tell me this instant, girl," he cried, catching her fiercely by the arm.

"Oh, don't, please, Mr. Dale," she whimpered. "You frighten me."

"Then speak."

"Yes, sir; but I shall holler if you pinch my arm, and that 'talian girl 'll hear me."

"Who was it, then?"

"Please, sir, it was a cracker."

"What?"

"A bit of a fib, sir. I knowed you wanted to

get rid of them two 'cause you'd got her as you're so fond on shut up in there."

" Silence ! "

" Yes, sir, but missus can't hear; she's down in the kitchen."

" Then nobody came ? "

" No, sir; I thought if I come and said that, you'd like it, because it would send them away. I've often done it for missus when some one's been bothering her for money."

" Go down," said Dale, writhing beneath the sense of degradation he felt at being under this obligation to the poor little slut before him.

" Yes, Mr. Dale, sir; but please don't you be cross with me. I don't mind missus, but it hurts me if you are."

" Go down."

" Yes, sir," said the girl, with a sob; and the tears began to make faint marks on her dirty face. " I wouldn't ha' done it, sir, on'y I knowed you was in love with her and wanted to be alone."

" Poor Cornel ! " muttered Dale as he turned away. " Fallen so low as this ! If you only knew ! "

" Please, Mr. Dale, sir, have I done very wrong ? " she whimpered.

" No; go down now."

" Keren—Hap—puch ! "

" Comin', mum," cried the girl, thrusting her head out of the door, and then turning back.

" Oh, thankye, sir. I don't mind now."

Dale fastened the door after her; and as he turned back, that of the inner room opened, and Valentina came out with her eyes flashing and a joyful look upon her face, as she took his arm and nestled to him.

" We must never forget that poor, brave little drudge, dear," she whispered fondly. " Don't look so serious. All that is nothing to us."

" Nothing ? " he said, as he bent down, fascinated by the beautiful eyes which gazed so tenderly into his.

" Nothing. I am glad they came, to show you how little cause for compunction you have. You see what she is—what the wretched woman is who gives me her sickly kisses and calls me her friend."

She clung to him, and passed her soft white hand over his brow as she looked into his eyes, her voice growing gentle like the cooing of some dove, as she almost whispered—

" I am going now for awhile, but when I am gone don't think of me as a mad, reckless woman, abandoned to her passion, false to her husband and her oaths. I never loved but you, Armstrong: I shall never love another. Try and think of me as one who was forced into a marriage with that despicable wretch who in one week taught me to loathe him; and till I saw you I was the wretched being whose life was void, a kind of gilded doll upon which he hung his jewels, and whom he paraded before his guests, while in private my life was a mockery. Wife? By law, yes, till we can break the tie, and then you will take me to your heart, dear, away from all that black despairing life, to a new one all delight and joy. For I shall be with you, my brave, noble—husband! May I call you husband then?"

She sank upon her knees, clasped her arms about him, and laid her cheeks against his hands, murmuring softly—

"If you will take me for your wife, dearest. If not, I should be always happy as your slave."

He would have been more than man if he had not raised the beautiful appealing woman to his breast, and held her tightly there.

"I love you—I love you!" she murmured, as her soft, swimming eyes gazed in his, "and it is misery to leave you now. But there is all that new joy in my heart to keep me waiting and hopeful till I come again."

"But the risk—for you?" he said.

"Risk?" she laughed softly. "You will protect me. I must go now, and you will wait till your poor Italian model is here once more—she whom you love so well."

He clasped her to his heart, and held her till

she faintly struggled to be free, and then laughingly covered her face with the thick veil her husband had thrown down.

"There," she said merrily. "Now I must go. Back to my faithful Jaggs."

"What!"

"He is my slave—"The Emperor," he says you call him. He has been my slave from the first day you sent him to the house. He told me everything about you in answer to my questions regarding the portrait you had painted from memory, and then—'Armstrong does love me with all his heart' I said to myself, and I was ready to risk everything to win that love."

"And did he suggest that you should be my model?" said Dale.

"No; that was my idea, when he told me how hard you were pressed. He helped me, and I came. And now, once more, I must go. It will not be like life until I am here again."

She gave him her white hands, which he held passionately to his lips. Then, covering them hastily with her common gloves, she drew her cloak about her.

"One moment," he whispered. "The address? Where are you now—for this?"

"Always in your heart," she said, in a passionate whisper. Then, "A rivederla," she said aloud, and was gone.

"Poor Cornel!" sighed Dale, as he sank into a chair. "Forgive me, dear. She is right; a boy and girl's pure gentle love, of which I am not worthy. It is fate, dear, and this is really love— a love for which a man might sacrifice honour— even sell his very soul."

So he said, for it has been written of old— "Love is blind."

CHAPTER XXII.

A LAST EFFORT.

"Corny, I've no patience with you," cried Dr. Thorpe, as they sat at dinner in their hotel with a guest that evening—Joe Pacey.

"Not to-night, dear," she said, with a quiet, grave smile.—"He has very little patience with me when he comes home tired from the hospitals," she continued, turning to Pacey. "He works too hard."

"Yes: he does seem a glutton over work; but we must work hard nowadays to succeed."

"Hah, you are right," said the young doctor. "It was all very well a hundred years ago. Plenty of medical men went through life then without half the knowledge I possess, while I'm a perfect baby to your big doctors."

"No, you are not, dear," said Cornel quietly. "You know that you stand first among our young medical men."

"Humph! not saying much that; but this is begging the question. I shall want to stay in

England another three months, and, as I was saying, the Hudsons go back by the next boat. I've been to the office: you can have a cabin, so you had better accompany them."

"No, dear, I shall stay and go back with you."

Thorpe pushed his chair away from the table impatiently.

"My dear sister, where is your pride?"

"My dear brother, where is your sympathy?"

"How can I have sympathy for a girl who is so blind to her own dignity! Now, my dear Pacey, do you not agree with me that my sister is behaving very foolishly?"

"No," said Pacey, holding his glass of wine to the light, shutting one eye and scowling at it with the other—"no, sir, I don't."

"Thank you, Mr. Pacey," said Cornel, laying her hand upon the table, so that he could take it in his and press it warmly.

"Can't kiss it before company," he said, in his abrupt way. "Please take it as being done—or owing."

"You are as bad over the scamp as she is," cried Thorpe sharply.

"Come, come, doctor," cried Pacey; "you are too hard. If Armstrong were suffering from a bodily disease, you would stand by him."

"Of course. But this——"

"Is a mental disease," cried Pacey, "so why blame your sister for standing by the patient?"

"Bah! Don't talk like that. I haven't patience with her. I thought her firm, self-reliant, and proud of her position as a woman."

"Quite right," said Pacey, turning and smiling at Cornel. "She's all that."

"I join issue," cried Thorpe. "No: she is neither one nor the other."

"And I say that she is all three," cried Pacey, bringing his fist down on the table with a thump, which drew the waiters' attention. "I beg pardon," he said hastily. "No, I don't. I'm not ashamed of my earnestness."

"Just eight," said Thorpe, looking at his watch. "I've a meeting to attend. You will stop and talk to my sister?"

"Of course."

Ten minutes later they were alone, and Cornel's manner changed.

"You will not mind my brother's manner to you?" she said earnestly.

"Not I," replied Pacey bluffly. "He's mad against Dale, naturally. Wouldn't be a good brother if he were not. I'm mad against him, and get worse every day."

"But tell me now—what news have you for me?"

Pacey looked at her with pitying thoughtfulness, and then said gravely—

"You have trusted me thoroughly since the first day we met, and made me your friend."

"Completely," she said earnestly.

"And a friend would be nothing unless sincere."

"No."

"I have no news, then, that is good."

Cornel sighed, and rested her head upon her hand.

"Can nothing be done?" she said at last. "Oh! it is too dreadful to let his whole career be blasted like this! Mr. Pacey, you are his friend; pray, pray, help me! Tell me what to do."

Pacey's brow wrinkled so that he looked ten years older, and he sat for some time with his eyes averted.

At last he spoke.

"I know what I ought to say to you as your friend."

"Yes; what?" she cried eagerly; but Pacey shook his head.

"Nothing but—be strong and bear your cruel disappointment like a true woman, proud of her dignity."

"I could bear all that," she said piteously, "even if it broke my heart, but I cannot bear the knowledge that the boy with whom I walked hand in hand as a child, grew up with as if he were my own brother, and whose child-love ripened into a sincere affection, should drift away like this.

Mr. Pacey—this woman! I know how beautiful she is, and how she has ensnared him. I ceased to wonder when we stood face to face. I know too what influence she has, but nothing but horror and misery can result from it all, and it cuts me to the heart to think of what he will suffer—of the bitter repentance to come."

Pacey sighed.

"To me, night and day, it is as if he were drowning—being swept away; and if—utterly worn out—I sleep for a few minutes, I wake up with a start, for his hands seem to be stretched out to me to save him before it is too late."

Pacey was silent still as he sat with his arms resting upon his knees, and his head bent, gazing at the carpet.

At last he looked up, to meet her appealing eyes fixed on his.

"Yes," he said, and he took a long deep breath: "there is no other way."

"You—you have thought of something?" she cried eagerly.

"It is a forlorn hope," he replied. "I ought not to advise it, and your brother will blame me, and tell me I am not acting as an honest friend."

"The danger sweeps away all ideas of worldly custom, Mr. Pacey," she cried with animation, her eyes sparkling, her cheeks flushed; and as he gazed at her, the artist mentally said that if his friend could see the woman he had so cruelly jilted, now, he would humbly ask her to pardon him, and take him back to her heart.

"Yes," he said firmly, "this is not time to study etiquette. Go to him, then. Don't look upon it as sinking your womanly dignity, but as a last effort to save the man you once loved from a deadly peril."

"Yes; and when I go," said Cornel faintly, "what can I say more than I have said?"

"Say nothing, child. If your face, and your reproachful forgiving eyes do not bring him to your feet, come away, and go down upon your knees to thank God for saving you from a man not worthy of a second thought."

CHAPTER XXIII.

"And my poor painting," said Armstrong, smiling, as Valentina, cloaked and ready to go once more, still clung to him—"not a step farther;" and he unlocked the door.

"No," she whispered softly, "not a step farther," and she looked up through her thick veil in his saddened face. "Let fate be kind to us and the work go on for years and years."

"Until I am old and grey."

"And I a bent, withered creature," she whispered. "No; you will never be old and grey in my eyes, but always the same as now. Can you say that to me?"

She laid her hands upon his shoulders, and forced him back, so that she could gaze searchingly in his eyes.

"Yes!" he cried passionately. "You know only too well."

"Yes, I know it well," she murmured. "And it shall go on and on. What is the praise of a fickle public worth? It is your masterpiece, but what of that? It might bring you fame and fortune, but it has already brought us love that can know no change."

"That can know no change, dearest. Now you must go, or you will be breaking faith with me again to-morrow, and you have made me so that I cannot live without you now."

"Yes, once more," she sighed, "I must go—back to my gilded prison."

She clung to him fondly again, and her voice was very soft and tender, as she rested her brow upon his breast.

"When will you say to me—'Stay; go back no more?' Armstrong, this life is killing me End all the miserable trickery and subterfuge. That woman is planning and plotting to take my place. Once it roused up all my pride and hatred; now all that is past. Let him sue for his divorce if Lady Grayson wishes, and then I shall have my revenge: for he will laugh in her false, deceitful face. Marry her?—Not he.—What is it, dearest?"

He had started back, and as she raised her eyes, she saw that he was looking angrily at something behind her.

She turned slowly, calling upon herself for readiness to meet the face of her husband, as she believed, but it was Cornel standing just within the doorway, flushed, proud, and stern, and she uttered a sigh of relief.

"A domani, signore," she said quietly to Armstrong, and then turned and took a step toward the door, but Cornel raised her hand, and the proud, haughty-looking figure shrank back a step or two in surprise.

"Stop!" said Cornel firmly; and she closed the door behind. "I wish to speak to you both."

"Cornel!" cried Armstrong, in a low and excited voice, "this is madness. For Heaven's sake, go. Have you no delicacy—no shame?"

"You ask me that!" she cried scornfully; and he shrank from her indignant eyes. "Man, where is your own delicacy?—woman, where is your shame? I claim the right—in the name of truth and honour—to come and upbraid you both."

Valentina made a gesture with her hands, and turned to Armstrong to say in French—

"What does the strange lady mean?"

Cornel took a step forward, with her eyes flashing.

"Mean, Lady Dellatoria!" she cried loudly; and her rival started and drew herself up.

"Cornel! Silence, for Heaven's sake."

"You invoke Heaven?" she cried; and she turned from him with a look of disgust and scorn. "It means," she cried, "that this is no scene in amateur theatricals played by your set, but real life. You are face to face with me—the woman whose love you have outraged, whose life you have wrecked as well as his. And for what? Your pastime for a few weeks."

"No!" said Valentina, throwing back her head and seizing Armstrong's hand, to hold it tightly between her own. "He is mine—my love for ever. I told you, when you came and defied me, that I could laugh at your girlish efforts to separate us—for it was fate. There, you have tracked me down and seen; now go."

"Yes, I have tracked you down and seen, and you throw off your contemptible disguise—this paltry cloaking and veiling. Armstrong, is this the type of the boasted British woman—an example to the world?"

"Cornel, silence! Pray go!"

"Not yet. I have a right here in the home of my affianced husband. I find him being dragged to ruin and despair by a heartless creature, devoid of love as she is of shame."

"You lie!" cried Valentina fiercely, as she made a quick movement toward Cornel, but Armstrong held her back. "Yes," she said, calming as quickly as she had flashed into rage; "poor child, she is half mad with misery and disappointment. I will not speak—but pity."

Cornel held out her hands to Armstrong as Lady

Dellatoria half turned away and linked her fingers upon his arm.

"Before it is too late, Armstrong," said Cornel softly. "No word of reproach shall ever come from those who love you."

He shook his head.

"Listen, dear," she whispered, but her voice thrilled both. "I come to you a weak woman, but strong in my armour of love and truth. They tell me it is lowering, weak, and contemptible—that I am utterly lost to a woman's sense of dignity and shame. But they do not know my love for you—yes, my love for you, I say it even before this creature, who cannot know the depth and truth of a true woman's love—I come, I say, once again to plead, to beg of you to come. Let her go back to her own people; come you to yours, before it is too late."

"It is too late, girl," said Valentina gently. "I forgive you all you have said in ignorance that my love is stronger, more womanly, than yours. In Heaven's sight this is my husband now. We sorrow for you, and can pity. But go now, and leave us in peace. I tell you again—it is too late."

"Yes," said Cornel, with a piteous sigh. "God forgive you, Armstrong! I am beaten." Then, as if inspired, her eyes flashed, and the colour left her cheeks, and she cried wildly, "Yes, it is too late."

There were voices on the stairs coming plainly

to them, for Cornel had in ignorance left the door unlatched, so that the sounds were uninterrupted.

"He's got a lady with him."

"I know, girl. Stand aside. Do you know who I am?"

"Yes, sir; Count Delly-tory, sir."

"Yes!" cried Cornel, with a wail of horror; "her husband. Then it is indeed too late."

"No!" cried Valentina fiercely; "your opportunity for revenge."

She drew back, and stood there erect and proud, with defiance flashing through her thick veil as the Conte entered, quickly followed by Lady Grayson. A heavy, gold-topped, ebony stick was in his hand, his lips were compressed, and it was plain to see in his pallid face and dilated nostrils that he was struggling with suppressed passion.

He was making straight for Armstrong when his eyes fell upon Cornel, who stood now white and calm, as if ready to interpose. Then he looked sharply at the cloaked and veiled figure just on the artist's right.

He stopped in astonishment, confused, and as if the supply of vital force which had urged him on had suddenly been checked.

It was Armstrong's opportunity. A few carelessly spoken, contemptuous utterances as to the meaning of this intrusion and the like would have sufficed

to send the Conte back, mortified, and in utter
ignorance, to vent his rage upon Lady Grayson,
who, in her malignant desire to cast down her
dearest confidante and friend from her throne,
had brought him on there to be a witness of
one of his wife's secret meetings with her lover,
such as she had vowed to him were taking place.
But Armstrong, in utter scorn of all subterfuge,
stood there manly and ready to meet the man in
full defiance, come what might.

A terrible silence followed, of moments that felt
to all like hours, while each waited for others to
speak.

It was Cornel's opportunity too, to bring her
rival to her knees and sweep her for ever from
her path, and Valentina felt it as she stood there
with her teeth clenched and face convulsed behind
the thick veil. For, after all, in spite of her bravery
and readiness to defy the man whose name she
bore, she was a woman still, and instinctively shrank
from the dénouement, knowing as she did that a
terrible scene must follow; and another later, in
spite of English laws, for it was an Italian pitted
against a man who would dare all.

But Cornel remained silent, and Lady Grayson
scanned all in turn, ending by fixing her eyes upon
the great canvas whose back was toward them
where they stood.

"I—I beg pardon—some mistake," stammered

the Conte. "I did not know that——Curse you," he whispered to Lady Grayson, and relapsing in his excitement into broken English, "You make me with you silly cock-bull tale a fool."

Armstrong still made no movement, said no word, but Lady Grayson read him as if he were an open page laid before her, and her eyes twinkled and flashed.

The keen-witted American girl saw it too, and with all her gentleness and love, she possessed the quick perception and readiness of a people born in a clearer air and warmer clime. In those moments, with all her hatred and scorn for the woman who was the blight upon her life, she shrank in all the tenderness of her nature from seeing her humbled to the very dust. More; she grasped the horror of the situation; how that, beneath the weak flippancy of the man of fashion, there smouldered the hot passions of his countrymen—passions which, once roused, are as hot and destructive as the lava of their great volcano. She saw in imagination, blows, and Armstrong injuring or injured, either being too horrible to be borne. Lastly, she grasped Lady Grayson's plan.

"It is for his sake," she said to herself, "not for hers;" and as, apparently prompted by a whisper from Lady Grayson, the blood flushed into the Conte's face again and he fixed his eyes on his wife, Cornel stepped forward and held out her hand.

" Good-bye, Mr. Dale," she said gently ; "you have business with this lady and gentleman ; we shall see you another time.   Come, signora."

She turned and held out her hand to Valentina, proving herself a better actress, for there was a smile upon her lip, and she bent forward as if whispering something through the veil, the only utterances being the words—

" Don't hesitate.   Quick ! "

Valentina stared at her—half stunned.   Then, as if moved by a stronger will than her own, she laid one white hand on Cornel's arm, and, just bending her head to Armstrong, they moved slowly toward the door.

It was the left hand, and ungloved.

Cornel saw it, and could not restrain a start.

The hand was ungloved, and upon it sparkled several rings—for there had been no need of late to keep up the disguise so closely—and one of those rings was of plain gold.

They were nearly at the door, the Conte drawing back on one side to let them pass, Lady Grayson on the other, Armstrong still motionless, and feeling as if a hand were compressing his throat, while Cornel, as she went on with the set smile upon her lip, felt that the hand upon her arm trembled, and fancied she heard a sob.

" It is for his sake," she said to herself, " for his sake ; " and the next minute they would have been outside the door, when, with one quick movement, Lady Grayson reached out her hand, and snatched the veil from Valentina's face.

The Conte uttered a cry of rage, and made a dash at her, but she avoided him, and sprang toward Armstrong, who caught her to his breast, but so as to have his right hand at liberty.

But it was not free in time, for the Conte, with a cry of rage, swung round, and brought down the heavy ebony stick with a sickening crash upon the artist's head, then caught Valentina from him as he fell inert and senseless upon the floor.

"Well, am I such a simple idiot and fool?" said Lady Grayson in a quick whisper.

"Yes; to talk now," was the fierce reply. "Help me; get her away, or I shall kill him."

Without another word she went to Valentina's side, and between them they dragged her, sick at heart, trembling, and half fainting, out of the studio and down the stairs to Lady Grayson's carriage, which was waiting at the door.

"Is anything the matter, miss? Can I do anything?" said a voice.

Cornel looked up from where she was kneeling on one of the rugs with Armstrong's head in her lap, and saw that the grimy little face of Keren-Happuch was peering in at the door.

Cornel looked at her wildly for a few moments, and then, in a low hoarse voice, whispered—

"Yes: quick, water!" Then, with a piteous sigh, "Oh, the blood—the blood! Help!—quick, quick! He is dying. Oh, my love, my love, that it should come to this!"

CHAPTER XXIV.

THE AWAKENING.

"Don't you be in a flurry, miss," said Keren-Happuch coolly; "he ain't so very bad. Here, you'll soon see."

She rushed into the bedroom, and returned with a basin, sponge, and towel, which, to her surprise and annoyance, were taken from her hand; and she saw Cornel, with deft manipulation, bathe the cut, examine it, and then take from her pocket a little case, out of which she drew a pair of scissors and a leaf of adhesive plaster. A minute later she had closely clipped away a little of the hair, pressed the cut together, and cleverly strapped it up.

"Hold this handkerchief pressed to it tightly, while I bathe his temples," said Cornel; and, as the little maid obeyed, she watched with wide open eyes the pulse felt and the temples bathed before a few drops from a stoppered bottle were added to a wine-glass full of water, and gently poured between the insensible man's lips.

"Lor', if she ain't one o' them female doctors," thought Keren-Happuch. "Wonder what she's give him to drink?"

There was a singular look of dislike condensed into a frown on the girl's brows as she watched Cornel, and a jealous scowl or two as she saw her take Armstrong's hand and kneel by his side, waiting for some signs of returning animation; but at last it seemed as if the girl could not keep her tongue quiet.

"I say," she whispered, "are you a doctor, miss?"

"No: my brother is a medical man, though, and I have been often to a hospital and helped him as a nurse."

"Oh, then you know what's right. But oughtn't he to have some beef-tea?"

Cornel shook her head, and Keren-Happuch was silent for a few minutes, but she could refrain no longer.

"You're the 'Merican lady he was engaged to, aren't you?"

Cornel bowed.

"I thought you was. I've took him your letters with Bosting on 'em, lots o' times."

Cornel sighed.

"You're going to marry him, ain't you?"

"No."

"Then it's all off?"

"Yes."

Keren-Happuch looked relieved. The scowl disappeared from her countenance, and she smiled at Cornel.

"Don't you take on about it, miss. It ain't worth it. I allers liked Mr. Dale, and he makes me feel as if I'd do anything for him, and I allus have done as much as missus'd let me; but it's no use to worry about artisses; they're all like Mr. Dale —all them as we've had here."

Cornel looked at her indignantly.

"Oh, it ain't my fault, miss. I never wanted him to have ladies come to see him. I've gone down into the kitchen along with our old cat, and had many a good cry about it. Not as he ever thought anything about me."

Cornel looked at the girl in wonder and horror.

"But he was allus kind to me, and never called me names, and made fun of me like the others did. On'y Mirandy, and I didn't mind that. Them others teased me orful, you know. Men ain't much good; but you can't help liking of 'em."

"Hush!" whispered Cornel; "he is coming to."

For there was a quivering about Dale's lips, and then his eyes opened wildly, to gaze vacantly upward for some moments before memory reasserted itself, and he gave a sudden start and looked sharply round.

Cornel suppressed a sigh.

"Not for me," she said to herself; and she was right. The look was not for her.

She knew it directly, for he turned to her, caught her wrist, and said excitedly—

"Gone?"

"Yes; they are gone."

"But Lady Dellatoria—gone—with him?"

The words seemed as if they would choke her, but Cornel spoke out quite plainly, and without a tremor in her voice, though there was a terrible compression at her breast.

"Yes," she said calmly, though every word she uttered caused her a pang; "she has gone back with her husband."

Armstrong lay perfectly still for a few minutes, thinking deeply. Then, as if resolved what to do, he said sharply—

"Help me up."

Cornel bent over him, but he turned from her.

"No, no, not you: Miranda."

The girl eagerly helped him to rise, and he leaned upon her as she guided him to a chair.

"Thanks," he said huskily. "Now, you wait there."

The girl stopped at the place he had pointed out, watching Armstrong as he signed to Cornel to approach, and held out his hand.

She took it mechanically, and held it fast.

"Thank you for what you have done," he said.

"Now go and forget me. You see I am hopelessly gone. It was to be, and it is of no use to fight against fate. Now go back to your brother."

"And leave you—sick ? "

"Yes; even if I were dying. God bless you, dear ! Think of me as I used to be."

"Armstrong !" she cried, with her hands extended toward him. But he waved her off.

"No, no. I am a scoundrel, but not black enough for that. Go back to your brother."

"Go ? "

"Yes; I insist. You cannot forgive me now."

She could bear no more. Her chin sank upon her breast, and with one low, heart-wrung sigh, she went quickly from the room.

"Thank Heaven ! that's over," muttered Armstrong. "Now for the end, and the quicker the better. Life is not worth living, after all."

He looked sharply round to where Keren-Happuch stood, wiping her eyes upon her apron.

"Here, girl !" he cried.

"Yes, Mr. Dale, sir."

"Go at once to Mr. Leronde's rooms—you know --in Poland Street, and ask him to come on here at once."

"But are you fit to leave, sir ? "

"Yes, yes. Go quickly."

The girl hurried off on her mission, leaving the artist thinking.

"He would challenge me if I did not challenge him. I suppose it ought to come from me after the blow, for me to prove that I am not 'un lâche,' as our French friends term it. A duel! What a mockery! Well, better so. Let him shoot me, and have done with it. There is not room here for us both. Poor Cornel! It will be like making some expiation. It will leave her free. She can deal more tenderly with my memory as dead than she could with me living still. I should be a blight upon her pure young life. Ah! if we had never met."

He lay back feverish and excited, for the blow had had terrible effect, and there were minutes when he was half delirious, and had hard work to control his thoughts.

For he was wandering away now with Cornel, who had forgiven him because Valentina was dead. Then it was Cornel who was dead, and he was with the Contessa far away in some glorious land of flowers, fruit, and sunshine; but the fruit was bitter, the flowers gave forth the scent of poison, and the sun beat down heavily upon his head, scorching his throbbing brain.

He woke up from a dream crowded with strange fancies, and uttered an ejaculation of satisfaction, for his brain was clear again, and the young Frenchman was standing before him, waiting to know why he had been fetched.

CHAPTER XXV.

THE SECOND SECOND.

"AH, oui, of course," said Leronde, exhaling a little puff of smoke. "It is so, of course. I know. If there had been no knog viz ze stique, ze huzziband would shallenge you. But viz ze knog viz ze stique—so big a knog, I sink you shallenge him, and satisfy l'honneur. I go at once and ask him to name his friends."

"Yes, I suppose that will be right," said Armstrong, after a few moments' thought.

"But I am not sure that you can fight so soon."

"Why?"

"You 'ave ze bad head."

"Bah! a mere nothing. I am ready; but of course, as you say, it cannot be here. Listen! Is not that some one on the stairs?"

They were not left in doubt, for Keren-Happuch came in, round-eyed and wondering, with a couple of cards held in her apron-guarded thumb and finger.

"Please, Mr. Dale, sir, here's two doctors come to see you."

"Ma foi! two," cried Leronde. "One is bad, too much. Send zem away, my friend."

"Bah! Show them up," said the artist; and Keren-Happuch hurried out. "Look," continued Armstrong; "Italians—his friends, I suppose."

"Aha! that is good," cried Leronde, holding out the cards. "He shallenge then. I am glad, for I was get in head muddled after all vezzer you ought to shallenge. Now we are quite square."

A minute later two important-looking men were ushered in, to whom Leronde at once advanced with a dignified mien, receiving them and listening to the declaration of their mission, and after a few exchanges of compliments on one side of the studio, away from where Armstrong sat scowling, they left with the understanding that Leronde was to wait upon them shortly to arrange all preliminaries.

"I am still not quite satisfy," said Leronde thoughtfully. "I ought to have been first, and take your shallenge to him.

"But what does it matter if we are to meet?"

"But you vas ze insulte."

"Indeed!" said Armstrong, with a bitter smile. "Opinions are various, boy. But let that rest. Help me to lie down on that couch, and give me a cigar."

Leronde obeyed, watching his friend anxiously.

"You vill not be vell enough to fight."

"I will be well enough to fight, man," cried Armstrong savagely. "There: wait a bit. It is too soon to follow them yet;" and for a while they sat and smoked, till Leronde burst out with—

"I am so glad you go to fight, my dear Dale."

"Are you?" said Armstrong gruffly.

"Yes; it do me good that you are ready to fight M'sieu le Conte like a gentleman. I thought all Englishmans degrade themself viz le boxe. Bah! it is not good. You have ze muscle great, but so have ze dustman and ze navigator; let them fight—so."

"But look here, Leronde; this must be kept a secret from every one."

"Oh, certainement, name of a visky and sodaire. I tell nobdis. You think I go blab and tell of ze meeting? Valkaire! Mums!"

"Have you ever seen one of these affairs at home?"

"Oh no, my friend, not chez-moi—at home. It was in the Bois de Boulogne."

"And you saw one there?"

"Four—five—and all were journalistes. I was in two as principal, in two as friend of my friend, and in ze oder one I go as ze friend of ze docteur."

"Then you quite understand how it should be carried out?"

"Yes, yes, yes," said Leronde, nearly closing his eyes, and nodding his head many times. "Soyez content. I mean make yourself sholly comfortable, and it shall all go off to ze marvel."

"Very well, then; I leave myself in your hands."

"That is good. Everything shall be done, as you say, first-class."

"And about weapons?"

"You are ze person insulte, and you have ze choice. Le sword, of course?" cried Leronde; and, throwing himself on guard, he foiled, parried, and hopped about the studio, as if he were encountering an enemy.

"Sit down, man," said Armstrong peevishly. "No; I choose the pistol."

"My friend! Oh!"

"It is shorter and sharper."

"But you do not vant to shoot ze man for stealing—fence like angels, and there will be a little gentlemanly play; you prick ze Conte in ze arm, honneur is satisfy, you embrace, and we return to Paris. What can be better than that?"

"Pistol!" said Armstrong sternly.

"But you do not want to shoot ze man for stealing away his vife."

"No," said Armstrong, in a low voice "I want him to shoot me."

"Ha, ha! You are a fonnay fellow, my dear Dale. You will not talk like zat when you meet. Ze sword?"

"Pistols."

"As you will," said the Frenchman, shrugging his shoulders. "You are my principal, and I see zat your honneur is satisfy. I go then to see ze friend of M'sieu le Conte, and to make all ze preparations for to cross to Belgium; but, my faith, my dear Dale, it is very awkward: I have not ze small shange for all ze preliminary. May I ask you to be my banker?"

"Yes, of course. I ought to have thought," said Armstrong.

He went to his desk and took out the necessary sum, passed it to the voluble little Frenchman, who rose, shook him by both hands, looked at him with tears in his eyes, told him he was proud of him, and then hurried off with his head erect his hat slightly cocked, and his eyes now sparkling with excitement.

"Step ze first to be in ordaire; whom shall ve ave for ze ozaire seconde?"

He frowned severely and walked on a few yards, looking very thoughtful. Then the idea came.

"Of course: Shoe Pacey. He vill be proud to go viz me to meet ze ozaire secondes."

Leronde had been in the lowest of low spirits

that morning. The news from Paris had been most disastrous for gentlemen of communistic principles, who, in spite of crying "Vive la Commune!" saw the unfortunate idol of their lives withering and dying daily. Money, too, had been very "shorts," as he called it, and he had gone to Armstrong Dale's in the most despondent manner. But now all that was altered. He had money in his purse, and walked as if on air. There was no opportunity for following the tracks of either "la gloire, or l'amour;" but here was "l'honneur," the other person of a Frenchman's trinity, calling him to the front; and on the strength of the funds in hand, he entered the first tobacconist's, bought a whole ninepenny packet of cigarettes, and then smoked in triumph all the way to Pacey's lodgings.

This gentleman was growling over a notice of the Old Masters' Exhibition which he had written for a morning paper, and with which, to use his own words, "the humbug of an editor had taken confounded liberties."

"Hallo! Signor Barricado, what's up? Republic gone to the dogs?"

"No, no, mon ami; but great news—a secret."

"Keep it, then."

"No, no; it is for you as well. An affaire of honneur."

"An affair of fluff! Bosh! we don't fight here."

"No," said Leronde, frowning fiercely. "Belgium."

"Why, you confounded young donkey, whom are you going to fight?"

"I fight? But, no; I am one seconde. I come to you as my dear friend to be ze ozaire."

"Oh, of course," cried Pacey ironically. "Exactly —just in my line."

"I knew you would," cried Leronde, lighting a fresh cigarette, and offering the packet, which was refused.

"Bah! I like a draught, not a spoonful," growled Pacey, taking up and filling his big meerschaum. "Now then, about this honour mania? Who's the happy man?"

"Armstrong Dale, of course, for certaine."

"What!" roared Pacey. "Who with?"

"Ze Conte Dellatoria, my friend."

"The devil. Has it come to that?"

"But, yes. Why not? Zes huzziband is sure to find out some ozaire day."

"Phew!" whistled Pacey, wiping his brow. Then striking a match, he began to smoke tremendously.

"And you will help our friend?" said Leronde.

"Help him? Certainly."

"I knew it. Pacey, my friend, you are one grand big brique."

"Oh yes, I am," cried Pacey banteringly. "Now then, how was it?"

"Ze Conte follow his vife to chez Armstrong, find zem togezzer, and knog our dear friend down viz a cane."

"Humph! Serious as that?"

"Oh yes. There is a great offence, of course. Zey meet in Belgium, and we go togezzer to see ze friend of ze Conte and arrange ze—ze—ze—vat you call zem?"

"Preliminaries?"

"Precisely. Now, my dear ole friend, you put on your boot an' ze ozaire coat, and brush your hair —oh! horreur; why do you not get zem cut short like mine?"

"Because I don't want to look like a convict. Come in here."

Pacey seized his tobacco-jar and a box of matches.

"Got any cigarette papers?"

"But yes, and plenty of cigarettes."

"Come in here, then."

He opened the door leading into his little bedroom, and Leronde followed him.

Pacey banged down the tobacco-jar upon the dressing-table, and then threw open the window.

"Come and look out here," he cried.

"But we have no time to spare, my friend."

"Come and look out here," roared Pacey.

As Leronde approached him wonderingly, Pacey seized him by the collar, and half dragged his head out.

"Look down there," he said, pointing into the square pit-like place formed by the backs of the neighbouring houses, from the second floor, where they stood, to the basement; "you can't jump down there?"

"My faith, no. It would be death."

"And there is no way of climbing on to the roof."

Leronde shook his head, and looked to see if his friend was mad.

"And you cannot fly?"

"No; I leave zat to your cocksparrow de Londres," said Leronde, trying to conceal his wonder and dread by a show of hilarity.

"That's right, then. You sit down there and smoke cigarettes till I come back."

"But, my friend, ze engagement, ze meeting viz ze amis of ze Conte. What go you to do?"

"See Armstrong Dale, and bring him to his senses. If I can't—go and break the Count's neck."

"But, mon cher Pacey!" cried Leronde, "l'honneur?"

"Hang honour!" roared his friend. "I'm going in for common-sense;" and before the Frenchman could arrest him, the door was banged to, locked, the key removed, and steps were heard on the landing; then the sitting-room door was locked, and, with his face full of perplexity, Leronde lit a fresh cigarette.

"Faith of a man, these English," he said, "zey are mad, as Shakspere did say about Hamlet, and I am sure, if zey do shave Shoe Pacey head, zey will find ze big crack right across him."

CHAPTER XXVI.

THE NEWS SPREADS.

"If I have sinned," muttered Armstrong, as he leaned back in his chair, for when from time to time he tried to walk about, a painful sensation of giddiness seized upon him, "I am having a foretaste of my punishment. How long he is—how long he is!"

But still Leronde did not come, and to occupy his mind, the sufferer sat and thought out a plan for their journey, which he concluded would mean a cab to Liverpool Street, then the express to Harwich, the boat to Ostend; next, where the seconds willed: and afterwards—

"What?" said the wretched man, with a strange smile. "Ah, who knows! If it could only be oblivion—rest from all this misery and despair!"

He rose to try and write a letter or two, notably one to Cornel, but the effort was painful, and he crept back to his chair.

"She will know—she will divine—that I preferred to die," he muttered. "Ah, at last! Why, he has been hours."

For there was a step outside, and then the door was thrown open, as he lay back, with his aching eyes shaded by his hand.

"Come at last, then!" he sighed; and the next moment he started, for the studio door was banged to, and locked. "You, Joe?"

"Yes, I've come at last," cried Pacey, thrusting his hands into his pockets, and striding up, to stand before him with his legs far apart.

"Well, then, shake hands and go," said Armstrong quietly. "I'm not well. I've had an accident."

"Accident?" roared Pacey. "Yes, you have had an accident, the same as a man has who goes and knocks his head against a wall."

"What do you mean?" cried Armstrong, starting.

"Mean? I mean that you're the biggest fool that fortune ever pampered and spoiled."

"Joe Pacey!"

"Hold your tongue, idiot, and listen to me. Here you are, gifted by nature with ten times the brains of an ordinary man; you can paint like Raphael or Murillo; fame and fortune are at your feet; and you have the love waiting for you of one of the sweetest, most angelic women who ever stepped this earth."

"Pacey!"

"Hold your tongue, boy! Haven't I been like a father to you ever since you came into this cursed village? Haven't I devoted myself to you as soon as I saw you were a good fellow, full of genius? I'm a fool to say so, but in my wretched, wrecked life, I felt that I'd found something to live for at last, and that I could be proud and happy in seeing you, who are as much an Englishman as I am in blood, rise to the highest pitch of triumph; while, if you grew proud then and forgot me, it wouldn't matter; I could afford it, for you had achieved success."

"You've been a good true adviser to me, Joe, ever since I have known you."

"And you have turned out the most ungrateful dog that ever breathed. Morals? You've no more morals than a mahlstick. You had everything man could wish for, and then you must kick it all over, and break the heart of an angel."

"Let her rest. Say what you like to bully me, Joe. It's all true. I don't fight against it. But you can't understand it all. Say what you like, only go and leave me. I want to be alone."

"Do you?" cried Pacey excitedly. "Then I don't want you to be. So the Conte gave you that crack on the head, did he?"

"What!" cried Armstrong, springing up. "How came you to think that?"

"How came I to think that? Why, I was told by a chattering French ape."

"Leronde? Told you?"

"Of course he did. Came to me to be your other second."

"The idiot! Where is he?"

"Locked up where he'll stay till I let him loose."

Armstrong used a strong expression.

"And so we must have a duel, must we? Go out to Belgium to fight this Italian organ-grinder. Curse him, and his Jezebel of a wife!"

"Silence, man!" cried Armstrong excitedly. "Pacey, no more of this! Where is Leronde? He must be set free at once. My honour is at stake."

"His what?" cried Pacey, bursting into a roar of ironical laughter. "My God! His honour! You adulterous dog, you talk to me of your honour and duelling, and all that cursed, sickly, contemptible code that ought to have been dead and buried, and wondered at by us as a relic of the dark ages—you talk to me of that? Why, do you know what it means? First and foremost, murdering Cornel Thorpe: for, as sure as heaven's above us, that organ-man will shoot you like the dog you are, and in killing you he'll kill that poor girl. I swear it. She can't help it. She gave her love to you, poor lassie, and she's the kind of woman who loves once

and for all. There's the first of it. As for you, well,
the best end of you is that you should be buried at
once, out of the way, as you would be if I let you
go to meet this man."

"If you let me?" raged Armstrong.

"Yes, if I let you; for I won't. Why, you're
mad. That Jezebel has turned your brain, and I'll
have you in a strait waistcoat, and then in a padded
room, before I'll let you go to save your honour and
his. Ha, ha! His honour! The Italian grey-
hound! He never took any notice of his wife till
he found she had a lover, but was after as many
light-famed creatures as there are cards in the
devil's books. Then — his honour! Ha, ha! his
honour! Why, the whole gang of French and
Italian monkeys never knew what honour is, and
never will. Now then, I said I'd thrash you, and
I have. I only wish Dellatoria had jolly well
fractured your skull, so as to make you an invalid
for six months. Look here; I've locked up Leronde,
I'll lock up you, and if the Conte comes here, I'll
kick him downstairs."

"You are mad. I must meet him."

"I'm not mad, and you shan't meet him."

"You mean well, Pacey, but it is folly to go on
like this. Run back and set Leronde at liberty."

"I'm going to do what I like, not what you
like," cried Pacey fiercely, pulling out a knife;
"and first of all, I'll finish that cursed picture."

He swung the great easel round, and in a few minutes had slashed the canvas to ribbons, and torn it from the frame.

"There's an end of that!" he roared.

"So much the better," said Armstrong, who had looked on unmoved.

"Oh! you like that, then?" cried Pacey. "You're coming round."

"Now go," said Armstrong, "and end this folly."

"You'll swear first of all that you will not meet this man?"

"I'll swear I will," said Armstrong coldly.

"He'll shoot you dead."

"I hope so."

"Armstrong, lad, listen to me," said Pacey, calming down. "You'll be sensible?"

"Yes."

"And give it up? For poor Cornel's sake?"

"Silence! or you'll drive me really mad."

"Now then, get your hat, and come with me."

"Will you go?"

"Will you come with me?"

"Look here," said Armstrong. "I can bear no more. I want to be cool and act like a man to the end, but you are pushing me to the very brink. —Will you go?"

"Yes," said Pacey, buttoning up his coat. "I'm off now, boy."

"Where?"

"Straight to the police. I'll swear a breach of the peace against you both, and have you seized, or bound over, or something. This meeting shan't take place. For Cornel's sake—do you hear? For her sake, so there!"

He strode to the door, unlocked it, opened, and banged it loudly behind him, and Armstrong stood thinking what course he ought to pursue, while Pacey went straight away, not to the police, but to Thorpe's hotel, where he told the doctor how matters stood.

"I don't know what you are to do, sir," said Thorpe coldly. "I wash my hands of the whole business. He has behaved horribly to my poor sister, and turned her brain. Let him go and be shot."

"Likely," growled Pacey. "Nice Christian advice to give. Why, it would kill her."

"Not it. She has too much womanly determination in her, poor girl. But I can do nothing. She has been to him again and again in opposition to my wishes—forgotten all her woman's dignity."

"To try and save your old schoolfellow, her lover."

"Bah! she has cast him off, sir, as the scoundrel deserves."

"Not she," said Pacey. "She loves him still in spite of all, and in time she would forgive him, if he behaved like a man."

"Not if I can prevent it," retorted Thorpe. "She shall not forgive him."

" Well, sir," said Pacey, " I have not come to dispute with you about that. He is almost your brother, and he is in deadly peril of his life. That Italian has challenged him; they will fight, as sure as we stand here, and the malignant, spiteful scoundrel will shoot Armstrong like a dog."

" Nonsense! What can he care for such a wife ? "

" Nothing; but his honour is at stake."

" His honour ! " cried Thorpe contemptuously.

" Exactly so. What such men call their honour. Armstrong will evade me somehow, and go off to Belgium, I am sure; and if he does, he is so careless of his own life now, in his despair, misery, and degradation, that he will never come back alive."

" Pish ! "

" It is a fact, sir. I have heard that Dellatoria is deadly with sword or pistol, and he has been out more than once before——Good heavens, Miss Thorpe! are you there ? "

" Yes," said Cornel slowly, as she came forward from the door leading into an inner room. " I have heard every word."

CHAPTER XXVII.

A POTENT DRUG.

WHAT to do? Leronde a prisoner; Pacey threatening legal steps. He must go somehow. The only way open appeared to be this; he must leave London at once, telegraphing to the Conte that he had gone on, and would meet him and his friends at the principal hotel in Ostend.

Armstrong, after much mental struggling, had come to this decision, when there was a knock at the door.

"Too late," he muttered. Then aloud, "Come in!" and Keren-Happuch entered.

"If you please, sir, there's———"

"I know," he said shortly. "Show them up."

"Please, sir, it ain't them; it's her."

"What?" he cried, starting. "Whom do you mean?"

"Her in the thick veil, sir, as come before."

"Great Heavens!" panted Armstrong; and his brain seemed to reel. "No. I cannot—I will not see her."

"'M I to tell her so, sir?" cried the girl joyfully, "and send her away?"

"Yes. I'll go no farther," he muttered. "Send her away at once."

The girl turned to the door, but, when she twisted the handle, it moved in her hand, the door was pushed against her, and as she gave way, the closely veiled and cloaked figure walked slowly into the room.

Armstrong turned savagely upon Keren-Happuch.

"Go!" he said sharply.

"I knowed it," muttered the girl as she went out. "Men can't keep to their words, and it's very hard on us poor girls."

Armstrong stood facing his visitor as the door closed, and then the giddiness came over him again. He staggered to a chair, dropped into it, and his head fell upon his hand.

"How could you be so mad!" he groaned. "Go back to your husband; we must never meet again. Woman, you have been a curse to me and ruined my poor life. But there, I will not reproach you."

He closed his eyes, for his senses nearly left him, and his visitor stood gazing sadly down at him not a yard away.

"I suppose you will despise me," he groaned, "but I cannot help that. You will think that I ought to hold to you now, and save you from your husband's anger. But I can do nothing. Broken, conscience-stricken, if ever poor wretch was in despair it is I. There, for God's sake, go back to him. He will forgive you, as I ask you to forgive me now."

He paused, and then went on as if she had just spoken something which coincided with his thoughts.

"You will despise me and think me weak, but I am near the end, and I do not shrink from speaking and telling you that I go to meet your husband with the knowledge that I have broken the heart of as pure and true a woman as ever breathed."

A low, pitiful sigh came from behind the veil.

"Don't, for Heaven's sake, don't, now. It is all over; the mad comedy is played out—all but the last scene. Try and forget it all, and go with the knowledge that his life is safe for me, for I will not raise my hand against him—that I swear."

He uttered a low moan, for the place seemed strange to him, and his words far distant, as if they were spoken by some one else. Incipient delirium was creeping in to assault his brain, and in another minute he would have been quite insensible; but a hand was laid upon his shoulder, and the touch electrified him, making him spring wildly from his seat with a cry.

"No, no," he cried passionately, and with his eyes flashing; "slave to you no more; I tell you, woman, all is over between us. For the few hours left to me, let me be in peace."

The veil was slowly drawn aside, and he clapped his hands to his temples and bent forward, gazing at his visitor.

"Cornel!" he muttered—"Cornel!—No, no! It is a dream."

He shook his head, and passed his hand across his eyes, to try and sweep away the mist that was gathering in his brain.

"No, no," he muttered again, in a low tone; "a dream—a dream."

"No," came softly to his ears, "it is not a dream, Armstrong. It is I—Cornel."

"Why have you come?" he cried, roused by her words, and staggering up to grasp the mantelpiece and save himself from falling.

"To try and save you," she said sadly. "Armstrong, you are going to fight this man?"

He was silent. The dreamy feeling was coming back.

"You do not deny it. Armstrong—brother—companion of my childhood—you must not, you shall not do this wicked thing. Think of it. Your life against his. The shame—the horror of the deed."

He laughed softly.

"I have sinned enough," he said. "He will not fall."

"Will the sin be less if you let him, in your despair, take his enemy's life? This is madness. Armstrong, you cannot—you shall not go."

He was silent.

"What am I to say to you again?" she pleaded. "You are like stone. Must I humble myself to you once more, and cast off all a woman's modesty and dignity? Armstrong, weak, doting as it is, I tell you I forgive you, dear—only promise me that you will not go."

He passed his hand across his eyes as he clung to the shelf to keep himself from falling, and said, in a low, dreamy voice—

"An insult to you—a degradation to me to take your pardon. No! Cornel, and once more, no. Now, if you have any feeling for me, leave me to myself, for I have much to do."

"You will prepare to go?"

He remained stubbornly silent, with his eyes half closed.

"Then," she cried passionately, as she saw him sway gently to and fro, as if prior to falling helpless upon the floor, "I will save you in spite of all. You shall not give away your life like this. You are weak, half-delirious, and cannot command even your thoughts. You shall not go."

He opened his eyes widely, and it was as if it took some moments for him to grasp her words. Then, with a little laugh, he said softly—

"How will you stop me?"

"I would sooner see you dead."

"Well, then—dead—dead—at rest. Why not! You are mistress of all his secrets—all his drugs. Why not? I have injured you; kill me now— at once."

"Are you really mad, Armstrong?" she said, looking at him wonderingly.

"Yes—I suppose so—my head swims. I can't— can't think. But it is time to go."

"Go?—go where?" she cried excitedly.

He uttered a low laugh and shook his head, as if to clear it again, but the vertigo increased.

She started and looked wildly round with her eyes flashing; and a strangely set look of deter- mination came over her face, as she took a step to a table upon which stood a carafe of water and a glass, which she rapidly filled. Then, going toward him again, she hesitated once more, and her whole manner changed.

"Armstrong!" she cried, but he did not hear her; "Armstrong!"

She shook him, and he sprang up, fully roused now.

"Ah!" he muttered. "Giddy from the blow."

He took a step or two aside, and caught the back of a chair.

"You are going!" she said mockingly.

He looked at her sharply.

"You will not go," she said. "It is all a

braggart's boast, to hide the cowardice in your heart."

"What!" he cried wildly.

"A man who is going to fight does not tell his friends for fear they should stop him."

"No," he groaned. "I'm not myself. What have I said?"

"Coward's words," she cried, "to frighten a weak girl. You bade me poison you to end your miserable life."

"I—I said that?" he cried. "Well, why not?"

"Why not?" she said, gazing at him fixedly, "why not? Look, then."

He bent forward wondering, as he struggled with the fit that was coming on again, while she took a bottle from the little satchel hanging from her wrist, snatched out the stopper, and poured a portion of its contents into the glass.

"There!" she cried triumphantly. "The test. Poison—one of our strongest drugs. Are you brave enough to drink?"

He took a step forward, seized the glass, tottered for a moment, and let a little splash over the side on to the floor. Then, drawing himself up, he placed the vessel to his lips, and drained it—the last drop seeming to scald his throat, and making him drop the tumbler, and clap his hands to his lips.

Then, half turning round, he thrust out his

hands again, as if feeling, like one suddenly struck blind, for something to save himself from falling. A little later, he lurched suddenly, his legs gave way beneath him, and he sank heavily upon the floor.

CHAPTER XXVIII.

TWO WOMEN'S LOVE.

A WOMAN—with the fierce lurid look of a tigress in her dark eyes, and in her action as lithe and elastic, she paced up and down her bedroom hour after hour. Now she threw herself upon a couch in utter exhaustion, but anon she sprang up again to resume the hurried walk to and fro.

At times she went to the door to open it and listen, for it was secured only by the locks and bolts of the Grundy Patent—Dellatoria, in spite of his newly awakened jealous rage, feeling that his wife would join with him in keeping the servants in ignorance of their terrible rupture.

But all was still downstairs; and at last, enforcing an outward appearance of composure, Valentina changed her dress, bathed her burning eyes with spirit-scented water, and descended to her boudoir, where she turned down the lamp beneath its rose-coloured shade, and rang the bell, before seating herself in a lounge with her back half turned from the door.

"Pretty well time," said the butler, who had been heading the discussion below stairs regarding the meaning of what had taken place. "There, cook, you may dish up."

The footman presented himself at the door.

"Your ladyship rang?"

"Yes. Where is your master?"

"In the lib'ry, my lady."

"Alone?"

"No, my lady. Colonel Varesti and Baron Gratz are with him again."

"That will do."

"Yes, my lady."

The man hesitated at the door.

"Well?"

"Does your ladyship wish the dinner to be served?"

"No: wait till your master orders it. I am unwell. Give me that flacon of salts."

The man handed the large cut-glass bottle, and went down.

The aspect of languor passed away in an instant, and Valentina sprang from the seat.

"I might have known it," she panted. "He is no coward when he is roused, despicable as he is at other times. Those men. It means a meeting. They will fight, and——"

She clapped her hands to her forehead as in imagination she saw Armstrong lying bleeding at her husband's feet. Strong and brave as he was, she doubted the artist's ability to stand before a man like the Conte, who had often boasted to her of his skill with the small sword, and ability as a marksman.

"And I have wasted all this time."

Then, after a few moments' thought, divining that the inevitable meeting would take place abroad, she went up at once to her bedroom and locked herself in.

Her brain was still misty and confused by the intense excitement through which she had passed, for upon reaching home, and savagely dismissing Lady Grayson, the Conte had turned upon her furiously. The passion of his southern nature had been aroused, and a mad jealousy developed itself respecting the woman whom of late he had utterly neglected.

In a few moments her mind was quite made up, and, taking a small dressing bag, she rapidly emptied into it the whole of the costly contents of her jewel-cases, unlocked a small cabinet, and took from it what money she possessed, and then hastily dressed for going out.

A very few minutes sufficed for this, and, after pausing for a few moments to collect herself, she took up the bag, and, unlocking the door, passed out silently on to the thickly carpeted landing, descended to the hall, where she paused again as she heard a low buzz of voices in the library, and then walked quickly to the door, passed out, and hurried up the wide street, breathing freely as she felt that she had been unobserved.

Not quite. Ladies in large establishments live beneath the observation of many eyes. Valentina had no sooner begun to descend the wide stairs than a white cap was thrust out from the door of a neighbouring room, and the eyes beneath it were immediately after looking down the great staircase, while a pair of ears twitched as they listened till the front door was heard to close.

The next minute the wearer of the cap was in the bed and dressing rooms, gazing at the empty jewel-cases, noting the absence of the bag, cloak, and bonnet, even to the veil; and then came the low ejaculation of the one word, " Well ! "

The Abigail ran down the backstairs and made her way into the hall, just in time to meet the butler returning from ushering out the Conte's two friends, who had been closeted with him, consulting as to what proceedings should be taken, as there had been no appearance put in by the other side.

The butler heard the lady's-maid's hurried communication, nodded sagely, and said oracularly that he wasn't a bit surprised; then coughed to clear his voice, waved the maid away, closed the baize door after her, and entered the library to repeat what he had heard.

The Conte did not even change countenance.

"Stop all tattling amongst the servants," he said. "Her ladyship is not well—a strange seizure to-day. It must be past the dinner hour."

"Yes, my lord."

"Let it be served at once."

The butler bowed, and went out solemnly.

The moment he was alone, a sharp grating sound was heard, and a strange look came over the Conte's face as he hastily opened a cabinet, took something from a drawer, and placed it in his breast pocket. Then, hurrying upstairs, he satisfied himself of the truth of all he had heard, and descended, took his hat from the stand and went out quietly, unheard, even by the servants.

Meanwhile Valentina had walked straight to the studio.

The street door was ajar, for Keren-Happuch had just gone into the next street to post a letter at the pillar, so the closely veiled woman passed in unseen, and went upstairs, stood for a few moments listening, and then softly entered.

She uttered a low sigh of relief, glad to have entered the place which, for the moment, felt to her like a sanctuary

It was many hours since she had been surprised there by her husband and Lady Grayson; but to

her then it seemed only a few minutes before, and
she looked round the great dim room quickly, with
a smile upon her lips.

But the smile froze there, and a horrible sensation of fear came over her. She had waited too
long. There must have been a challenge from her
husband, and Armstrong had responded. The street-
door open; the studio unfastened; and this dim
light! Then she was too late: he had gone. But
where? Belgium? France? The thought was horrible—almost more than she could bear.

"No, no," she murmured. "It cannot be."

She advanced into the great dim place excitedly,
with the many grim-looking plaster figures and
busts seeming to watch her furtively out of the
gloom; and as she looked quickly from side to side,
she fancied that the faces were menacing and full
of reproach, as if telling her that she had sent her
lover to his death.

She had nearly crossed the room when she
started and shrank back in horror, for one of the
rugs had been kicked slightly aside, and there was
a wet dark mark upon the boards which she knew
at a glance to be blood—his blood, for it was
here he had fallen when her husband struck him
down.

With the faintest of hopes amid her despair that
she might still be in time, she went on to the inner
door, seized the handle, and was pressing it, but

it was twisted from her fingers, the door opened, and she was about to fling herself into Armstrong's arms, but only shrank back with a look of jealous rage and despair.

For Cornel stood framed in the opening and closed the door, then looked her firmly and defiantly in the face.

Neither spoke for a full minute, and as Valentina gazed in the blanched countenance before her, she read here so stony and despairing a look, that she shrank away in horror, certain that either there was some terrible revelation awaiting her beyond the door which had been so carefully closed, or else that Cornel's eyes were confirming her worst dread, and that Armstrong had gone forth to meet his death.

It was some moments before the Contessa could command herself sufficiently to speak aloud. She wished to get from Cornel's lips the truth, and to show her how, possessed as she was of Armstrong's love, she could treat her with calm, contemptuous tolerance, as one almost beneath her notice. But the stern disdain in those large flashing eyes mastered her and kept her silent. There was a magnetism in their glance, and she felt that if she spoke it would be in a broken feeble manner, which would lower her in her rival's eyes.

She fought against it, struggled for a long time

vainly, and moment by moment felt how strong in her innocence and truth her rival stood before her. It was not until she had lashed herself into a state of fury that she could force herself to speak.

"Mr. Dale — where is he?" she cried at last imperiously.

"How dare you come and ask?" said Cornel fiercely, her whole manner changed.

"Because I have a right," cried Valentina, who, stung now by her rival's words, began to recover herself. Her eyes too dilated as she went on, and something of her old hauteur and contempt flashed out.

"You!—a right?"

"Yes; the right of the woman he loves—who has given up everything for his sake."

"Loves! The woman he loves!" cried Cornel contemptuously.

"Yes, and who loves him as such a woman as I can love. Do you think that you, in your girlish coldness, could ever have won him as I have? Tell me where he is."

"That you may join him?" cried Cornel. "You would give him over to your husband—to that horror—and his death."

"Ah!" cried Valentina excitedly; "then he has not gone yet. He is safe." And, in spite of herself, she gave way to a hysterical burst of tears.

"What is it to you?" said Cornel coldly. "He has escaped from your hands. You have no right here, woman. Go."

"I am right, then," cried the Contessa, mastering her weakness once more. "You are trying to keep us apart. He is mine, I tell you, mine for ever. He is there, then; I am not too late—there in that room. Armstrong!" she cried loudly, "come to me. I am here."

She made for the door again, but Cornel seized her, and strove with all her might to keep the furious woman back, but she was like a child in her hands, and was rudely flung aside. Valentina thrust open the door, entered the study, and passed through it to the chamber beyond, to utter a wild cry, and fall upon her knees beside the bed on which Armstrong lay cold and still.

Then, starting up, she bent over him, laid her hand upon his brow, her cheek against his lips, and staggered back.

"Dead!" she cried, "dead!"

For his eyes were closed, and the bandaged cut upon his brow gave him a ghastly look, seen as he was by the shaded light of a lamp upon the table by the bed's head.

She rushed back through the little room to the studio, where Cornel stood, wild-eyed, and white as the figure upon the bed.

"Wretch! you have killed him in your insane

jealousy. It could not have been that blow. Tell me! confess!" she cried, seizing her by the arms.

"Better so than that he should have fallen back into your power," said Cornel bitterly.

"Ah! You own it, then? Oh, it is too horrible!"

Her face convulsed with agony, the Contessa seized Cornel by the arm, threw down the bag, which flew open, so that the jewels scattered on the floor, and tried to drag her toward the studio door, calling hoarsely for help. But her voice rose to the ceiling, and not a sound was heard below.

But Cornel resisted now with all her might, and in the struggle which ensued wrested herself away, ran across the studio, darted through the door of the little room, dashed it to, and had time to slip the bolt before her rival flung herself against it, and then beat heavily against the panel with her hand.

Pale as ashes, and panting with excitement, Cornel stood with her left shoulder pressed against the panel, feeling the blows struck upon it through the wood, as, with her eyes fixed and strained, she felt about for the key, her hand trembling so that she could hardly turn it in the lock.

"No, no!" she muttered. "I'll die sooner than she shall touch him again."

Then she held her breath, listening, for she

fancied she heard a sound in the studio above the beating on the panel, which suddenly culminated in one strangely given blow, accompanied by a wild shriek of agony, followed by a heavy fall and a piteous groan.

CHAPTER XXIX.

STARTLED beyond bearing by the sounds of mortal suffering, Cornel unfastened the door, drew it toward her, and then stopped, utterly paralysed by the scene in the studio.

There, not a yard away from the door, lay the beautiful woman, her face drawn in agony and horror, with the blood welling from a wound in her throat: her bonnet was back on her shoulders, and her hair torn down, as if a hand had suddenly been savagely laid upon her brow, her head dragged back, and a blow struck at her from behind; while standing upon the other side, with his compressed lips drawn away from his set teeth, eyes nearly closed, and brow contracted, was the Conte, looking down at his work.

For a few moments Cornel could not stir. The studio, with its many casts, seemed to perform a ghastly dance round her, and she felt as if this were some horrible nightmare. Then the deathly sickness passed off, and she cried wildly to the

Conte, who did not even seem aware of her presence—

"O Heaven! What have you done?"

Her piteous appeal made him start back into consciousness, and with a hasty motion he hurled something across the studio, where it fell with a tinkling, metallic sound.

"I—I struck her," he gasped, in a harsh cracked voice. "I loved her—ah! how I loved her; and she was false. Look: she had even robbed me, and fled with all her jewels—to him. See where they lie, scattered upon his floor. Ah, signora," he cried passionately, and growing more and more Italian in his excitement, "I poured out wealth at her feet. There was nothing I would not have done to gratify her. For I loved her—I loved her. Dio mio, how I loved!"

"Hush!" cried Cornel, recovering herself somewhat in the presence of suffering and danger, her medical education asserting itself. "Go quickly and call help. Send for a surgeon."

"No, no!" he cried excitedly, as his face blanched with dread. "If I call, it means the police, and—oh! horror—they will say I have murdered her."

"Man!" cried Cornel, in disgust at his sudden display of selfishness, "have you no feeling?—Is this your love? Quick!—your handkerchief. Mine too; take it from my pocket. God help me, and give me strength," she whispered, as her busy fingers staunched the wound by closing the cut. Then, as the Conte stood looking on, trembling like a leaf, she bade him fetch a large wide lotah from where it stood upon a bracket, pour water into it from the carafe, and place it upon the floor beside the Contessa's head.

And as she knelt there all hatred and horror of the beautiful woman passed away. It was an erring sister and sufferer for sin, bleeding to death; and, knowing how precious minutes were at such a time, she tore up the handkerchiefs and portions of the Contessa's attire, as, with skilled hands, she checked the bleeding, and securely bandaged the wound.

She was so intent upon her work, that, after he had obeyed her orders, she was hardly conscious of the Conte's presence, while he, after watching her acts for some minutes, suddenly looked round, startled by some sound which penetrated to where they were. Then, trembling visibly, he began to examine the front of his clothes, passing his hands over them, and examining his palms for traces of the deed, but finding none.

Then a fresh thought struck him, and after keenly watching Cornel to see if she noticed the action, he crept on tip-toe—a miserably bent, decrepit-looking figure—to where the tinkling sound had been heard, picked up a little ivory-handled stiletto, examined its blade in the faint light, with his back to the group by the inner room door, and, catching up a piece of Moorish scarf, wiped it quickly, and hid the weapon in his breast pocket.

Then creeping on tip-toe to the studio door, he listened, his face full of abject fear, and hearing nothing, he turned the key.

He glanced toward Cornel, whose back was toward him, as she busily went on with her task, hiding too his wife's face from him by her position.

Hesitating for a moment or two, he then drew a deep breath, and crossed softly to where the bag lay open with some of the glittering jewels still hanging to its edge: great strings of pearls, and a necklet of diamonds.

These he hurriedly thrust back, and then went quickly and silently about, picking up rings, bracelets, brooches, and tiaras of emerald, ruby, diamond, and sapphire, till, with a sigh of satisfaction, he closed the morocco bag, the fastening giving forth a loud snap.

"Is—is she dead?" he whispered; and his lips were so close to Cornel's ear that she started round, and let fall the wrist upon whose pulse her fingers were pressed.

"No," she whispered. "I have staunched the wound till you can get proper help, but I fear internal bleeding."

At that moment there was a piteous sigh, followed by a low moan, and the beautiful dark eyes opened, to gaze vacantly for a few moments. Then intelligence came into them, as they rested upon Cornel, who was now bending over her.

"Ah," she said softly, as her hand felt for Cornel's, which was laid upon her brow; "you? Good for evil;" and she drew Cornel's hand to her lips and kissed it. "Forgive me," she whispered, "before I die. I loved him so."

A curiously harsh low cry escaped from the Conte, who literally writhed in his jealous agony, and Valentina turned her eyes upon him where he stood dimly seen, as if looking at her from out of a mist.

"You there!" she said bitterly, as Cornel once more grasped her wrist. "Well, are you satisfied? You have killed my body, as you killed my love, when, as a young innocent girl, I was sold to you for your wealth and title, and Heaven knows I would have tried to be your true loving wife."

"Oh, Valentina! my beautiful—my own!" he groaned; and he stooped to take her hand.

"Pah! don't touch me!" she cried hoarsely; and she raised the hand she had snatched away, and pointed to the bag he held. "Take them to your mistresses whose smiles you have always bought. Let me die in peace."

"No, no; live!" he cried.

"To save you from the punishment you merit?" she whispered scornfully.

"No, no! to be my dearest love and wife again. Let us go back to sunny Italy, away from all this miserable city."

"Too late!" she said sadly. "You should have said that years ago."

"For pity's sake don't speak," whispered Cornel.

"Why not, little doctor?" said Valentina softly. "Better so. Ah, I was not all bad, dear. I loved him before I knew of you. How could I help looking on you with jealous hate? Let me kiss you once—before I go. Be loving to him and forgive him—it was all my fault—tell me you will forgive him—when I am gone."

"With all my heart," said Cornel softly; and she bent down to press her lips to those of the suffering woman, while the tears over-ran her brimming eyelids, and her heart swelled with pity for one so deeply punished for her sin.

But as if the Contessa recollected the scene of a short time before, she thrust the gentle face away before lips touched lips, and with a loud cry—

"No, no! I had forgotten. I remember now. How could you be so base? No! don't touch me. I will see him once again. Armstrong!—my love —my own."

She dragged herself over, and began to crawl to the door, when the Conte's face became convulsed with passion once more, his hand sought his breast, the bag fell to the ground, and with an oath he cried—

"Then he is in there!—in hiding."

Springing over the crawling figure, he dashed through to the inner room, and, as Valentina uttered a piteous moan, the Conte flung open the bedroom door.

"Dog!—Coward!" he yelled, and then stopped, petrified at the sight of the motionless figure upon the bed. Then the door swung to between them, and he thrust back the little blade, and came stealthily out, muttering softly to himself as he bent over his wife, insensible to all that passed.

He was trembling violently now.

"I did not know," he muttered to Cornel. "I struck him when I found them together, but I did not know. I—I must go—away. Your laws are bad. An affair of honour. Will—will she die too?"

"I cannot say," replied Cornel coldly. "She must have better surgical help. I am only a nurse."

"Yes," he said hastily. "Better help. A great surgeon. She must not die. I will get a carriage and take her away."

"It would be dangerous to move her."

"More dangerous far to leave her here," he

muttered. Then aloud, "It must be risked, madam. But listen. You are his friend?"

"Yes."

"This is a terrible misfortune, but a private matter—not for the police. You will not tell them how—by accident—I struck my wife?"

"No," said Cornel, after a pause; and a shudder ran through her.

"Hah! Then the law need not meddle with what was a private quarrel—a mistake. My wife, here, shall live, and you who are so good and beautiful and kind, you shall be silent, and—one moment."

He fumbled with the clasp of the bag he had picked up, opened it, and, as Cornel's brows contracted with horror, he searched within and drew out a magnificent diamond and sapphire bracelet.

"Hah!" he cried. "You will wear that for both our sakes, and be silent, and blind to the past."

"I will be silent and blind, for the sake of the man I loved," she said to herself, as she thrust back the jewel and shook her head.

"But you will not tell?" he said.

"No, sir; your secret is safe."

The Conte uttered a sigh of satisfaction, threw back the bracelet, and closed the bag with a snap, while Cornel eyed him with disgust.

"Do you intend to risk removing this lady?"

"Certainly," he said firmly; "it must be done. Lock the door after me," he whispered, as he crossed the studio.

Cornel followed and obeyed, listening to his descending steps. Then, returning to where Valentina lay insensible, she satisfied herself of the security of the bandages, and once more felt her pulse.

"If there is no internal bleeding she will live. Yes, I will forgive you. Some day you may know the truth. And then? Ah, who can tell?"

She bent down and kissed the broad forehead, and then knelt there for a few moments before rising and going quickly into Armstrong's bedroom to gaze at him for a minute, and return, carefully closing after her both the doors.

She kept her vigil there for a few minutes before there were steps again, and a soft tap at the door.

She admitted the Conte.

"I have a carriage waiting, and a man here to help," he said.

"I am not clever and experienced," said Cornel anxiously. "Let a doctor see her first."

For answer the Conte gave her a quick nod.

"It is secrecy, is it not?"

"Oh yes, but——"

"The best London can give," he whispered. "When I have her back at home. And you understand that was nonsense which I said about striking him?"

The bag was on his arm, with his hand pushed far through, as he went back to the door, and signalled to a man to come in. Then seeing that this removal was inevitable, Cornel rapidly replaced the cloak well round the insensible figure, and rearranged the head.

"Don't—don't waste time," said the Conte impatiently, and signing to the man, the latter bent down and lifted the motionless figure as easily as if it had been a child.

"Be careful, my friend. A sad accident. Be careful. Mind."

He opened the door for the man to pass through, and Cornel followed them, to listen to the heavy descending steps, till all was silent. Then came the rattle of wheels, and she knew that they were gone.

Closing the door of the studio, she walked across it, dropped upon her knees, and clasped her hands.

"Have I done rightly?" she murmured. "I don't know. It seems like madness now." Then a weary sigh, as she laid her head against the door leading to the chamber. "Armstrong! what I have suffered for your sake!"

CHAPTER XXX.

"And you gave him enough to keep him in that insensible state?" said Dr. Thorpe next night, after seeing and treating Armstrong, who lay in a weak, half-delirious state.

Cornel nodded and gazed wildly at her brother, who continued—

"To keep him from going abroad to fight this duel?"

"Yes, I felt sure that the Conte would kill him."

"And serve him right. Well," he went on, as his sister winced at his harsh words, "this proves the truth of the saying—'A little knowledge is a dangerous thing.' You know a bit about narcotics and anæsthetics, and you may congratulate yourself upon not having killed him. But there, perhaps, it was right; and anyhow, you have saved him."

"You think he will recover now?" she cried eagerly.

"Think so? Oh yes! of course. Nothing to prevent him. Only wants time. But it's nothing to you."

"How is the Contessa?"

"Getting better, I hear. Fact is, I met the surgeon who is attending her at the society. But never mind them. I shall have done all I want here in less than a fortnight. That is when the *Spartania* sails, so be ready, and let's get back."

"Yes, dear," said Cornel quietly, "I shall have finished my task, too."

.   .   .

Two years later Armstrong Dale went back home, but only for a visit, for his fame was increasing rapidly, and he had more commissions than he could undertake. He wanted help and counsel, and he brought them back with him, for he did not return to London alone.

.   .   .   .   .   .

Four more years had elapsed, and that season there was a great deal of talk about Armstrong Dale's big picture at the Academy. The press had praised it unanimously; society had endorsed the critics' words; and it was sold for a heavy sum. But though he was importuned to take portraits, Armstrong sternly refused.

The picture that year was a fanciful subject of a beautiful woman reclining upon a tiger skin, with a huge cluster of orange maculated lilies thrust, as if by careless hands, into a magnificent repoussé copper vase. And as he painted it, he had turned to his wife one day, and said, "I can't help it, Little Heart; it will come so like her. I shall paint it out and give up."

Then he seized a cloth to pass across the fresh paint, but Cornel caught his wrist.

"Absurd!" she cried. "That magnificent piece of work—and because of a fancied resemblance?"

"Then you do not mind?" he said sadly.

Palette, brushes, and mahlstick were slowly and softly taken from his hands, which were drawn round Cornel's neck, and she nestled closely in his breast.

"Mind? No," she said gently; "let the dead past bury its dead."

The picture went to the Academy then, and was the most discussed work of the year.

One sunny morning early, so as to be before the crush, Armstrong and his wife walked through the principal room, joined together by a little fairy-like golden-haired link, whose bright eyes flashed with delight as she clung to the hand on either side, for she was at her urgent request being taken "to see papa's picture—'The Tiger Lily.'"

The trio had been standing in front of it for some minutes, when, after playfully responding to the happy child's many questions, Cornel and

Armstrong turned to take her round the room, but both stopped short as if petrified.

For within a couple of yards stood Valentina, pale as death, her eyes abnormally large, and her whole countenance telling of bodily suffering and mental pain.

Beside her was an invalid chair, occupied by a wasted, prematurely old man, wrapped in furs—in May—and attended by a servant, who stood motionless behind.

The meeting was a surprise, and all present save one remained fascinated by some spell.

The silence was broken by Valentina, who took a step forward, and held out her hand, while Armstrong saw at a glance that the Conte was gazing vacantly at the pictures, his eyes dull and glazed, the light of recognition being absent.

"It is six years since we met, Mrs. Dale," said the Contessa softly, but the tones of her voice were changed, and she turned her head slightly to let her eyes rest upon Armstrong. "As in all human probability we shall never meet again, I cannot resist referring once to the past—to thank your sweet wife for the life she saved."

"Oh, pray," whispered Cornel in a tremulous voice, "no more."

"No," said Valentina, holding Cornel's hand tightly, and gazing wildly in her eyes, though her voice was very calm. "We go back to Italy at once. My husband, who is a great invalid, seems better there."

She paused for a moment, as if to gain strength to continue; and then, in a low, passionate whisper, full of the maternal longing of an unsatisfied heart—

"Your child ? May I kiss her once ? "

Cornel bowed her head—she could not speak, but held the child a little forward, and Valentina bent down.

"Will you kiss me ? " she asked.

The bright, innocent eyes looked smilingly up, and the silvery voice said, as the soft little arms clasped her neck—

"Yes, I'll give you two." Then, as she was held tightly for a few moments, "Do you like dear papa's picture? I saw him make it. Is it you ?"

The eager, wondering question sent a pang through three breasts, but not another word was uttered, till the invalid-chair and its attendants had passed through the door close by.

It was the child who broke the silence just as Cornel had stolen her hand to her husband's side to press his with a long, firm, trusting grasp.

"Why did that lady cry when she kissed me, mamma? I know:" the child added quickly. "It was because that poor gentleman is so ill."

It was the winter of the same year when Armstrong was seated by his studio fire with his child upon his knee, and Cornel upon the rug, with the warm light of the fire upon her cheek—not in the old studio, but the great, artistically furnished salon in Kensington. The door opened, and a gruff voice exclaimed—

"May I come in?"

The child uttered a cry of delight, sprang from her father's knee, and dashed across the studio, to begin dragging forward the rough grey-beard in a shabby velvet coat, and soft black hat.

He raised her in his arms, and bore her forward caressingly, to sit chatting for some time. Then Cornel rose and took the child's hand.

"Come, dear," she said. "Your tea-time."

"No, no. I want to stop with Uncle Joe."

"Uncle Joe wants to talk to papa about business," said Cornel, with a nod and a smile, as she drew the little one away. "You shall come in to dessert if you are good."

She nodded, smiling at the rough-looking old friend, and then tripped out playfully with the child.

"Light your pipe, old man," said Armstrong. "Is it business?"

"Yes. Your wife reads my face like a book. Have you seen to-day's paper?"

"No. Been growling all day at the bad light and playing with Tiny."

"Read that, then."

Pacey passed a crumpled newspaper, folded small, and under the Paris news Armstrong read—

"M. Leronde has been appointed French Consul at Constantinople, and leaves Marseilles by the Messageries Maritimes steamer *Corne d'Or* on Friday."

"Well, I am glad. Hang it, Joe, I could find it in my heart to run over to Paris to have one dinner with him, and say 'Good-bye.'"

"No time," said Pacey gruffly. "Now read that."

He took back the paper and doubled it again, so that the front page was outward, and pointed to the column of deaths.

Armstrong started, and for some moments held the paper with his eyes fixed upon his friend, in whose countenance he seemed to divine what was to come.

He was in no wise surprised, when he looked down, to find the name Dellatoria, and he began to read the announcement with the remembrance that the Conte's face, when they last met, bore the stamp of impending death; but he was not prepared for what he did read. The type was blurred, and the paper quivered a little as he saw as through a mist the name Valentina, the age thirty, Rome, and then the last words stood out clearly—"Only surviving the Conte Dellatoria four days."

"Chapter the last, boy," said Pacey, taking back the paper, and folding it tightly before replacing it in his breast pocket.

"Yes," said Armstrong slowly, as he mentally looked backward through the golden mists of six years, "chapter the last."

THE END.

Printed by BALLANTYNE, HANSON & Co.
Edinburgh and London

MARIE ANTOINETTE ON THE EVE OF HER EXECUTION.

"All hope of Succour, but from Thee, is lost."

WHAT IS MORE TERRIBLE THAN REVOLUTION?

" As clouds of adversity gathered around, *Marie Antoinette* displayed a Patience and Courage in *Unparalleled Sufferings* such as few Saints and *Martyrs have equalled.*
The *Pure Ore* of her nature was but hidden under the cross of worldliness, and the scorching fire of suffering revealed one of the tenderest hearts, and one of the *Bravest Natures* that history records.

(Which will haunt all who have studied that tremendous drama,
" THE FRENCH REVOLUTION.")

" When one reflects that a century which considered itself enlightened, of the most refined civilization, *ends* with public acts of such *barbarity*, one begins to *doubt* of *Human Nature itself, and fear* that the *brute which is always* in *Human Nature, has the ascendancy !"*—GOWER.

THE UNSPEAKABLE GRANDEUR OF THE HUMAN HEART.
THE DRYING UP OF A SINGLE TEAR HAS MORE HONEST FAME THAN SHEDDING SEAS OF GORE!!!

What Is Ten Thousand Times more Horrible than Revolution or War?

OUTRAGED NATURE!

" O World! O men! what are we, and our best designs, that we must work by crime to punish crime, and slay, as if death had but this one gate ? "—BYRON.
" What is Ten Thousand Times more Terrible than *Revolution* or War? Outraged Nature ! She kills and kills, and is never tired of killing, till she has taught man the terrible lesson he is so slow to learn—that Nature is only conquered by obeying her.
Man has his courtesies in Revolution and War ; he spares the *woman and child.* But Nature is fierce when she is offended ; she spares neither *woman nor child.* She has no pity, for some awful but most good reason. She is *not* allowed to have any pity.
Silently she strikes the sleeping child with as little remorse as she would strike the strong man with musket or the pickaxe in his hand. Oh ! would to God that some man had the pictorial eloquence to put before the mothers of England the *mass of preventable suffering,* the mass of preventable agony of mind which exists in England year after year."—KINGSLEY.

MORAL.—Life is a Battle, not a Victory. Disobey ye who will, but ye who disobey must suffer.

JEOPARDY OF LIFE, THE GREAT DANGER OF DELAY.

You can change the trickling stream, but not the Raging Torrent.

How important it is to have at hand some simple, effective, and palatable remedy, such as **ENO'S "FRUIT SALT,"** to check disease at the onset ! ! For this is the time. With very little trouble you can change the course of the trickling mountain stream, but not the rolling river. It will defy all your efforts. I cannot sufficiently impress this important information upon all householders, ship captains, or Europeans generally, who are visiting or residing in hot or foreign climates. Whenever a change is contemplated likely to disturb the condition of health, let **ENO'S "FRUIT SALT"** be your companion, for under any circumstances its use is beneficial, and never can do harm. When you feel out of sorts, restless, sleepless, yet unable to say why, frequently without warning you are seized with lassitude, disinclination for bodily or mental exertion, loss of appetite, sickness, pain in the forehead, dull aching of back and limbs, coldness of the surface, and often shivering, &c., then your whole body is out of order, the spirit of danger has been kindled, but you do not know where it may end ; it is a real necessity to have a simple remedy at hand. The common idea is : "I will wait and see, perhaps I shall be better to-morrow," whereas had a supply of ENO'S "FRUIT SALT" been at hand, and use made of it at the onset, all calamitous results might have been avoided. What dashes to the earth so many hopes, breaks so many sweet alliances, blasts so many auspicious enterprises, as untimely Death ?

" I used my ' FRUIT SALT' in my last severe attack of fever, and I have every reason to say I believe it saved my life."—J. C. ENO.

Small Pox, Scarlet Fever, Pyæmia, Erysipelas, Measles, Gangrene, and almost every mentionable disease.—" I have been a nurse for upwards of ten years, and in that time have nursed cases of scarlet fever, pyæmia, erysipelas, measles, gangrene, cancer, and almost every mentionable disease. During the whole time I have not been ill myself for a single day, and this I attribute in a great measure to the use of ENO'S 'FRUIT SALT,' which has kept my blood in a pure state. I recommend it to all my patients during convalescence. Its value as a means of health cannot be over-estimated.—April 21, 1894, A PROFESSIONAL NURSE.

LIST OF BOOKS PUBLISHED BY

CHATTO & WINDUS

214 PICCADILLY, LONDON, W.

About (Edmond).—The Fellah: An Egyptian Novel. Translated by Sir RANDAL ROBERTS. Post 8vo, illustrated boards, 2s.

Adams (W. Davenport), Works by.
A Dictionary of the Drama: being a comprehensive Guide to the Plays, Playwrights, Players, and Playhouses of the United Kingdom and America, from the Earliest Times to the Present Day. Crown 8vo, half-bound, 12s. 6d. [*Preparing.*
Quips and Quiddities. Selected by W. DAVENPORT ADAMS. Post 8vo, cloth limp, 2s. 6d.

Agony Column (The) of 'The Times,' from 1800 to 1870. Edited, with an Introduction, by ALICE CLAY. Post 8vo, cloth limp, 2s. 6d.

Aïdé (Hamilton), Novels by. Post 8vo, illustrated boards, 2s. each.
Carr of Carrlyon. | Confidences.

Albert (Mary).—Brooke Finchley's Daughter. Post 8vo, picture boards, 2s. ; cloth limp, 2s. 6d.

Alden (W. L.).—A Lost Soul: Being the Confession and Defence of Charles Lindsay. Fcap. 8vo, cloth boards, 1s. 6d.

Alexander (Mrs.), Novels by. Post 8vo, illustrated boards, 2s. each.
Maid, Wife, or Widow? | Valerie's Fate.

Allen (F. M.).—Green as Grass. With a Frontispiece. Crown 8vo, cloth, 3s. 6d.

Allen (Grant), Works by.
The Evolutionist at Large. Crown 8vo, cloth extra, 6s.
Post-Prandial Philosophy. Crown 8vo, art linen, 3s. 6d.
Moorland Idylls. Crown 8vo, cloth decorated, 6s. [*Shortly.*

Crown 8vo, cloth extra, 3s. 6d. each ; post 8vo, illustrated boards, 2s. each.

Philistia.	In all Shades.	Dumaresq's Daughter.
Babylon. 12 Illustrations.	The Devil's Die.	The Duchess of Powysland
Strange Stories. Frontis.	This Mortal Coil.	Blood Royal.
The Beckoning Hand.	The Tents of Shem. Frontis.	Ivan Greet's Masterpiece.
For Maimie's Sake.	The Great Taboo.	The Scallywag. 24 Illusts.

Crown 8vo, cloth extra, 3s. 6d. each.

At Market Value. | Under Sealed Orders. [*Shortly.*

Dr. Palliser's Patient. Fcap. 8vo, cloth boards, 1s. 6d.

Anderson (Mary).—Othello's Occupation: A Novel. Crown 8vo, cloth, 3s. 6d.

Arnold (Edwin Lester), Stories by.
The Wonderful Adventures of Phra the Phœnician. Crown 8vo, cloth extra, with 12 Illustrations by H. M. PAGET, 3s. 6d. ; post 8vo, illustrated boards, 2s.
The Constable of St. Nicholas. With Frontispiece by S. L. WOOD. Crown 8vo, cloth, 3s. 6d.

Artemus Ward's Works. With Portrait and Facsimile. Crown 8vo, cloth extra, 7s. 6d.—Also a POPULAR EDITION, post 8vo, picture boards, 2s.
The Genial Showman: The Life and Adventures of ARTEMUS WARD. By EDWARD P HINGSTON. With a Frontispiece. Crown 8vo, cloth extra, 3s. 6d.

Ashton (John), Works by. Crown 8vo, cloth extra, 7s. 6d. each.
History of the Chap-Books of the 18th Century. With 334 Illustrations.
Social Life in the Reign of Queen Anne. With 85 Illustrations.
Humour, Wit, and Satire of the Seventeenth Century. With 82 Illustrations.
English Caricature and Satire on Napoleon the First. With 115 Illustrations.
Modern Street Ballads. With 57 Illustrations.

Bacteria, Yeast Fungi, and Allied Species, A Synopsis of. By
W. B. GROVE, B.A. With 87 Illustrations. Crown 8vo, cloth extra, 3s. 6d.

Bardsley (Rev. C. Wareing, M.A.), Works by.
English Surnames: Their Sources and Significations. Crown 8vo, cloth, 7s. 6d.
Curiosities of Puritan Nomenclature. Crown 8vo, cloth extra, 6s.

Baring Gould (Sabine, Author of 'John Herring,' &c.), Novels by.
Crown 8vo, cloth extra, 3s. 6d. each; post 8vo, illustrated boards, 2s. each.
Red Spider. | Eve.

Barr (Robert: Luke Sharp), Stories by. Cr. 8vo, cl., 3s. 6d. each.
In a Steamer Chair. With Frontispiece and Vignette by DEMAIN HAMMOND.
From Whose Bourne, &c. With 47 Illustrations by HAL HURST and others.

A Woman Intervenes. With 8 Illustrations by HAL HURST. Crown 8vo, cloth extra, 6s.
Revenge! With numerous Illustrations. Crown 8vo, cloth extra, 6s.   [Shortly.

Barrett (Frank), Novels by.
Post 8vo, illustrated boards, 2s. each; cloth, 2s. 6d. each.

Fettered for Life.	A Prodigal's Progress.
The Sin of Olga Zassoulich.	John Ford; and His Helpmate.
Between Life and Death.	A Recoiling Vengeance.
Folly Morrison.	Honest Davie.	Lieut. Barnabas.	Found Guilty.
Little Lady Linton.	For Love and Honour.

The Woman of the Iron Bracelets. Cr. 8vo. cloth, 3s. 6d.; post 8vo, boards, 2s.; cl. limp, 2s. 6d.

Barrett (Joan).—Monte Carlo Stories. Fcap. 8vo, cloth, 1s. 6d.

Beaconsfield, Lord. By T. P. O'CONNOR, M.P. Cr. 8vo, cloth, 5s.

Beauchamp (Shelsley).—Grantley Grange. Post 8vo, boards, 2s.

Beautiful Pictures by British Artists: A Gathering of Favourites
from the Picture Galleries, engraved on Steel. Imperial 4to, cloth extra, gilt edges, 21s.

Besant (Sir Walter) and James Rice, Novels by.
Crown 8vo, cloth extra, 3s. 6d. each; post 8vo, illustrated boards, 2s. each; cloth limp, 2s. 6d. each.

Ready-Money Mortiboy.	By Celia's Arbour.
My Little Girl.	The Chaplain of the Fleet.
With Harp and Crown.	The Seamy Side.
This Son of Vulcan.	The Case of Mr. Lucraft, &c.
The Golden Butterfly.	'Twas in Trafalgar's Bay, &c.
The Monks of Thelema.	The Ten Years' Tenant, &c.

*** There is also a LIBRARY EDITION of the above Twelve Volumes, handsomely set in new type on a large crown 8vo page, and bound in cloth extra, 6s. each; and a POPULAR EDITION of The Golden Butterfly, medium 8vo, 6d.; cloth, 1s.—NEW EDITIONS, printed in large type on crown 8vo laid paper, bound in figured cloth, 3s. 6d. each, are also in course of publication.

Besant (Sir Walter), Novels by.
Crown 8vo, cloth extra, 3s. 6d. each; post 8vo, illustrated boards, 2s. each; cloth limp, 2s. 6d. each.
All Sorts and Conditions of Men. With 12 Illustrations by FRED. BARNARD
The Captains' Room, &c. With Frontispiece by E. J. WHEELER.
All in a Garden Fair. With 6 Illustrations by HARRY FURNISS.
Dorothy Forster. With Frontispiece by CHARLES GREEN.
Uncle Jack, and other Stories. | Children of Gibeon.
The World Went Very Well Then. With 12 Illustrations by A. FORESTIER.
Herr Paulus: His Rise, his Greatness, and his Fall. | The Bell of St. Paul's.
For Faith and Freedom. With Illustrations by A. FORESTIER and F. WADDY.
To Call Her Mine, &c. With 9 Illustrations by A. FORESTIER.
The Holy Rose, &c. With Frontispiece by F. BARNARD.
Armorel of Lyonesse: A Romance of To-day. With 12 Illustrations by F. BARNARD.
St. Katherine's by the Tower. With 12 Illustrations by C. GREEN.
Verbena Camellia Stephanotis, &c. With a Frontispiece by GORDON BROWNE.
The Ivory Gate. | The Rebel Queen.

Beyond the Dreams of Avarice. Crown 8vo, cloth extra, 6s.
In Deacon's Orders, &c. With Frontispiece by A. FORESTIER. Crown 8vo, cloth, 6s.
The Master Craftsman. 2 vols., crown 8vo, 10s. net.   [May.

Fifty Years Ago. With 144 Plates and Woodcuts. Crown 8vo, cloth extra, 5s.
The Eulogy of Richard Jefferies. With Portrait. Crown 8vo, cloth extra, 6s.
London. With 125 Illustrations. Demy 8vo, cloth extra, 7s. 6d.
Westminster. With Etched Frontispiece by F. S. WALKER, R.P.E., and 130 Illustrations by
WILLIAM PATTEN and others. Demy 8vo, cloth, 18s.
Sir Richard Whittington. With Frontispiece. Crown 8vo, art linen, 3s. 6d.
Gaspard de Coligny. With a Portrait. Crown 8vo, art linen, 3s. 6d.
As We Are: As We May Be: Social Essays. Crown 8vo, linen, 6s.   [Shortly.

Bechstein (Ludwig).—As Pretty as Seven, and other German Stories. With Additional Tales by the Brothers GRIMM, and 98 Illustrations by RICHTER. Square 8vo, cloth extra, 6s. 6d.; gilt edges, 7s. 6d.

Beerbohm (Julius).—Wanderings in Patagonia; or, Life among the Ostrich-Hunters. With Illustrations. Crown 8vo, cloth extra, 3s. 6d.

Bellew (Frank).—The Art of Amusing: A Collection of Graceful Arts, Games, Tricks, Puzzles, and Charades. With 300 Illustrations. Crown 8vo, cloth extra, 4s. 6d.

Bennett (W. C., LL.D.).—Songs for Sailors. Post 8vo, cl. limp, 2s.

Bewick (Thomas) and his Pupils. By AUSTIN DOBSON. With 95 Illustrations. Square 8vo, cloth extra, 6s.

Bierce (Ambrose).—In the Midst of Life: Tales of Soldiers and Civilians. Crown 8vo, cloth extra, 6s.; post 8vo, illustrated boards, 2s.

Bill Nye's History of the United States. With 146 Illustrations by F. OPPER. Crown 8vo, cloth extra, 3s. 6d.

Bire (Edmond). — Diary of a Citizen of Paris during 'The Terror.' Translated and Edited by JOHN DE VILLIERS. With 2 Photogravures. Two Vols., 8vo, cloth, 21s.　[*Shortly.*

Blackburn's (Henry) Art Handbooks.

Academy Notes, 1875, 1877-86, 1889, 1890, 1892-1895, Illustrated, each 1s.
Academy Notes, 1875-79. Complete in One Vol., with 600 Illustrations. Cloth, 6s.
Academy Notes, 1880-84. Complete in One Vol., with 700 Illustrations. Cloth, 6s.
Academy Notes, 1890-94. Complete in One Vol., with 800 Illustrations. Cloth, 7s. 6d.
Grosvenor Notes, 1877. 6d.
Grosvenor Notes, separate years from **1878-1890,** each 1s.
Grosvenor Notes, Vol. I., **1877-82.** With 300 Illustrations. Demy 8vo, cloth, 6s.
The Paris Salon, 1895. With 300 Facsimile Sketches. 3s.

Grosvenor Notes, Vol. II., **1883-87.** With 300 Illustrations. Demy 8vo, cloth, 6s.
Grosvenor Notes, Vol. III., **1888-90.** With 230 Illustrations. Demy 8vo cloth, 3s. 6d.
The New Gallery, 1888-1895. With numerous Illustrations, each 1s.
The New Gallery, Vol. I., **1888-1892.** With 250 Illustrations. Demy 8vo, cloth, 6s.
English Pictures at the National Gallery. With 114 Illustrations. 1s.
Old Masters at the National Gallery. With 128 Illustrations. 1s. 6d.
Illustrated Catalogue to the National Gallery. With 242 Illusts. Demy 8vo, cloth, 3s.

Blind (Mathilde), Poems by.
The Ascent of Man. Crown 8vo, cloth, 5s.
Dramas in Miniature. With a Frontispiece by F. MADOX BROWN. Crown 8vo, cloth, 5s.
Songs and Sonnets. Fcap. 8vo, vellum and gold, 5s.
Birds of Passage: Songs of the Orient and Occident. Second Edition. Crown 8vo, linen, 6s. net.

Bourget (Paul).—A Living Lie. Translated by JOHN DE VILLIERS. Crown 8vo, cloth, 3s. 6d.　[*Shortly.*

Bourne (H. R. Fox), Books by.
English Merchants: Memoirs in Illustration of the Progress of British Commerce. With numerous Illustrations. Crown 8vo, cloth extra, 7s. 6d.
English Newspapers: Chapters in the History of Journalism. Two Vols., demy 8vo, cloth, 25s.
The Other Side of the Emin Pasha Relief Expedition. Crown 8vo, cloth, 6s.

Bowers (George).—Leaves from a Hunting Journal. Coloured Plates. Oblong folio, half-bound, 21s.

Boyle (Frederick), Works by. Post 8vo, illustrated bds., 2s. each.
Chronicles of No-Man's Land. | **Camp Notes.** | **Savage Life.**

Brand (John).—Observations on Popular Antiquities; chiefly illustrating the Origin of our Vulgar Customs, Ceremonies, and Superstitions. With the Additions of Sir HENRY ELLIS, and numerous Illustrations. Crown 8vo, cloth extra, 7s. 6d.

Brewer (Rev. Dr.), Works by.
The Reader's Handbook of Allusions, References, Plots, and Stories. Seventeenth Thousand. Crown 8vo, cloth extra, 7s. 6d.
Authors and their Works, with the Dates: Being the Appendices to 'The Reader's Handbook,' separately printed. Crown 8vo, cloth limp, 2s.
A Dictionary of Miracles. Crown 8vo, cloth extra, 7s. 6d.

Brewster (Sir David), Works by. Post 8vo, cloth, 4s. 6d. each.
More Worlds than One: Creed of the Philosopher and Hope of the Christian. With Plates.
The Martyrs of Science: GALILEO, TYCHO BRAHE, and KEPLER. With Portraits.
Letters on Natural Magic. With numerous Illustrations.

Brillat-Savarin.—Gastronomy as a Fine Art. Translated by R. E. ANDERSON, M.A. Post 8vo, half-bound, 2s.

Brydges (Harold).—Uncle Sam at Home. With 91 Illustrations

Buchanan (Robert), Works by. Crown 8vo, cloth extra, 6s. each.
Selected Poems of Robert Buchanan. With Frontispiece by T. DALZIEL.
The Earthquake; or, Six Days and a Sabbath.
The City of Dream: An Epic Poem. With Two Illustrations by P. MACNAB.
The Wandering Jew: A Christmas Carol.

The Outcast: A Rhyme for the Time. With 15 Illustrations by RUDOLF BLIND, PETER MACNAB, and HUME NISBET. Small demy 8vo, cloth extra, 8s.
Robert Buchanan's Poetical Works. With Steel-plate Portrait. Crown 8vo, cloth extra, 7s. 6d.

Crown 8vo, cloth extra, 3s. 6d. each; post 8vo, illustrated boards, 2s. each.

The Shadow of the Sword.	Love Me for Ever. With Frontispiece.
A Child of Nature. With Frontispiece.	Annan Water. Foxglove Manor.
God and the Man. With 11 Illustrations by FRED. BARNARD.	The New Abelard.
	Matt: A Story of a Caravan. With Frontispiece.
The Martyrdom of Madeline. With Frontispiece by A. W. COOPER.	The Master of the Mine. With Frontispiece.
	The Heir of Linne. Woman and the Man.

Crown 8vo, cloth extra, 3s. 6d. each.

Red and White Heather.	Rachel Dene.

Lady Kilpatrick. Crown 8vo, cloth extra, 6s.

The Charlatan. By ROBERT BUCHANAN and HENRY MURRAY. With a Frontispiece by T. H ROBINSON. Crown 8vo, cloth, 3s. 6d.

Burton (Richard F.).—The Book of the Sword. With over 400 Illustrations. Demy 4to, cloth extra, 32s.

Burton (Robert).—The Anatomy of Melancholy. With Translations of the Quotations. Demy 8vo, cloth extra, 7s. 6d.
Melancholy Anatomised: An Abridgment of BURTON'S ANATOMY. Post 8vo, half-bd., 2s. 6d.

Caine (T. Hall), Novels by. Crown 8vo, cloth extra, 3s. 6d. each.; post 8vo, illustrated boards, 2s. each; cloth limp, 2s. 6d. each.
  The Shadow of a Crime. | A Son of Hagar. | The Deemster.
A LIBRARY EDITION of The Deemster is now ready; and one of The Shadow of a Crime is in preparation, set in new type, crown 8vo, cloth decorated, 6s. each.

Cameron (Commander V. Lovett).—The Cruise of the 'Black Prince' Privateer. Post 8vo, picture boards, 2s.

Cameron (Mrs. H. Lovett), Novels by. Post 8vo, illust. bds. 2s. ea.
  Juliet's Guardian. | Deceivers Ever.

Carlyle (Jane Welsh), Life of. By Mrs. ALEXANDER IRELAND. With Portrait and Facsimile Letter. Small demy 8vo, cloth extra, 7s. 6d.

Carlyle (Thomas).—On the Choice of Books. Post 8vo, cl., 1s. 6d.
Correspondence of Thomas Carlyle and R. W. Emerson, 1834-1872. Edited by C. E. NORTON. With Portraits. Two Vols., crown 8vo, cloth, 24s.

Carruth (Hayden).—The Adventures of Jones. With 17 Illustrations. Fcap. 8vo, cloth, 2s.

Chambers (Robert W.), Stories of Paris Life by. Long fcap. 8vo, cloth, 2s. 6d. each.
  The King in Yellow. | In the Quarter.

Chapman's (George), Works. Vol. I., Plays Complete, including the Doubtful Ones.—Vol. II., Poems and Minor Translations, with Essay by A. C. SWINBURNE.—Vol. III., Translations of the Iliad and Odyssey. Three Vols., crown 8vo, cloth, 6s. each.

Chapple (J. Mitchell).—The Minor Chord: The Story of a Prima Donna. Crown 8vo, cloth, 3s. 6d.

Chatto (W. A.) and J. Jackson.—A Treatise on Wood Engraving, Historical and Practical. With Chapter by H. G. BOHN, and 450 fine Illusts. Large 4to, half-leather, 28s.

Chaucer for Children: A Golden Key. By Mrs. H. R. HAWEIS. With 8 Coloured Plates and 30 Woodcuts. Crown 4to, cloth extra, 3s. 6d.
Chaucer for Schools. By Mrs. H. R. HAWEIS. Demy 8vo, cloth limp, 2s. 6d.

Chess, The Laws and Practice of. With an Analysis of the Openings. By HOWARD STAUNTON. Edited by R. B. WORMALD. Crown 8vo, cloth, 5s.
The Minor Tactics of Chess: A Treatise on the Deployment of the Forces in obedience to Strategic Principle. By F. K. YOUNG and E. C. HOWELL. Long fcap. 8vo, cloth, 2s. 6d.
The Hastings Chess Tournament Book (Aug.-Sept., 1895). Containing the Official Report of the 231 Games played in the Tournament, with Notes by the Players, and Diagrams of Interesting Positions; Portraits and Biographical Sketches of the Chess Masters; and an Account of the Congress and its surroundings. Crown 8vo, cloth extra, 7s. 6d. net.   [Shortly.

Clare (Austin).—For the Love of a Lass. Post 8vo, 2s. ; cl., 2s. 6d.

Clive (Mrs. Archer), Novels by. Post 8vo, illust. boards, 2s. each.
Paul Ferroll. | Why Paul Ferroll Killed his Wife.

Clodd (Edward, F.R.A.S.).—Myths and Dreams. Cr. 8vo, 3s. 6d.

Cobban (J. Maclaren), Novels by.
The Cure of Souls. Post 8vo, Illustrated boards, 2s.
The Red Sultan. Crown 8vo, cloth extra, 3s. 6d. ; post 8vo, Illustrated boards, 2s.
The Burden of Isabel. Crown 8vo, cloth extra, 3s. 6d.

Coleman (John).—Players and Playwrights I have Known. Two
Vols., demy 8vo, cloth, 24s.

Coleridge (M. E.).—The Seven Sleepers of Ephesus. Cloth, 1s. 6d.

Collins (C. Allston).—The Bar Sinister. Post 8vo, boards, 2s.

Collins (John Churton, M.A.), Books by.
Illustrations of Tennyson. Crown 8vo, cloth extra, 6s.
Jonathan Swift: A Biographical and Critical Study. Crown 8vo, cloth extra, 8s.

Collins (Mortimer and Frances), Novels by.
Crown 8vo, cloth extra, 3s. 6d. each ; post 8vo, illustrated boards, 2s. each.
From Midnight to Midnight. | Blacksmith and Scholar.
Transmigration. | You Play me False. | A Village Comedy.
Post 8vo, illustrated boards, 2s. each.
Sweet Anne Page. | A Fight with Fortune. | Sweet and Twenty. | Frances

Collins (Wilkie), Novels by.
Crown 8vo, cloth extra, 3s. 6d. each ; post 8vo, illustrated boards, 2s. each ; cloth limp, 2s. 6d. each.
Antonina. With a Frontispiece by Sir JOHN GILBERT, R.A.
Basil. Illustrated by Sir JOHN GILBERT, R.A., and J. MAHONEY.
Hide and Seek. Illustrated by Sir JOHN GILBERT, R.A., and J. MAHONEY.
After Dark. With Illustrations by A. B. HOUGHTON. | The Two Destinies.
The Dead Secret. With a Frontispiece by Sir JOHN GILBERT, R.A.
Queen of Hearts. With a Frontispiece by Sir JOHN GILBERT, R.A.
The Woman in White. With Illustrations by Sir JOHN GILBERT, R.A., and F. A. FRASER.
No Name. With Illustrations by Sir J. E. MILLAIS, R.A., and A. W. COOPER.
My Miscellanies. With a Steel-plate Portrait of WILKIE COLLINS.
Armadale. With Illustrations by G. H. THOMAS.
The Moonstone. With Illustrations by G. DU MAURIER and F. A. FRASER.
Man and Wife. With Illustrations by WILLIAM SMALL.
Poor Miss Finch. Illustrated by G. DU MAURIER and EDWARD HUGHES.
Miss or Mrs.? With Illustrations by S. L. FILDES, R.A., and HENRY WOODS, A.R.A.
The New Magdalen. Illustrated by G. DU MAURIER and C. S. REINHARDT.
The Frozen Deep. Illustrated by G. DU MAURIER and J. MAHONEY.
The Law and the Lady. With Illustrations by S. L. FILDES, R.A., and SYDNEY HALL.
The Haunted Hotel. With Illustrations by ARTHUR HOPKINS.
The Fallen Leaves. | Heart and Science. | The Evil Genius.
Jezebel's Daughter. | 'I Say No.' | Little Novels. Frontis.
The Black Robe. | A Rogue's Life. | The Legacy of Cain.
Blind Love. With a Preface by Sir WALTER BESANT, and Illustrations by A. FORESTIER.
POPULAR EDITIONS. Medium 8vo, 6d. each ; cloth, 1s. each.
The Woman in White. | The Moonstone.

Colman's (George) Humorous Works: 'Broad Grins,' 'My Night-
gown and Slippers,' &c. With Life and Frontispiece. Crown 8vo, cloth extra, 7s. 6d.

Colquhoun (M. J.).—Every Inch a Soldier. Post 8vo, boards, 2s.

Colt-breaking, Hints on. By W. M. HUTCHISON. Cr. 8vo, cl., 3s. 6d.

Convalescent Cookery. By CATHERINE RYAN. Cr. 8vo, 1s. ; cl., 1s. 6d.

Conway (Moncure D.), Works by.
Demonology and Devil-Lore. With 65 Illustrations. Two Vols., demy 8vo, cloth, 28s.
George Washington's Rules of Civility. Fcap. 8vo, Japanese vellum, 2s. 6d.

Cook (Dutton), Novels by.
Paul Foster's Daughter. Crown 8vo, cloth extra, 3s. 6d. ; post 8vo, illustrated boards, 2s.
Leo. Post 8vo, illustrated boards, 2s.

Cooper (Edward H.).—Geoffory Hamilton. Cr. 8vo, cloth, 3s. 6d.

Cornwall.—Popular Romances of the West of England; or, The
Drolls, Traditions, and Superstitions of Old Cornwall. Collected by ROBERT HUNT, F.R.S. With
two Steel Plates by GEORGE CRUIKSHANK. Crown 8vo, cloth, 7s. 6d.

Cotes (V. Cecil).—Two Girls on a Barge. With 44 Illustrations by
F. H. TOWNSEND. Post 8vo, cloth, 2s. 6d.

Craddock (C. Egbert), Stories by.
The Prophet of the Great Smoky Mountains. Post 8vo, illustrated boards, 2s.
His Vanished Star. Crown 8vo, cloth extra, 3s. 6d.

Crellin (H. N.) Books by.
Romances of the Old Seraglio. With 28 Illustrations by S. L. WOOD. Crown 8vo, cloth, 3s. 6d.
Tales of the Caliph. Crown 8vo, cloth, 2s.
The Nazarenes: A Drama. Crown 8vo, 1s.

Cram (Ralph Adams).—Black Spirits and White. Fcap. 8vo, cloth, 1s. 6d.

Crim (Matt.).—Adventures of a Fair Rebel. Crown 8vo, cloth extra, with a Frontispiece by DAN. BEARD, 3s. 6d. ; post 8vo, illustrated boards, 2s.

Crockett (S. R.) and others. — Tales of Our Coast. By S. R. CROCKETT, GILBERT PARKER, HAROLD FREDERIC, 'Q.,' and W. CLARK RUSSELL. With 12 Illustrations by FRANK BRANGWYN. Crown 8vo, cloth, 3s. 6d. [Shortly.

Croker (Mrs. B. M.), Novels by. Crown 8vo, cloth extra, 3s. 6d. each; post 8vo, illustrated boards 2s. each; cloth limp, 2s. 6d. each.

Pretty Miss Neville.	Diana Barrington.	A Family Likeness.
A Bird of Passage.	Proper Pride.	'To Let.'

Village Tales and Jungle Tragedies.
Crown 8vo, cloth extra, 3s. 6d. each.

Mr. Jervis.	The Real Lady Hilda.

Married or Single? Three Vols., crown 8vo, 15s. net.

Cruikshank's Comic Almanack. Complete in TWO SERIES: The FIRST, from 1835 to 1843; the SECOND, from 1844 to 1853. A Gathering of the Best Humour of THACKERAY, HOOD, MAYHEW, ALBERT SMITH, A'BECKETT, ROBERT BROUGH, &c. With numerous Steel Engravings and Woodcuts by GEORGE CRUIKSHANK, HINE, LANDELLS, &c. Two Vols., crown 8vo, cloth gilt, 7s. 6d. each.
The Life of George Cruikshank. By BLANCHARD JERROLD. With 84 Illustrations and a Bibliography. Crown 8vo, cloth extra, 6s.

Cumming (C. F. Gordon), Works by. Demy 8vo, cl. ex., 8s. 6d. ea.
In the Hebrides. With an Autotype Frontispiece and 23 Illustrations.
In the Himalayas and on the Indian Plains. With 42 Illustrations.
Two Happy Years in Ceylon. With 28 Illustrations.
Via Cornwall to Egypt. With a Photogravure Frontispiece. Demy 8vo, cloth, 7s. 6d.

Cussans (John E.).—A Handbook of Heraldry; with Instructions for Tracing Pedigrees and Deciphering Ancient MSS., &c. Fourth Edition, revised, with 408 Woodcuts and 2 Coloured Plates. Crown 8vo, cloth extra, 6s.

Cyples (W.).—Hearts of Gold. Cr. 8vo, cl., 3s. 6d. ; post 8vo, bds., 2s.

Daniel (George).—Merrie England in the Olden Time. With Illustrations by ROBERT CRUIKSHANK. Crown 8vo, cloth extra, 3s. 6d.

Daudet (Alphonse).—The Evangelist; or, Port Salvation. Crown 8vo, cloth extra, 3s. 6d. ; post 8vo, illustrated boards, 2s.

Davenant (Francis, M.A.).—Hints for Parents on the Choice of a Profession for their Sons when Starting in Life. Crown 8vo, 1s. ; cloth, 1s. 6d.

Davidson (Hugh Coleman).—Mr. Sadler's Daughters. With a Frontispiece by STANLEY WOOD. Crown 8vo, cloth extra, 3s. 6d.

Davies (Dr. N. E. Yorke-), Works by. Cr. 8vo, 1s. ea.; cl., 1s. 6d. ea.
One Thousand Medical Maxims and Surgical Hints.
Nursery Hints: A Mother's Guide in Health and Disease.
Foods for the Fat: A Treatise on Corpulency, and a Dietary for its Cure.
Aids to Long Life. Crown 8vo, 2s. ; cloth limp, 2s. 6d.

Davies' (Sir John) Complete Poetical Works. Collected and Edited, with Introduction and Notes, by Rev. A. B. GROSART, D.D. Two Vols., crown 8vo, cloth, 12s.

Dawson (Erasmus, M.B.).—The Fountain of Youth. Crown 8vo, cloth extra, with Two Illustrations by HUME NISBET, 3s. 6d. ; post 8vo, illustrated boards, 2s.

De Guerin (Maurice), The Journal of. Edited by G. S. TREBUTIEN. With a Memoir by SAINTE-BEUVE. Translated from the 20th French Edition by JESSIE P. FROTHINGHAM. Fcap. 8vo, half-bound, 2s. 6d.

De Maistre (Xavier).—A Journey Round my Room. Translated by Sir HENRY ATTWELL. Post 8vo, cloth limp, 2s. 6d.

De Mille (James).—A Castle in Spain. Crown 8vo, cloth extra, with a Frontispiece, 3s. 6d. ; post 8vo, illustrated boards, 2s.

Derby (The) : The Blue Ribbon of the Turf. With Brief Accounts of THE OAKS. By LOUIS HENRY CURZON. Crown 8vo, cloth limp, 2s. 6d.

Derwent (Leith), Novels by. Cr. 8vo, cl., 3s. 6d. ea.; post 8vo, 2s. ea.
Our Lady of Tears. | Circe's Lovers.

Dewar (T. R.).—A Ramble Round the Globe. With 220 Illustrations. Crown 8vo, cloth extra, 7s. 6d.

Dickens (Charles), Novels by. Post 8vo, illustrated boards, 2s. each.
Sketches by Boz. | Nicholas Nickleby. | Oliver Twist.

About England with Dickens. By ALFRED RIMMER. With 57 Illustrations by C. A. VANDER-HOOF, ALFRED RIMMER. and others. Square 8vo, cloth extra, 7s. 6d.

Dictionaries.
A Dictionary of Miracles: Imitative, Realistic, and Dogmatic. By the Rev. E. C. BREWER, LL.D. Crown 8vo, cloth extra, 7s. 6d.
The Reader's Handbook of Allusions, References, Plots, and Stories. By the Rev. E. C. BREWER, LL.D. With an ENGLISH BIBLIOGRAPHY. Crown 8vo, cloth extra, 7s. 6d.
Authors and their Works, with the Dates. Crown 8vo, cloth limp, 2s.
Familiar Short Sayings of Great Men. With Historical and Explanatory Notes by SAMUEL A. BENT, A.M. Crown 8vo, cloth extra, 7s. 6d.
The Slang Dictionary: Etymological, Historical, and Anecdotal. Crown 8vo, cloth, 6s. 6d.
Words, Facts, and Phrases: A Dictionary of Curious, Quaint, and Out-of-the-Way Matters. By ELIEZER EDWARDS. Crown 8vo, cloth extra, 7s. 6d.

Diderot.—The Paradox of Acting. Translated, with Notes, by WALTER HERRIES POLLOCK. With Preface by Sir HENRY IRVING. Crown 8vo, parchment, 4s. 6d.

Dobson (Austin), Works by.
Thomas Bewick and his Pupils. With 95 Illustrations. Square 8vo, cloth, 6s.
Four Frenchwomen. With Four Portraits. Crown 8vo, buckram, gilt top, 6s.
Eighteenth Century Vignettes. TWO SERIES. Crown 8vo, buckram, 6s. each.—A THIRD SERIES is in preparation.

Dobson (W. T.).—Poetical Ingenuities and Eccentricities. Post 8vo, cloth limp, 2s. 6d.

Donovan (Dick), Detective Stories by.
Post 8vo, illustrated boards, 2s. each; cloth limp, 2s. 6d. each.
The Man-Hunter. | Wanted. | A Detective's Triumphs.
Caught at Last. | In the Grip of the Law.
Tracked and Taken. | From Information Received.
Who Poisoned Hetty Duncan? | Link by Link. | Dark Deeds.
Suspicion Aroused. | Riddles Read.

Crown 8vo, cloth extra, 3s. 6d. each; post 8vo, illustrated boards, 2s. each; cloth, 2s. 6d. each.
The Man from Manchester. With 23 Illustrations.
Tracked to Doom. With Six full-page Illustrations by GORDON BROWNE.

The Mystery of Jamaica Terrace. Crown 8vo, cloth, 3s. 6d.

Doyle (A. Conan).—The Firm of Girdlestone. Cr. 8vo, cl., 3s. 6d.

Dramatists, The Old. Crown 8vo, cl. ex., with Portraits, 6s. per Vol.
Ben Jonson's Works. With Notes, Critical and Explanatory, and a Biographical Memoir by WILLIAM GIFFORD. Edited by Colonel CUNNINGHAM. Three Vols.
Chapman's Works. Three Vols. Vol. I. contains the Plays complete; Vol. II., Poems and Minor Translations, with an Essay by A. C. SWINBURNE; Vol. III., Translations of the Iliad and Odyssey.
Marlowe's Works. Edited, with Notes, by Colonel CUNNINGHAM. One Vol.
Massinger's Plays. From GIFFORD'S Text. Edited by Colonel CUNNINGHAM. One Vol.

Duncan (Sara Jeannette: Mrs. EVERARD COTES), Works by.
Crown 8vo, cloth extra, 7s. 6d. each.
A Social Departure. With 111 Illustrations by F. H. TOWNSEND.
An American Girl in London. With 80 Illustrations by F. H. TOWNSEND.
The Simple Adventures of a Memsahib. With 37 Illustrations by F. H. TOWNSEND.

Crown 8vo, cloth extra, 3s. 6d. each.
A Daughter of To-Day. | Vernon's Aunt. With 47 Illustrations by HAL HURST.

Dyer (T. F. Thiselton).—The Folk=Lore of Plants. Cr. 8vo, cl., 6s.

Early English Poets. Edited, with Introductions and Annotations, by Rev. A. B. GROSART, D.D. Crown 8vo, cloth boards, 6s. per Volume.
Fletcher's (Giles) Complete Poems. One Vol.
Davies' (Sir John) Complete Poetical Works. Two Vols.
Herrick's (Robert) Complete Collected Poems. Three Vols.
Sidney's (Sir Philip) Complete Poetical Works. Three Vols.

Edgcumbe (Sir E. R. Pearce).—Zephyrus: A Holiday in Brazil and on the River Plate. With 41 Illustrations. Crown 8vo, cloth extra, 5s.

Edison, The Life and Inventions of Thomas A. By W. K. L. and ANTONIA DICKSON. With 200 Illustrations by R. F. OUTCALT, &c. Demy 4to, cloth gilt, 18s.

Edwardes (Mrs. Annie), Novels by.
Post 8vo, illustrated boards, 2s. each.
Archie Lovell. | A Point of Honour.

Edwards (Eliezer).—Words, Facts, and Phrases: A Dictionary of Curious, Quaint, and Out-of-the-Way Matters. Crown 8vo, cloth, 7s. 6d.

Edwards (M. Betham-), Novels by.
Kitty. Post 8vo, boards, 2s. ; cloth, 2s. 6d. | Felicia. Post 8vo, illustrated boards, 2s.

Egerton (Rev. J. C., M.A.). — Sussex Folk and Sussex Ways. With Introduction by Rev. Dr. H. WACE, and Four Illustrations. Crown 8vo, cloth extra, 5s.

Eggleston (Edward).—Roxy: A Novel. Post 8vo, illust. boards, 2s.

Englishman's House, The: A Practical Guide for Selecting or Building a House. By C. J. RICHARDSON. Coloured Frontispiece and 534 Illusts. Cr. 8vo, cloth, 7s. 6d.

Ewald (Alex. Charles, F.S.A.), Works by.
The Life and Times of Prince Charles Stuart, Count of Albany (THE YOUNG PRETENDER). With a Portrait. Crown 8vo, cloth extra, 7s. 6d.
Stories from the State Papers. With Autotype Frontispiece. Crown 8vo, cloth, 6s.

Eyes, Our: How to Preserve Them. By JOHN BROWNING. Cr. 8vo, 1s.

Familiar Short Sayings of Great Men. By SAMUEL ARTHUR BENT, A.M. Fifth Edition, Revised and Enlarged. Crown 8vo, cloth extra, 7s. 6d.

Faraday (Michael), Works by. Post 8vo, cloth extra, 4s. 6d. each.
The Chemical History of a Candle: Lectures delivered before a Juvenile Audience. Edited by WILLIAM CROOKES, F.C.S. With numerous Illustrations.
On the Various Forces of Nature, and their Relations to each other. Edited by WILLIAM CROOKES, F.C.S. With Illustrations.

Farrer (J. Anson), Works by.
Military Manners and Customs. Crown 8vo, cloth extra, 6s.
War: Three Essays, reprinted from 'Military Manners and Customs.' Crown 8vo, 1s. ; cloth, 1s. 6d.

Fenn (G. Manville), Novels by.
Crown 8vo, cloth extra, 3s. 6d. each ; post 8vo, illustrated boards, 2s. each.
The New Mistress. | Witness to the Deed.
The Tiger Lily: A Tale of Two Passions.
The White Virgin. Crown 8vo, cloth extra, 3s. 6d.

Fin-Bec.—The Cupboard Papers: Observations on the Art of Living and Dining. Post 8vo, cloth limp, 2s. 6d.

Fireworks, The Complete Art of Making; or, The Pyrotechnist's Treasury. By THOMAS KENTISH. With 267 Illustrations. Crown 8vo, cloth, 5s.

First Book, My. By WALTER BESANT, JAMES PAYN, W. CLARK RUSSELL, GRANT ALLEN, HALL CAINE, GEORGE R. SIMS, RUDYARD KIPLING, A. CONAN DOYLE, M. E. BRADDON, F. W. ROBINSON, H. RIDER HAGGARD, R. M. BALLANTYNE, I. ZANGWILL, MORLEY ROBERTS, D. CHRISTIE MURRAY, MARY CORELLI, J. K. JEROME, JOHN STRANGE WINTER, BRET HARTE, 'Q.,' ROBERT BUCHANAN, and R. L. STEVENSON. With a Prefatory Story by JEROME K. JEROME, and 185 Illustrations. Small demy 8vo, cloth extra, 7s. 6d.

Fitzgerald (Percy), Works by.
The World Behind the Scenes. Crown 8vo, cloth extra, 3s. 6d.
Little Essays: Passages from the Letters of CHARLES LAMB. Post 8vo, cloth, 2s. 6d.
A Day's Tour: A Journey through France and Belgium. With Sketches. Crown 4to, 1s.
Fatal Zero. Crown 8vo, cloth extra, 3s. 6d. ; post 8vo, illustrated boards, 2s.

Post 8vo, illustrated boards, 2s. each.
Bella Donna. | The Lady of Brantome. | The Second Mrs. Tillotson.
Polly. | Never Forgotten. | Seventy-five Brooke Street.

The Life of James Boswell (of Auchinleck). With Illusts. Two Vols., demy 8vo, cloth, 24s.
The Savoy Opera. With 60 Illustrations and Portraits. Crown 8vo, cloth, 3s. 6d.
Sir Henry Irving: Twenty Years at the Lyceum. With Portrait. Crown 8vo, 1s. ; cloth, 1s. 6d.

Flammarion (Camille), Works by.
Popular Astronomy: A General Description of the Heavens. Translated by J. ELLARD GORE, F.R.A.S. With Three Plates and 288 Illustrations. Medium 8vo, cloth, 16s.
Urania: A Romance. With 87 Illustrations. Crown 8vo, cloth extra, 5s.

Fletcher's (Giles, B.D.) Complete Poems: Christ's Victorie in Heaven, Christ's Victorie on Earth, Christ's Triumph over Death, and Minor Poems. With Notes by Rev. A. B. GROSART, D.D. Crown 8vo, cloth boards, 6s.

Fonblanque (Albany).—Filthy Lucre. Post 8vo, illust. boards, 2s.

Francillon (R. E.), Novels by.
Crown 8vo, cloth extra, 3s. 6d. each; post 8vo, illustrated boards, 2s. each.

One by One. | A Real Queen. | King or Knave.
Ropes of Sand. Illustrated. | | A Dog and his Shadow.

Post 8vo, illustrated boards, 2s. each.

Queen Cophetua. | Olympia. | Romances of the Law.

Jack Doyle's Daughter. Crown 8vo, cloth, 3s. 6d.
Esther's Glove. Fcap. 8vo, picture cover, 1s.

Frederic (Harold), Novels by. Post 8vo, illust. boards, 2s. each.
Seth's Brother's Wife. | The Lawton Girl.

French Literature, A History of. By HENRY VAN LAUN. Three
Vols., demy 8vo, cloth boards, 7s. 6d. each.

Friswell (Hain).—One of Two: A Novel. Post 8vo, illust. bds., 2s.

Frost (Thomas), Works by. Crown 8vo, cloth extra, 3s. 6d. each.
Circus Life and Circus Celebrities. | Lives of the Conjurers.
The Old Showmen and the Old London Fairs.

Fry's (Herbert) Royal Guide to the London Charities. Edited
by JOHN LANE. Published Annually. Crown 8vo, cloth, 1s. 6d.

Gardening Books. Post 8vo, 1s. each; cloth limp. 1s. 6d. each.
A Year's Work in Garden and Greenhouse. By GEORGE GLENNY.
Household Horticulture. By TOM and JANE JERROLD. Illustrated.
The Garden that Paid the Rent. By TOM JERROLD.

My Garden Wild. By FRANCIS G. HEATH. Crown 8vo, cloth extra, 6s.

Gardner (Mrs. Alan).—Rifle and Spear with the Rajpoots: Being
the Narrative of a Winter's Travel and Sport in Northern India. With numerous Illustrations by the
Author and F. H. TOWNSEND. Demy 4to, half-bound, 21s.

Garrett (Edward).—The Capel Girls: A Novel. Crown 8vo, cloth
extra, with two Illustrations, 3s. 6d.; post 8vo, illustrated boards, 2s.

Gaulot (Paul).—The Red Shirts: A Story of the Revolution. Trans-
lated by JOHN DE VILLIERS. With a Frontispiece by STANLEY WOOD. Crown 8vo, cloth, 3s. 6d.

Gentleman's Magazine, The. 1s. Monthly. Contains Stories,
Articles upon Literature, Science, Biography, and Art, and 'Table Talk' by SYLVANUS URBAN.
*** Bound Volumes for recent years kept in stock, 8s. 6d. each. Cases for binding, 2s.

Gentleman's Annual, The. Published Annually in November. 1s.

German Popular Stories. Collected by the Brothers GRIMM and
Translated by EDGAR TAYLOR. With Introduction by JOHN RUSKIN, and 22 Steel Plates after
GEORGE CRUIKSHANK. Square 8vo, cloth, 6s. 6d.; gilt edges, 7s. 6d.

Gibbon (Charles), Novels by.
Crown 8vo, cloth extra, 3s. 6d. each; post 8vo, illustrated boards, 2s. each.

Robin Gray. Frontispiece. | The Golden Shaft. Frontispiece. | Loving a Dream.

Post 8vo, illustrated boards, 2s. each.

The Flower of the Forest. | In Love and War.
The Dead Heart. | A Heart's Problem.
For Lack of Gold. | By Mead and Stream.
What Will the World Say? | The Braes of Yarrow.
For the King. | A Hard Knot. | Fancy Free. | Of High Degree.
Queen of the Meadow. | In Honour Bound.
In Pastures Green. | Heart's Delight. | Blood-Money.

Gibney (Somerville).—Sentenced! Crown 8vo, 1s.; cloth, 1s. 6d.

Gilbert (W. S.), Original Plays by. In Three Series, 2s. 6d. each.
The FIRST SERIES contains: The Wicked World—Pygmalion and Galatea—Charity—The Princess—
The Palace of Truth—Trial by Jury.
The SECOND SERIES: Broken Hearts—Engaged—Sweethearts—Gretchen—Dan'l Druce—Tom Cobb
—H.M.S. 'Pinafore'—The Sorcerer—The Pirates of Penzance.
The THIRD SERIES: Comedy and Tragedy—Foggerty's Fairy—Rosencrantz and Guildenstern—
Patience—Princess Ida—The Mikado—Ruddigore—The Yeomen of the Guard—The Gondoliers—
The Mountebanks—Utopia.

Eight Original Comic Operas written by W. S. GILBERT. Containing: The Sorcerer—H.M.S.
'Pinafore'—The Pirates of Penzance—Iolanthe—Patience—Princess Ida—The Mikado—Trial by
Jury. Demy 8vo, cloth limp, 2s. 6d.
The Gilbert and Sullivan Birthday Book: Quotations for Every Day in the Year, selected
from Plays by W. S. GILBERT set to Music by Sir A. SULLIVAN. Compiled by ALEX. WATSON.
Royal 16mo, Japanese leather, 2s. 6d.

Gilbert (William), Novels by. Post 8vo, illustrated bds., 2s. each.
Dr. Austin's Guests. | James Duke, Costermonger.
The Wizard of the Mountain.

Glanville (Ernest), Novels by.
Crown 8vo, cloth extra, 3s. 6d. each; post 8vo, illustrated boards, 2s. each.
The Lost Heiress: A Tale of Love, Battle, and Adventure. With Two Illustrations by H. NISBET.
The Fossicker: A Romance of Mashonaland. With Two Illustrations by HUME NISBET.
A Fair Colonist. With a Frontispiece by STANLEY WOOD.

The Golden Rock. With a Frontispiece by STANLEY WOOD. Crown 8vo, cloth extra, 3s. 6d.
Kloof Yarns. Crown 8vo, picture cover, 1s.; cloth, 1s. 6d. [Shortly.

Glenny (George).—A Year's Work in Garden and Greenhouse:
Practical Advice as to the Management of the Flower, Fruit, and Frame Garden. Post 8vo, 1s.; cloth, 1s. 6d.

Godwin (William).—Lives of the Necromancers. Post 8vo, cl., 2s.

Golden Treasury of Thought, The: An Encyclopædia of QUOTA-
TIONS. Edited by THEODORE TAYLOR. Crown 8vo, cloth gilt, 7s. 6d.

Gontaut, Memoirs of the Duchesse de (Gouvernante to the Chil-
dren of France), 1773-1836. With Two Photogravures. Two Vols., demy 8vo, cloth extra, 21s.

Goodman (E. J.).—The Fate of Herbert Wayne. Cr. 8vo, 3s. 6d.

Graham (Leonard).—The Professor's Wife: A Story. Fcp. 8vo, 1s.

Greeks and Romans, The Life of the, described from Antique
Monuments. By ERNST GUHL and W. KONER. Edited by Dr. F. HUEFFER. With 545 Illustrations. Large crown 8vo, cloth extra, 7s. 6d.

Greenwood (James), Works by. Crown 8vo, cloth extra, 3s. 6d. each.
The Wilds of London. | Low-Life Deeps.

Greville (Henry), Novels by.
Nikanor. Translated by ELIZA E. CHASE. Post 8vo, illustrated boards, 2s.
A Noble Woman. Crown 8vo, cloth extra, 5s.; post 8vo, illustrated boards, 2s.

Griffith (Cecil).—Corinthia Marazion: A Novel. Crown 8vo, cloth
extra, 3s. 6d.; post 8vo, illustrated boards, 2s.

Grundy (Sydney).—The Days of his Vanity: A Passage in the
Life of a Young Man. Crown 8vo, cloth extra, 3s. 6d.; post 8vo, illustrated boards, 2s.

Habberton (John, Author of 'Helen's Babies'), **Novels by.**
Post 8vo, illustrated boards, 2s. each; cloth limp, 2s. 6d. each.
Brueton's Bayou. | Country Luck.

Hair, The: Its Treatment in Health, Weakness, and Disease. Translated from the German of Dr. J. PINCUS. Crown 8vo, 1s.; cloth, 1s. 6d.

Hake (Dr. Thomas Gordon), Poems by. Cr. 8vo, cl. ex., 6s. each.
New Symbols. | Legends of the Morrow. | The Serpent Play.

Maiden Ecstasy. Small 4to, cloth extra, 8s.

Hall (Owen).—The Track of a Storm. Crown 8vo, cloth, 6s.

Hall (Mrs. S. C.).—Sketches of Irish Character. With numerous
Illustrations on Steel and Wood by MACLISE, GILBERT, HARVEY, and GEORGE CRUIKSHANK.
Small demy 8vo, cloth extra, 7s. 6d.

Halliday (Andrew).—Every-day Papers. Post 8vo, boards, 2s.

Handwriting, The Philosophy of. With over 100 Facsimiles and
Explanatory Text. By DON FELIX DE SALAMANCA. Post 8vo, cloth limp, 2s. 6d.

Hanky-Panky: Easy and Difficult Tricks, White Magic, Sleight of
Hand, &c. Edited by W. H. CREMER. With 200 Illustrations. Crown 8vo, cloth extra, 4s. 6d.

Hardy (Lady Duffus).—Paul Wynter's Sacrifice. Post 8vo, bds., 2s.

Hardy (Thomas).—Under the Greenwood Tree. Crown 8vo, cloth
extra, with Portrait and 15 Illustrations, 3s. 6d.; post 8vo, illustrated boards, 2s. cloth limp, 2s. 6d.

Harper (Charles G.), Works by. Demy 8vo, cloth extra, 16s. each.
The Brighton Road. With Photogravure Frontispiece and 90 Illustrations.
From Paddington to Penzance: The Record of a Summer Tramp. With 105 Illustrations.

Harte's (Bret) Collected Works. Revised by the Author. LIBRARY
EDITION, In Eight Volumes, crown 8vo, cloth extra, 6s. each.
Vol.   I. COMPLETE POETICAL AND DRAMATIC WORKS. With Steel-plate Portrait.
  „   II. THE LUCK OF ROARING CAMP—BOHEMIAN PAPERS—AMERICAN LEGENDS.
  „   III. TALES OF THE ARGONAUTS—EASTERN SKETCHES.
  „   IV. GABRIEL CONROY. | Vol. V. STORIES—CONDENSED NOVELS, &c.
  „   VI. TALES OF THE PACIFIC SLOPE.
      VII. TALES OF THE PACIFIC SLOPE—II. With Portrait by JOHN PETTIE, R.A.
  „ VIII. TALES OF THE PINE AND THE CYPRESS.

The Select Works of Bret Harte, in Prose and Poetry. With Introductory Essay by J. M.
  BELLEW, Portrait of the Author, and 50 Illustrations. Crown 8vo, cloth extra, 7s. 6d.
Bret Harte's Poetical Works. Printed on hand-made paper. Crown 8vo, buckram, 4s. 6d.
The Queen of the Pirate Isle. With 28 Original Drawings by KATE GREENAWAY, reproduced
  in Colours by EDMUND EVANS. Small 4to, cloth, 5s.

Crown 8vo, cloth extra, 3s. 6d. each ; post 8vo, picture boards, 2s. each.
A Waif of the Plains. With 60 Illustrations by STANLEY L. WOOD.
A Ward of the Golden Gate. With 59 Illustrations by STANLEY L. WOOD.

Crown 8vo, cloth extra, 3s. 6d. each.
A Sappho of Green Springs, &c. With Two Illustrations by HUME NISBET.
Colonel Starbottle's Client, and Some Other People. With a Frontispiece.
Susy: A Novel. With Frontispiece and Vignette by J. A. CHRISTIE.
Sally Dows, &c. With 47 Illustrations by W. D. ALMOND and others.
A Protegee of Jack Hamlin's. With 26 Illustrations by W. SMALL and others.
The Bell-Ringer of Angel's, &c. With 39 Illustrations by DUDLEY HARDY and others
Clarence: A Story of the American War. With Eight Illustrations by A. JULE GOODMAN.

Post 8vo, illustrated boards, 2s. each.

Gabriel Conroy.	**The Luck of Roaring Camp,** &c.
An Heiress of Red Dog, &c.	**Californian Stories.**

Post 8vo, illustrated boards, 2s. each ; cloth, 2s. 6d. each.

Flip.	**Maruja.**	**A Phyllis of the Sierras.**

Fcap. 8vo, picture cover, 1s. each.

Snow-Bound at Eagle's.	**Jeff Briggs's Love Story.**

Haweis (Mrs. H. R.), Books by.
  The Art of Beauty. With Coloured Frontispiece and 91 Illustrations. Square 8vo, cloth bds., 6s.
  The Art of Decoration. With Coloured Frontispiece and 74 Illustrations. Sq. 8vo, cloth bds., 6s.
  The Art of Dress. With 32 Illustrations. Post 8vo, 1s. ; cloth, 1s. 6d.
  Chaucer for Schools. Demy 8vo, cloth limp, 2s. 6d.
  Chaucer for Children. With 38 Illustrations (8 Coloured). Crown 4to, cloth extra, 3s. 6d.

Haweis (Rev. H. R., M.A.), Books by.
  American Humorists: WASHINGTON IRVING, OLIVER WENDELL HOLMES, JAMES RUSSELL
    LOWELL, ARTEMUS WARD, MARK TWAIN, and BRET HARTE. Third Edition. Crown 8vo,
    cloth extra, 6s.
  Travel and Talk, 1885, 1893, 1895: America—New Zealand—Tasmania—Ceylon. With Pho-
    togravure Frontispieces. Two Vols., crown 8vo, cloth, 21s.   [Shortly.

Hawthorne (Julian), Novels by.
Crown 8vo, cloth extra, 3s. 6d. each   post 8vo, illustrated boards, 2s. each.

Garth.	**Ellice Quentin.**	**Beatrix Randolph.** With Four Illusts.
Sebastian Strome.		**David Poindexter's Disappearance.**
Fortune's Fool.	**Dust.** Four Illusts.	**The Spectre of the Camera.**

Post 8vo, illustrated boards, 2s. each.

Miss Cadogna.	**Love—or a Name.**

Mrs. Gainsborough's Diamonds. Fcap. 8vo, illustrated cover, 1s.

Hawthorne (Nathaniel).—Our Old Home. Annotated with Pas-
sages from the Author's Note-books, and Illustrated with 31 Photogravures. Two Vols., cr. 8vo, 15s.

Heath (Francis George).—My Garden Wild, and What I Grew
There. Crown 8vo, cloth extra, gilt edges, 6s.

Helps (Sir Arthur), Works by. Post 8vo, cloth limp, 2s. 6d. each.

Animals and their Masters.	**Social Pressure.**

Ivan de Biron: A Novel. Crown 8vo, cloth extra, 3s. 6d. ; post 8vo, illustrated boards, 2s.

Henderson (Isaac). — Agatha Page: A Novel. Cr. 8vo, cl., 3s. 6d.

Henty (G. A.), Novels by.
  Rujub the Juggler. With Eight Illustrations by STANLEY L. WOOD. Crown 8vo, cloth, 3s. 6d.;
    post 8vo, illustrated boards, 2s.
  Dorothy's Double. Crown 8vo, cloth, 3s. 6d.

Herman (Henry).—A Leading Lady. Post 8vo, bds., 2s. ; cl., 2s. 6d.

Herrick's (Robert) Hesperides, Noble Numbers, and Complete
Collected Poems. With Memorial-Introduction and Notes by the Rev. A. B. GROSART, D.D.,
Steel Portrait, &c. Three Vols., crown 8vo, cloth boards, 18s.

Hertzka (Dr. Theodor).—Freeland: A Social Anticipation. Translated by ARTHUR RANSOM. Crown 8vo, cloth extra, 6s.

Hesse=Wartegg (Chevalier Ernst von).—Tunis: The Land and the People. With 22 Illustrations. Crown 8vo, cloth extra, 3s. 6d.

Hill (Headon).—Zambra the Detective. Post 8vo, bds., 2s.; cl., 2s. 6d.

Hill (John), Works by.
Treason-Felony. Post 8vo, boards, 2s. | The Common Ancestor. Cr. 8vo, cloth, 3s. 6d.

Hindley (Charles), Works by.
Tavern Anecdotes and Sayings: Including Reminiscences connected with Coffee Houses, Clubs, &c. With Illustrations. Crown 8vo, cloth extra, 3s. 6d.
The Life and Adventures of a Cheap Jack. Crown 8vo, cloth extra, 3s. 6d.

Hodges (Sydney).—When Leaves were Green. 3 vols.,15s. net.

Hoey (Mrs. Cashel).—The Lover's Creed. Post 8vo, boards, 2s.

Hollingshead (John).—Niagara Spray. Crown 8vo, 1s.

Holmes (Gordon, M.D.)—The Science of Voice Production and Voice Preservation. Crown 8vo, 1s.; cloth, 1s. 6d.

Holmes (Oliver Wendell), Works by.
The Autocrat of the Breakfast-Table. Illustrated by J. GORDON THOMSON. Post 8vo, cloth limp, 2s. 6d.—Another Edition, post 8vo, cloth, 2s.
The Autocrat of the Breakfast-Table and The Professor at the Breakfast-Table. In One Vol. Post 8vo, half-bound, 2s.

Hood's (Thomas) Choice Works in Prose and Verse. With Life of the Author, Portrait, and 200 Illustrations. Crown 8vo, cloth extra, 7s. 6d.
Hood's Whims and Oddities. With 85 Illustrations. Post 8vo, half-bound, 2s.

Hood (Tom).—From Nowhere to the North Pole: A Noah's Arkæological Narrative. With 25 Illustrations by W. BRUNTON and E. C. BARNES. Cr. 8vo, cloth, 6s.

Hook's (Theodore) Choice Humorous Works; including his Ludicrous Adventures, Bons Mots, Puns, and Hoaxes. With Life of the Author, Portraits, Facsimiles, and Illustrations. Crown 8vo, cloth extra, 7s. 6d.

Hooper (Mrs. Geo.).—The House of Raby. Post 8vo, boards, 2s.

Hopkins (Tighe).—''Twixt Love and Duty.' Post 8vo, boards, 2s.

Horne (R. Hengist). — Orion: An Epic Poem. With Photograph Portrait by SUMMERS. Tenth Edition. Crown 8vo, cloth extra, 7s.

Hungerford (Mrs., Author of ' Molly Bawn '), Novels by.
Post 8vo, Illustrated boards, 2s. each; cloth limp, 2s. 6d. each.

A Maiden All Forlorn.	In Durance Vile.	A Mental Struggle.
Marvel.	A Modern Circe.	The Red-House Mystery.

The Three Graces. With 6 Illustrations. Crown 8vo, cloth extra, 3s. 6d.   [Shortly.
Lady Verner's Flight. Crown 8vo, cloth, 3s. 6d.; post 8vo, illustrated boards, 2s.
The Professor's Experiment. Three Vols., crown 8vo, 15s. net.
A Point of Conscience. Three Vols., crown 8vo, 15s. net.

Hunt's (Leigh) Essays: A Tale for a Chimney Corner, &c. Edited by EDMUND OLLIER. Post 8vo, half-bound, 2s.

Hunt (Mrs. Alfred), Novels by.
Crown 8vo, cloth extra, 3s. 6d. each; post 8vo, illustrated boards, 2s. each.

The Leaden Casket.	Self-Condemned.	That Other Person.

Thornicroft's Model. Post 8vo, boards, 2s. | Mrs. Juliet. Crown 8vo, cloth extra, 3s. 6d.

Hutchison (W. M.).—Hints on Colt-breaking. With 25 Illustrations. Crown 8vo, cloth extra, 3s. 6d.

Hydrophobia: An Account of M. PASTEUR'S System; The Technique of his Method, and Statistics. By RENAUD SUZOR, M.B. Crown 8vo, cloth extra, 6s.

Hyne (C. J. Cutcliffe).—Honour of Thieves. Cr. 8vo, cloth, 3s. 6d.

Idler (The): An Illustrated Magazine. Edited by J. K. JEROME. 1s.

Impressions (The) of Aureole. Crown 8vo, printed on blush-rose paper and handsomely bound, 6s.

Indoor Paupers. By ONE OF THEM. Crown 8vo, 1s. ; cloth, 1s. 6d.

Ingelow (Jean).—Fated to be Free. Post 8vo, illustrated bds., 2s.

Innkeeper's Handbook (The) and Licensed Victualler's Manual. By J. TREVOR-DAVIES. Crown 8vo, 1s. ; cloth, 1s. 6d.

Irish Wit and Humour, Songs of. Collected and Edited by A. PERCEVAL GRAVES. Post 8vo, cloth limp, 2s. 6d.

Irving (Sir Henry): A Record of over Twenty Years at the Lyceum. By PERCY FITZGERALD. With Portrait. Crown 8vo, 1s. ; cloth, 1s. 6d.

James (C. T. C.). — A Romance of the Queen's Hounds. Post 8vo, picture cover, 1s. ; cloth limp, 1s. 6d.

Jameson (William).—My Dead Self. Post 8vo, bds., 2s. ; cl., 2s. 6d.

Japp (Alex. H., LL.D.).—Dramatic Pictures, &c. Cr. 8vo, cloth, 5s.

Jay (Harriett), Novels by. Post 8vo, illustrated boards, 2s. each.
The Dark Colleen.	The Queen of Connaught.

Jefferies (Richard), Works by. Post 8vo, cloth limp, 2s. 6d. each.
Nature near London.	The Life of the Fields.	The Open Air.

*** Also the HAND-MADE PAPER EDITION, crown 8vo, buckram, gilt top, 6s. each.

　　The Eulogy of Richard Jefferies. By Sir WALTER BESANT. With a Photograph Portrait. Crown 8vo, cloth extra, 6s.

Jennings (Henry J.), Works by.
Curiosities of Criticism. Post 8vo, cloth limp, 2s. 6d.
Lord Tennyson: A Biographical Sketch. With Portrait. Post 8vo, 1s. ; cloth, 1s. 6d.

Jerome (Jerome K.), Books by.
Stageland. With 64 Illustrations by J. BERNARD PARTRIDGE. Fcap. 4to, picture cover, 1s.
John Ingerfield, &c. With 9 Illusts. by A. S. BOYD and JOHN GULICH. Fcap. 8vo, pic. cov. 1s. 6d.
The Prude's Progress: A Comedy by J. K. JEROME and EDEN PHILLPOTTS. Cr. 8vo, 1s. 6d.

Jerrold (Douglas).—The Barber's Chair; and The Hedgehog Letters. Post 8vo, printed on laid paper and half-bound, 2s.

Jerrold (Tom), Works by. Post 8vo, 1s. ea. ; cloth limp, 1s. 6d. ea.
The Garden that Paid the Rent.
Household Horticulture: A Gossip about Flowers. Illustrated.

Jesse (Edward).—Scenes and Occupations of a Country Life. Post 8vo, cloth limp, 2s.

Jones (William, F.S.A.), Works by. Cr. 8vo, cl. extra, 7s. 6d. ea.
Finger-Ring Lore: Historical, Legendary, and Anecdotal. With nearly 300 Illustrations. Second Edition, Revised and Enlarged.
Credulities, Past and Present. Including the Sea and Seamen, Miners, Talismans, Word and Letter Divination, Exorcising and Blessing of Animals, Birds, Eggs, Luck, &c. With Frontispiece.
Crowns and Coronations: A History of Regalia. With 100 Illustrations.

Jonson's (Ben) Works. With Notes Critical and Explanatory, and a Biographical Memoir by WILLIAM GIFFORD. Edited by Colonel CUNNINGHAM. Three Vols. crown 8vo, cloth extra, 6s. each.

Josephus, The Complete Works of. Translated by WHISTON. Containing 'The Antiquities of the Jews' and 'The Wars of the Jews.' With 52 Illustrations and Maps. Two Vols., demy 8vo, half-bound, 12s. 6d.

Kempt (Robert).—Pencil and Palette: Chapters on Art and Artists. Post 8vo, cloth limp, 2s. 6d.

Kershaw (Mark). — Colonial Facts and Fictions: Humorous Sketches. Post 8vo, illustrated boards, 2s. ; cloth, 2s. 6d.

Keyser (Arthur).—Cut by the Mess. Crown 8vo, 1s. ; cloth, 1s. 6d.

King (R. Ashe), Novels by. Cr. 8vo, cl., 3s. 6d. ea.; post 8vo, bds., 2s. ea.
A Drawn Game.	'The Wearing of the Green.'

Post 8vo, illustrated boards, 2s. each.
Passion's Slave.	Bell Barry.

Knight (William, M.R.C.S., and Edward, L.R.C.P.). — The
Patient's Vade Mecum : How to Get Most Benefit from Medical Advice. Cr. 8vo, 1s.; cl., 1s. 6d.

Knights (The) of the Lion : A Romance of the Thirteenth Century.
Edited, with an Introduction, by the MARQUESS OF LORNE, K.T. Crown 8vo, cloth extra, 6s.

Lamb's (Charles) Complete Works in Prose and Verse, including
'Poetry for Children' and 'Prince Dorus.' Edited, with Notes and Introduction, by R. H. SHEP-
HERD. With Two Portraits and Facsimile of the 'Essay on RoastPig.' Crown 8vo, half-bd., 7s. 6d.
The Essays of Elia. Post 8vo, printed on laid paper and half-bound, 2s.
Little Essays : Sketches and Characters by CHARLES LAMB, selected from his Letters by PERCY
FITZGERALD. Post 8vo, cloth limp, 2s. 6d.
The Dramatic Essays of Charles Lamb. With Introduction and Notes by BRANDER MAT-
THEWS, and Steel-plate Portrait. Fcap. 8vo, half-bound, 2s. 6d.

Landor (Walter Savage).—Citation and Examination of William
Shakspeare, &c., before Sir Thomas Lucy, touching Deer-stealing, 19th September, 1582. To which
is added, **A Conference of Master Edmund Spenser** with the Earl of Essex, touching the
State of Ireland, 1595. Fcap. 8vo, half-Roxburghe, 2s. 6d.

Lane (Edward William).—The Thousand and One Nights, com-
monly called in England **The Arabian Nights' Entertainments.** Translated from the Arabic,
with Notes. Illustrated with many hundred Engravings from Designs by HARVEY. Edited by EDWARD
STANLEY POOLE. With Preface by STANLEY LANE-POOLE. Three Vols., demy 8vo, cloth, 7s. 6d. ea.

Larwood (Jacob), Works by.
The Story of the London Parks. With Illustrations. Crown 8vo, cloth extra, 3s. 6d.
Anecdotes of the Clergy. Post 8vo, laid paper, half-bound, 2s.

Post 8vo, cloth limp, 2s. 6d. each.

Forensic Anecdotes.	**Theatrical Anecdotes.**

Lehmann (R. C.), Works by. Post 8vo, 1s. each ; cloth, 1s. 6d. each.
Harry Fludyer at Cambridge.
Conversational Hints for Young Shooters : A Guide to Polite Talk.

Leigh (Henry S.), Works by.
Carols of Cockayne. Printed on hand-made paper, bound in buckram, 5s.
Jeux d'Esprit. Edited by HENRY S. LEIGH. Post 8vo, cloth limp, 2s. 6d.

Lepelletier (Edmond). — Madame Sans-Gène. Translated from
the French by JOHN DE VILLIERS. Crown 8vo, cloth extra, 3s. 6d.

Leys (John).—The Lindsays : A Romance. Post 8vo, illust. bds., 2s.

Lindsay (Harry).—Rhoda Roberts : A Welsh Mining Story. Crown
8vo, cloth, 3s. 6d.

Linton (E. Lynn), Works by.

Crown 8vo, cloth extra, 3s. 6d. each ; post 8vo, illustrated boards, 2s. each.

Patricia Kemball. | **Ione.**	**Under which Lord ?** With 12 Illustrations.
The Atonement of Leam Dundas.	**'My Love!'** | **Sowing the Wind.**
The World Well Lost. With 12 Illusts.	**Paston Carew,** Millionaire and Miser
The One Too Many.	

Post 8vo, illustrated boards, 2s. each.

The Rebel of the Family.	**With a Silken Thread.**

Post 8vo, cloth limp, 2s. 6d. each.

Witch Stories.	**Ourselves :** Essays on Women.
Freeshooting : Extracts from the Works of Mrs. LYNN LINTON.	

Lucy (Henry W.).—Gideon Fleyce : A Novel. Crown 8vo, cloth
extra, 3s. 6d. ; post 8vo, illustrated boards, 2s.

Macalpine (Avery), Novels by.
Teresa Itasca. Crown 8vo, cloth extra, 1s.
Broken Wings. With Six Illustrations by W. J. HENNESSY. Crown 8vo, cloth extra, 6s.

MacColl (Hugh), Novels by.
Mr. Stranger's Sealed Packet. Post 8vo, illustrated boards, 2s.
Ednor Whitlock. Crown 8vo, cloth extra, 6s.

Macdonell (Agnes).—Quaker Cousins. Post 8vo, boards, 2s.

MacGregor (Robert).—Pastimes and Players : Notes on Popular
Games. Post 8vo, cloth limp, 2s. 6d.

Mackay (Charles, LL.D.). — Interludes and Undertones; or,
Music at Twilight. Crown 8vo, cloth extra, 6s.

McCarthy (Justin, M.P.), Works by.

A History of Our Own Times, from the Accession of Queen Victoria to the General Election of 1880. Four Vols., demy 8vo, cloth extra, 12*s.* each.—Also a POPULAR EDITION, in Four Vols., crown 8vo, cloth extra, 6*s.* each.—And the JUBILEE EDITION, with an Appendix of Events to the end of 1886, in Two Vols., large crown 8vo, cloth extra, 7*s.* 6*d.* each.

A Short History of Our Own Times. One Vol., crown 8vo, cloth extra, 6*s.*—Also a CHEAP POPULAR EDITION, post 8vo, cloth limp, 2*s.* 6*d.*

A History of the Four Georges. Four Vols., demy 8vo, cl. ex., 12*s.* each. [Vols. I. & II. *ready.*

Crown 8vo, cloth extra, 3*s.* 6*d.* each ; post 8vo, illustrated boards, 2*s.* each ; cloth limp, 2*s.* 6*d.* each.

The Waterdale Neighbours.	**Donna Quixote.** With 12 Illustrations.
My Enemy's Daughter.	**The Comet of a Season.**
A Fair Saxon.	**Maid of Athens.** With 12 Illustrations.
Linley Rochford.	**Camiola:** A Girl with a Fortune.
Dear Lady Disdain.	**The Dictator.**
Miss Misanthrope. With 12 Illustrations.	**Red Diamonds.**

' The Right Honourable.' By JUSTIN MCCARTHY, M.P., and Mrs. CAMPBELL PRAED. Crown 8vo, cloth extra, 6*s.*

McCarthy (Justin Huntly), Works by.

The French Revolution. (Constituent Assembly, 1789–91). Four Vols., demy 8vo, cloth extra, 12*s.* each.   Vols. I. & II. *ready;* Vols. III. & IV. *in the press.*

An Outline of the History of Ireland. Crown 8vo, 1*s.* ; cloth, 1*s.* 6*d.*

Ireland Since the Union: Sketches of Irish History, 1798–1886. Crown 8vo, cloth, 6*s.*

Hafiz in London: Poems. Small 8vo, gold cloth, 3*s.* 6*d.*

Our Sensation Novel. Crown 8vo, picture cover, 1*s.* ; cloth limp, 1*s.* 6*d.*
Doom: An Atlantic Episode. Crown 8vo, picture cover, 1*s.*
Dolly: A Sketch. Crown 8vo, picture cover, 1*s.* ; cloth limp, 1*s.* 6*d.*
Lily Lass: A Romance. Crown 8vo, picture cover, 1*s.* ; cloth limp, 1*s.* 6*d.*
The Thousand and One Days. With Two Photogravures. Two Vols., crown 8vo, half-bd., 12*s.*
A London Legend. Crown 8vo, cloth, 3*s.* 6*d.*

MacDonald (George, LL.D.), Books by.

Works of Fancy and Imagination. Ten Vols., 16mo, cloth, gilt edges, in cloth case, 21*s.* ; or the Volumes may be had separately, in Grolier cloth, at 2*s.* 6*d.* each.

Vol.   I. WITHIN AND WITHOUT.—THE HIDDEN LIFE.
  ,,   II. THE DISCIPLE.—THE GOSPEL WOMEN.—BOOK OF SONNETS.—ORGAN SONGS.
  ,, III. VIOLIN SONGS.—SONGS OF THE DAYS AND NIGHTS.—A BOOK OF DREAMS.—ROADSIDE POEMS.—POEMS FOR CHILDREN.
  ,,   IV. PARABLES.—BALLADS.—SCOTCH SONGS.
  ,, V. & VI. PHANTASTES: A Faerie Romance. | Vol. VII. THE PORTENT.
  ,, VIII. THE LIGHT PRINCESS.—THE GIANT'S HEART.—SHADOWS.
  ,,   IX. CROSS PURPOSES.—THE GOLDEN KEY.—THE CARASOYN.—LITTLE DAYLIGHT.
  ,,   X. THE CRUEL PAINTER.—THE WOW O' RIVVEN.—THE CASTLE.—THE BROKEN SWORDS. —THE GRAY WOLF.—UNCLE CORNELIUS.

Poetical Works of George MacDonald. Collected and Arranged by the Author. Two Vols., crown 8vo, buckram, 12*s.*

A Threefold Cord. Edited by GEORGE MACDONALD. Post 8vo, cloth, 5*s.*

Phantastes: A Faerie Romance. With 25 Illustrations by J. BELL. Crown 8vo, cloth extra, 3*s.* 6*d.*
Heather and Snow: A Novel. Crown 8vo, cloth extra, 3*s.* 6*d.* ; post 8vo, illustrated boards, 2*s.*
Lilith: A Romance. SECOND EDITION. Crown 8vo, cloth extra, 6*s.*

Maclise Portrait Gallery (The) of Illustrious Literary Characters: 85 Portraits by DANIEL MACLISE; with Memoirs—Biographical, Critical, Bibliographical, and Anecdotal—illustrative of the Literature of the former half of the Present Century, by WILLIAM BATES, B.A. Crown 8vo, cloth extra, 7*s.* 6*d.*

Macquoid (Mrs.), Works by. Square 8vo, cloth extra, 6*s.* each.

In the Ardennes. With 50 Illustrations by THOMAS R. MACQUOID.
Pictures and Legends from Normandy and Brittany. 34 Illusts. by T. R. MACQUOID.
Through Normandy. With 92 Illustrations by T. R. MACQUOID, and a Map.
Through Brittany. With 35 Illustrations by T. R. MACQUOID, and a Map.
About Yorkshire. With 67 Illustrations by T. R. MACQUOID.

Post 8vo, illustrated boards, 2*s.* each.

The Evil Eye, and other Stories.	**Lost Rose,** and other Stories.

Magician's Own Book, The: Performances with Eggs, Hats, &c. Edited by W. H. CREMER. With 200 Illustrations. Crown 8vo, cloth extra, 4*s.* 6*d.*

Magic Lantern, The, and its Management: Including full Practical Directions. By T. C. HEPWORTH. With 10 Illustrations. Crown 8vo, 1*s.* ; cloth, 1*s.* 6*d.*

Magna Charta: An Exact Facsimile of the Original in the British Museum, 3 feet by 2 feet, with Arms and Seals emblazoned in Gold and Colours, 5*s.*

Mallory (Sir Thomas). — Mort d'Arthur: The Stories of King Arthur and of the Knights of the Round Table. (A Selection.) Edited by B. MONTGOMERIE RANKING. Post 8vo, cloth limp, 2*s.*

Mallock (W. H.), Works by.
The New Republic. Post 8vo, picture cover, 2s. ; cloth limp, 2s. 6d.
The New Paul & Virginia: Positivism on an Island. Post 8vo, cloth, 2s. 6d.
A Romance of the Nineteenth Century. Crown 8vo, cloth 6s. ; pos 8vo, illust. boards, 2s.

Poems. Small 4to, parchment, 8s.
Is Life Worth Living? Crown 8vo, cloth extra, 6s.

Mark Twain, Books by. Crown 8vo, cloth extra, 7s. 6d. each.
The Choice Works of Mark Twain. Revised and Corrected throughout by the Author. With Life, Portrait, and numerous Illustrations.
Roughing It; and The Innocents at Home. With 200 Illustrations by F. A. FRASER.
Mark Twain's Library of Humour. With 197 Illustrations.

Crown 8vo, cloth extra (Illustrated), 7s. 6d. each ; post 8vo, Illustrated boards, 2s. each.
The Innocents Abroad; or, The New Pilgrim's Progress. With 234 Illustrations. (The Two Shilling Edition is entitled Mark Twain's Pleasure Trip.)
The Gilded Age. By MARK TWAIN and C. D. WARNER. With 212 Illustrations.
The Adventures of Tom Sawyer. With 111 Illustrations.
A Tramp Abroad. With 314 Illustrations.
The Prince and the Pauper. With 190 Illustrations.
Life on the Mississippi. With 300 Illustrations.
The Adventures of Huckleberry Finn. With 174 Illustrations by E. W. KEMBLE.
A Yankee at the Court of King Arthur. With 220 Illustrations by DAN BEARD.

Crown 8vo, cloth extra, 3s. 6d. each.
The American Claimant. With 81 Illustrations by HAL HURST and others.
Tom Sawyer Abroad. With 26 Illustrations by DAN. BEARD.
Pudd'nhead Wilson. With Portrait and Six Illlustrations by LOUIS LOEB.
Tom Sawyer, Detective, &c. With numerous Illustrations.   *[Shortly.*

The £1,000,000 Bank-Note. Crown 8vo, cloth, 3s. 6d. ; post 8vo, picture boards 2s.

Post 8vo, illustrated boards, 2s. each.
The Stolen White Elephant. | Mark Twain's Sketches.

Marks (H. S., R.A.), Pen and Pencil Sketches by. With Four
Photogravures and 126 Illustrations. Two Vols. demy 8vo, cloth, 32s.

Marlowe's Works. Including his Translations. Edited, with Notes
and Introductions, by Colonel CUNNINGHAM. Crown 8vo, cloth extra, 6s.

Marryat (Florence), Novels by. Post 8vo, illust. boards, 2s. each.
A Harvest of Wild Oats. | Fighting the Air.
Open! Sesame! | Written in Fire.

Massinger's Plays. From the Text of WILLIAM GIFFORD. Edited
by Col. CUNNINGHAM. Crown 8vo, cloth extra, 6s.

Masterman (J.).—Half-a-Dozen Daughters. Post 8vo, boards, 2s.

Matthews (Brander).—A Secret of the Sea, &c. Post 8vo, illustrated boards, 2s. ; cloth limp, 2s. 6d.

Mayhew (Henry).—London Characters, and the Humorous Side
of London Life. With numerous Illustrations. Crown 8vo, cloth, 3s. 6d.

Meade (L. T.), Novels by.
A Soldier of Fortune. Crown 8vo, cloth, 3s. 6d. ; post 8vo, illustrated boards, 2s.
In an Iron Grip. Crown 8vo. cloth, 3s. 6d.
The Voice of the Charmer. Three Vols., 15s. net.

Merrick (Leonard).—The Man who was Good. Post 8vo, illustrated boards, 2s.

Mexican Mustang (On a), through Texas to the Rio Grande. By
A. E. SWEET and J. ARMOY KNOX. With 265 Illustrations. Crown 8vo, cloth extra, 7s. 6d.

Middlemass (Jean), Novels by. Post 8vo, illust. boards, 2s. each.
Touch and Go. | Mr. Dorillion.

Miller (Mrs. F. Fenwick).—Physiology for the Young; or, The
House of Life. With numerous Illustrations. Post 8vo, cloth limp, 2s. 6d.

Milton (J. L.), Works by. Post 8vo, 1s. each ; cloth, 1s. 6d. each.
The Hygiene of the Skin. With Directions for Diet, Soaps, Baths, Wines, &c.
The Bath in Diseases of the Skin.
The Laws of Life, and their Relation to Diseases of the Skin.

Minto (Wm.).—Was She Good or Bad? Cr. 8vo, 1s. ; cloth, 1s. 6d.

Mitford (Bertram), Novels by. Crown 8vo, cloth extra, 3s. 6d. each.
The Gun-Runner: A Romance of Zululand. With a Frontispiece by STANLEY L. WOOD.
The Luck of Gerard Ridgeley. With a Frontispiece by STANLEY L. WOOD.
The King's Assegai. With Six full-page Illustrations by STANLEY L. WOOD.
Renshaw Fanning's Quest. With a Frontispiece by STANLEY L. WOOD.

Molesworth (Mrs.), Novels by.
Hathercourt Rectory. Post 8vo, illustrated boards, 2s.
That Girl in Black. Crown 8vo, cloth, 1s. 6d.

Moncrieff (W. D. Scott-).—The Abdication: An Historical Drama.
With Seven Etchings by JOHN PETTIE, W. Q. ORCHARDSON, J. MACWHIRTER, COLIN HUNTER,
R. MACBETH and TOM GRAHAM. Imperial 4to, buckram. 21s.

Moore (Thomas), Works by.
The Epicurean; and Alciphron. Post 8vo, half-bound, 2s.
Prose and Verse; including Suppressed Passages from the MEMOIRS OF LORD BYRON. Edited
  by R. H. SHEPHERD. With Portrait. Crown 8vo, cloth extra, 7s. 6d.

Muddock (J. E.) Stories by.
Stories Weird and Wonderful. Post 8vo, illustrated boards, 2s.; cloth, 2s. 6d.
The Dead Man's Secret. Frontispiece by F. BARNARD. Cr. 8vo, cloth, 5s.; post 8vo, boards, 2s.
From the Bosom of the Deep. Post 8vo, illustrated boards, 2s.
Maid Marian and Robin Hood. With 12 Illusts. by STANLEY WOOD. Cr. 8vo, cloth extra, 3s. 6d.
Basile the Jester. With Frontispiece by STANLEY WOOD. Crown 8vo, cloth, 3s. 6d.   [Shortly.

Murray (D. Christie), Novels by.
Crown 8vo, cloth extra, 3s. 6d. each; post 8vo, illustrated boards, 2s. each.

A Life's Atonement.	A Model Father.	First Person Singular.
Joseph's Coat. 12 Illusts.	Old Blazer's Hero.	Bob Martin's Little Girl.
Coals of Fire. 3 Illusts.	Cynic Fortune. Frontisp.	Time's Revenges.
Val Strange.	By the Gate of the Sea.	A Wasted Crime.
Hearts.	A Bit of Human Nature.	In Direst Peril.
The Way of the World.		

Mount Despair, &c. With Frontispiece by GRENVILLE MANTON. Crown 8vo, cloth, 3s. 6d.
The Making of a Novelist: An Experiment in Autobiography. With a Collotype Portrait and
  Vignette. Crown 8vo, art linen, 6s.

Murray (D. Christie) and Henry Herman, Novels by.
Crown 8vo, cloth extra, 3s. 6d. each; post 8vo, illustrated boards, 2s. each.
One Traveller Returns. | The Bishops' Bible.
Paul Jones's Alias, &c. With Illustrations by A. FORESTIER and G. NICOLET.

Murray (Henry), Novels by.
Post 8vo, illustrated boards, 2s. each; cloth, 2s. 6d. each.
A Game of Bluff. | A Song of Sixpence.

Newbolt (Henry).—Taken from the Enemy. Fcp. 8vo, cloth, 1s. 6d.

Nisbet (Hume), Books by.
'Bail Up.' Crown 8vo, cloth extra, 3s. 6d.; post 8vo, illustrated boards, 2s.
Dr. Bernard St. Vincent. Post 8vo, illustrated boards, 2s.

Lessons in Art. With 21 Illustrations. Crown 8vo, cloth extra, 2s. 6d.
Where Art Begins. With 27 Illustrations. Square 8vo, cloth extra, 7s. 6d.

Norris (W. E.), Novels by. Crown 8vo, cloth, 3s. 6d. each.
Saint Ann's. | Billy Bellew. With Frontispiece.   [Shortly.

O'Hanlon (Alice), Novels by. Post 8vo, illustrated boards, 2s. each.
The Unforeseen. | Chance? or Fate?

Ouida, Novels by. Cr. 8vo, cl., 3s. 6d. ea.; post 8vo, illust. bds., 2s. ea.

Held in Bondage.	Folle-Farine.	Moths. | Pipistrello.
Tricotrin.	A Dog of Flanders.	In Maremma. | Wanda.
Strathmore.	Pascarel. | Signa.	Bimbi. | Syrlin.
Chandos.	Two Wooden Shoes.	Frescoes. | Othmar.
Cecil Castlemaine's Gage	In a Winter City.	Princess Napraxine.
Under Two Flags.	Ariadne. | Friendship.	Guilderoy. | Ruffino.
Puck. | Idalia.	A Village Commune.	Two Offenders.

Square 8vo, cloth extra, 5s. each.
Bimbi. With Nine Illustrations by EDMUND H. GARRETT.
A Dog of Flanders, &c. With Six Illustrations by EDMUND H. GARRETT.

Santa Barbara, &c. Square 8vo, cloth, 6s.; crown 8vo, cloth, 3s. 6d.; post 8vo, illustrated boards, 2s.
Under Two Flags. POPULAR EDITION. Medium 8vo, 6d.; cloth, 1s.   [May.

Wisdom, Wit, and Pathos, selected from the Works of OUIDA by F. SYDNEY MORRIS. Post
  8vo, cloth extra, 5s.—CHEAP EDITION, illustrated boards, 2s.

Ohnet (Georges), Novels by. Post 8vo, illustrated boards, 2s. each.
Doctor Rameau. | A Last Love.

A Weird Gift. Crown 8vo, cloth, 3s. 6d.; post 8vo, picture boards, 2s.

Oliphant (Mrs.), Novels by. Post 8vo, illustrated boards, 2s. each.
The Primrose Path. | Whiteladies.
The Greatest Heiress in England.

O'Reilly (Mrs.).—Phœbe's Fortunes. Post 8vo, illust. boards, 2s.

Page (H. A.), Works by.
Thoreau: His Life and Aims. With Portrait. Post 8vo, cloth limp, 2s. 6d.
Animal Anecdotes. Arranged on a New Principle. Crown 8vo, cloth extra, 5s.

Pandurang Hari; or, Memoirs of a Hindoo. With Preface by Sir
BARTLE FRERE. Crown 8vo, cloth, 3s. 6d.; post 8vo, illustrated boards, 2s.

Pascal's Provincial Letters. A New Translation, with Historical
Introduction and Notes by T. M'CRIE, D.D. Post 8vo, cloth limp, 2s.

Paul (Margaret A.).—Gentle and Simple. Crown 8vo, cloth, with
Frontispiece by HELEN PATERSON, 3s. 6d.; post 8vo, illustrated boards, 2s.

Payn (James), Novels by.
Crown 8vo, cloth extra, 3s. 6d. each; post 8vo, illustrated boards, 2s. each.

Lost Sir Massingberd.	Holiday Tasks.
Walter's Word.	The Canon's Ward. With Portrait.
Less Black than We're Painted.	The Talk of the Town. With 12 Illusts.
By Proxy.	For Cash Only.	Glow-Worm Tales.
High Spirits.	The Mystery of Mirbridge.
Under One Roof.	The Word and the Will.
A Confidential Agent. With 12 Illusts.	The Burnt Million.
A Grape from a Thorn. With 12 Illusts.	Sunny Stories.	A Trying Patient.

Post 8vo, illustrated boards, 2s. each.

Humorous Stories.	From Exile.	Found Dead.
The Foster Brothers.	Gwendoline's Harvest.
The Family Scapegrace.	A Marine Residence.
Married Beneath Him.	Mirk Abbey.
Bentinck's Tutor.	Some Private Views.
A Perfect Treasure.	Not Wooed, But Won.
A County Family.	Two Hundred Pounds Reward.
Like Father, Like Son.	The Best of Husbands.
A Woman's Vengeance.	Halves.
Carlyon's Year.	Cecil's Tryst.	Fallen Fortunes.
Murphy's Master.	What He Cost Her.
At Her Mercy.	Kit: A Memory.
The Clyffards of Clyffe.	A Prince of the Blood.

In Peril and Privation. With 17 Illustrations. Crown 8vo, cloth, 3s. 6d.
Notes from the ' News.' Crown 8vo, portrait cover, 1s.; cloth, 1s. 6d.

Pennell (H. Cholmondeley), Works by. Post 8vo, cloth, 2s. 6d. ea.
Puck on Pegasus. With Illustrations.
Pegasus Re-Saddled. With Ten full-page Illustrations by G. DU MAURIER.
The Muses of Mayfair: Vers de Société. Selected by H. C. PENNELL.

Phelps (E. Stuart), Works by. Post 8vo, 1s. ea.; cloth, 1s. 6d. ea.
Beyond the Gates. | An Old Maid's Paradise. | Burglars in Paradise.

Jack the Fisherman. Illustrated by C. W. REED. Crown 8vo, 1s.; cloth, 1s. 6d.

Phil May's Sketch-Book. Containing 50 full-page Drawings. Imp.
4to, art canvas, gilt top, 10s. 6d.

Pirkis (C. L.), Novels by.
Trooping with Crows. Fcap. 8vo, picture cover, 1s.
Lady Lovelace. Post 8vo, illustrated boards, 2s.

Planche (J. R.), Works by.
The Pursuivant of Arms. With Six Plates and 209 Illustrations. Crown 8vo, cloth, 7s. 6d.
Songs and Poems, 1819-1879. With Introduction by Mrs. MACKARNESS. Crown 8vo, cloth, 6s.

Plutarch's Lives of Illustrious Men. With Notes and a Life of
Plutarch by JOHN and WM. LANGHORNE, and Portraits. Two Vols., demy 8vo, half-bound 10s. 6d.

Poe's (Edgar Allan) Choice Works in Prose and Poetry. With Introduction by CHARLES BAUDELAIRE, Portrait and Facsimiles. Crown 8vo, cloth, 7s. 6d.

Pope's Poetical Works. Post 8vo, cloth limp, 2s.

Praed (Mrs. Campbell), Novels by. Post 8vo, illust. bds., 2s. each.

The Romance of a Station. | The Soul of Countess Adrian.

Crown 8vo, cloth, 3s. 6d. each; post 8vo, boards, 2s. each.

Outlaw and Lawmaker. | Christina Chard. With Frontispiece by W. PAGET.

Mrs. Tregaskiss. Three Vols., crown 8vo, 15s. net.

Price (E. C.), Novels by.

Crown 8vo, cloth extra, 3s. 6d. each; post 8vo, illustrated boards, 2s. each.

Valentina. | The Foreigners. | Mrs. Lancaster's Rival.

Gerald. Post 8vo, illustrated boards, 2s.

Princess Olga.—Radna: A Novel. Crown 8vo, cloth extra, 6s.

Proctor (Richard A., B.A.), Works by.

Flowers of the Sky. With 55 Illustrations. Small crown 8vo, cloth extra, 3s. 6d.
Easy Star Lessons. With Star Maps for every Night in the Year. Crown 8vo, cloth, 6s.
Familiar Science Studies. Crown 8vo, cloth extra, 6s.
Saturn and its System. With 13 Steel Plates. Demy 8vo, cloth extra, 10s. 6d.
Mysteries of Time and Space. With numerous Illustrations. Crown 8vo, cloth extra, 6s.
The Universe of Suns, &c. With numerous Illustrations. Crown 8vo, cloth extra, 6s.
Wages and Wants of Science Workers. Crown 8vo, 1s. 6d.

Pryce (Richard).—Miss Maxwell's Affections. Crown 8vo, cloth, with Frontispiece by HAL LUDLOW, 3s. 6d.; post 8vo, illustrated boards, 2s.

Rambosson (J.).—Popular Astronomy. Translated by C. B. PITMAN. With Coloured Frontispiece and numerous Illustrations. Crown 8vo, cloth extra, 7s. 6d.

Randolph (Lieut.-Col. George, U.S.A.).—Aunt Abigail Dykes: A Novel. Crown 8vo, cloth extra, 7s. 6d.

Reade's (Charles) Novels.

Crown 8vo, cloth extra, mostly Illustrated, 3s. 6d. each; post 8vo, illustrated boards, 2s. each.

Peg Woffington. | Christie Johnstone.
'It is Never Too Late to Mend.'
The Course of True Love Never Did Run
  Smooth.
The Autobiography of a Thief; Jack of
  all Trades; and James Lambert.
Love Me Little, Love Me Long.
The Double Marriage.
The Cloister and the Hearth.
Hard Cash | Griffith Gaunt.
Foul Play. | Put Yourself in His Place.
A Terrible Temptation.
A Simpleton. | The Wandering Heir.
A Woman-Hater.
Singleheart and Doubleface.
Good Stories of Men and other Animals.
The Jilt, and other Stories.
A Perilous Secret. | Readiana.

A New Collected LIBRARY EDITION, complete in Seventeen Volumes, set in new long primer type, printed on laid paper, and elegantly bound in cloth, price 3s. 6d. each, is now in course of publication. The volumes will appear in the following order:—

1. Peg Woffington; and Christie Johnstone.
2. Hard Cash.
3. The Cloister and the Hearth. With a Preface by Sir WALTER BESANT.
4. 'It is Never too Late to Mend.'
5. The Course of True Love Never Did Run Smooth; and Singleheart and Doubleface.
6. The Autobiography of a Thief; Jack of all Trades; A Hero and a Martyr; and The Wandering Heir.
7. Love Me Little, Love me Long. [Mar.
8. The Double Marriage. [April.
9. Griffith Gaunt. [May.
10. Foul Play. [June.
11. Put Yourself in His Place. [July.
12. A Terrible Temptation. [August.
13. A Simpleton. [Sept.
14. A Woman-Hater. [Oct.
15. The Jilt, and other Stories; and Good Stories of Men & other Animals. [Nov.
16. A Perilous Secret. [Dec.
17. Readiana; & Bible Characters. [Jan. '97

POPULAR EDITIONS, medium 8vo, 6d. each: cloth, 1s. each.

'It is Never Too Late to Mend.' | The Cloister and the Hearth.
Peg Woffington; and Christie Johnstone.

Christie Johnstone. With Frontispiece. Choicely printed in Elzevir style. Fcap. 8vo, half-Roxb. 2s. 6d.
Peg Woffington. Choicely printed in Elzevir style. Fcap. 8vo, half-Roxburghe, 2s. 6d.
The Cloister and the Hearth. In Four Vols., post 8vo, with an Introduction by Sir WALTER BESANT, and a Frontispiece to each Vol., 14s. the set; and the ILLUSTRATED LIBRARY EDITION, with Illustrations on every page. Two Vols., crown 8vo, cloth gilt, 42s. net.
Bible Characters. Fcap. 8vo, leatherette, 1s.

Selections from the Works of Charles Reade. With an Introduction by Mrs. ALEX. IRELAND. Crown 8vo, buckram, with Portrait, 6s.; CHEAP EDITION, post 8vo, cloth limp, 2s. 6d.

Riddell (Mrs. J. H.), Novels by.

Weird Stories. Crown 8vo, cloth extra, 3s. 6d.; post 8vo, illustrated boards, 2s.

Post 8vo, illustrated boards, 2s. each.

The Uninhabited House.
The Prince of Wales's Garden Party.
The Mystery in Palace Gardens.
Fairy Water.
Her Mother's Darling.
The Nun's Curse. | Idle Tales.

Rimmer (Alfred), Works by. Square 8vo, cloth gilt, 7s. 6d. each.
Our Old Country Towns. With 55 Illustrations by the Author.
Rambles Round Eton and Harrow. With 50 Illustrations by the Author.
About England with Dickens. With 58 Illustrations by C. A. VANDERHOOF and A. RIMMER.

Rives (Amelie).—Barbara Dering. Crown 8vo, cloth extra, 3s. 6d.;
post 8vo, illustrated boards, 2s.

Robinson Crusoe. By DANIEL DEFOE. With 37 Illustrations by
GEORGE CRUIKSHANK. Post 8vo, half-cloth, 2s.; cloth extra, gilt edges, 2s. 6d.

Robinson (F. W.), Novels by.
Women are Strange. Post 8vo, illustrated boards, 2s.
The Hands of Justice. Crown 8vo, cloth extra, 3s. 6d.; post 8vo, illustrated boards, 2s.

The Woman in the Dark. Two Vols., 10s. net.

Robinson (Phil), Works by. Crown 8vo, cloth extra, 6s. each.
The Poets' Birds. | The Poets' Beasts.
The Poets and Nature: Reptiles, Fishes, and Insects.

Rochefoucauld's Maxims and Moral Reflections. With Notes
and an Introductory Essay by SAINTE-BEUVE. Post 8vo, cloth limp, 2s.

Roll of Battle Abbey, The: A List of the Principal Warriors who
came from Normandy with William the Conqueror, 1066. Printed in Gold and Colours, 5s.

Rosengarten (A.).—A Handbook of Architectural Styles. Translated by W. COLLETT-SANDARS. With 639 Illustrations. Crown 8vo, cloth extra, 7s. 6d.

Rowley (Hon. Hugh), Works by. Post 8vo, cloth, 2s. 6d. each.
Puniana: Riddles and Jokes. With numerous Illustrations.
More Puniana. Profusely Illustrated.

Runciman (James), Stories by. Post 8vo, bds., 2s. ea.; cl., 2s. 6d. ea.
Skippers and Shellbacks. | Grace Balmaign's Sweetheart.
Schools and Scholars.

Russell (Dora), Novels by. Crown 8vo, cloth, 3s. 6d. each.
A Country Sweetheart. | The Drift of Fate.   [Shortly.

Russell (W. Clark), Books and Novels by.
Crown 8vo, cloth extra, 6s. each; post 8vo, illustrated boards, 2s. each; cloth limp, 2s. 6d. each.
Round the Galley-Fire. | A Book for the Hammock.
In the Middle Watch. | The Mystery of the 'Ocean Star.'
A Voyage to the Cape. | The Romance of Jenny Harlowe.

Crown 8vo, cloth extra, 3s. 6d. each; post 8vo, illustrated boards, 2s. each; cloth limp, 2s. 6d. each.
An Ocean Tragedy. | My Shipmate Louise. | Alone on a Wide Wide Sea.

Crown 8vo, cloth, 3s. 6d. each.
Is He the Man? | The Phantom Death, &c. With Frontispiece.
The Good Ship 'Mohock.' | The Convict Ship.   [Shortly.

On the Fo'k'sle Head. Post 8vo, illustrated boards, 2s.; cloth limp, 2s. 6d.
Heart of Oak. Three Vols., crown 8vo, 15s. net.
The Tale of the Ten. Three Vols., crown 8vo, 15s. net.   [Shortly.

Saint Aubyn (Alan), Novels by.
Crown 8vo, cloth extra, 3s. 6d. each; post 8vo, illustrated boards, 2s. each.
A Fellow of Trinity. With a Note by OLIVER WENDELL HOLMES and a Frontispiece.
The Junior Dean. | The Master of St. Benedict's. | To His Own Master.
Orchard Damerel.

Fcap. 8vo, cloth boards, 1s. 6d. each.
The Old Maid's Sweetheart. | Modest Little Sara.

Crown 8vo, cloth extra, 3s. 6d. each.
In the Face of the World. | The Tremlett Diamonds.   [Shortly.

Sala (George A.).—Gaslight and Daylight. Post 8vo, boards, 2s.

Sanson. — Seven Generations of Executioners: Memoirs of the
Sanson Family (1688 to 1847). Crown 8vo, cloth extra, 3s. 6d.

Saunders (John), Novels by.
Crown 8vo, cloth extra, 3s. 6d. each; post 8vo, illustrated boards, 2s. each.
Guy Waterman. | The Lion in the Path. | The Two Dreamers.

Bound to the Wheel. Crown 8vo, cloth extra, 3s. 6d.

Saunders (Katharine), Novels by.

Crown 8vo, cloth extra, 3s. 6d. each; post 8vo, illustrated boards, 2s. each.

Margaret and Elizabeth. | Heart Salvage.
The High Mills. | Sebastian.

Joan Merryweather. Post 8vo, illustrated boards, 2s.
Gideon's Rock. Crown 8vo, cloth extra, 3s. 6d.

Scotland Yard, Past and Present: Experiences of Thirty-seven Years.

By Ex-Chief-Inspector CAVANAGH. Post 8vo, illustrated boards, 2s.; cloth, 2s. 6d.

Secret Out, The: One Thousand Tricks with Cards; with Entertaining Experiments in Drawing-room or 'White' Magic. By W. H. CREMER. With 300 Illustrations. Crown 8vo, cloth extra, 4s. 6d.

Seguin (L. G.), Works by.

The Country of the Passion Play (Oberammergau) and the Highlands of Bavaria. With Map and 37 Illustrations. Crown 8vo, cloth extra, 3s. 6d.
Walks in Algiers. With Two Maps and 16 Illustrations. Crown 8vo, cloth extra, 6s.

Senior (Wm.).—By Stream and Sea. Post 8vo, cloth, 2s. 6d.

Sergeant (Adeline).—Dr. Endicott's Experiment. Crown 8vo, buckram, 3s. 6d.

Shakespeare for Children: Lamb's Tales from Shakespeare.

With Illustrations, coloured and plain, by J. MOYR SMITH. Crown 4to, cloth gilt, 3s. 6d.

Sharp (William).—Children of To-morrow. Crown 8vo, cloth, 6s.

Shelley's (Percy Bysshe) Complete Works in Verse and Prose.

Edited, Prefaced, and Annotated by R. HERNE SHEPHERD. Five Vols., crown 8vo, cloth, 3s. 6d. each.
Poetical Works, in Three Vols.:
Vol. I. Introduction by the Editor; Posthumous Fragments of Margaret Nicholson; Shelley's Correspondence with Stockdale; The Wandering Jew; Queen Mab, with the Notes; Alastor, and other Poems; Rosalind and Helen; Prometheus Unbound; Adonais, &c.
  II. Laon and Cythna; The Cenci; Julian and Maddalo; Swellfoot the Tyrant; The Witch of Atlas; Epipsychidion; Hellas.
  III. Posthumous Poems; The Masque of Anarchy; and other Pieces.
Prose Works, in Two Vols.:
Vol. I. The Two Romances of Zastrozzi and St. Irvyne; the Dublin and Marlow Pamphlets; A Refutation of Deism; Letters to Leigh Hunt, and some Minor Writings and Fragments.
  II. The Essays; Letters from Abroad; Translations and Fragments, edited by Mrs. SHELLEY. With a Biography of Shelley, and an Index of the Prose Works.
*** Also a few copies of a LARGE-PAPER EDITION, 5 vols., cloth, £2 12s. 6d.

Sherard (R. H.).—Rogues: A Novel. Crown 8vo, 1s.; cloth, 1s. 6d.

Sheridan (General P. H.), Personal Memoirs of. With Portraits,

Maps, and Facsimiles. Two Vols., demy 8vo, cloth, 24s.

Sheridan's (Richard Brinsley) Complete Works, with Life and

Anecdotes. Including his Dramatic Writings, his Works in Prose and Poetry, Translations, Speeches, and Jokes. With 10 Illustrations. Crown 8vo, half-bound, 7s. 6d.
The Rivals, The School for Scandal, and other Plays. Post 8vo, half-bound, 2s.
Sheridan's Comedies: The Rivals and The School for Scandal. Edited, with an Introduction and Notes to each Play, and a Biographical Sketch, by BRANDER MATTHEWS. With Illustrations. Demy 8vo, half-parchment, 12s. 6d.

Sidney's (Sir Philip) Complete Poetical Works, including all

those in 'Arcadia.' With Portrait, Memorial-Introduction, Notes, &c., by the Rev. A. B. GROSART, D.D. Three Vols., crown 8vo, cloth boards, 18s.

Sims (George R.), Works by.

Post 8vo, illustrated boards, 2s. each; cloth limp, 2s. 6d. each.

Rogues and Vagabonds. | Tales of To-day.
The Ring o' Bells. | Dramas of Life. With 60 Illustrations.
Mary Jane's Memoirs. | Memoirs of a Landlady.
Mary Jane Married. | My Two Wives.
Tinkletop's Crime. | Scenes from the Show.
Zeph: A Circus Story, &c. | The Ten Commandments: Stories. [Shortly.

Crown 8vo, picture cover, 1s. each; cloth, 1s. 6d. each.

How the Poor Live; and Horrible London.
The Dagonet Reciter and Reader: Being Readings and Recitations in Prose and Verse, selected from his own Works by GEORGE R. SIMS.
The Case of George Candlemas. | Dagonet Ditties. (From The Referee.)

Dagonet Abroad. Crown 8vo, cloth, 3s. 6d.

Signboards: Their History, including Anecdotes of Famous Taverns and Remarkable Characters. By JACOB LARWOOD and JOHN CAMDEN HOTTEN. With Coloured Frontispiece and 94 Illustrations. Crown 8vo, cloth extra, 7s. 6d.

Sister Dora: A Biography. By MARGARET LONSDALE. With Four Illustrations. Demy 8vo, picture cover, 4d.; cloth, 6d.

Sketchley (Arthur).—A Match in the Dark. Post 8vo, boards, 2s.

Slang Dictionary (The): Etymological, Historical, and Anecdotal. Crown 8vo, cloth extra, 6s. 6d.

Smart (Hawley).—Without Love or Licence: A Novel. Crown 8vo, cloth extra, 3s. 6d.; post 8vo, illustrated boards, 2s.

Smith (J. Moyr), Works by.
The Prince of Argolis. With 130 Illustrations. Post 8vo, cloth extra, 3s. 6d.
The Wooing of the Water Witch. With numerous Illustrations. Post 8vo, cloth, 6s.

Society in London. Crown 8vo, 1s.; cloth, 1s. 6d.

Society in Paris: The Upper Ten Thousand. A Series of Letters from Count PAUL VASILI to a Young French Diplomat. Crown 8vo, cloth, 6s.

Somerset (Lord Henry).—Songs of Adieu. Small 4to, Jap. vel., 6s.

Spalding (T. A., LL.B.).— Elizabethan Demonology: An Essay on the Belief in the Existence of Devils. Crown 8vo, cloth extra, 5s.

Speight (T. W.), Novels by.
Post 8vo, illustrated boards, 2s. each.

The Mysteries of Heron Dyke.	Back to Life.
By Devious Ways, &c.	The Loudwater Tragedy.
Hoodwinked; & Sandycroft Mystery.	Burgo's Romance.
The Golden Hoop.	Quittance in Full.

Post 8vo, cloth limp, 1s. 6d. each.

A Barren Title.	Wife or No Wife?

Crown 8vo, cloth extra, 3s. 6d. each.

A Secret of the Sea.	The Grey Monk.

The Sandycroft Mystery. Crown 8vo, picture cover, 1s.
The Master of Trenance. Three Vols., crown 8vo, 15s. net.   [Shortly.
A Husband from the Sea. Post 8vo, illustrated boards, 2s.   [Shortly.

Spenser for Children. By M. H. TOWRY. With Coloured Illustrations by WALTER J. MORGAN. Crown 4to, cloth extra, 3s. 6d.

Starry Heavens (The): A POETICAL BIRTHDAY BOOK. Royal 16mo, cloth extra, 2s. 6d.

Stedman (E. C.), Works by. Crown 8vo, cloth extra, 9s. each.
Victorian Poets. | The Poets of America.

Stephens (Riccardo, M.B.).—The Cruciform Mark: The Strange Story of RICHARD TREGENNA, Bachelor of Medicine (Univ. Edinb.) Crown 8vo, cloth, 6s. [Shortly.

Sterndale (R. Armitage).—The Afghan Knife: A Novel. Crown 8vo, cloth extra, 3s. 6d.; post 8vo, illustrated boards, 2s.

Stevenson (R. Louis), Works by. Post 8vo, cloth limp, 2s. 6d. ea.
Travels with a Donkey. With a Frontispiece by WALTER CRANE.
An Inland Voyage. With a Frontispiece by WALTER CRANE.

Crown 8vo, buckram, gilt top, 6s. each.

Familiar Studies of Men and Books.
The Silverado Squatters. With Frontispiece by J. D. STRONG.
The Merry Men. | Underwoods: Poems.
Memories and Portraits.
Virginibus Puerisque, and other Papers. | Ballads. | Prince Otto.
Across the Plains, with other Memories and Essays.

New Arabian Nights. Crown 8vo, buckram, gilt top, 6s.; post 8vo, illustrated boards, 2s.
The Suicide Club; and The Rajah's Diamond. (From NEW ARABIAN NIGHTS.) With Eight Illustrations by W. J. HENNESSY. Crown 8vo, cloth, 5s.
Father Damien: An Open Letter to the Rev. Dr. Hyde. Cr. 8vo, hand-made and brown paper, 1s.
The Edinburgh Edition of the Works of Robert Louis Stevenson. Twenty-seven Vols., demy 8vo. This Edition (which is limited to 1,000 copies) is sold only in Sets, the price of which may be learned from the Booksellers. The First Volume was published Nov., 1894.

Songs of Travel. Crown 8vo, buckram, 5s.   [Shortly.
Weir of Hermiston. (R. L. STEVENSON'S LAST WORK.) Large crown 8vo, 6s.   [May.

Stoddard (C. Warren).—Summer Cruising in the South Seas. Illustrated by WALLIS MACKAY. Crown 8vo, cloth extra, 3s. 6d.

Stories from Foreign Novelists. With Notices by HELEN and ALICE ZIMMERN. Crown 8vo, cloth extra, 3s. 6d.; post 8vo, illustrated boards, 2s.

Strange Manuscript (A) Found in a Copper Cylinder. Crown 8vo, cloth extra, with 19 Illustrations by GILBERT GAUL, 5s.; post 8vo, illustrated boards, 2s.

Strange Secrets. Told by PERCY FITZGERALD, CONAN DOYLE, FLORENCE MARRYAT, &c. Post 8vo, illustrated boards, 2s.

Strutt (Joseph). — The Sports and Pastimes of the People of England; including the Rural and Domestic Recreations, May Games, Mummeries, Shows, &c., from the Earliest Period to the Present Time. Edited by WILLIAM HONE. With 140 Illustrations. Crown 8vo, cloth extra, 7s. 6d.

Swift's (Dean) Choice Works, in Prose and Verse. With Memoir, Portrait, and Facsimiles of the Maps in 'Gulliver's Travels.' Crown 8vo, cloth, 7s. 6d.
Gulliver's Travels, and **A Tale of a Tub.** Post 8vo, half-bound, 2s.
Jonathan Swift: A Study. By J. CHURTON COLLINS. Crown 8vo, cloth extra, 8s.

Swinburne (Algernon C.), Works by.

Selections from the Poetical Works of A. C. Swinburne. Fcap. 8vo, 6s.
Atalanta in Calydon. Crown 8vo, 6s.
Chastelard: A Tragedy. Crown 8vo, 7s.
Poems and Ballads. FIRST SERIES. Crown 8vo, or fcap. 8vo, 9s.
Poems and Ballads. SECOND SERIES. Crown 8vo, 9s.
Poems & Ballads. THIRD SERIES. Cr. 8vo, 7s.
Songs before Sunrise. Crown 8vo, 10s. 6d.
Bothwell: A Tragedy. Crown 8vo, 12s. 6d.
Songs of Two Nations. Crown 8vo, 6s.
George Chapman. (See Vol. II. of G. CHAPMAN'S Works.) Crown 8vo, 6s.
Essays and Studies. Crown 8vo, 12s.
Erechtheus: A Tragedy. Crown 8vo, 6s.
A Note on Charlotte Bronte. Cr. 8vo, 6s.
A Study of Shakespeare. Crown 8vo, 8s.
Songs of the Springtides. Crown 8vo, 6s.
Studies in Song. Crown 8vo, 7s.
Mary Stuart: A Tragedy. Crown 8vo, 8s.
Tristram of Lyonesse. Crown 8vo, 9s.
A Century of Roundels. Small 4to, 8s.
A Midsummer Holiday. Crown 8vo, 7s.
Marino Faliero: A Tragedy. Crown 8vo, 6s.
A Study of Victor Hugo. Crown 8vo, 6s.
Miscellanies. Crown 8vo, 12s.
Locrine: A Tragedy. Crown 8vo, 6s.
A Study of Ben Jonson. Crown 8vo, 7s.
The Sisters: A Tragedy. Crown 8vo, 6s.
Astrophel, &c. Crown 8vo, 7s.
Studies in Prose and Poetry. Cr. 8vo, 9s.

Syntax's (Dr.) Three Tours: In Search of the Picturesque, in Search of Consolation, and in Search of a Wife. With ROWLANDSON'S Coloured Illustrations, and Life of the Author by J. C. HOTTEN. Crown 8vo, cloth extra, 7s. 6d.

Taine's History of English Literature. Translated by HENRY VAN LAUN. Four Vols., small demy 8vo, cloth boards, 30s.—POPULAR EDITION, Two Vols., large crown 8vo, cloth extra, 15s.

Taylor (Bayard). — Diversions of the Echo Club: Burlesques of Modern Writers. Post 8vo, cloth limp, 2s.

Taylor (Dr. J. E., F.L.S.), Works by. Crown 8vo, cloth, 5s. each.
The Sagacity and Morality of Plants: A Sketch of the Life and Conduct of the Vegetable Kingdom. With a Coloured Frontispiece and 100 Illustrations.
Our Common British Fossils, and Where to Find Them. With 331 Illustrations.
The Playtime Naturalist. With 366 Illustrations.

Taylor (Tom). — Historical Dramas. Containing 'Clancarty,' 'Jeanne Darc,' ''Twixt Axe and Crown,' 'The Fool's Revenge,' Arkwright's Wife,' 'Anne Boleyn,' 'Plot and Passion.' Crown 8vo, cloth extra, 7s. 6d.
⁎ The Plays may also be had separately, at 1s. each.

Tennyson (Lord): A Biographical Sketch. By H. J. JENNINGS. Post 8vo, portrait cover, 1s.; cloth, 1s. 6d.

Thackerayana: Notes and Anecdotes. With Coloured Frontispiece and Hundreds of Sketches by WILLIAM MAKEPEACE THACKERAY. Crown 8vo, cloth extra, 7s. 6d.

Thames, A New Pictorial History of the. By A. S. KRAUSSE. With 340 Illustrations. Post 8vo, 1s.; cloth, 1s. 6d.

Thiers (Adolphe). — History of the Consulate and Empire of France under Napoleon. Translated by D. FORBES CAMPBELL and JOHN STEBBING. With 36 Steel Plates. 12 Vols., demy 8vo, cloth extra, 12s. each.

Thomas (Bertha), Novels by. Cr. 8vo, cl., 3s. 6d. ea.; post 8vo, 2s. ea.
The Violin-Player.　　　　　　　　　| Proud Maisie.

Cressida. Post 8vo, Illustrated boards, 2s.

Thomson's Seasons, and The Castle of Indolence. With Introduction by ALLAN CUNNINGHAM, and 48 Illustrations. Post 8vo, half-bound, 2s.

Thornbury (Walter), Books by.
The Life and Correspondence of J. M. W. Turner. With Illustrations in Colours. Crown 8vo, cloth extra, 7s. 6d.

Post 8vo, illustrated boards, 2s. each.
Old Stories Re-told.　　　　　　　　| Tales for the Marines.

Timbs (John), Works by. Crown 8vo, cloth extra, 7s. 6d. each.
The History of Clubs and Club Life in London: Anecdotes of its Famous Coffee-houses, Hostelries, and Taverns. With 42 Illustrations.
English Eccentrics and Eccentricities: Stories of Delusions, Impostures, Sporting Scenes, Eccentric Artists, Theatrical Folk, &c. With 48 Illustrations.

Trollope (Anthony), Novels by.
Crown 8vo, cloth extra, 3s. 6d. each; post 8vo, illustrated boards, 2s. each.
The Way We Live Now.　　　　　　| Mr. Scarborough's Family.
Frau Frohmann.　　　　　　　　　　| The Land-Leaguers.

Post 8vo, illustrated boards, 2s. each.
Kept in the Dark.　　　　　　　　　| The American Senator.
The Golden Lion of Granpere.　　　| John Caldigate.　　　| Marion Fay.

Trollope (Frances E.), Novels by.
Crown 8vo, cloth extra, 3s. 6d. each; post 8vo, illustrated boards, 2s. each.
Like Ships Upon the Sea. | Mabel's Progress.　　　| Anne Furness.

Trollope (T. A.).—Diamond Cut Diamond. Post 8vo, illust. bds., 2s.

Trowbridge (J. T.).—Farnell's Folly. Post 8vo, illust. boards, 2s.

Tytler (C. C. Fraser-).—Mistress Judith: A Novel. Crown 8vo, cloth extra, 3s. 6d.; post 8vo, illustrated boards, 2s.

Tytler (Sarah), Novels by.
Crown 8vo, cloth extra, 3s. 6d. each; post 8vo, illustrated boards, 2s. each.
Lady Bell.　　　　　　　| Buried Diamonds.　　　| The Blackhall Ghosts.

Post 8vo, illustrated boards, 2s. each.
What She Came Through.　　　　| The Huguenot Family.
Citoyenne Jacqueline.　　　　　　| Noblesse Oblige.
The Bride's Pass.　　　　　　　　| Beauty and the Beast.
Saint Mungo's City.　　　　　　　| Disappeared.

The Macdonald Lass. With Frontispiece. Crown 8vo, cloth, 3s. 6d.

Upward (Allen), Novels by.
The Queen Against Owen. Crown 8vo, cloth, with Frontispiece, 3s. 6d.; post 8vo, boards, 2s.
The Prince of Balkistan. Crown 8vo, cloth extra, 3s. 6d.
A Crown of Straw. Crown 8vo, cloth, 6s.　　　　　　　　　　　　　　[Shortly

Vashti and Esther. By the Writer of 'Belle's' Letters in *The World*. Crown 8vo, cloth extra, 3s. 6d.

Villari (Linda).—A Double Bond: A Story. Fcap. 8vo, 1s.

Vizetelly (Ernest A.).—The Scorpion: A Romance of Spain. With a Frontispiece. Crown 8vo, cloth extra, 3s. 6d.

Walton and Cotton's Complete Angler; or, The Contemplative Man's Recreation, by IZAAK WALTON; and Instructions How to Angle, for a Trout or Grayling in a clear Stream, by CHARLES COTTON. With Memoirs and Notes by Sir HARRIS NICHOLAS, and 61 Illustrations. Crown 8vo, cloth antique, 7s. 6d.

Walt Whitman, Poems by. Edited, with Introduction, by WILLIAM M. ROSSETTI. With Portrait. Crown 8vo, hand-made paper and buckram, 6s.

Ward (Herbert), Books by.
Five Years with the Congo Cannibals. With 92 Illustrations. Royal 8vo, cloth, 14s.
My Life with Stanley's Rear Guard. With Map. Post 8vo, 1s.; cloth, 1s. 6d.

Walford (Edward, M.A.), Works by.

Walford's County Families of the United Kingdom (1896). Containing the Descent, Birth, Marriage, Education, &c., of 12,000 Heads of Families, their Heirs, Offices, Addresses, Clubs, &c. Royal 8vo, cloth gilt, 50s.
Walford's Shilling Peerage (1896). Containing a List of the House of Lords, Scotch and Irish Peers, &c. 32mo, cloth, 1s.
Walford's Shilling Baronetage (1896). Containing a List of the Baronets of the United Kingdom, Biographical Notices, Addresses, &c. 32mo, cloth, 1s.
Walford's Shilling Knightage (1896). Containing a List of the Knights of the United Kingdom, Biographical Notices, Addresses, &c. 32mo, cloth, 1s.
Walford's Shilling House of Commons (1896). Containing a List of all the Members of the New Parliament, their Addresses, Clubs, &c. 32mo, cloth, 1s.
Walford's Complete Peerage, Baronetage, Knightage, and House of Commons (1896). Royal 32mo, cloth, gilt edges, 5s.

Tales of our Great Families. Crown 8vo, cloth extra, 3s. 6d.

Warner (Charles Dudley).—A Roundabout Journey. Crown 8vo, cloth extra, 6s.

Warrant to Execute Charles I. A Facsimile, with the 59 Signatures and Seals. Printed on paper 22 in. by 14 in. 2s.
Warrant to Execute Mary Queen of Scots. A Facsimile, including Queen Elizabeth's Signature and the Great Seal. 2s.

Washington's (George) Rules of Civility Traced to their Sources and Restored by MONCURE D. CONWAY. Fcap. 8vo, Japanese vellum, 2s. 6d.

Wassermann (Lillias), Novels by.
The Daffodils. Crown 8vo, 1s.; cloth, 1s. 6d.

The Marquis of Carabas. By AARON WATSON and LILLIAS WASSERMANN. Post 8vo, illustrated boards, 2s.

Weather, How to Foretell the, with the Pocket Spectroscope.
By F. W. CORY. With Ten Illustrations. Crown 8vo, 1s.; cloth, 1s. 6d.

Webber (Byron).—Fun, Frolic, and Fancy. With 43 Illustrations by PHIL MAY and CHARLES MAY. Fcap. 4to, cloth, 5s.

Westall (William), Novels by.
Trust-Money. Post 8vo, illustrated boards, 2s.; cloth, 2s. 6d.
Sons of Belial. Two Vols., crown 8vo, 10s. net.

Whist, How to Play Solo. By ABRAHAM S. WILKS and CHARLES F. PARDON. Post 8vo, cloth limp, 2s.

White (Gilbert).—The Natural History of Selborne. Post 8vo, printed on laid paper and half-bound, 2s.

Williams (W. Mattieu, F.R.A.S.), Works by.
Science in Short Chapters. Crown 8vo, cloth extra, 7s. 6d.
A Simple Treatise on Heat. With Illustrations. Crown 8vo, cloth, 2s. 6d.
The Chemistry of Cookery. Crown 8vo, cloth extra, 6s.
The Chemistry of Iron and Steel Making. Crown 8vo, cloth extra, 9s.
A Vindication of Phrenology. With Portrait and 43 Illusts. Demy 8vo, cloth extra, 12s. 6d.

Williamson (Mrs. F. H.).—A Child Widow. Post 8vo, bds., 2s.

Wilson (Dr. Andrew, F.R.S.E.), Works by.
Chapters on Evolution. With 259 Illustrations. Crown 8vo, cloth extra, 7s. 6d.
Leaves from a Naturalist's Note-Book. Post 8vo, cloth limp, 2s. 6d.
Leisure-Time Studies. With Illustrations. Crown 8vo, cloth extra, 6s.
Studies in Life and Sense. With numerous Illustrations. Crown 8vo, cloth extra, 6s.
Common Accidents: How to Treat Them. With Illustrations. Crown 8vo, 1s.; cloth, 1s. 6d.
Glimpses of Nature. With 35 Illustrations. Crown 8vo, cloth extra, 3s. 6d.

Winter (J. S.), Stories by. Post 8vo, illustrated boards, 2s. each; cloth limp, 2s. 6d. each.
Cavalry Life. | **Regimental Legends.**

A Soldier's Children. With 34 Illustrations by E. G. THOMSON and E. STUART HARDY. Crown 8vo, cloth extra, 3s. 6d.

Wissmann (Hermann von). — My Second Journey through Equatorial Africa. With 92 Illustrations. Demy 8vo, cloth, 16s.

Wood (H. F.), Detective Stories by. Post 8vo, boards, 2s. each.
The Passenger from Scotland Yard. | The Englishman of the Rue Cain.

Wood (Lady).—Sabina: A Novel. Post 8vo, illustrated boards, 2s.

Woolley (Celia Parker).—Rachel Armstrong; or, Love and The-
ology. Post 8vo, illustrated boards, 2s. ; cloth, 2s. 6d.

Wright (Thomas), Works by. Crown 8vo, cloth extra, 7s. 6d. each.
The Caricature History of the Georges. With 400 Caricatures, Squibs, &c.
History of Caricature and of the Grotesque in Art, Literature, Sculpture, and
    Painting. Illustrated by F. W. FAIRHOLT, F.S.A.

Wynman (Margaret).—My Flirtations. With 13 Illustrations by
J. BERNARD PARTRIDGE. Post 8vo, cloth, 3s. 6d.

Yates (Edmund), Novels by. Post 8vo, illustrated boards, 2s. each.
Land at Last. | The Forlorn Hope. | Castaway.

Zangwill (I.). — Ghetto Tragedies. With Three Illustrations by
A. S. BOYD. Fcap. 8vo, picture cover, 1s. net.

Zola (Emile), Novels by. Crown 8vo, cloth extra, 3s. 6d. each.
The Fat and the Thin. Translated by ERNEST A. VIZETELLY.
Money. Translated by ERNEST A. VIZETELLY.
The Downfall. Translated by E. A. VIZETELLY.
The Dream. Translated by ELIZA CHASE. With Eight Illustrations by JEANNIOT.
Doctor Pascal. Translated by E. A. VIZETELLY. With Portrait of the Author.
Lourdes. Translated by ERNEST A. VIZETELLY.
Rome. Translated by ERNEST A. VIZETELLY.
[Shortly.

SOME BOOKS CLASSIFIED IN SERIES.

₊ *For fuller cataloguing, see alphabetical arrangement, pp. 1-26.*

The Mayfair Library. Post 8vo, cloth limp, 2s. 6d. per Volume.

A Journey Round My Room. By X. DE MAISTRE. Translated by Sir HENRY ATTWELL.
Quips and Quiddities. By W. D. ADAMS.
The Agony Column of ' The Times.'
Melancholy Anatomised: Abridgment of BURTON.
Poetical Ingenuities. By W. T. DOBSON.
The Cupboard Papers. By FIN-BEC.
W. S. Gilbert's Plays. Three Series.
Songs of Irish Wit and Humour.
Animals and their Masters. By Sir A. HELPS.
Social Pressure. By Sir A. HELPS.
Curiosities of Criticism. By H. J. JENNINGS.
The Autocrat of the Breakfast-Table. By OLIVER WENDELL HOLMES.
Pencil and Palette. By R. KEMPT.
Little Essays: from LAMB'S LETTERS.
Forensic Anecdotes. By JACOB LARWOOD.

Theatrical Anecdotes. By JACOB LARWOOD.
Jeux d'Esprit. Edited by HENRY S. LEIGH.
Witch Stories. By E. LYNN LINTON.
Ourselves. By E. LYNN LINTON.
Pastimes and Players. By R. MACGREGOR.
New Paul and Virginia. By W. H. MALLOCK.
The New Republic. By W. H. MALLOCK.
Puck on Pegasus. By H. C. PENNELL.
Pegasus Re-saddled. By H. C. PENNELL.
Muses of Mayfair. Edited by H. C. PENNELL.
Thoreau: His Life and Aims. By H. A. PAGE.
Puniana. By Hon. HUGH ROWLEY.
More Puniana. By Hon. HUGH ROWLEY.
The Philosophy of Handwriting.
By Stream and Sea. By WILLIAM SENIOR.
Leaves from a Naturalist's Note-Book. By Dr. ANDREW WILSON.

The Golden Library. Post 8vo, cloth limp, 2s. per Volume.

Diversions of the Echo Club. BAYARD TAYLOR.
Songs for Sailors. By W. C. BENNETT.
Lives of the Necromancers. By W. GODWIN.
The Poetical Works of Alexander Pope.
Scenes of Country Life. By EDWARD JESSE.
Tale for a Chimney Corner. By LEIGH HUNT.

The Autocrat of the Breakfast Table. By OLIVER WENDELL HOLMES.
La Mort d'Arthur: Selections from MALLORY.
Provincial Letters of Blaise Pascal.
Maxims and Reflections of Rochefoucauld.

The Wanderer's Library. Crown 8vo, cloth extra, 3s. 6d. each.

Wanderings in Patagonia. By JULIUS BEERBOHM. Illustrated.
Merrie England in the Olden Time. By G. DANIEL. Illustrated by ROBERT CRUIKSHANK.
Circus Life. By THOMAS FROST.
Lives of the Conjurers. By THOMAS FROST.
The Old Showmen and the Old London Fairs. By THOMAS FROST.
Low-Life Deeps. By JAMES GREENWOOD.
The Wilds of London. By JAMES GREENWOOD.

Tunis. By Chev. HESSE-WARTEGG. 22 Illusts.
Life and Adventures of a Cheap Jack.
World Behind the Scenes. By P. FITZGERALD.
Tavern Anecdotes and Sayings.
The Genial Showman. By E. P. HINGSTON.
Story of London Parks. By JACOB LARWOOD.
London Characters. By HENRY MAYHEW.
Seven Generations of Executioners.
Summer Cruising in the South Seas. By C. WARREN STODDARD. Illustrated.

THE PICCADILLY (3/6) NOVELS—*continued.*

By J. LEITH DERWENT.
Onr Lady of Tears. | Oirce's Lovers.

By DICK DONOVAN.
Tracked to Doom. | The Mystery of Jamaica
Man from Manchester. | Terrace.

By A. CONAN DOYLE.
The Firm of Girdlestone.

By S. JEANNETTE DUNCAN.
A Daughter of To-day. | Vernon's Annt.

By G. MANVILLE FENN.
The New Mistress. | The Tiger Lily.
Witness to the Deed. | The White Virgin.

By PERCY FITZGERALD.
Fatal Zero.

By R. E. FRANCILLON.
One by One. | King or Knave ?
A Dog and his Shadow. | Ropes of Sand.
A Real Queen. | Jack Doyle's Daughter.

Prefaced by Sir BARTLE FRERE.
Pandurang Hari.

BY EDWARD GARRETT.
The Capel Girls.

By PAUL GAULOT.
The Red Shirts.

By CHARLES GIBBON.
Robin Gray. | The Golden Shaft.
Loving a Dream. |

By E. GLANVILLE.
The Lost Heiress. | The Fossicker.
A Fair Colonist. | The Golden Rock.

By E. J. GOODMAN.
The Fate of Herbert Wayne.

By Rev. S. BARING GOULD.
Red Spider. | Eve.

By CECIL GRIFFITH.
Corinthia Marazion.

By SYDNEY GRUNDY.
The Days of his Vanity.

By THOMAS HARDY.
Under the Greenwood Tree.

By BRET HARTE.
A Waif of the Plains. | Susy.
A Ward of the Golden | Sally Dows.
Gate. | A Protégée of Jack
A Sappho of Green | Hamlin's.
Springs. | Bell-Ringer of Angel's.
Col. Starbottle's Client. | Clarence.

By JULIAN HAWTHORNE.
Garth. | Beatrix Randolph.
Ellice Quentin. | David Poindexter's Dis-
Sebastian Strome. | appearance.
Dust. | The Spectre of the
Fortune's Fool. | Camera.

By Sir A. HELPS.
Ivan de Biron.

By I. HENDERSON.
Agatha Page.

By G. A. HENTY.
Rujub the Juggler. | Dorothy's Double.

By JOHN HILL.
The Common Ancestor.

By Mrs. HUNGERFORD.
Lady Verner's Flight. | The Red-House Mystery.
The Three Graces. |

By Mrs. ALFRED HUNT.
The Leaden Casket. | Self-Condemned.
That Other Person. | Mrs. Juliet.

By C. J. CUTCLIFFE HYNE.
Honour of Thieves.

By R. ASHE KING.
A Drawn Game.
'The Wearing of the Green.

By EDMOND LEPELLETIER.
Madame Sans-Gêns.

By HARRY LINDSAY.
Rhoda Roberts.

By E. LYNN LINTON.
Patricia Kemball. | Sowing the Wind.
Under which Lord ? | The Atonement of Leam
'My Love !' | Dundas.
Ione. | The World Well Lost.
Paston Carew. | The One Too Many.

By HENRY W. LUCY.
Gideon Fleyce.

By JUSTIN McCARTHY.
A Fair Saxon. | Miss Misanthrope.
Linley Rochford. | Donna Quixote.
Dear Lady Disdain. | Red Diamonds.
Camiola. | Maid of Athens.
Waterdale Neighbours. | The Dictator.
My Enemy's Daughter. | The Comet of a Season.

By JUSTIN H. McCARTHY.
A London Legend.

By GEORGE MACDONALD.
Heather and Snow. | Phantastes.

By L. T. MEADE.
A Soldier of Fortune. | In an Iron Grip.

By BERTRAM MITFORD.
The Gun-Runner. | The King's Assegai.
The Luck of Gerard | Renshaw Fanning's
Ridgeley. | Quest.

By J. E. MUDDOCK.
Maid Marian and Robin Hood.
Basile the Jester.

By D. CHRISTIE MURRAY.
A Life's Atonement. | First Person Singular
Joseph's Coat. | Cynic Fortune.
Coals of Fire. | The Way of the World.
Old Blazer's Hero. | Bob Martin's Little Girl.
Val Strange. | Hearts. | Time's Revenge.
A Model Father. | A Wasted Crime.
By the Gate of the Sea. | In Direst Peril.
A Bit of Human Nature. | Mount Despair.

By MURRAY and HERMAN.
The Bishops' Bible. | Paul Jones's Alias.
One Traveller Returns. |

By HUME NISBET.
'Bail Up !'

By W. E. NORRIS.
Saint Ann's. | Billy Bellew.

By G. OHNET.
A Weird Gift.

By OUIDA.
Held in Bondage. | Two Little Wooden
Strathmore. | Shoes.
Chandos. | In a Winter City.
Under Two Flags. | Friendship.
Idalia. | Moths.
Cecil Castlemaine's | Rnffino.
Gage. | Pipistrello.
Tricotrin. | A Village Commune.
Puck. | Bimbi.
Folle Farine. | Wanda.
A Dog of Flanders. | Frescoes. | Othmar.
Pascarel. | In Maremma.
Signa. | Syrlin. | Guilderoy.
Princess Napraxine. | Santa Barbara.
Ariadne. | Two Offenders.

By MARGARET A. PAUL.
Gentle and Simple.

By JAMES PAYN.
Lost Sir Massingberd. | High Spirits.
Less Black than We're | Under One Roof.
Painted. | Glow-worm Tales.
A Confidential Agent. | The Talk of the Town.
A Grape from a Thorn. | Holiday Tasks.
In Peril and Privation. | For Cash Only.
The Mystery of Mir- | The Burnt Million.
By Proxy. [bridge. | The Word and the Will.
The Canon's Ward. | Sunny Stories.
Walter's Word. | A Trying Patient.

Two-Shilling Novels—*continued.*

By FREDERICK BOYLE.

Camp Notes. | Chronicles of No-man's
Savage Life. | Land.

BY BRET HARTE.

Californian Stories. | Flip. | Maruja.
Gabriel Conroy. | A Phyllis of the Sierras.
The Luck of Roaring | A Waif of the Plains.
  Camp. | A Ward of the Golden
An Heiress of Red Dog. | Gate.

By HAROLD BRYDGES.

Uncle Sam at Home.

By ROBERT BUCHANAN.

Shadow of the Sword. | The Martyrdom of Ma-
A Child of Nature. | deline.
God and the Man. | The New Abelard.
Love Me for Ever. | Matt.
Foxglove Manor. | The Heir of Linne.
The Master of the Mine. | Woman and the Man.
Annan Water.

By HALL CAINE.

The Shadow of a Crime. | The Deemster.
A Son of Hagar.

By Commander CAMERON.

The Cruise of the 'Black Prince.'

By Mrs. LOVETT CAMERON.

Deceivers Ever. | Juliet's Guardian.

By HAYDEN CARRUTH.

The Adventures of Jones.

By AUSTIN CLARE.

For the Love of a Lass.

By Mrs. ARCHER CLIVE.

Paul Ferroll.
Why Paul Ferroll Killed his Wife.

By MACLAREN COBBAN.

The Cure of Souls. | The Red Sultan.

By C. ALLSTON COLLINS.

The Bar Sinister.

By MORT. & FRANCES COLLINS.

Sweet Anne Page. | Sweet and Twenty.
Transmigration. | The Village Comedy.
From Midnight to Mid- | You Play me False.
  night. | Blacksmith and Scholar
A Fight with Fortune. | Frances.

By WILKIE COLLINS.

Armadale. | AfterDark. | My Miscellanies.
No Name. | The Woman in White.
Antonina. | The Moonstone.
Basil. | Man and Wife.
Hide and Seek. | Poor Miss Finch.
The Dead Secret. | The Fallen Leaves.
Queen of Hearts. | Jezebel's Daughter.
Miss or Mrs.? | The Black Robe.
The New Magdalen. | Heart and Science.
The Frozen Deep. | 'I Say No!'
The Law and the Lady | The Evil Genius.
The Two Destinies. | Little Novels.
The Haunted Hotel. | Legacy of Cain.
A Rogue's Life. | Blind Love.

By M. J. COLQUHOUN.

Every Inch a Soldier.

By DUTTON COOK.

Leo. | Paul Foster's Daughter.

By C. EGBERT CRADDOCK.

The Prophet of the Great Smoky Mountains.

By MATT CRIM.

The Adventures of a Fair Rebel.

By B. M. CROKER.

Pretty Miss Neville. | Proper Pride.
Diana Barrington. | A Family Likeness.
'To Let.' | Village Tales and Jungle
A Bird of Passage. | Tragedies.

By W. CYPLES.

Hearts of Gold.

By ALPHONSE DAUDET.

The Evangelist; or, Port Salvation.

By ERASMUS DAWSON.

The Fountain of Youth.

By JAMES DE MILLE.

A Castle in Spain.

By J. LEITH DERWENT.

Our Lady of Tears. | Circe's Lovers.

By CHARLES DICKENS.

Sketches by Boz. | Nicholas Nickleby.
Oliver Twist.

By DICK DONOVAN.

The Man-Hunter. | In the Grip of the Law.
Tracked and Taken. | From Information Re-
Caught at Last! | ceived.
Wanted! | Tracked to Doom.
Who Poisoned Hetty | Link by Link
  Duncan? | Suspicion Aroused.
Man from Manchester. | Dark Deeds.
A Detective's Triumphs | Riddles Read.

By Mrs. ANNIE EDWARDES.

A Point of Honour. | Archie Lovell.

By M. BETHAM-EDWARDS.

Felicia. | Kitty.

By EDWARD EGGLESTON.

Roxy.

By G. MANVILLE FENN.

The New Mistress. | The Tiger Lily.
Witness to the Deed.

By PERCY FITZGERALD.

Bella Donna. | Second Mrs. Tillotson.
Never Forgotten. | Seventy-five Brooke
Polly. | Street.
Fatal Zero. | The Lady of Brantome.

By P. FITZGERALD and others.

Strange Secrets.

By ALBANY DE FONBLANQUE.

Filthy Lucre.

By R. E. FRANCILLON.

Olympia. | King or Knave?
One by One. | Romances of the Law.
A Real Queen. | Ropes of Sand.
Queen Cophetua. | A Dog and his Shadow

By HAROLD FREDERIC.

Seth's Brother's Wife. | The Lawton Girl.

Prefaced by Sir BARTLE FRERE.

Pandurang Hari.

By HAIN FRISWELL.

One of Two.

By EDWARD GARRETT.

The Capel Girls.

By GILBERT GAUL.

A Strange Manuscript.

By CHARLES GIBBON.

Robin Gray. | In Honour Bound.
Fancy Free. | Flower of the Forest
For Lack of Gold. | The Braes of Yarrow.
What will World Say? | The Golden Shaft.
In Love and War. | Of High Degree.
For the King. | By Mead and Stream.
In Pastures Green. | Loving a Dream.
Queen of the Meadow. | A Hard Knot.
A Heart's Problem. | Heart's Delight.
The Dead Heart. | Blood-Money.

By WILLIAM GILBERT.

Dr. Austin's Guests. | The Wizard of the
James Duke. | Mountain.

By ERNEST GLANVILLE.

The Lost Heiress. | The Fossicker.
A Fair Colonist.

By Rev. S. BARING GOULD.

Red Spider. | Eve.

By HENRY GREVILLE.

A Noble Woman. | Nikanor.

By CECIL GRIFFITH.

Corinthia Marazion.

By SYDNEY GRUNDY.

The Days of his Vanity.

By JOHN HABBERTON.

Brueton's Bayou. | Country Luck.

By ANDREW HALLIDAY.

Every-day Papers.

By Lady DUFFUS HARDY.

Paul Wynter's Sacrifice.

Two-Shilling Novels—*continued*.

By JAMES PAYN.

Bentinck's Tutor.	The Talk of the Town.
Murphy's Master.	Holiday Tasks.
A County Family.	A Perfect Treasure.
At Her Mercy.	What He Cost Her.
Cecil's Tryst.	A Confidential Agent.
The Clyffards of Clyffe.	Glow-worm Tales.
The Foster Brothers.	The Burnt Million.
Found Dead.	Sunny Stories.
The Best of Husbands.	Lost Sir Massingberd.
Walter's Word.	A Woman's Vengeance.
Halves.	The Family Scapegrace.
Fallen Fortunes.	Gwendoline's Harvest.
Humorous Stories.	Like Father, Like Son.
£200 Reward.	Married Beneath Him.
A Marine Residence.	Not Wooed, but Won.
Mirk Abbey.	Less Black than We're
By Proxy.	Painted.
Under One Roof.	Some Private Views.
High Spirits.	A Grape from a Thorn.
Carlyon's Year.	The Mystery of Mir-
From Exile.	bridge.
For Cash Only.	The Word and the Will.
Kit.	A Prince of the Blood.
The Canon's Ward.	A Trying Patient.

By CHARLES READE.

It is Never Too Late to Mend.	A Terrible Temptation.
Christie Johnstone.	Foul Play.
The Double Marriage.	The Wandering Heir.
Put Yourself in His Place	Hard Cash.
Love Me Little, Love Me Long.	Singleheart and Double-face.
The Cloister and the Hearth.	Good Stories of Men and other Animals.
The Course of True Love.	Peg Woffington.
The Jilt.	Griffith Gaunt.
The Autobiography of a Thief.	A Perilous Secret.
	A Simpleton.
	Readiana.
	A Woman-Hater.

By Mrs. J. H. RIDDELL.

Weird Stories.	The Uninhabited House.
Fairy Water.	The Mystery in Palace.
Her Mother's Darling.	Gardens.
The Prince of Wales's Garden Party.	The Nun's Curse.
	Idle Tales.

By AMELIE RIVES.

Barbara Dering.

By F. W. ROBINSON.

Women are Strange.	The Hands of Justice.

By JAMES RUNCIMAN.

Skippers and Shellbacks. | Schools and Scholars.
Grace Balmaign's Sweetheart.

By W. CLARK RUSSELL.

Round the Galley Fire.	The Romance of Jenny Harlowe.
On the Fo'k'sle Head.	An Ocean Tragedy.
In the Middle Watch.	My Shipmate Louise.
A Voyage to the Cape.	Alone on a Wide Wide Sea.
A Book for the Hammock.	
The Mystery of the 'Ocean Star.'	

By GEORGE AUGUSTUS SALA.

Gaslight and Daylight.

By JOHN SAUNDERS.

Guy Waterman.	The Lion in the Path.
The Two Dreamers.	

By KATHARINE SAUNDERS.

Joan Merryweather.	Sebastian.
The High Mills.	Margaret and Eliza-beth.
Heart Salvage.	

By GEORGE R. SIMS.

Rogues and Vagabonds.	Tinkletop's Crime.
The Ring o' Bells.	Zeph.
Mary Jane's Memoirs.	My Two Wives.
Mary Jane Married.	Memoirs of a Landlady.
Tales of To-day.	Scenes from the Show.
Dramas of Life.	The 10 Commandments

By ARTHUR SKETCHLEY.

A Match in the Dark.

By HAWLEY SMART.

Without Love or Licence.

By T. W. SPEIGHT.

The Mysteries of Heron Dyke.	Back to Life.
The Golden Hoop.	The Loudwater Tragedy.
Hoodwinked.	Burgo's Romance.
By Devious Ways.	Quittance in Full.
	A Husband from the Sea

By ALAN ST. AUBYN.

A Fellow of Trinity.	To His Own Master.
The Junior Dean.	Orchard Damerel.
Master of St. Benedict's	

By R. A. STERNDALE.

The Afghan Knife.

By R. LOUIS STEVENSON.

New Arabian Nights. | Prince Otto.

By BERTHA THOMAS.

Cressida.	The Violin-Player.
Proud Maisie.	

By WALTER THORNBURY.

Tales for the Marines. | Old Stories Retold.

By T. ADOLPHUS TROLLOPE.

Diamond Cut Diamond.

By F. ELEANOR TROLLOPE.

Like Ships upon the Sea.	Anne Furness.
	Mabel's Progress.

By ANTHONY TROLLOPE.

Frau Frohmann.	The Land-Leaguers.
Marion Fay.	The American Senator.
Kept in the Dark.	Mr. Scarborough's Family.
John Caldigate.	
The Way We Live Now.	GoldenLion of Granpere

By J. T. TROWBRIDGE.

Farnell's Folly.

By IVAN TURGENIEFF, &c.

Stories from Foreign Novelists.

By MARK TWAIN.

A Pleasure Trip on the Continent.	Life on the Mississippi.
The Gilded Age.	The Prince and the Pauper.
Huckleberry Finn.	A Yankee at the Court of King Arthur.
Mark Twain's Sketches.	The £1,000,000 Bank-Note.
Tom Sawyer.	
A Tramp Abroad.	
Stolen White Elephant.	

By C. C. FRASER-TYTLER.

Mistress Judith.

By SARAH TYTLER.

The Bride's Pass.	The Huguenot Family.
Buried Diamonds.	The Blackhall Ghosts.
St. Mungo's City.	What She Came Through
Lady Bell.	Beauty and the Beast.
Noblesse Oblige.	Citoyenne Jaqueline.
Disappeared.	

By ALLEN UPWARD.

The Queen against Owen.

By AARON WATSON and LILLIAS WASSERMANN.

The Marquis of Carabas.

By WILLIAM WESTALL.

Trust-Money.

By Mrs. F. H. WILLIAMSON.

A Child Widow.

By J. S. WINTER.

Cavalry Life.	Regimental Legends.

By H. F. WOOD.

The Passenger from Scotland Yard.
The Englishman of the Rue Cain.

By Lady WOOD.

Sabina.

By CELIA PARKER WOOLLEY.

Rachel Armstrong; or, Love and Theology.

By EDMUND YATES.

The Forlorn Hope.	Castaway.
Land at Last.